THE TAPESTRY SHOP

THE TAPESTRY SHOP

JOYCE ELSON MOORE

FIVE STAR
A part of Gale, Cengage Learning

GALE
CENGAGE Learning·

Detroit • New York • San Francisco • New Haven, Conn • Waterville, Maine • London

GALE
CENGAGE Learning

LIBRARY OF CONGRESS CATALOGING-IN-PUBLICATION DATA

Moore, Joyce Elson, 1934–.
  The tapestry shop / Joyce Elson Moore. — 1st ed.
     p. cm.
  ISBN-13: 978-1-59414-899-6 (hardcover)
  ISBN-10: 1-59414-899-6 (hardcover)
  1. Adam, de La Halle, ca. 1235-ca. 1288—Fiction. I. Title.
PS3613.O5628T37 2010
813'.6—dc22   2010024712

First Edition. First Printing: October 2010.
Published in 2010 in conjunction with Tekno Books.

Printed in the United States of America
1 2 3 4 5 6 7 14 12 11 10

To my daughter, Schella

ACKNOWLEDGMENTS

I am indebted to the following people upon whose work I drew when piecing together what few facts are known about Adam's life.

Dr. Deborah Nelson-Campbell is Professor of French at Rice University. Her research and teaching areas are Philology and Medieval French and Occitan Literature, and I am grateful for her permission to use excerpts from *Lyrics and Melodies of Adam de la Halle* in my novel.

Professor Carol Symes teaches in the Department of History and the Program in Medieval Studies at the University of Illinois. Her book, *A Common Stage: Theater and Public Life in Medieval Arras* (Cornell University Press, 2007), gave me insight as to the community in which Adam lived his early years.

Anne Stone, who studied at the University of Paris and holds a Master of Arts from Middlebury College in Paris, kindly translated excerpts from Adam's *Le Jeu de Robin et Marion*.

My thanks also to all the librarians who spent countless hours searching for books from which I could recreate the life of an obscure musician who left behind a wealth of medieval literature and music.

Venés apres moi, venés le sentele,
Le sentele, le sentele, lés le bos.
Follow me, come down the path,
The path, the path along the wood.
—Adam de la Halle, *Robin et Marion*

CHAPTER ONE

Arras, France: 1265

On the morning of his judgment, Adam lay in bed, listening to Madame Crespin's rooster and contemplating his own fate. The fowl's raspy *arrk-ah-aaark* blended with the bells at Saint-Vaast and the parish church at Saint Géry and the eleven other belfries in Arras ringing the hour of Prime.

He glanced out the open window. Between branches of the chestnut tree, tall as a church nave and as somber, a pearlescent glow signaled a new dawn, the day he both dreaded and longed for.

The cock crowed again and he wondered if Madame Crespin's tonic had worked on the rooster's damaged craw which, according to her, was the direct result of its having supped poisoned water from ditches where cloth dyers' on the hill emptied their vats into the street. She planned to lodge a protest but he doubted there was a village anywhere in France that would entertain such a complaint, as taxes from the lucrative weaving industry were what paid the officials' salaries.

A goat bleated, followed by another and another as the goat herder approached, leading his five does along the cobblestoned street outside, their bells jingling like gypsy bracelets. "M-ilk?" the herder called. "Fresh goat m-ilk?"

Adam closed his eyes, willing sleep to return its black comfort. Today he would stand like a common thief in the

11

square before his accusers and listen to some arrogant magistrate pronounce his sentence.

Now that the day was finally here, he wondered if his friends had been right when they'd prodded him to ask Count Robert to intervene. But that would have meant sending a courier on a three-day ride and interrupting Robert's hunting. He had not the money for one, nor the desire for the other, even though a word from his patron would have ended it all. Too, involving Robert would have lent credence to the accusation, one the simplest peasant would know contrived. Besides, he'd felt righteous at the time: the spectacle might help other members of the Puy and serve as a warning to lesser *jongleurs* who had no royal patron and simply wanted to sing their songs.

The goat herder passed and a sudden stillness descended. In the quiet, Adam heard beetles scurrying in the rafters overhead, gnawing inside their caverns, a familiar sound in the timber-framed house. He wondered how much damage had been done in the few years since he and Maroie had married and moved in. Once this business with his punishment was behind him, he would enlist the aid of the carpenter who doubled as the night watchman at the currency exchange on the Petit Marché. Together they could check the roof beams.

Maroie turned her back, then tugged at the narrow coverlet, exposing his feet to the cool night air that never left the room before midday, not in April, which was still part of winter if you lived north of Paris.

With a flapping of wings and a gurgle, the rooster landed on the sill and commenced tapping his beak on the wood, a brazen move for a sick rooster and one that gave Adam a moment of amusement.

The pallet shook and Maroie sat up, her face silhouetted in the soft light.

Her black hair was unbound, and he remembered the silky

feel of it: how it flowed through his fingers, flowed like a song, winding down beside her ears, resting like a final note on her slim shoulders.

She leaned over and retrieved a small block of wood that held the melted remains of a rush candle. Cursing, she took aim at the open shutter. The rooster flapped his wings and flew from the window, squawking loudly.

Adam sat up, reached for his woolen hose and could feel her watching him.

"Is this the morning you find out what your brashness will cost us?" Her voice sounded sleepy and thick like he remembered, from earlier days when they made love, and he had a rushing sense of loss for the promises that had dissolved between them.

"Yes. An hour after sunrise." His sentencing? He thought she had forgotten. They hadn't spoken of it since her bitter reproach when he had first confided in her, and she had sided with his accusers.

She wrapped the blanket around her shoulders and padded to the front room. After pulling on his boots, he slipped the tunic over his head and followed her out.

She took kindling from a basket and tossed it on cold ashes. "It was foolish to sing songs that mocked the authorities—and in front of unknown foreigners. The burghers will entertain anyone, you've said that yourself."

He stared into the fire and waited for the branches to ignite. "Be that as it may, Maroie, I'd like you to come. We will show them we're not afraid."

"I've promised Juliane to help sew her daughter's wedding gown. It was not me, in any case, who offended the officials." Her voice was no longer sleepy, but clear and accusing. She covered her bare arm with the blanket, pulling it taut across her chest like a shield to protect her from his foolishness.

"It was a song, Maroie, a *song*. A satire of sorts, about excessive taxes. Some of us think these new councilmen are imposters, not sent here by King Louis, as they claim. They would ostracize those of us who speak the truth."

"Nonsense. The *enquêteurs* would find them out."

"Maroie, the king only sends *enquêteurs* once yearly now." He paused, lowered his head, then looked up at her. There was so much she didn't know, or would not admit. "These opportunists will be gone by then, replaced with new ones."

"No matter. We have our own fees to worry about, and you go looking for more misfortune, ridiculing the authorities." She picked up scraps of dry bread from the table, rubbed them into crumbs in her palm and threw them to the three hens pecking in dirt near the door. "Go by yourself."

She walked outside and past what would be a hedge of lilies come June, but now were slender leaves, vulnerable to hares and insects. The hens trailed at her feet as she turned right and took the path to Madame Crespin's.

He glanced at the table where a few sheets of parchment lay, an unfinished *chanson* about youthful love, and the beginning lines of a play, the theme of which laid bare the commonly held belief that Arras had too many officials and that quarrels between the monks at Saint-Vaast and the canons at the cathedral were more about gaining revenue from the relics than about spirituality.

He rolled the leaves together, thinking that his indictment was only the first in a long line of groundless accusations that would dissuade poets and musicians from exercising their talents when faced with condemnation and fines.

When the church bells rang the hour of *terce*, Adam stood beside the fishmonger's stand. The smithy was already at work, sparks flying from the heated iron as he struck red-hot metal, a spade slowly forming from the molten mass. Directly across the square, a worker struggled to set up a trestle table on the makeshift podium. Nearby, a golden banner hung limply from its frame, a scowling Lion of Arras embroidered on it, paw raised, ready to crush its enemies.

Vendors had opened their shops early, hoping to make sales to the onlookers. Adam glanced at the baker's stall, smelled the aroma of cooked tarts, and wondered why he wasn't tempted.

A trained bear, tied to its master, danced across the square. With each step, the bells on its collar tinkled, adding a monotonous, annoying distraction to the carnival atmosphere.

Adam rubbed his eyes, wished he had gotten more sleep. He dreaded the impending disclosure of his punishment, yet some part of him wanted to hear it, to have it finished.

Someone touched his shoulder, and he turned to see Michael, a childhood friend, standing beside the dwarf Liegart who was engrossed in feeding his pet monkey.

Adam smiled, noticing Michael's scruffy black curls and red-rimmed eyes. "It is plain to see you spent the evening with one of the ladies from the tavern."

Michael grinned and squinted into the sun at the activity across the square. "Are these the ones, then, who dictate the fate of all Arras?" He tilted his chin toward a group of busy clerks. "Is that the magistrate, the red-robed one?"

"Yes, between the two redheaded bodyguards."

Liegart tugged on the hem of Adam's tunic. "Here come the others now," the dwarf said, pointing to one corner of the square. He took a bite of plum and gave the rest to his monkey. A group of townspeople, led by the chair-mender and butcher, crossed the square to Adam. A horn sounded and clerks approached the table. A bailiff handed a rolled parchment to the magistrate, and the smithy put down his hammer. The hawkers grew quiet. A slight breeze flapped the Lion of Arras. He appeared to be rolling on a golden sea, placid, listening.

Adam looked closer at the magistrate, thinking he knew him from some other time, another place, away from this bitter morning with its judgments. Clerks unrolled parchment and quoted ordinances. The magistrate referred to new laws to defend their decision.

The air grew still; the Lion ceased rolling. Pigeons cooed from perches beneath the roofs of the open-air stalls.

"Citizen Adam de la Halle, present yourself to the magistrate," a bailiff called out.

Adam thought the magistrate looked uneasy. After all, the man had little protection, as this was to be a minor sentencing for civil disobedience, not like a hanging or public beating that would bring crowds of townspeople and *gens d'armes*.

As Adam studied the magistrate's face, something wet hit the man's cheek. The magistrate glanced down, then up at the smithy. The smithy smiled, wiped his mouth with the back of his hand as if to claim victory for so accurate an aim. Someone in the crowd laughed, and Adam shifted, hoping the gathering mob would not resort to a riot in his defense and make matters worse.

The magistrate looked away, evidently deciding to ignore the smithy's brazen challenge and gave a sharp command to his guards. "Push these bystanders away. We've business to conduct." He kicked a hapless mongrel that had wandered onto the platform. The crowd hushed as the hated official cast his eyes over the sea of faces.

Anxious to have done with the preliminaries, to learn his sentence, Adam squared his shoulders and stepped forward to stand near the platform. The magistrate's gaze pinned him and he suddenly regretted his choice of clothes: a simple brown tunic and hooded cape. He had wanted to blend with the crowd and appear no different than an ordinary peasant come to market, but he would not grovel. In fact, he felt oddly defiant. After all, he had entertained royalty. His poetry was known throughout France.

"You, here. Are you the accused? Step forward, then, do you hear?" The magistrate pointed to a spot directly in front of him, his red brocade sleeves unfolding to show thick pink arms, mounds of flesh adorned with gold bracelets where his wrists would be.

Adam swallowed a reply. He dared not speak, as this court controlled the severity of his punishment and could change it at will. He felt a familiar embarrassing warmth rise on his neck, his ears, as it always did with irritation or discomfiture. Holding his head high he took another step forward, not blinking, the sun almost blinding him. He looked into those rheumy eyes, and remembered.

At court, not two months ago this fleshy little man with his bulbous countenance had sat grinning, watching the entertainment, fingering the neck of a young girl beside him. Adam recalled the silent endurance, her rigid posture in contrast with the man's contentment. Like her, he was at the magistrate's mercy. Did the man thrive on others' discomfort? Obviously he had misled the Paris officials, convinced them he could enforce the collection of taxes, in a village where no one knew who was in charge.

The townspeople crowded behind Adam, hardly breathing, waiting, like him, to see what rebuke would come from the lips of this hated intruder.

A clerk handed another scroll to the magistrate. He unrolled the parchment and held it before him, the sun glinting from golden rings on his stubby fingers, and read. "By the order of *Le bailli d'Arras et Les magistrats urbain,* bearing in mind the accused is from a family respected in Arras, the following is hereby ordered: For aiding those who would knowingly withhold fair

17

taxes levied upon certain households by the honorable town magistrates, and for encouraging these same households to defy the lawful collectors of funds to support the sacred cause of our beloved King Louis's crusade, we sentence him to a period of four months' exile in Douai, where he will be imprisoned for the duration of his exile."

Hisses rose from the crowd like a swarm of bees driven from their hive. Catcalls interrupted the magistrate, becoming louder, spreading across the square, first from the baker, followed by the card reader, the fish merchant, the dealer in wines, the stableman.

The magistrate lifted his pudgy face and waited, looking from beneath his hooded lids at Adam, then blinked in recognition. His lips trembled; sweat broke out on his upper lip and he blotted his face with his sleeve.

Adam experienced a moment's satisfaction. The man now recognized him as a friend of the royal family.

The magistrate lowered his head and continued reading, evidently trying to ignore the insistent objections of the townspeople which had become loud enough almost to drown out his words. "By the authority of King Louis, this fourteenth day of April in the year of our Lord twelve hundred sixty-five."

He laid the parchment on the table and spoke in low tones to the guards. They nodded.

Near Adam, a clerk unrolled a document and signaled him to sign.

While he wrote his name, a shadow fell across the parchment. Adam looked up. The magistrate's two guards grinned down at him. One held a coil of rope.

CHAPTER TWO

In a town not far from Arras, Guillaume Ridaut adjusted his riding breeches and pulled a wool cloak across his chest, shutting out the northern wind that held Ypres in its grip. He walked past his storehouse and headed to the stable, anticipating what lay ahead. He had waited the last six of his twenty-two years for this day. Nothing could stop him now.

A worker glanced up, watched his master pass by, then looked away and continued loading the dung cart, steam rising from the odorous pile as he lifted it with his shovel.

Guillaume continued on, half-amused at the servant's averted gaze, a gesture he had gotten used to since becoming one of the town's respected landowners. Inside the stable, he bent to tighten the spurs around his ankles, then tramped through the hay to where the stallion waited in his stall. The early sun glinted off the dark mane of the horse, whose nostrils blew misty clouds onto the beam of light slanting through the thatched roof. A groom, caught unawares, ran quickly to saddle him.

"A fine morning for a ride, Master Guillaume," the stableman said as Guillaume mounted.

The servant held up leather straps. Guillaume glanced at the man's callused hands and black nails, pulled his riding gloves from the waist of his riding breeches and slid them on before taking the reins. He adjusted the bridle and spurred his horse to a canter. They passed the workers' huts, the orchards, the serfs carrying sickles into the field, finally descending into the valley below.

Beyond the stand of beech trees bordering his land, he rode, down the grassy slope and onto the path that would take him to Vitry-en-Artois.

Slowing the horse to a walk, he passed grazing sheep and post mills, their sails turning slowly in the wind from the Scarpe, and within two hours Guillaume saw the church spire that marked the village of Vitry. Beyond that lay the Hall of Cloth.

The horse's hooves clicked on the uneven cobblestones as he crossed the town square. Dismounting in front of the hall, he secured his horse to a beech tree and went inside. He removed his cloak, brushed road dust from his boots, and scanned the hallway. The old building no longer boasted tables of colorful cloth. Ancient murals had faded, and pigeons cooed in the rafters. Ornamental lanterns had long ago vanished when vagrants lived here, before the mayor had decided to convert the abandoned building to offices, but the faded interior did nothing to calm Guillaume's quickening pulse. A newly painted sign indicated the city clerk's office.

His heart pounded, matching his heavy footfalls, steps away from his destiny.

Inside the assigned meeting room, he found Phillipe Durant already there. Phillipe swung around with a pleasant smile, and it flashed through Guillaume's mind that the man had treated him like a son.

Quickly discarding the thought, he concentrated on Phillipe's demeanor, that of a man who knew what he wanted from life and had worked to get it. He felt the older man's gaze, steady and wise. Guillaume wondered if, after all his careful planning, Catherine's father would raise some last-minute objection.

Guillaume bowed his head to the father of his soon-to-be fiancée. "Phillipe."

Phillipe accorded him a similar bow, and Guillaume took a chair.

A clerk walked in and laid papers on the desk. He ran a hand over his bald head, and then, as if remembering why he was there, he handed each man a quill. "I'm obliged to read this to you both, although you, *Monsieur* Durant, have already seen it." He cleared his throat.

Guillaume realized he'd been holding his breath. "No need for all that," he said, tapping his fingers on the desk. "We've already agreed."

The clerk looked reluctant at having his protocol interrupted. "Then please, sir, allow me to summarize." The clerk shifted his eyes from Guillaume to Phillipe. "*Monsieur* Durant, by signing this, you are giving *Monsieur* Ridaut the right to use, invest, and manage your daughter's dowry and your holdings after your death, effective upon the date of her marriage. If you or your daughter should change your mind, *Monsieur* Ridaut would be entitled to half the receipts of the tapestry shop for the next five years to compensate for the breach of promise. Should their union later be dissolved for any other reason, the dowry would revert to your estate."

Phillipe nodded. "Guillaume's father and I were lifelong friends. It was his dying wish that our families be bound by marriage. Catherine has always known she and Guillaume would wed, and I see no obstacles to their marriage. I am blessed with so good a daughter." He turned to Guillaume. "I have been remiss in not becoming better-acquainted with you, but that will change. I'm not so busy now, for my capable book-keeper, Gérard, helps me more and more with the records. Under your guidance, the business will remain safely bound to Catherine, to be inherited by the sons I hope she bestows on you."

"Rest assured, that is my intention," Guillaume said, reaching for the quill. "To have many sons, and secure a comfortable life for Catherine."

"Then you're agreed." The clerk signed his name with a flourish and slid the parchment to Phillipe.

Phillipe signed as well, then leaned back while Guillaume made his mark where the clerk indicated.

After folding the vellum and sealing it with melted wax, the clerk placed it in a wood box. Guillaume rose, shook hands with Phillipe, and strode confidently from the Hall of Cloth. On the ride back, Guillaume could hardly contain his glee. With the stroke of a quill, he had not only guaranteed the future respect of the townspeople, but ensured the income from a thriving shop in a neighboring town. Phillipe had lost his youth, was no longer the robust man he'd been, so it was only a matter of time before he turned it over to his son-in-law. The biggest prize, though, was Catherine; no more sleazy brothels or unclean wenches. Instead, he would now have in his bed a beautiful woman with lively green eyes and a winning smile.

In the tapestry shop, the front part of a timber-framed house on the main street of Vitry, Catherine walked between the piles of tapestries, glad to be done with the day's work. Sorting and hanging tapestries by color was no easy task; the local dyes made her sneeze, and the imported ones smelled musty and made her throat hurt.

She sat on the shorter of two stools and watched dusty particles floating in rectangles of sun that splashed against the rough-hewn walls. As if a new shipment wasn't enough trouble, she had discovered a sparrow nest in the rafters, one sure to bring disaster to the tapestries directly below. It had taken the better part of an hour to scare the birds away and discard the twigs to discourage future settlements.

Her best friend, Francino, dipped a ladle into the water barrel. If not for him, she thought, moving the tapestries from beneath the nest would have been an impossible job. "Have some?" he asked. His dark eyes conveyed an expression of tiredness, instead of the usual mischievous glint.

She took the ladle and brought it to her mouth, mindless of water trickling down both sides of her chin. After handing it back, she rubbed her back. "Ooh, the next time I see packhorses and a wagon of tapestries, I'm going to plead illness."

Francino laughed. "Little good that will do. Your father knows you're healthy as a mule. Besides, how could I work without you?"

She laughed. Surely, she thought, there was no better friend than Francino. Not only that, he had a girl of his own, eliminating that complication.

A wagon drawn by two horses rolled past, and she heard a woman's laughter.

"You're quiet," Francino said. "What are you thinking? Scheming some foolish plan like you instigated before to avoid your marriage?"

She swiped at a fly buzzing around her head and narrowed her eyes. "I never should have told you about that."

He chuckled. "Why not? The incident is long past."

"I felt foolish, afterward."

"It was four years ago, Catherine. You were a child, and brave, to sneak out in the dead of night like that in an attempt to escape. I only wish I'd seen your face when the constable awakened you, out there on the edge of town barefoot, wearing pilgrim's weeds and huddling like some poor waif." He shook his head.

"It was not funny, Francino, not then. I was hot and hungry, and he made me walk back here to Papa. I know now the constable contrived the whole spectacle, purely for show and to teach a lesson."

"And you haven't learned?" He shifted on the stool.

She cast him a disgusted glance.

He stood, adjusting his worn coat around his shoulders. "I can see you're in no mood to talk, and I'm hungry."

He wrapped a shawl around his neck and lifted a sack, one she knew contained a sizeable portion of meat her father had insisted they didn't need. It was her father's way. They weren't rich, not by any standards, but they ate well enough. And Francino had worked his way into both their hearts.

Catherine propped her chin on her hand and stared out the door, long after Francino had disappeared from sight. He was right, of course. She had been trying to think of something—anything—that would keep her from having to marry Guillaume Ridaut. She'd talked to her father over and over, but each time, when she'd thought she had him convinced, he had given her that reassuring smile, meeting each of her objections with some rational explanation, then assuring her that her worries were baseless. More than once, she'd been tempted to tell him her secret. Thankfully, she'd stopped short of dooming her soul.

The worst part of all was that she, unlike others, knew what Guillaume was really like—she had seen it with her own eyes. The secret haunted her dreams. How could she marry a man she feared?

By the next morning, Catherine had worried herself to a state of near-panic. Yesterday's talk to Francino had not helped, and last evening her worst fears had been confirmed. Over dinner, her father told her that he and Guillaume had signed papers that legalized her betrothal. She had been about to blurt out a refusal, stopping short of revealing the whole truth, and bluntly stating that she would not marry Guillaume, not ever, when her father's next words had stopped her cold.

"I'm relieved," he'd said, taking another serving of pudding, "that you'll be in good hands when I'm not around."

"Papa, don't talk like that!"

He laid down his spoon and looked directly into her eyes. "I don't want you to worry, Catherine, so I didn't tell you before, but lately I'm bedeviled my some new miseries. I'm no longer young, so I tossed them off as the pains that come with old age, but the doctor worries that I never quite recovered from that prolonged illness this past winter. He warned me to slow down—no excitement at all. I'm supposed to eat radishes with salt, and sit, like a fool, in vapor baths. He even told me not to ride, but I told him what I thought of that." He chuckled and turned his attention to the pudding.

His confession had made the food stick in her throat. She should have known. The doctor's visits had become more frequent, but she had passed it off as simple companionship. The two men had been friends for years.

All that evening, her thoughts loomed dark. Perhaps the physician was wrong—others had been proven wrong. They couldn't know everything. Still, she remembered grimly, not long ago her father had come home complaining again of that pain in his chest and shoulder. Now, the memory floated back to haunt her. She turned over in bed and bunched the goose-feather pillow into a ball. When had he become so ill? What would she do without her dear Papa?

CHAPTER THREE

After a sleepless night of troubling dreams, Catherine woke the next morning, determined to keep a careful eye on her father. Beyond that, she would question the doctor more closely next time she saw him.

She dressed and went downstairs. Francino had already opened the shop, and when she came from behind the line of tapestries, he thrust a branch of newly opened blossoms her way, then stuck the stems in her hair, laughing.

Thank goodness for Francino's good humor, she thought. She broke a hunk of cheese in half and sat down. Thursdays were always slow. Besides, they'd done two days' work yesterday.

She had almost finished the cheese when the branch fell from her hair and scratched her nose. She flung it at a side wall, narrowly missing a candlestand. She shifted on the stool and sighed. Long and hard.

"What's wrong with you today?" Francino asked.

"Everything." She decided not to say anything about her father's health. If Papa wanted Francino to know, he'd tell him himself. It wasn't a daughter's place. But she *could* tell him the other bad news. "Papa made an agreement with Guillaume yesterday. They signed the papers in Ypres. Guillaume wanted the dowry terms witnessed, I suppose, as if Papa had ever cheated anyone."

"I don't understand you," Francino said. "The man is rich. He promises to take care of you and evidently likes the idea of having an interest in a tapestry shop."

She started to tell Francino some gossip she'd heard, about how part of Guillaume's lands were ill-gotten, but decided against it. After all, there may not be a speck of truth to it.

"You do not know him, Francino. Not like I do." She watched a pigeon pecking at the crumbs of cheese on the table, shredding them to bits, a perfect image of her life. In spite of eating the cheese, her stomach felt hollow.

"Why? What don't I know?"

She twisted the hem of her tunic, not sure how, or even if, she should tell what she'd seen. Still, hadn't Francino told her about the tavern wench? In fact, described it in great detail, down to where the man's hands had touched, and how the girl had flung ale in the patron's face? Besides, the incident with Guillaume was long ago, and Francino's name had not been mentioned in the oath-taking.

She decided to take a chance. Perhaps, if Francino knew just what kind of person Guillaume really was, he would help her figure something out, although that hope diminished with each passing day.

"It happened a few years after Mother died, so I must have been about ten. We lived in the bigger house, down the road. Guillaume's father died that year and he was all alone. His mother had died years before. Anyway, Father said Guillaume could stay with us, until he was old enough to manage the Ridaut estate on his own. Guillaume was about sixteen." She shifted, feeling like one of the orators who frequented the square on holy days.

"Go ahead, Catherine. You can trust me, you know that."

"You must never repeat this—ever." She tucked her legs further beneath the stool. "On this particular day, Father was at the docks, supervising the unloading of some tapestries. No one was in the house but the kitchen maid, and Guillaume, and me.

I was upstairs, and I heard a noise in the kitchen, so I called out. When there was no answer, I was afraid someone had come to rob us so I crept downstairs, staying in the shadows." She pressed her lips together, looked down, then continued. "Guillaume had the girl pressed against the table. His hand was over her mouth and he pushed her to the floor, then—you know—he pulled up her clothes. I wanted to stop him, but thought maybe she wanted him to, but when he was finished, she cried and cursed him. There was nothing I could do. Guillaume is strong, stronger when he's angry. I learned that right then."

She trembled, reliving the terrible scene. She, too, could have been a victim, like the maid, trapped beneath his sweating body, unable to move. Try as she may, she could not remember what happened next; maybe she cried out, or he heard her whimper. Something had made him spin around and advance toward her as he tied the rope of his braies. He'd come so close that his dark eyes had pierced her thoughts like daggers. She knew then—they both knew—he could do with her what he liked.

Francino cleared his throat and she looked up. The room had suddenly become warm and she blotted her face with her sleeve. "Anyway, like I said, I knew I was no match for Guillaume. And when he grabbed my arm, I thought my life was over—that I'd be like the kitchen maid. But he had other intentions. He dragged me over to Mother's Psalter and shoved it in my face." 'Swear! Swear on your Mother's Bible that you'll not tell anyone, or, so help me, I'll do the same thing to you.' " She swallowed hard, remembering the cruel lines of his face. She'd known he meant it.

"I was so afraid, but I told him I was going to tell Father and he couldn't make me promise anything. By then I had stopped shaking and was angry instead. He must have seen that I meant every word. Both of us knew Father would have killed him if he'd touched me. I knew right then I didn't want to marry

Guillaume, and I guess I thought if he were gone I'd be spared. So we made a bargain. I said I would swear not to tell if he would leave and never come back." She shook her head. "I was really dumb back then."

"Why didn't you tell your father after it happened?"

"Francino! Didn't you hear me? I swore on my mother's holy book." She narrowed her eyes. "Oh, Guillaume was clever. He held the Bible and made me put my hand on it and swear I would never tell Father. He must have read my mind, because then he made me swear I'd never tell Gérard, or the neighbors. He made me repeat a long list of names, everyone we knew, and that seemed to satisfy him. Then he reminded me I would spend my life in Purgatory if I swore on a Psalter and didn't keep my oath, as if I didn't know that." She grimaced, picturing what she knew about Purgatory, where people burned and devils prodded you with pitchforks for punishment. Never, never would she do anything to risk being sent there. Father Bretel had talked about temptation and wicked deeds. She had no intention of going against God's will, which was fair as long as you tried to do right. But Evil was always waiting down below, waiting for souls who had done something exactly like breaking an oath given on a holy book.

Francino frowned, then a grin spread across his face. "Well, I didn't swear anything. I can tell him."

She grabbed his arm. "No, Francino. I'd go to Purgatory. It's the same thing as me telling him—because I told you. You'd damn me to life in Purgatory!"

"Okay, okay. You're right. I suppose if I'd sworn on my mother's prayer book, I'd not tell either." He frowned, as if he were sorting it all out. "And the girl? What did she do?"

"What could she do? You know they always take a man's word—they'd say she brought it on herself. And because of the oath, I could not have helped her anyway. No one saw but me.

29

She had no proof." Catherine looked down at her hands, shamed that she'd been helpless to make it right for the girl.

Francino must have guessed what she was thinking, because he leaned forward and gave her a smile. "Catherine, you were only ten."

She wiped a tear. Francino was trying to help.

"So," he said, "Guillaume kept his part of the bargain?"

"Yes. He told Father he was ready to run the estate. Father helped him hire some workers, and he's lived there ever since."

Francino blotted his brow with his sleeve. "Whew, that's quite a story. But, you know, that was a long time ago. Guillaume could have changed."

"No, I can see it in his eyes. When he looks at me, I always think of the girl. And I can see that he does, too. He'll exact his revenge for that bargain." She shivered at what might lie ahead. She'd relived the horror of that day so many times, she sometimes thought she'd dreamed it, simply because she wished it a dream. In her memory, the scene had taken on an illusory quality, the faces of perpetrator and victim blurred and formless.

She had long ago realized Guillaume was two separate people: the Guillaume he presented to the villagers, the one who treated the ladies courteously and gave alms in abundance to the parish church, asking nothing but that a small stone with his name be set into the wall near the entrance to the new chapel.

And the Guillaume who had raped the maiden, and had threatened to do the same to her.

She recalled the last time she had been alone with him. She had talked incessantly to cover her fear of him, asking about his orchards, when the fruit ripened, where he sold it. He had brushed off her questions like so many loose feathers. "It's not your concern, Catherine. I have able foremen to handle that."

Silenced, like a prisoner.

Over the last few months, her father had dropped little reminders of what was to come: how he and Guillaume's father had been close friends, how they had made a pact, and of the promise he'd made to her mother on her deathbed, that he would marry their daughter to someone who could provide well for her, someone like Guillaume.

At first, she had offered objections, laying the groundwork, hoping to convince her father that she and Guillaume were not suited to be man and wife, but when that didn't seem to dissuade him, she said she had no desire to live in Ypres, where winters were long and bitter. She had proposed every excuse she could think of, and in the end had gotten desperate and considered ending her long silence, but in the light of day, decided the punishment for breaking an oath given on a holy book would be worse than any marriage, even this one. Her reward would come in the afterlife.

Soon, Catherine thought, I will be Guillaume's prisoner for real, not just for a few moments of discourse. Her fate was sealed. Guillaume had made sure of that. And her father, trusting by nature, had evidently signed the agreement without a second thought.

She chewed her lip. Francino was a good listener, but had offered no practical help. She wondered if she dared confide in Gérard, who was more like an uncle than her father's accountant, and who always had answers to everything, but could she persuade him to take her side in this? If she confided her reluctance to marry Guillaume, perhaps Gérard could think of some way to avoid the wedding, to get around the signed agreement. Still, with her father's health the way it was, this was no time to risk a confrontation. Guillaume, it appeared, would win out, unless Gérard could pull off a miracle. He had to. There was no other way out.

CHAPTER FOUR

The wagon lurched forward, and Adam braced himself. He felt sorry for the driver, forced to abandon most of his cabbages on the road and not daring to protest as the guards demanded he drive them to Douai. Now the few cabbages the farmer had not yet unloaded rolled on the floor of the wagon as it tumbled eastward.

The two redheaded guards sat facing Adam, one watching him warily, the other one, taller by a hand, alternately chewing nutmeat and drinking wine from a flagon tied at his waist while purple juice ran down his sleeve. The one who sat opposite appeared to be younger, and never took his eyes off Adam. Four fingers were missing from his left hand, and Adam wondered how he'd lost them. It was no act of nature, not blunted like that—more likely chopped for some offense, or a painful accident. The likeness between the men was unmistakable; the two must be brothers.

Adam turned away, could hear the guard beside him still guzzling wine. The sound reminded Adam of his thirst, tempting him to ask for a drink, but he said nothing. Soon all this unpleasantness would be behind him. A few months at a monastery, the usual place for a political prisoner, would give him time to write.

The road followed the winding Scarpe River. Adam tried not to think of others who were exiled to Douai. Some were rogues and murderers, but lately he'd hear stories of political arrests.

"Stop here," yelled the one who seemed to be in charge. "Now, we walk." He tossed the empty wine flagon from the cart and wiped his mouth.

The wagon slowed. Adam's captors wound a rope around his waist and tied the ends to each of their belts.

They jumped from the wagon, pulling Adam with them. "C'mon, Hunchback." The wine drinker yanked on the rope. "That's what they call you, the Hunchback of Arras, isn't it? Where's the hump? Keep it hidden, eh?"

Determined to ignore the query, Adam said nothing. The guard pulled at the rope. "Answer us. You're not around your royal friends now. We're in charge."

"It's a family name. As you see I have no hump," he answered, hoping to end the man's sadistic taunting. An ancestor perhaps. . . .

"No hump, eh? We could put one there, unless you make this easy for us." The threat had come from the younger guard, who until now had said nothing, but seemed to be looking at his brother for approval. "Walk along, now," he continued, "and show some respect."

Secured between them as he was, he could not avoid the rancid breath of the wine drinker; he felt sick, but knew it would only anger them both if he stopped to rid himself of the sour taste in his throat. They walked the dirt path, following the winding road as it turned north. A fresh breeze blew from the water, and Adam took deep breaths, grateful for the river wind that pushed the man's odor behind them.

They passed beside the quay, and he shifted his thoughts to the Douai of his childhood, when the smell of fresh-caught fish mingled with odorous refuse the townspeople discarded in the river under cover of darkness, for a law had been passed levying a steep fine on Douaisians caught emptying pots into the Scarpe.

On the bank, an old woman yelled at a fishmonger. "You

worthless cheat—you gave me two that were rotten." She shoved an empty basket his way. He lost his footing on the slippery bank and sat down hard. The two guards laughed loudly at the fishmonger's misfortune, but Adam glanced away, refusing to be part of their ridicule.

The guards led him past a weathered building, one he remembered housed the tribunal and bankers on one end, the public scales on the other. The town remained unchanged from when he had come here as a boy with his father.

The rope at his waist chafed his skin, but he clenched his jaw, refusing to let them see his discomfort. Instead, he concentrated on the sights: the chapel of Notre Dame, silhouetted in the glow from the horizon, and the adjacent cemetery. Beyond that stood the burghers' houses, lined in a row beside the cobbled road.

Children watched idly from the doorways, probably wondering if this new prisoner would go to the gallows. Just beyond, where the path turned again to follow the river, he saw the sandstone facade of the old monastery. He shivered and pulled his tunic, damp from perspiration and river wind, closer to his chest.

Dusk had settled over the town as the guards led him to a side courtyard, a shadowy nook that smelled of herbs. Small animals scuttled to safety as they crossed the cobbles. Strange, Adam thought, they would lead him here instead of through the main entrance. He was about to object when he felt a splintering blow on his skull. Pain blacked out light as his legs collapsed beneath him.

He lay still, unable to see, afraid he'd been blinded. After a few minutes he turned his head up and saw a crescent moon. He was in the courtyard of the monastery, probably left for dead. Why would the guards attack him, when all he'd done was to go along with what they wanted?

Suddenly remembering his purse, he reached to his waist. The bastards had robbed him and fled, not caring if he were dead or alive.

Rubbing his fingers across his head he touched a sticky mass in his hair, then followed the line of a gaping cut. He shivered, wrapped his arms across his chest, and wondered how long he'd been there. He closed his eyes and lost consciousness again.

Something tickled his ear. He swiped at it and missed. The tickling continued. He reached up and his fingers closed around a hard-shelled insect. He slung it away, a move that brought new pain to his head.

From somewhere he heard a rooster crow.

He thought again of the purse and felt a moment of satisfaction. Before leaving Arras, he had given most of his money to Maroie, knowing he would have no use for coins at the monastery. Then he remembered; his father's ring was in the purse. He had intended leaving the ring at the goldsmith's for repair, but events had driven it from his head.

They had stolen his father's prized possession—a ring given him by a wealthy businessman in appreciation of his service. Modest by royal standards, and set with a common stone, it was the only ornament his father ever wore, and the only keepsake Adam had to remember him by. Adam recalled the ring's golden gleam reflected from candlelight as his father worked on the ledgers and accounts that consumed his life. Even when his fingers became gnarled and twisted, he had worn it proudly, and had promised it to Adam, as if it were a token from a king.

Adam realized the memory had misted his eyes. He swiped a hand across them. His father had not been able to leave him much, but he'd left him the ring, and a sense of honor, which was now outraged by his loss. *I'll get your ring back, Father,* he murmured. *May their lecherous souls rot in hell.*

A slow drizzle set in and he struggled to stand upright. He had almost come to the corner of the building when he stumbled and fell. Making his way on hands and knees, he reached a portico and beat on the door with his fists.

When he thought no one would answer, the door flew open and, just before he blacked out again, he saw two sandaled feet and the hem of a tunic.

He woke in a dimly lit room to the sound of bells. When he touched his head, he felt a bandage. The cot he lay on was comfortable enough, and the glow of candles filled him with a sense of warm comfort. At least he was among friends, and they had dressed his wound.

As he drifted in and out of sleep, he dreamed, strange dreams that made him wonder if they had given him something for pain. A pelting rain drove against the outside wall. The rain turned into rivulets of wine. He was playing hide-and-seek in the limestone tunnels below Arras, giggling as Michael and André opened spigots releasing rivers of dark liquid from the barrels, transfixed as it flowed on the dirt trickling toward his feet. The wine merchants jumped from the darkness, flailing sticks and shouting. He fled in terror, running through the passageways, hiding in the labyrinth.

Wakened momentarily by some small sound he turned his head on the pillow and wondered why he'd dreamed of his childhood. Perhaps the loss of the ring, or the way he'd left the town of his birth, bound like a common criminal. Arras had changed from those carefree days. He smiled, remembering the merchants had finally installed an iron plate at the opening to the tunnels, a clever move that prevented further mischief.

A throbbing pain in his head jarred him awake. He licked his parched lips, then froze. Footsteps approached.

Adam turned toward the sound of the door latch. Suddenly,

the room filled with light. He cursed the pain that lanced his eyes.

A boy wearing the white tunic of a novice monk walked toward the bed carrying a candle and a bowl smelling of fish and pungent herbs. "I didn't mean to frighten you."

"No harm was done. I've been in the dark too long."

"Perhaps it was the drought they gave you. Makes some people vomit, or have bad dreams. I suspect it only affected your eyesight. It's temporary. Here." The novice set the bowl on a nearby table and lit two more candles. "They said you should eat something. The cook sent some broth." The youth fanned his face with one hand. "It's warmer in here than in the travelers' room." He nodded at the chamber pot. "When you feel up to it, no need of that. The latrine is outside by the stables, and there's a fountain beside the back entrance."

Adam suppressed a smile. Evidently emptying the pot was another duty of the novice.

The youth retrieved two plump pillows from a high shelf. "Lean forward a bit." He stuffed the pillows behind Adam's shoulders, pulled a stool next to the bed, and fetched the bowl of soup.

"Do you know who I am?" Adam asked.

The boy nodded. "I was told you were exiled, sent here from Arras, but evidently you were attacked by highwaymen at our very doors."

Adam touched the bandage, thinking the guards worse than highwaymen who usually stole and fled. "Who bandaged me?" he asked, changing the subject.

"Why, the monastery physician—with the help of our herbalist, of course. His salves work miracles—with God's help, of course."

The novice took the empty bowl and was pulling the stool from the bed when Adam heard the jingle of keys.

Another man joined the first. As he approached Adam's bed, his slippers crunched the fresh rushes that covered the floor, and his sizeable frock rustled with every step. He wore a robe with a collar of squirrel fur that trimmed the neck and hem. At his expansive waist, a yellow cord held a chain, hung with keys on both sides of his belly. His eyes looked kind, with deep lines at the corners. His face bore a short stubble of growth. "You must be Adam de la Halle."

Adam nodded, aware the prior had come to visit. No one else dressed so fine in a priory. How much, Adam mused, did this man know about the reasons for his exile, and how he came to be attacked?

The prior stood gazing down at Adam. "I think I remember the name . . . de la Halle." He scratched his forehead. "Your father has passed this way. Yes, I remember; he stayed with us many times. He bequeathed a sizable amount to be distributed each year as alms to the poor."

The prior dismissed the novice, then turned back to Adam and lifted an index finger as if to chastise. "I think I remember you, too. You stayed here with some noblemen."

Adam searched his mind, then remembered another night, long ago, the first night he had met Count Robert, a chance encounter that had led to a lasting friendship.

"We could hear you singing," the prior continued, "even from the apprentices' hall, though I forbade my monks to listen as it was not the proper music to be sung in sacred places." He paused, evidently amused at the recollection.

The prior took a seat next to the bed. "We have political exiles, from time to time. I understand your misdeed was a minor one. I'm sorry you had such a misfortune on your way here."

"No matter," Adam said. "Thanks to the talents of your physician, I seem to be recovering."

"Well, if you're up to it, please join us for the evening meal tomorrow. Since you're a musician, you might enjoy our music. After the meal, I will take you to the nave where you can hear the brothers chant at *compline.*" He rose, gathering his robe at the sides and adjusting the cord. "Shortly the hours of silence will be upon us. And now, I feel a damp wind blows upon the land, and you are in need of warmth and rest."

He resumed rubbing his stubble and left the room without another word.

The following evening, after the prior took him to the nave, Adam settled back. The darkened cubicle offered peace and seclusion, guarded as it was by solemn-faced wooden statues above a row of candles. When the music began, he closed his eyes and listened to the chants he recognized from mass. He began to nod, but was startled when he heard a familiar chant interrupted with a *trope.*

Strange, he thought. *Troping* had been abolished in many abbeys, considered too much of an embellishment to the music and an addition tending toward the secular.

He suppressed a smile. The music director here had a mind of his own.

Shifting his weight on the hard bench, he made a mental note to compliment the monk who had written such a fine addition to their worship.

An unfamiliar chant drew his attention and he listened to the melodic line, picturing the *neumes.* He heard some of the monks stray from the accustomed mode; there were always brothers whose voices could not follow the melody, try as they may, but as long as they knew the words. . . .

They sang the *Alleluia,* a moving rendition that brought tears to his eyes.

After the benediction, Adam stepped from the nave. The

guest-master walked with him back to his room on the east wing of the priory.

Adam sank onto the mattress, tired from the exertion and hoping the pounding in his head would soon stop. He pulled the covers to his chin. An earlier song, one he'd worked on in Arras, came to him again.

> *I rue the day that I went to the fountain*
> *Where I saw you the other day,*
> *For without my heart I returned.*
> *Now it is in this way*
> *That I will await mercy.*

He turned, saw a sliver of moonlight in the black sky, and fell into a restless sleep.

The next morning, walking into the main room, he saw two monks preparing for the noon meal, poking at embers that surrounded a cauldron. A novice scattered straw underneath tables and benches to cover dropped food.

One of the brothers left the fire and walked in to the refectory. "Here. Try some of this. It's my own invention." He pushed a small pot of jam toward Adam. "Aren't you our visitor from Arras?"

Adam nodded. "Yes, and I shouldn't have slept so long." He laid the knife beside the jam pot and finished the bread. "Delicious. Tell me, is there a quill I could use? I have my own parchment."

The monk nodded. "Come, I'll show you to the scriptorium. They will give you what you need."

"May I show him?" the novice asked. "May I, Brother Cosset?"

"Go, go. Of course, show our traveler above. They are already at work, so you'll need no key."

Adam followed the young novice up to the scriptorium, where

the distinctive odor of old leather and lampblack assailed his nostrils. He climbed onto a high stool and laid his parchment on the desk.

Light poured in from openings on both sides of the room. Adam glanced around the room at the monks, their heads bent over the tasks before them. Except for an occasional cough or belch, the only sounds were quills scratching on parchment, a scribe smoothing vellum with pumice, and the flapping of wings as a novice shooed doves from the rafters with a long pole.

Adam took the quill in hand, looked down at the parchment and closed his eyes, remembered the beginning words of the verse he wanted to write. He propped both feet on the rung of the stool, dipped the quill into the ink pot, and began to write.

With the spring season
I must sing

He paused, waiting for the familiar rush, the words that came from nowhere. Instead, an irritating melancholia washed over him. He looked out an open window, stared at the shafts of light playing against stone, and waited for inspiration. When none came, he left the room, careful not to disturb the monks, whose inspiration he envied. Had the blow to his head done something to his mind? Why else this void, this lack of creativity, when before he had only to pick up a quill and hum a melody, and begin? Cold fear washed over him, remembering he had had no motivation to write since the attack. What would his future be like if he'd lost the last meaningful thing in his life?

CHAPTER FIVE

A north wind stirred through Vitry, swinging the sign that hung outside the tapestry shop and blowing clouds light as meringues to the south, toward Paris. Spring rains had not yet come, and winter had not quite left. The streets of the city were filled with journeying merchants and traders, and shopkeepers opened their doors early, welcoming the additional business. In years like this, in which Easter came early to signal the beginning of a new trading season, shops along the main street enjoyed unparalleled trade, and this April was no different. Noblemen, frequenting the path from Douai to Arras, found the village to be a welcome stop. Businesses thrived, including the tapestry shop, and so it was that a full week had passed before Catherine found an opportunity to speak with Gérard about her predicament, in the hopes of enlisting his help.

She and Francino were arranging tapestries by size when she spotted her father's bookkeeper through the window, his brown hooded surcoat flapping at his ankles with each step. He trudged up the path that wound between the shop and the neighboring house, his head bent against the wind.

Catherine grabbed her cloak. "I'll be back in a few minutes, Francino." Outside, she gathered her courage and joined Gérard. "May I speak with you? Please."

At the urgency in her voice he stopped midstride and turned to wait. "Of course. Is there a problem in the shop?"

"No, no. Nothing like that." She fell in step beside him. Why hadn't she thought all this out, instead of scrambling out with no plan in mind? He would think her addled.

They came to the corner and he pointed to the lane that ran behind the row of houses. "Such a beautiful day. Let's walk a while."

They had nearly reached the end of the street before she'd decided there was nothing to do but be straightforward. "I have a problem."

"I suspected as much." They stopped at a bench near the back door of the cobbler's shop. Using the hem of his cloak, he dusted away some fallen leaves. "Sit, and tell me about it."

"I do not want to marry Guillaume. I never have."

"That does not surprise me. I've seen you two together. Why haven't you discussed this with him?"

Her mind raced, searching for an answer that was partly truthful; she could not lie to Gérard. "I did before, after that time I left home, but I was younger then. And when Papa held me and didn't punish me for leaving, and said everything would work out and I'd be fine, I let it go. I did not really understand, until—a year or so ago. He invited Guillaume to dinner, and that's when I realized what might happen. Before that, it seemed so far away—the marriage, I mean. Even Mother used to say I would someday marry Guillaume, but I suppose I thought the time would never come, that things would change."

Gérard nodded. "To children, a day is a year long. When you're my age, a year is a day long." He smiled and crossed his legs. "And now that you see the day is here, you know you should have spoken up long ago and not allowed him to hope."

She nodded. "Exactly."

"How can I help?"

She tilted her head and shot him a sidelong glance. "I don't know. I thought perhaps you could think of something— something that won't make Papa angry and upset. He listens to me, but you know how he is. He has an answer for everything, like you."

Gérard smiled. "I cannot interfere, Catherine. I am his employee, not a family member."

A door slammed shut nearby and she jumped. Why was Gérard always right?

"You know, Catherine, most times, people come to love each other after they marry. And all brides are fretful as their wedding day approaches."

"That's what he always says." Her heart sank. Gérard wasn't going to help. And she could not tell him about Guillaume. Even if she could, he would say what Francino said: that Guillaume had changed, that everyone changed as they grew to manhood.

She watched as a hare nibbled on some weeds, directly across from them. The hare appeared content, with not a care in the world.

If Gérard could not help, there was only one other place to turn. Perhaps she should have gone there first.

She rose from the bench. "I suppose you're right, Gérard. Things will work out. And now we should go back. Father will be expecting you."

Gérard patted her arm. "You will be fine, you'll see. And don't worry, I'll not mention a word of this to your father. It would only give him something to worry about."

"Exactly," she said, keeping pace with Gérard's long strides while her mind raced ahead.

When the path divided, he turned to take the short way to the back entrance. She continued to the front of the house. It was foolish of her to think Gérard could do anything different. Had she not done everything possible, short of telling her father the truth? Besides, from what she'd learned about the agreement, there was no way out anyway. Guillaume had outwitted them all. As she reached the end of the footpath, she glanced at the woodbine that grew next to the shop. An idea struck. She broke off several pieces from a rotted stump.

Entering the shop, she heard Francino discussing the merits of a tapestry with a customer. She hung her cloak on a peg, gathered up the woodbine, and sat on her favorite stool.

Deftly weaving the woody cords into a garland, she decided the best place to put it was right at the feet of the Holy Mother at Saint Mark's. The saint would guide her—perhaps even perform a miracle.

After the customer had left, Francino pulled up a stool. "Mind if I watch?"

"No." She stripped the leaves from one twisting stem.

"What is that for? Your hair?"

She laughed. "No. It's a simple offering—to Mary."

"I see." The silence grew between them while she worked. When the garland was finished, she laid it aside. "Do you believe in miracles, Francino?"

"I'm not sure. I pray, and some of my prayers have been answered. Miracles? Possibly, though it's a bit like magic if you think about it. But, you know, prayer can't hurt."

Francino paused, as if deciding whether or not to trust her, then leaned forward conspiratorially. "Sometimes, I've made a compact with God."

"That's blasphemous!"

"Not really. Think of it this way. Instead of so many prayers, which He probably gets tired of hearing, why not offer something else to God? He may reward you with a solution to your problem."

Catherine propped her heels on the legs of the stool. "That sounds like foolishness."

Francino shrugged. "Very well. Forget I said it. Now I need to get back to work."

Later that evening, after her father had gone to bed, she lit the oil lamp, intent on mending a tear in her tunic. She'd almost finished when she heard rain hitting the side of their timber-framed house. She tossed the tunic aside and hurried to close the shutters.

Returning to her chair, her glance fell on the small silver box Guillaume had sent her months ago. She opened the lid. The light from the lamp reflected the luster of the amethyst—costly, he had emphasized, when she had thanked him later for sending it. She withdrew the token from its crimson nest. Some believed the stone stained dark from Bacchus's wine-colored tears, a fitting image for Guillaume's gift, considering the tears she would shed unless Someone answered her prayers and performed a miracle.

It had to happen soon. The wedding date was only six months away.

CHAPTER SIX

On a warm July day, with only a few weeks of his exile remaining, Adam sat reading in his cell-like room, a sparse, clean place he'd called home for almost three months. A bell rang, signaling the hour, and he turned another page. Finally, he placed the bound book atop the pile of manuscripts he'd borrowed from the vast collection in the monastery. He'd hoped that by reading, he would gain inspiration, some morsel to feed his starving creativity, but the idea had proven futile. There was nothing left but to take quill in hand and make another try.

He took the steps to the scriptorium two at a time, arriving with a sense of hope, but after an hour of dipping and re-dipping the quill into the ink pot, of trying to force the words, he laid the quill aside, put both elbows on the desktop, and rested his chin on his fists, fighting a feeling of desperation. A hand grasped his shoulder and he turned to see the prior.

"They said you were here. I thought perhaps you'd fallen asleep. The quiet up here is conducive to napping."

Adam looked around the room and saw the others had left. "No, I guess I was . . . thinking."

The prior stood on his toes and peered at the desk. "Ah, I see you've been busy." He smiled, looking at the empty parchment.

"No, I . . . words fail me this morning."

"Well, come below. Perhaps you sit too long. I like to show our visitors the vineyards, if you feel like walking."

They left the scriptorium, the only sounds the padding of

leather shoes on the flat stones and the jingle of the keys at the prior's waist.

Outside the monastery Adam breathed the smell of hay and dung. He heard stable noises, whickers, and the sound of hooves against the wooden enclosure. Past the stable was a well-worn path leading uphill through a pasture.

"Tell me—your family, Adam—they're in Arras? Slow down. I can't walk this hill so fast."

Adam paused, and for a while neither man spoke. Then, his eyes fixed on a distant hill, Adam decided to confide in the prior. "I . . . have a wife. But she is not happy with a *trouvère*'s life. We have no children. We only share a house."

They reached the top of the slope, and the prior pointed below. "Look, there are the vineyards. We take great pride in them. They support the monastery well as you tasted from our cellars last evening."

The vineyard covered the entire valley and swept up the next hillside where the forest, a darker green, abutted the last row of grapevines. Adam breathed deeply and glanced at the smiling prior, envying him this refuge, then he glanced at the keys, hung from the prior's waist, and the moment passed as quickly as it had come.

"Now to your problem," the prior said, rubbing the stubble on his face as they headed back down the hill toward the main building. "What are you to do? You don't travel together? That must be a lonesome life for you both." He mopped his face with a piece of linen and continued. "I have known others, wandering minstrels who stop here regularly. They are a carefree lot, bent on enjoying themselves, visiting the brothels in villages along the way, I suspect. But you're different. I don't mean to pry, but sometimes men have a quest—be it for God or some other spiritual manifestation. Until that is found, anguish accompanies one through life."

They reached the stone walkway, and the prior bent to pet a dog that blocked the path. "At least here," he continued, "we have the company of the other brothers and the eternal presence of God. Have you considered the religious life?"

"I admire you and the good brothers here—the work you do—but it is not the life for me. I hope before too long to study in Paris. I have a patron who has encouraged me to go there."

"Ah, yes, the university. By all means, if you can, you should. Most of the scholars are young men, and your wife would love Paris."

"I'm afraid she will have nothing of Paris. She wants to stay in Arras."

"Then you would have to go alone. Is that what bothers you, Adam, the solitude? Or perhaps you only wish to cherish something, or someone. For us it is easy. We have a road to follow, a simple path. Yours is more difficult."

Adam swallowed, trying to rid himself of the tightness in his throat, but said nothing.

The prior looked away. "I must go now." He lifted the white linen of his robe and climbed the few steps that led into the refectory. "I'll pray for you."

"Father, thank you for . . . everything."

"Nonsense. I have done nothing, only offered the rantings of an old man." He turned to leave. "Remember, you're always welcome here."

As the time for his release grew near, Adam made a conscious decision to abandon his writing for now. Perhaps he'd been trying too hard. Besides, there was a gnawing issue that needed resolution. During his stay at the monastery, he'd had time to think and to plan; his first goal upon leaving would be to recover what the guards had stolen. No one had a right to that ring, especially not two ruffians unfit to clean his father's boots.

First, he would go to the magistrate, and, if he received no satisfaction, he would seek out the thieves himself. He mulled over his plan, wishing he knew a scoundrel he could ask for advice, for in all his life he had never dealt with thieves.

No matter. It was a simple enough plan, and hopefully it could be done without violence. If not, he was prepared to do whatever was necessary.

On the last morning of his exile, he woke with a start, dismayed he hadn't heard the bells at prime. It was a full day's walk to Arras and he had hoped to be there by dusk. Later, after breaking his fast and bidding good-bye to the prior and to each of the monks he had come to know personally, Adam picked up his bundle and left the monastery.

He walked down the main street, reflecting on what might lie ahead. Once past the gates of Douai, he followed the winding path northeast, stopping only once to rest. He leaned against the base of a tree and scratched his back against the bark. A wolf howled, a lonesome, lonely echo coming from the forest behind him. He swallowed, trying to ignore the vague, clawing feeling of isolation. For the moment he was free, but what awaited him in Arras?

Maroie, the only person allowed to visit him during his exile, had never come. Perhaps she was glad to be alone.

What lay ahead for them both? He only wanted freedom to write and perform, to exercise his talents in the cities of France, but she wanted her feet planted firmly in Arras. He refused to believe the gossips who linked her name with another, refused to acknowledge what his heart whispered when he lay awake at home waiting for her to tiptoe in, long after the tavern had closed.

A cart rattled by. He picked up his bundle and headed north to a ridge. Below lay a village, one he had not noticed on his ride here in the cabbage farmer's cart with the two villainous guards. He shook his head. That seemed like a lifetime ago.

Fat sheep grazed in a side pasture, and he thought it a perfect setting for the *pastourelle* he had begun earlier, before his exile, when he could still write.

> *This morning I was riding along the edge of a wood;*
> *Found a pretty shepherdess, so lovely no king ever*
> *saw.*

He hummed to the rhythm of his footsteps.

> *Little shepherdess, sweet little girl,*
> *Give me your garland of flowers,*
> *Give me your garland of flowers.*
>
> *Robin, do you want me to put it*
> *On your head as a token of love?*
>
> *Yes, and you will be my sweetheart.*

Three merchants riding mules passed by, then two knights rode southwest, the direction he was heading, their horses kicking up clouds of dust.

After crossing a moat he turned left and made his way down the cobbled street of Vitry-en-Artois, the only village between Douai and Arras. The shopping section lay past a stone church.

A crudely drawn sign drew his attention to the stables. Weariness had him counting his money. He could not afford a horse, but he could rent a mule. As the stableman adjusted the harness, Adam heard someone singing. He glanced to the source of the sound and was surprised that it came from inside a rug vendor's shop.

> *Song, go where I would not dare to go:*
> *Go to greet for me the smiling eyes. . . .*

He paused to listen. The singer's voice had a wistful sound, childlike, yet held a vibrato of compelling strength.

On impulse, he led the mule across the road and tied it to a post.

"*Bonjour, Monsieur.*" A girl's voice rang out.

"*Bonjour, Mademoiselle.*"

She stood beside the open door. Her cheeks rounded into a smile and he caught his breath. She was slender, just past girl-hood, with the most charming face he had ever encountered. Unlike the courtiers, she wore no paint on her lips, but she seemed to glow with an inner expression of joy mixed with an air of impertinence. Everything about her was golden and warm, from the hair that framed her face like a halo to her simple brown tunic that did little to hide her curves. He wanted to leave, and he wanted to dance with her. He wanted to buy her costly slippers and a cup of good wine.

No longer in a hurry to pass through town, he tried to formulate a plausible excuse to stay.

CHAPTER SEVEN

From habit, Adam bowed low, then quickly realized the gesture was out of place. He hoped she did not take offense to his exaggerated court manners. He'd quite forgotten he stood in front of a tapestry shop.

"Come inside. Take a look around."

He followed her through the door, feeling like an intruder. What was wrong with him?

"How may I help?"

"I—I heard you singing. It was a sad *chanson*, but I see you are not sad."

She shrugged. "It's only a song."

He pretended to examine the rugs, then walked to a row of tapestries, unmistakably from the finest weavers in Arras. "How much?"

"Ah, I see you appreciate quality."

Adam saw a movement in the shadows and, a moment later, a dark-skinned youth appeared at her side carrying a wooden flute. "*Bonjour, Monsieur.* I am Francino."

Adam nodded, thinking the youth was letting him know the girl was spoken for. "*Bonjour.* I am Adam de la Halle, from Arras." He turned to the girl. "Your brother, *Mademoiselle?*"

Her laughter set his heart singing. "*Mais non!* I have no brother. He works here."

Adam tried to think of something to say, some reason not to leave her.

Francino broke the silence. "Did you come for the music?"

"Yes. I heard her singing. But, no—I only wanted to look at the tapestries."

She laughed, and Adam felt his face flush.

"No, Francino means the music, tonight in the square. We were practicing. That's what you heard."

Adam's heart leaped. This was the opening he wanted. What was another day's delay in returning to Arras?

"A celebration of some kind in the square? I was just passing through. But I could stay the night. So, yes, if there's music, I will be there."

She climbed onto the stool, never taking her gaze from him. "Can you sing?"

He paused. How much should he tell her? That he had written songs for kings, that he had entertained at the French palace? He decided that might frighten her away. Villagers usually stood in awe of royalty and their ilk, forgetting they were only men. "Yes, I sing. I write a bit of poetry too. Sometimes, I entertain noblemen."

She clapped her hands. "Then you must perform! We've no poet tonight, only Francino and me and a few others. The women cook for everyone, and there's always too much to eat."

"Then, by all means, I'll be there." He laughed, and she joined in, and he thought again that her laughter lit the afternoon. "What name do they call you?"

"I am Catherine Durant. My father owns the shop."

"*Enchanté.* Now, does your village have an innkeeper?"

"Straight ahead, on the right, at the other end of town."

He hated to leave, but he couldn't stand there forever, not with Francino watching, and not when he wanted to kiss her.

That evening, as the late August sun slid behind the forest to the west, leaving behind a pink glow above the trees, Catherine walked beside Francino to the square. Cooks basted meat above flaming pits. Vegetables and soups simmered in pots hung over braziers.

"Why don't you take back some food for Isabel?" she said. "It will let her know you were thinking of her, and not of the other young maidens."

"Isabel trusts me. She knows if I had my way, we'd be married by now, but her father wants me to save more."

"Well, that aside, you know how she loves Madame Chaffier's cooking."

"I'll take her something, but she may not be up to eating. She's much better today, though. I'm just grateful her illness turned out to be mild. We were worried it was something more serious."

Catherine nodded. "That's all the more reason to bring her some good stew."

They had reached the square, where the townspeople were gathered in clusters. Her father sat at a long table of men. She smiled, thinking their discussion no different from their wives: gossip, pouting complaints of sullen servants from the better-off parishioners, even talk of the latest births. When Guillaume joined her father's table, her heart sank. Of course, he would not miss out on a chance to claim her as his, in front of everyone. He wouldn't let her forget, not even for one evening.

Francino headed toward his friends.

To one side, a group of young girls called out. "Come, Catherine. See what we have."

Catherine joined them, curious as to what held their attention; usually they were only concerned with the village youths who gathered now at the far side of the square.

She sat down, and realized the excitement was about a round disk trimmed with filigree. "My brother brought it to me," one girl said. "See, you can see yourself clearly."

They passed it around and, when it reached Catherine, she held it up, fascinated that it reflected a clear image. Was that what she looked like? She stared at the disc. *I look just like Mother did, before she got sick.*

She handed the trinket to the girl beside her. How would her mother have felt tonight? She wished they had talked more, but back then. . . . She sighed, impatient with her thoughts. When you're eight years old and your mother is dying, one does not think to ask a question about a suitor.

The village wives gathered at another table, laughing as they carried trenchers to the men. *That,* Catherine thought, should be what I want to do. Was there something wrong with her that she felt no desire to be one of them, content to cook meals and live and die in Vitry-en-Artois while others visited faraway places and saw the great cathedrals and even the sea to the south?

Laughter and shouts came from the table where Guillaume sat beside her father. To her embarrassment, someone shouted a toast: "To Phillipe Durant and all his friends—and most importantly, to our newly betrothed couple."

Catherine wanted to be somewhere else, anywhere but here, but there was no escape now. Why hadn't someone warned her?

Before she could object, the ladies were passing a horn of wine around the table. "To your marriage!"

Guillaume stood then. "We thank you, both of us. And now, a toast to my bride to be."

She felt a sudden chill in spite of the warm evening and stared down at the wood table, not wanting to look at him, hoping her averted eyes would be taken for shyness. As shouts and toasts continued, she began to imagine the entire square was full of jostling, persistent jokers, a garish masquerade. She felt herself near hysteria.

Then, someone rang a bell, a signal the meal would begin, and the jokers fell silent. Catherine was so relieved that she embraced the girl to her left.

After a meal of roast pig with vegetables, followed by fruit-filled tarts, the entertainment began. A nimble youth, whose father was the local tanner, ran onto the makeshift stage dressed as a joker. Catherine glanced at Francino, making sure he remembered they were next. He nodded at her, and she rose.

As they approached the stage, she saw Adam waiting, not far away. She had almost forgotten having invited him, but evidently he would perform right after them.

When the joker finished, she walked on stage to cheers and applause. She and Francino joined hands and sang . . .

> *Song, go where I would not dare to go:*
> *Go to greet for me the smiling eyes.* . . .

The song ended, and she walked to the front of the stage so those in the back could hear. "Tonight we have a visitor passing through. I invited him here. He says he is a poet. Or a singer, I'm not sure which." She laughed at her own ineptitude. "At any rate he agreed to perform for us. May I present Adam from Arras."

He walked on stage. Someone had loaned him a *vielle*. She climbed down to stand beside Francino and waited to hear the minstrel, wondering if he truly sang for noblemen. He looked a bit noble himself, with his broad shoulders and upright stature. His cheeks and carriage spoke of good health and ample food, and his high forehead below a head of thick brown hair was supposed to be a sign of breeding and intellect. He adjusted the strings on the *vielle*, and to her surprise, he glanced her way and gave her a tentative lopsided smile; it began on one side of his mouth, then spread to the other side. The man was a charmer. Perhaps, as he said, he was a poet. Besides, he had the poise of an experienced performer, with a bit of modesty thrown in, no doubt to engage the listeners.

He cleared his throat, strummed the *vielle,* and began:

> *For such great pleasure I take*
> *In the sweet suffering of love*
> *That the more I feel, the more joyful I am;*
> *I do not wish at all to be cured,*
> *For my hope equals the joy of another.*

As he sang the last stanza, townspeople joined in, hesitantly at first, then louder, as his deft fingers strummed the *vielle* for accompaniment.

When he finished, cheers rose from the crowd. "Sing *Merchi, Amors. Merchi, Amors!*"

Catherine glanced at the audience; all eyes were on him. *This musician has smitten all the ladies and probably cannot see past his own Norman nose, pampered as he is in court circles.*

Francino leaned to whisper in her ear. "I overheard the men. They call him the Hunchback from Arras."

She studied Adam's shoulders but could see no hump, only the beguiling tilt of his head and his uncommon poise. He wore his cap at a rakish angle, decorated by a bright feather. His tunic was no different than other men's—no jewels, no ornaments. She decided she liked this mixture of modesty and pride.

As he finished the second song, Catherine heard thunder rumbling in the distance. The wind gathered strength. Trees whipped about, and a squall pelted the onlookers as they dismantled the tables and gathered their belongings.

She hurried to help the women collect the food and saw Guillaume approaching, wiping sauce from his lips.

"Catherine!" He reached for her hand and clasped it in both of his. "Have a good evening, dear." As he bent to kiss her wrist she saw bits of fruit in his beard and smelled the wild onion cooks had stuffed into the meat.

He turned away to join the men. She felt a choking fullness

in her throat and regretted eating the rich food.

Later, back in her room above the rug shop, she crossed to the altar, dropped to her knees and sobbed. Her tears fell on the small wooden statue of a smiling blue-robed Virgin that had belonged to her mother.

The days were passing fast—too fast—and her prospects for a speedy miracle had dimmed. Was she destined, after all, to spend her life with Guillaume?

CHAPTER EIGHT

The next morning Adam approached the village square, where the previous evening he had learned that Catherine was betrothed to Guillaume Ridaut. At first, he'd not recognized the bridegroom, but as the evening wore on, he remembered a young Guillaume Ridaut from his childhood. The boy was pitied in Arras, the brunt of childish jokes, taunted mercilessly about his drunken father. To make matters worse, the youth had assumed defiant airs while attempting to hide the ever-present bruises on his face and neck. Later, when his father inherited land outside Arras, the family had moved away, but shortly thereafter Guillaume's father died in a tavern brawl. The fact that Guillaume was betrothed now to Catherine, and seemed to be a prosperous landowner, said much for a man with such a childhood.

The square, this morning, looked to Adam like any other square in any number of small villages like Vitry. All signs of the community gathering had been removed: tables, benches, and even the makeshift stage. He continued on to the stables, having resolved to clear his mind of all thoughts of the girl. Besides, was it not a pretty ankle that had turned his head before, and what had that done but lead two people into a cycle of bitterness?

As he approached the main street, he heard her from across the way, humming a song. *I should bid her farewell.*

He dismounted and tied the mule to a beech tree that offered shade from the August heat. A path led to a low wall of rocks, a modest divide bordered by herbs and purple flowers that separated the shop from the street.

When he reached the open door he paused. She sat on a stool with her back to the door and plucked the strings of a lute. He held his breath and listened.

> *It is proper to act moderately.*
> *Daedalus, who works in that way,*
> *Proves it,*
> *And also his son, who through his foolishness*
> *Was totally burned by flying too high.*

She stopped playing, evidently startled by the scrunch of his footsteps in the leaves. He stepped. back. She would scowl at his eavesdropping.

When she turned, her eyes locked with his. She laid the lute in her lap. He thought she had the greenest eyes he'd ever seen, green as a Picardy meadow.

"So, they said you are famous. They said everyone knows of Adam de la Halle, but I didn't."

"That's understandable. I'm not famous, not yet. It's true, a few have admired my work, but I've written nothing memorable." He smiled and propped his bundle near an empty table, trying to remember what foolish notion had brought him here again. He searched his mind for something to say, something safe that would hide his unease. "So, your parents own the shop?"

"*Oui.*" She frowned. "Well, with my father. My mother is dead."

"I'm sorry."

"It's fine. You couldn't know." She looked away, curiously disturbed by the kindness in his eyes, then gathered her composure. "Now, do you want to buy a tapestry?"

He'd made a fool of himself, and wanted to flee.

"I am a *trouvère*, as you must have learned. I have no real home, not now—nowhere to hang a tapestry." He rubbed his hand across a weave that depicted an angel blowing a trumpet. "But I will take this one." He pulled out the purse the prior had pressed on him, insisting he might need it before reaching home, and after paying her in *sous*, he rolled the tapestry tight. *A reckless purchase,* he thought, *but what better keepsake?* "I only stopped again to compliment you on your singing. It's not often I hear my songs sung so well. I wish the *jongleurs* could do justice to my music as you do." He stepped back and bowed. "And now I will take my leave."

"Come, sit if you can. Francino is never on time." She nodded to the empty stool. "You have a thousand songs in your head, I think, and I'd like to hear another one."

He climbed onto the stool, and to his consternation he felt suddenly inept. "I will sing *Au Repairier en la Douce Contree*, if you will sing along. Do you know it?"

"Yes. I mean no, I don't think so. Here, use this." She handed him the lute.

He plucked at the strings. Was her discomfiture the same as his? What was happening to them both?

He ended the song and handed back the lute.

"Do you write them down—the songs?" she asked.

"Sometimes, yes. The words, too, though most of the *jongleurs* cannot read. They learn them by listening."

"I could read your words. I can read, you know. Father taught me. He learned from the monks."

"Quite an accomplishment for someone so young."

He looked away, discomfited by her innocent youthfulness, her vulnerability. "And now I should go. Thank you for singing my music." He stood, bowed slightly, then picked up his bundle from where it leaned against the bench. He walked to the door.

"And thank you for inviting me to join the gathering last evening—and for singing my song."

"It is I who should thank you for the songs." She watched him tighten the knot on his bundle. "So you're traveling to Arras now?"

She slid down from the stool, still holding the lute, and followed him to the door.

He nodded. He wanted to tell her about Douai, but she might think him a *fraude*. "Yes, to Arras. I—travel a lot."

"To Paris? To the king?"

"Sometimes. More often, I go to a manor in Cambrai."

"To sing?"

"Yes, and to write. There is a count there. He is generous to poets and musicians—to any artists."

"He must be rich." She plucked a string on the lute, her eyes round and thoughtful.

"His father was the king's brother."

She formed an O with her lips and raised her brows.

He chuckled and stepped outside. Just past the door, his bundle caught in a flowering vine, and he stopped to untangle it. His face colored and he ducked away, straightening his cap. "I really must go. But I come this way often. Perhaps we will meet again."

She smiled. "Be safe on your trip, and watch for thieves."

Her words reminded him of the tasks that lay ahead: to recover his father's ring and face Maroie head-on about their future.

He waved and watched her walk back inside. She turned around. Their eyes met and he had the feeling his life would never be the same.

Catherine took the path behind their house, then turned left down the alley that led to Isabel's. No one understood her quite like Isabel. Not even Francino, who tried, but he was a man. Isabel had been her friend for years; she knew everything . . . except the real reason she didn't want to marry Guillaume. Isabel had even helped her think of reasons to persuade her father about the marriage, but none had worked. For that reason alone, she knew Isabel would back her plan. Everyone deserved a little happiness.

Catherine rapped on the door, and once inside, she set the fresh tart on a table. Isabel looked her old self. She'd even smeared a bit of rouge on her cheeks, which seemed a waste of time to Catherine, but it did make Isabel's blue eyes stand out, especially when she wore blue, like today. Evidently Isabel expected Francino to stop by later. "Francino said you were better. I thought you might eat some of this."

"I am. I think it was only from eating bad food. But I'll have some of that tart, if you'll share." Isabel rustled in a wood chest and handed a knife to Catherine. "Francino told me about last night's gathering in the square, how it stormed before the cooks could cover their pots." She sat down and took the proffered sweet. "And he told me about your *trouvère.*" She licked her fingers and winked at Catherine.

"Pay Francino no mind, Isabel. His tongue wags like Madame Mileaux's. Besides, I'm betrothed, and there's nothing to be done about it. We've gone over this before. They've recorded an agreement. Everything is in place."

"Tell me about the musician, the one who Francino says took a liking to you."

"Oh, pshaw, Isabel. We are simply friends." She nudged a piece of dried apple with her spoon. Would Isabel laugh if she told her how she really felt? She decided to take a chance. "Did Francino tell you much about him? He entertains royalty. But you'd never know, not from how he dresses or acts. Why, he bragged not at all, not like Guillaume. And his eyes—he's very kind, Isabel. You can tell from his smile. I even saw him nuzzle the mule. I liked that about him."

"You sound enamored of him, Catherine. You'd better be thinking about Guillaume."

Yes, Catherine thought bitterly. What Isabel said was right. Her life was about to end, and nothing could change that.

"I thought you were going to tell your father straight-out that you'd rather die than marry Guillaume. We both decided he'd have no answer for that. He loves you, Catherine. If he thought you'd rather be dead, I think he'd see you were serious. All these other excuses sounded weak next to that."

"I intended to, Isabel. But Father told me last evening—well, he's sicker than I thought. Don't tell Francino. I think Father wants to keep it to himself as long as he can."

"Just like a man," Isabel said, evidently trying to sound worldly. "They don't want to seem weak, so they refuse to admit when they're not well." She clamped her hand over her mouth. "Oh, Catherine, I didn't mean your father. I only meant—"

"It's alright, Isabel. You're right, but also, he doesn't want people to worry about him. It's just his way."

Isabel nodded thoughtfully, then licked the back of her spoon. "So you never told him what we talked about, that you'd rather be dead?"

"No. Besides, I'm trapped. Somehow Guillaume got Father to sign the dowry papers. I learned about that the same time I learned about Father's health. If I back out now, Father would have to give Guillaume a lot of money, and how would he live? Besides, he loves that shop. In spite of all that, I *was* tempted to go ahead anyway, hoping maybe Gérard would be able to pay off a clerk or something, but when I found out Papa was worse than I thought, I couldn't risk his health. He's not supposed to get angry or upset." She wondered how one could subdue anger. Didn't it come from inside, like hers? How could she keep from feeling cheated?

She wished she could tell Isabel everything, so she would understand better, but she had been one of the names Guillaume had made her say, that fateful day when she made an oath that had ended any chance of happiness. Perhaps someone very brave would risk Purgatory, but not her. Nothing was worth eternal damnation. If it weren't for the oath, maybe she and Adam could go somewhere together. He was the kind of man she'd always dreamed of marrying.

"Oh, Isabel, I feel like my life will end when I marry Guillaume. I will become his wife and that will be it, whereas with the *trouvère,* well, I can just imagine what his life is like. He goes through the countryside, singing his songs, and is respected by everyone." She looked up at her friend. "But all that doesn't matter, does it?"

She rinsed her hands and sat back down. "I have a plan, though. I've decided, since Guillaume insists on an elaborate wedding ceremony, that I will invite Adam to sing at the wedding."

"You can't, Catherine. You said he sings at the king's court. He probably earns more in an evening than a smithy makes in a week. Besides, Guillaume will be suspicious if he finds out about this. And what makes you think this musician will come?"

"Well, it's worth trying. Besides, Papa said he would spare no expense to make it a memorable event."

"Fine, but you're only stirring an empty pot. Why see him again when there's no future there? I'm warning you, Catherine, this is a dangerous plan that could lead anywhere. You've said you're a little afraid of Guillaume, which I never understood, but for sure, this would give him reason to be angry." She leaned forward, as if to give emphasis to her next words, and kept her voice low. "For all you know, your musician may be married. Did you even ask?"

"No, but I could tell he liked me. I didn't pry. He would have thought me rude, don't you think?"

Isabel rolled her eyes. "Well, like I said, you're just making things worse. If he did come, which I doubt he would, then what? He can't do anything to help, if that's what you think."

"That's not it. I just want to see him, one more time."

"Catherine, it's not like you're going to die or anything. You're just getting married. You're wasting your time with this— wandering singer."

"We'll see, Isabel." She rose to leave. "Possibly nothing will come of it. Likely he has better things to do, but what does it hurt to try? He can only say no."

"Fine. Go ahead, but remember what I said."

Catherine kissed Isabel good-bye, then returned to the shop to help Francino close for the day. After he left, she sat down and stared out the window, still mulling over Isabel's warning. Was it, as Isabel insisted, pure folly to think of bringing a royal entertainer to perform for a commoner's wedding? Perhaps. But there was no other way to see him again, and see him again she must, if only for an hour or so. After that, she would put his image in the back of her mind, only bringing it out when she was alone, when no one would suspect, especially Guillaume. The memory would comfort her in the dark days that surely lay ahead.

Determined to move ahead with her plan, she gathered her courage and took the back stairs to her father's study. She found him bent over his desk, where light from two tall candles illuminated the wax tablet on which he wrote.

"You stay too long at the records, Papa. You should let Gérard keep them now. You said he understands them as well as you do." She hugged him and kissed his cheek. He felt thinner, somehow, and the doctor's words rose like a shadow.

His face, once ruddy from riding through his small plot at

the edge of town, had paled to the color of parchment. She hoped it was only from staying inside more, as the doctor had ordered.

He laid the quill aside and turned to look at her. "I mean to have my entries in order before your wedding, so I can make Guillaume aware of our situation, the orchard, the shop inventory and merchants who can be trusted. . . ." His voice trailed off. "But, yes, I'm tired now, and will put this aside, if you will tell me why you come to me this cold afternoon. I'm dressed more warmly than you, and these walls give off dampness. Here, use this." He tossed her a shawl the color of ripened grapes. "It was your mother's."

She wrapped herself in the soft dyed wool and noticed that the fabric had tiny oval-shaped holes which marred its once perfect weave. It smelled of smoke and, curiously, like her father's gloves. She wondered if he held it often, as she did now, a ribbon tying her to the past.

Seated on the three-legged stool near his desk, she repeated her carefully chosen words. "Papa, I would like to plan the wedding entertainment. It would give me something to do to pass the time, and you've said yourself we enjoy the same songs. I'll get the best, the ones you like." Looking down, she wrapped the hem of her *cotehardie* around her ankles, then looked up at him. "You see, you've spoiled me, Papa."

"Indeed, Catherine, and that gives me joy. Only I have to wonder—why this sudden desire to help plan the wedding? Before, you said you had no interest in the ceremony. You wanted Gérard to handle everything."

He studied her face, and she felt her heart pound. Did he suspect? For a long moment, she wanted to tell him everything. He would take her in his arms and say he understood, that of course, she was a young girl with hopes and dreams of her own. He would cancel the wedding outright, and. . . .

68

Suddenly she remembered all the reasons that was impossible. The blasted agreement would make them beholden to Guillaume, for half the proceeds of the store. Her father would be reduced to the status of a serf. But, more importantly, the revelation would likely harm her father's health, which seemed to decline each passing day. No, confiding in him was out of the question.

She licked her lips, uncomfortable under his trusting gaze. "I—I've decided it's time I grow up. It's my wedding, and it's unseemly for Gérard to have to—"

"My dear, I didn't mean to scold, and of course you can choose your musicians, if that makes you happy. Gérard is quite out of his element, planning a wedding like Guillaume envisions. Select anyone you like. I'll give the list to Gérard, and he can contact them."

She rose and kissed him on the cheek, then lifted the shawl from her shoulders and draped it around his neck, looping the ends over his chest. She blinked back tears, almost wishing he had turned her down. His trust hurt more than anything, and she felt a rising anger at what she'd just done. While it wasn't an out-and-out lie, she'd not been truthful.

She swallowed, hoping her voice did not betray her feelings. "And now, do rest. I will fix you a cup of hippocras with the spices you like." She turned to go, then paused. "I'll bring some wood, too. You need a fire in here, Papa."

He smiled at her and turned back to his desk.

Back in her room, she knelt at her corner altar and bowed her head. *Holy Mary, pray for me. I am betrothed to marry. Look not with scorn upon me, but give me wisdom and grace . . . and, if it pleases you, ask Him to remember the miracle.*

A shutter banged against the window casing. She rose and crossed to the opening. A rainstorm was approaching from the north. Warning clouds gathered in the distance, and the sky turned angry gray, and a moment later a bolt of white light ripped through the room, raising the hair on her head.

She shuddered. What if it all was a warning not to tamper with fate?

CHAPTER NINE

As Adam neared Arras, he tried to put the girl from his mind. Fate had played a cruel joke; not only was she betrothed, but he was married to another. Still, some part of him was glad they'd met. Perhaps he would stop there again, on his next trip to Paris. Did he dare?

He looked ahead, forcing his thoughts to the task of getting back his father's ring. Until he did, he would have no peace.

The glistening white wall that surrounded the town of Arras seemed more brilliant than ever. Built of sandstone, it guarded the city like a competent army, and bore a plaque designating the donor, Count Robert, Adam's patron and friend. After building a mansion in the cathedral section of the city, Robert had commissioned the wall to connect the city's seven gates.

From the corner of his eye, Adam caught sight of something moving above the high wall. He rode closer and saw a figure on the horizontal timber that secured the vertical beams of a mangonel, the city's main defense against invading legions.

A bemused smile crossed his lips. He had seen that mangonel in action, loaded from the ample pile of stones nearby, and when the flying boulders failed to deter the attackers, the townspeople had used the deadly carcass of an infected animal to spread disease among those who would dare invade Arras.

He paused inside the gates and looked overhead. The figures high on the mangonel were Liegart and his monkey. Adam mused that the dwarf probably liked it up there, where he could look down upon the townspeople instead of they on him.

The dwarf scrambled down. "Adam! You're back," he called out. "I'll swear, an ale is not the same without you. That fat pig has kept low since your exile." He chuckled. "I believe he feared an uprising."

Adam laughed, then quickly grew serious. "He's still here?"

Liegart nodded. "Evidently assigned some minor position. He took an office near the square."

Then my job may be easier, Adam thought. He patted the mule's rump. "Want a ride?"

Liegart looked doubtful as he neared the animal. The monkey screeched and bared his teeth, and the dwarf stepped back. "We'll walk, thanks. He doesn't like mules." He reached for the two paws that dangled beside his neck, then ran ahead. "Meet you at the tavern."

Adam shouted an objection, but his words were drowned in the rumbling of a passing cart.

He rode the mule to the designated stable, and as the mule tender led the animal to a stall, he told Adam the additional fee was for the return of the mule. "I have to feed him, and it may be weeks before I have another rider going to Vitry."

Adam nodded, grateful to be rid of the beast, which had balked at every command along the way. If he had known the mule's temperament, he'd have chosen to walk.

The ale had been too warm, the tavern too hot, and after two cups, he went home. That evening, after a solitary meal, he went to bed. While the city slept, he lay awake, listening for Maroie's footsteps which never came.

The following morning, he made his way to the square, intent on seeing the magistrate. Adam proceeded past the bowery where two monks from Saint-Vaast kept a guarded watch on the relics and a shiny offering bowl placed prominently in front of the bowery. He tossed in a coin and continued to the Petit Marché, where noise from the taverns drowned out the shopkeepers' complaints. Beyond the row of guildhalls, he came to the Monetary Exchange, the lower part of which was taken up with offices for the town's officials.

When he stepped inside the office of the magistrate, a clerk scooted from behind a desk and hurried down a hallway.

A moment later, the magistrate from Paris greeted Adam, extending his hand like an old friend. "Ah, yes. Nice of you to visit. Sit, sit." The magistrate turned to the clerk. "Bring a vessel of wine for our visitor."

Before Adam could recover from the surprise, the magistrate hurried to offer his apologies. "I'm only one man, you see. I was sent to rout out the troublemakers. It was only later I learned my error—a week ago, actually. A clerk told me who you were. I thought, that morning in the square, that I'd seen you somewhere. I've no wish to anger your patron. I would have sent a messenger, but by then I knew your exile was nearly over." He wiped his face with his sizeable sleeve. "May I extend my apologies?" He shrugged. "What can I say? I'm truly sorry."

"It's not that that I've come about," Adam said, his mind racing. So, the rotund magistrate had discovered Adam's association with the count and was trying to make amends for his mistake. That should make the job that much easier.

"I need to see the two guards who escorted me to Douai. Since they're not from Arras, I assume they came from Paris with you."

The magistrate seemed to relax, now that he knew his visitor's intention. He sipped wine and leaned back against the wall. "On the contrary, they approached me for work. Seems they were employed by the city governor of Liévin as hangmen." He shook his head. "A tough breed, to be sure, but they needed money, so I hired them. Strange," he said, scratching his chin.

"They never came back for their last week's pay. Could I ask what interest you'd take in two ruffians?"

Adam felt heat rising to his face as he tried to control his voice. "They have something of mine."

"Thieves? Did I employ thieves?" He wiped his brow again. "This is most unfortunate. How can I help?"

"I only need some information: their names, where they can be found."

"I'm afraid I can be of little help." The magistrate frowned, then held one stubby finger in the air as if testing the wind. "Wait! They did say something about returning to Liévin, how they could earn more there than working in a community where citizens were an industrious lot." He chuckled, showing yellowed teeth. "I suppose Arras, with its open markets and docile monks proved to be a bit boring for their taste—considering their past, I mean." He circled his neck with his hands and sputtered another laugh.

"Liévin, you say? You're sure of that?"

"I only know that's where they lived before coming here. As far as their whereabouts now, I cannot say. I'm sorry."

Adam rose from the hard bench. "Then I shall begin in Liévin."

"Fine, fine. Let me know if I can be of further service."

Adam suppressed a grimace, remembering the episode in the monastery courtyard. "No, thank you. You've done quite enough."

He walked out of the magistrate's office and headed home, thinking he would have to rent a horse from the stableman for the journey to Liévin. Thank goodness he had a generous patron, whose monthly stipend had arrived just at the right time. Liévin was too far to walk.

That evening, having waited for hours for Maroie to return home, he let the fire die out and went to bed. The next morning he woke alone. Evidently Maroie had chosen another's bed. So be it. The time had come for a permanent separation. If he had to live by himself, it would not be like this. He had half-hoped she would confront him, but she seemed content to go on as they were. For him, that was unthinkable. Once this business in Liévin was over, he would tell her his plans. If she wanted to be a part of his life, there would be new rules. If not, he could accept that too. He'd waited too long, overlooked too much, but it had to end—not that he had not been partly to blame. Women wanted their men at home, not traipsing to Paris, or wherever he may be sent. He rose and dressed, wondering if the girl in the tapestry shop had had anything to do with his newfound resolution, but quickly rejected the idea. After all, Catherine would be married soon, and never give him a thought.

He stepped outside, closed the door behind him, and took a deep breath of air. The smell from the dye vats mingled with a breeze from the river, a peculiar mixture that would probably send Madame Crespin straight to the authorities again. He came to the baker's stall, purchased a warm tart, and walked to the stable. A mule was the only spare beast available. It would be a slow ride to Liévin.

The mule proved to be an obstinate beast, stopping at will to paw the ground or munch on a leaf. Earlier, while paying the stableman, Adam had remarked on a mule's stubbornness. The stableman assured him it was the animal's superior wisdom, a sense of self-preservation that made them seem obstinate. Adam, however, wasn't so sure. What should have been a four-hour journey had taken a better part of the day and evening, but by midnight, he had tethered the mule safely in the inn's stable, and rented the last remaining room.

The next morning Adam woke to the sound of bells calling the people of Liévin to mass. His business had nothing to do with God, though, but rather with the devil's rogues. He put on a clean tunic, went to the kitchen and reached for the breadbasket, admiring the innkeeper's invention. The basket hung from the rafters on a greased twine threaded through a wooden disk that prevented hungry mice from raiding it.

"Help yourself," the innkeeper called from a corner. "We're going to the garden. Leave the fee on the table when you go, unless you plan to return."

"I have business in Liévin, and I may be here all day. I'll be back tonight for some more of your wife's good stew."

"Very well. Tonight then." The innkeeper picked up a basket and followed his wife outside.

Adam broke off a hunk of bread and spread stewed cherries on it while two dogs begged at his feet. He reached for his cape and beret, tossed the crust to the dogs, then walked under the archway and into the street.

For the third time that morning he checked his purse, a new one purchased from a traveling merchant who had stopped by the monastery in Douai for a night's sleep. Reassured that the folded notice of safe passage from Robert was still there, Adam tucked the purse at his waist. Hopefully, he'd not need the document. He would rather not rely on his patron's influence, but if need be, a glimpse at a royal signature sometimes aided the memory.

He ignored a wine hawker's offer of samples and walked away from the creek front into one of the better sections of Liévin. Here, the streets were cleaned, gardens were tended. He made his way to the magistrate's house, following the directions of the innkeeper, and paused at the entrance, wondering how much he needed to confide in this stranger, then boldly lifted the knocker on the oak door.

A servant answered, bowing, and Adam followed him into the first of two adjoining rooms. A gaunt man sat behind a table, his bony fingers stroking a black bird.

He looked up. "Isn't he pretty?" The man indicated an empty bench across from where he sat.

Adam paused, looking first at the bird, whose eyes were closed, then at the man who continued stroking the dark feathers. "Indeed, he is a handsome one." He walked to the bench, wondering if the man were addled or simply unwise. "I need to see the magistrate."

"That would be me. You see, the bird is blind in both eyes. I found him just outside the door, hardly able to stand upright. I've nursed him back to health, and my wife says I must keep him away from the bed, so I bring him out here. What can I do for you?"

He had wasted his time. The man would know nothing. Still, no harm in trying. "I have a concern, and I need your help. I'm looking for two brothers—red hair, one taller than the other. The short one is missing four fingers, so they're easily recognizable. They used to work as hangmen here. I'm told you would know where to contact them."

The magistrate peered at Adam with dull eyes, then looked back at his pet. "I'm sorry. If it's not pertaining to the town's ordinances, I can't help you. Wait until the officials meet next Tuesday. They can be more help." He resumed stroking the bird perched near his hand.

"It is in your jurisdiction. You see, a magistrate from Paris sent me here, sure you could help."

"Indeed." He leaned back in his sturdy chair, obviously disinterested, even after the mention of a Paris official. "I'm sorry. I cannot account for every man who crosses into town. They may frequent Madame Fuente's place, or any of the prostitutes, who mostly stay on the other side of the river. Or perhaps you can find them in a tavern." He leaned closer to the bird, examined a wing feather, and resumed his petting. "But my advice is to ask around at the meeting next week. I'd like to help, but my work piles up each day. A Parisian expects me to keep track of everyone in the city?"

Adam reached inside his purse and retrieved Count Robert's notice of safe passage.

"Here," he said, laying it on the table beside the bird. He had never used Robert's name before, not in all his business dealings or at any time when it may have helped him, but had chosen instead to keep his professional and private life separate. After all, Robert was his patron, and as such had no responsibility to him beyond that. Later, he would explain to Robert what had happened. He shoved the folded parchment across the desk.

The magistrate picked it up with his free hand, unfolded it, and studied the broken seal. He turned it over and read silently.

"I see," he said, taking his hand from the bird. "You know the king's nephew?" He turned the parchment again and folded it, bringing the broken seal together, matching the edges. "And how do I know this is authentic?" He scratched his chin.

The man was beyond lazy. Or else—Adam's eyes narrowed—he was in league with the scoundrels he sought. "You see the seal for yourself. Of course, it's authentic. I merely showed this to you in hopes it might jog your memory as to where the two hangmen might be found."

"Very well." The magistrate handed the folded parchment back to Adam. "I'll try to help, though don't hope for success. I can't control every man who lives in Liévin. I still have . . . contacts, but lately the village is overrun with foreigners, making it difficult to locate anyone. Half the town are strangers to me."

Adam tucked the parchment in his purse. "I'm sure you'll find a way to help. Redheaded hangmen are not easily forgotten." He ignored the magistrate's scowl. "They have something of mine I intend to get."

"Oh? The belongings of one whose execution they carried out?"

"Not at all. It is a ring, not valuable by most standards, but of great value to me. If you come upon these two, tell them they may keep the coins. I want the ring returned."

The magistrate stroked the bird faster. "Does the count know they have this—this ring?"

"Not yet." Adam turned to leave, then paused by the door and looked directly into the man's eyes. "I'd like to take care of this peaceably if possible, without involving the count and his army of trained men. I'm staying at the Inn of the Hare. You can reach me there. I need an answer before nightfall Wednesday, or I'll take matters into my own hands."

The magistrate rose and gently picked up the bird, holding it to his chest, and bowed slightly. Adam thanked him and stepped outside, closing the door behind him. A light mist began to fall and he paused under an apple tree to adjust his cloak. When a door slammed shut behind him, he turned to see the magistrate crossing the yard, hurrying in the opposite direction, the bird tucked under one arm.

Adam clutched his cape against the cool wind blowing from the north. When he reached the creek road he turned and walked past the burghers' homes. Flocks of birds rose from the rushing stream. Dark clouds rolled in from the east, and thunder rumbled in the distance.

He reached the archway that opened to the small courtyard of the inn just as a pelting rain drove the cheese hawker under a beech tree. The dogs cowered by the door, waiting to be let in as rivulets of water cascaded from the thatched roof into the courtyard, washing the abandoned pig bones into the street. He stepped inside, believing he knew where the magistrate was heading in such a hurry.

CHAPTER TEN

Adam remained in Liévin for two days, waiting to hear from the magistrate. After no word, he finally decided that he would need to find the thieves himself. A bottle of wine might loosen a few lips in the local taverns. He would pose as a friend of the red-haired scoundrels. Questions would have to be carefully worded so as not to reveal his true motive.

Adam paid the innkeeper and headed for the square, having determined that the most popular tavern would be there. He took an alleyway between two wooden structures and was about to step into the square when a young beggar rose from his spot at the corner. "Please, *Monsieur*, can I have a coin?" He clasped Adam's waist with both hands. Adam tried to pull away and was about to reach into his purse when he saw the flick of a knife. In the blink of an eye, Adam grabbed the urchin's wrist, and the knife dropped to the ground. The next moment, Adam stepped on the knife, and he managed to grip the boy's arms behind his thin frame.

"For shame, boy. Begging is one thing. Thievery will get you to prison."

"Please, please don't call the *sergeant*. He'll send me to jail for sure!"

"As well he should." Adam held tight to the boy's arms and led him to the doorway of an abandoned building, away from the shoppers who were making their way to the vendors' stalls. Slowly he released his grip on one of the boy's arms, careful to keep one eye on the urchin's quick hands.

The youth seemed to be trembling, and Adam knew he was about to run for freedom, fearful of the authorities. "Tell you what. I'm looking for someone, and if you help me, you'll earn not only a coin, but my promise not to turn you in."

The boy's eyes widened and he bit his lip. "Is this some kind of trick?"

"Not at all. I thought, since you must see everything that goes on in the town—"

"Yes, yes, I do. I see everything." The boy appeared to relax a bit and Adam continued.

"I'm looking for two red-haired men. One has no fingers on his right hand. Have you ever seen anyone like that?"

The boy's face spread into a grin. "How much will you pay?"

Adam shook his head. "I told you, I'd not report you for thievery. As to the coins, it will depend on what you have to tell me."

The waif let out a sigh, as if he knew Adam had the upper hand. "I know of them. I even know where they live. But the one with a ruined hand—he's in jail." He leaned forward. "I saw it all. They stole from the coin bowl, the one people put coins in to view the relics. The big man was guilty too, but he blamed it on his brother. The magistrate let him go. Later, I saw something passed between the bigger hangman and the magistrate. I bet he paid the magistrate. Wonder why he didn't save his brother, too." The boy looked up at Adam. "If you buy me a tart, I'll take you to the place where he stays."

Adam nodded toward a baker's stall, and together they crossed the square.

While the urchin ate the second of a basket of tarts, he described the public trial, how he had wanted to speak up but knew that the authorities wouldn't believe a street beggar, especially one his age.

The dirt path led past a row of hovels. They came to what looked like an abandoned stable. Part of the roof had fallen in, but one side remained covered. A mounting block near the door and a coiled rope confirmed Adam's suspicions; the two brothers had taken over the abandoned building as their own.

Adam's footsteps crunched in layers of dried leaves, accumulated from the beech tree that shaded the entryway. He paused in the shadows. "Run along now, back to the square." He handed the boy a coin, and the youth turned away.

A door to the darkened building stood ajar. Crafted of sturdy planks, it contrasted with the weathered boards supporting what remained of the roof. Adam's heart beat fast. He anticipated a confrontation, but hopefully this could be settled peaceably.

He knocked on the door. When there was no answer, he pushed the door wider and called out. "Anyone home?"

After several minutes he set one foot inside and leaned into the darkness. "Yo! Anyone here?"

When there was no answer, Adam stepped inside. The room held the smell of spoiled food and unwashed bedding. The only light came from an opening on an outside wall. As his eyes adjusted to the dim light, he saw a cot in one corner, piled high with what looked like a tangle of clothing and bedding. Strewn carelessly on the floor were food wrappers, some of which had contained fish, Adam thought, judging by the smell.

He spotted a lamp, and decided to light it and look around. Perhaps the ring could be found and he'd be gone before anyone returned home.

He had only begun his search when he heard quick footsteps outside. The urchin burst into the room. "Here he comes, heading this way. Quick, *Monsieur*. He's been at the tavern, and I know from experience he gets mean when he's drunk."

Adam scowled. "I told you to leave. This is no place for boys."

"You may need help, *Monsieur*. Once he pushed me into a

ditch when I asked for money. I felt his boot on my face."

Adam was about to reply when he saw a shadow fall across the path, too late for the boy to disappear.

Stepping outside, Adam decided to confront the man boldly. Remembering the chaffing rope, the insults they had thrown his way gave him courage.

The red-haired hangman braced himself, rather unsteadily, and squinted at Adam. "Whatcha want?"

"My ring. I'll leave quietly once I get what is mine."

The man seemed to be trying to focus his eyes. Adam's heart sank. Would he have to come back in the morning, before the taverns opened? How could he reason with a man so full of wine?

The thief gave a grunt, then walked to one of the uprights that supported the roof. He wrapped one arm around the post, an effort Adam judged might keep him vertical. "Whatcha want?" he repeated. "You some kind of official? I've done nothin' wrong."

Adam stepped closer. "A few months back, you robbed me of my purse—in Douai. I only came for the ring that was in it." He hoped the drunk could remember back that far.

The man picked a splinter from the post and picked at his teeth. Finally, he lifted his head. "Now I remember—the monastery. Ah, you must mean my brother. He's a thief alright. In jail right now for stealin' from the monks." He leaned to spit, then glanced at the open door. "You been in my house? Lookin' around, were you?" He took his arm from the post and balled his fists.

Adam took a step forward and crossed his arms. "I mean to get my ring back one way or the other."

The man's face broke into a grin. He reached with surprising speed to the belt at his waist. A flash of light on metal warned Adam the thief had a dagger clasped in his hand. With the speed of a man experienced with a blade, he swung his huge arm at the side of Adam's head. The blade narrowly missed its target.

The thrust sent the man staggering, off balance, and Adam moved in, taking advantage of the man's drunkenness. A cuff to the side of his head was all it took. He crumpled to the ground, cursing and slobbering.

Adam's gaze flicked to a movement at his side, and before he could gather his thoughts, the urchin ran from the shadows and picked the knife from the dirt. He wiped it on his threadbare tunic, then handed it to Adam, never taking his eyes from the man's still body.

Adam knelt beside his tormentor, whose eyes seemed to be searching for some unseen object in the air. "Where's my ring?"

The man shook his head from side to side. Adam, judging the man by now too weak to fight back, held the dagger near his throat. "Speak up, or so help me. . . ." He pressed the sharpened tip against the man's skin. "In the house? In your purse?"

The waif by now had turned the man's coin purse inside out. Two coins rolled into the dirt. He shot a glance at Adam, who nodded.

Adam had about decided that either the ring had been sold, or the drunk could truly not remember, but he suddenly lifted a hand and pointed to the door, careful not to move his head. "Inside . . . clay pot." He closed his eyes, his head lolled to the side, and Adam knew he'd gotten all the information he was going to get.

He rose and walked inside. The waif trailed behind. After searching the room, Adam had almost given up when the boy crawled from beneath the cot, triumphantly holding a clay pot aloft and handing it to Adam.

He emptied the contents onto the table—an assortment of coins, trinkets, and jewelry. There, lying among the coins, was the ring, gleaming in the light from the lamp, and for one incongruous moment Adam was back in Arras, watching his father making notes, the ring reflecting firelight.

The boy cleared his throat. "Can I have these?" he asked, pointing to the coins.

"Only a few. After all, we're not sure they were all stolen." Adam extinguished the lamp.

"They were," the boy replied knowingly.

They stepped outside, walked past the sleeping red-haired thief. When they reached the square, Adam admonished the boy for attempting to take what was not his, knowing all the while that the youth would probably follow in the ways of the thief they'd just bested.

After listening patiently, the boy nodded, gave Adam a broad smile, then walked off in the direction of his chosen spot. He'd almost reached the corner when Adam saw two well-dressed men, obviously visiting officials from Paris, heading for a cobbler's shop. The boy blocked their path, and Adam saw them both reach to their purse and drop coins into the waif's outstretched hand.

Adam shook his head. How difficult life was for those like the young beggar, doing any man's bidding for a coin to buy food. Was a man's fate decided at the moment of birth? Evidently so. The youth most likely had been born in a cold hovel, and from the moment of his first gasp for air, had struggled to keep warm and get food in his belly. Was there hope for men like him? Could he, with determination and wit, rise to a better life?

Adam headed toward Arras. There was still time to get partway before sunset. He wondered again what would become of the boy. Perhaps, even in the echelon of street waifs, there was a hierarchy that would propel a determined man to succeed. After all, weren't there knights who had come from low-born parents, but who, with determination, had risen to lofty ranks others only dreamed of? So perhaps birth had nothing to do with it, but only passion and initiative and the will to change one's fate. And a smile, in the worst of times, like that on the face of the young beggar. But did he have the courage of the street waif to face what lay ahead? His thoughts ran together like inferior tapestry dye. First, he had to deal with his shattered marriage. Only then could both he and Maroie find happiness, a happiness, he thought recklessly, like he could have had with Catherine, had she not been promised to another.

Dusk had settled when he stopped at an inn which offered nothing more than a narrow mat in a noisy room. The next morning Adam woke to the clamor of the two bells at Notre Dame, announcing the Feast of the Assumption. A single bell rang one final reverberating tone, reminding him of the looming fear he'd had in the monastery, the fear that the fountain of creativity he'd always enjoyed might have dried up.

He dressed and reached for his bundle. The safe passage document lay atop a parchment that held a verse he had started. He rolled both together and slid them into a horn given to him by an ivory trader who had stayed at the inn. After laying the room fee on the table, he mounted the mule and started down the path back to Arras. Recovering his father's ring was a stroll in the square compared with confronting Maroie, but it had to be done.

Chapter Eleven

Adam passed through the gates of Arras late that afternoon. Eddies of dust blew across the road. He drank the last of his water, thinking the farmers here could have used some of Liévin's downpour.

He dismounted and led the mule to the stable door, settled the account, and headed toward his house.

"Yo! Adam!" It was the high-pitched voice of the dwarf.

Liegart scrambled down a pile of rocks to land in front of Adam. He hugged Adam's legs, and the monkey gripped Liegart's shoulder.

Adam smiled. The dwarf's pet resembled an irate child, frowning as it did with brows drawn together over glaring round eyes. Adam embraced the dwarf, careful to avoid the monkey's outstretched paw.

Liegart peppered him with questions that he deflected, too focused on what lay ahead with Maroie to concentrate on anything else. Liegart finally fell silent, giving Adam time to collect his thoughts. He glanced at the familiar toolmaker's stall, the casket maker's modest house. True, he had friends here, but his life would never be the same. Even before his exile, other members of the Puy, fearful they, too, would be accused of civil disobedience, had expressed reluctance to perform publicly. Who was to say that what was satire one day would not be a punishable offense the next? All of that, he mused, would have eventually blown over, but his biggest concern, the failure of his marriage, would not go away. Months ago, their friends seemed to have chosen sides, as if they knew who shouldered the blame, something he didn't know himself. What he did know, and what the whole town knew, was that Maroie preferred to spend her time sitting in taverns with her unmarried friends. Until now, he had rejected subtle hints from his friends, about the cloth buyer from Paris, but the thoughtful abbot at the monastery had forced him to think about his future. No longer would he put aside his own ambitions, hoping to placate Maroie. He would go to Paris to study, something he knew she would scorn. So be it. Her refusal to go with him would be proof enough of her infidelity, as if he needed more. He had been blinded by what he wanted to believe, in spite of what his friends told him candidly. When had he decided to end the charade? Was it in the tapestry shop, when Catherine had teased him into buying a tapestry he didn't need? He smiled, in spite of what lay ahead.

The five bells at Saint-Vaast rang, a steady funereal peal, bringing him back to the present.

"Who died?" Adam asked.

"Only yesterday, the councilman's wife . . . um, Lantsier," the dwarf explained in his hoarse high-pitched voice. "She was old and sick—almost fifty-five, I was told. I overheard some women. They say she went quite mad." He looked up at Adam. "They think because I'm short, I can't hear." His face registered amusement at his own joke.

They neared the square. "You're deep in thought, Adam. What's wrong?"

"Nothing, nothing. I was just thinking of being back here again." He reached to stroke the monkey who rode on the dwarf's shoulder; the animal glared as if daring him to come closer.

They approached a tavern, and Liegart nodded toward the entrance. "Let's have an ale, to celebrate your return."

Adam heard a woman's laughter coming from inside the tavern. The sound reminded him of Catherine's silvery laughter when she had discovered he sang for royalty.

"What do you say, Adam?"

"Maybe we can share an ale tonight. I need to put this bundle down. I feel as if it grows from my back."

"Very well. Tonight then." The dwarf disappeared through the arched doorway. Above it, a faded sign swung monotonously to and fro on rusty hooks.

He neared the house. The chickens scratched in discarded straw between the buildings. Maroie's marigolds bloomed by the door, and she had opened the wood shutters to the autumn air. A wave of regret and sadness at what might have been dissipated all thoughts of Catherine and unfaithfulness and resentment. The memory of earlier dreams he and Maroie had shared hurt like a deep wound.

He walked inside, put his bundle and *vielle* on the table, and removed his beret. She stood with her back to him and continued folding a cloth. "Oh, you're back?"

He went to her, rested his hands on her shoulders, and felt her body tense under his touch. He wanted to tell her about Douai, about the guards and how he recovered his father's ring. She moved away, then shooed a chicken from the bench and sat down at the table.

"Tonight, they are having a contest in the square. I am going with Henriette." She leaned over the table and reached into a basket of nuts. Sorting through, she took out two walnuts, then tapped them lightly with the small iron mallet he had bought for her. Axial cracks appeared on both dimpled surfaces, and she closed her fist around them, then sat looking up at him, her dark eyes obstinate. She looked back at her open palm and nonchalantly began picking through the shattered pieces, selecting the choice bites now exposed, separated neatly from their protective covering.

He sat down across the table and closed his eyes, rubbing his hands through his hair. Then he reached for the horn that held his rolled parchment. Nothing had changed. The icy truce that had allowed them to live together was still intact. He'd half-hoped she would ask him to leave, but evidently she had no such intention. It would be up to him to initiate the end of their marriage, something he had avoided for too long.

Tired from the mule ride and his troubling thoughts, he decided to wait one more day. He hadn't the heart for it tonight.

Later, lying in bed, he listened to the owls in the tree outside the window, and the shouts of the old thimble maker who passed outside arguing drunkenly at some imagined adversary.

He repeated a verse he'd written months before, words that now seemed prophetic.

> *Bitterness dwells in love*
> *And originates in there, to speak the truth. . . .*
> *Love makes one credulous and causes it to appear*
> *That it is sensible to persist in*
> *That which is foolishness,*
> *And sensible that which is foolish:*
> *And he who knows the most sees the least clearly.*

The next morning he woke early. Without disturbing her, he slipped from the bed, dressed, and padded to the kitchen area. A few minutes later, while smearing butter on a piece of bread, he heard the familiar morning sounds: the chamber pot, the splash of water in the basin, the *flep, flep* as she plumped the feather pillows.

She walked past him, not speaking, and went outside. He heard her call to Madame Crespin, heard their voices fade as they walked to the nests in the back, and wondered idly if she talked to Madame Crespin about him.

He unrolled parchment, as if that familiar act would quiet his mind. A few minutes later she came back in holding three brown eggs.

He laid the quill aside.

She placed the eggs gingerly in a bowl beside the hearth, then took a loaf of bread from the shelf and laid it on the table. Swallowing, he forced the words to leave his lips. "Maroie, I am going to Paris. If you want to come along, you're welcome. Perhaps we can piece together something of what we had."

She turned and looked at him, blinking, and he watched her eyes narrow, ovals transformed to slits. He tried to see beyond that look, beyond the pressed lips, to see into her mind. He only saw a steady pulse at the side of her white throat. He'd been so sure she would not go to Paris, but she seemed to be considering it. And where would that leave them? She remained silent so long he began to think she would make no reply at all.

A hen that had followed her in began clucking under the table for hidden crumbs of food buried beneath the rushes. A dog barked just outside.

Finally she spoke. "Paris!" she hissed. "Paris!" Her voice rose. "I am tired of hearing the word."

She moved toward the table and picked up the loaf that lay between them, breaking it first into one piece and then another, throwing the scraps at the nut basket. She lowered her voice and demanded, "Why would you think of being a student when you can be a clerk here in Arras, hmm? And why should I care?" She leaned close, her face within arm's reach, daring him, then with a swift motion of her hand scattered the leaves of parchment across the table. "It is little time we are together anyway, when your head is not bent over your songs and poems, or singing with your useless friends."

He recoiled, stunned by the profound bitterness of her words. As he reached to collect the pages the quill splattered ink onto a page. He blotted it with his sleeve as she continued, her back to him, her voice level now. "I have to leave; the market is already opened." She poured wine from a larger vessel into an earthenware pitcher. "No, I won't go to Paris. I prefer the life of the townspeople here. We never should have married." She wiped the spout with a cloth. "I miss the dancing, and am turning old before my time." She turned to face him and slammed the pitcher of wine down, splashing some onto the table, cracking the earthen pot. "Go! If you are gone when I return, it will be so much the better for me. I was none the worse when you were in Douai. Go to Paris! Will they teach you at the university how to be a husband?" She left the room, returning in a few moments carrying her shoes.

He looked at the small sheepskin boots, at her feet in the dark hose, and remembered them dancing in the square.

She sat on the bench across from him and leaned over, pulling on her shoes, brown hair falling forward across her cheek, then straightened, her face flushed. "Go, and I will stay in Arras and enjoy life as I did before our unlucky union."

"With Andrieu? Is what I've heard true, after all?"

Her face colored and he saw her hands tremble, the slightest move that gave away her secret even before she spoke. "Yes, it's true. I come first with him. What did you expect, all this time? I'm surprised no one told you before."

"They did. I didn't want to think that of you."

She picked up a chunk of bread, laughing, then threw it on the table, gathered her skirt, and walked into the street, not looking back.

Adam sat staring at the bread, then broke off a piece and tried to soak up the spilled wine. Her words had stung, though in truth, he had known for some time. Strange, how one can fool oneself, he thought bitterly. He clenched his fist and looked upward. *I vow never again to place myself at the mercy of a beauti-*

ful woman. How can she not know that I cannot write when sitting in a tavern or dancing in the street?

Never, he thought, should he have ever asked someone to share his destiny. Better to be a *trouvère* alone.

He recalled the two of them dancing when musicians gathered at the square, how he had been taken by her comeliness. She had never been interested in his poetry and knew nothing of his music, but he had hoped their mutual attraction would grow into love.

That had been childish foolishness, like the words of courtly love written by idealistic troubadours. Now their vows were broken beyond repair; they were the gossip of Arras. The sooner he left the town, the better for them both.

He ran his finger along the crack of the vessel which now seeped wine. *The shards always show what the pot was like.*

CHAPTER TWELVE

The confrontation he had dreaded had only served to strengthen his resolve. Finally, the end of their marriage had been openly discussed. They had aired their separate grievances, a useless conversation that had left them both exhausted, but the impossibility of living together had been settled. After seeing his friends one final time, he would leave immediately for Paris.

It was late afternoon when he heard footsteps outside, an interruption that any other time would have annoyed, but today, seeing friends at the door, his heart lifted. "Ah, Michael. And you, Thomas. *Bonjour.*"

"If I hadn't seen the dwarf we wouldn't know you were back," Thomas said. "No matter. But you must come to the tavern with us this evening, Adam. The owner's fat wife has promised us a surprise." He poured wine into a bowl and slid it across to Adam, a gesture that made Adam chuckle; Thomas had little patience with formalities. "The other night, some of the officials even asked about you."

Adam grinned. "Could it be they have sent away so many that they have no music?"

"A surprise, Thomas?" Michael said, and Adam suspected his friend was trying to change the subject. "The surprise she promises is probably that daughter of hers. She's been gone, you know. Went to a nunnery in Douai. Strange, it seemed to me—and right after she took up with crazy Pierre, that stable-boy." He wiped his mouth on his sleeve. "Seems they were caught in the straw, and she was sent to a convent the next day. I, for one, would guess she is to be raffled off tonight. This is what I would pay for her." Laughing, he reached into the purse at his waist, drew out a coin, and held it between his thumb and first finger. "And that would be too much." He turned to Adam. "Drink up, my friend. You look as if the inquisitor himself is coming."

Thomas interrupted. "The dart-throwing contest is behind the square tonight. It has taken the place of cockfighting since Gustave was caught cheating and hanged with his roosters beside the tower. Sad, and he was to marry the chair maker's daughter soon."

Adam broke a piece from a yellow cheese that lay on the table between them. "I may come later."

Thomas pushed the bench back from the table. "No, we'll come back for you. If Maroie isn't back, you'll stay here all night and write if you can. We will come at dark, walk to the dart games, and then to the tavern. Who knows who might be there, eh?" He winked at Michael and reached for his hat.

Adam watched his friend smooth the two feathers between his fingers, then roll up the back of the hat and pull it on, back to front, as he had seen him do a thousand times. Thomas walked out the door, and a neighbor's gander ran pecking at his legs, as it always did.

Watching from the table, Adam said, "Life in Arras is always predictable."

Michael rose. "Are you coming with us tonight?"

"No. I'll meet you in the square in the morning. Tonight, I want to see my old friend André."

"Then I'll come with you. We can leave now. The tavern can wait."

Torches illuminated every house of the burghers. Adam and

Michael, passing beside strolling magistrates, waved to merchants and bankers gossiping in the dusk.

"Our lives have become uncertain—ours and other *trouvères*, haven't they, Adam?"

"Indeed, and complex. When we tell stories we must be careful of the audience; one never knows when there are unfriendly ears. Otherwise how would the counsel have known what songs I sing?"

They greeted a cloth merchant who stood gossiping with the wine importer.

"But I don't blame the merchants," Adam continued. "You know we always exchanged verse and comedy freely, and their imitations of kings and queens are amusing and harmless."

Michael nodded, rubbing one cheek thoughtfully. "But we perform for nobility, and performance implies support." He sighed. "That complicates our lives."

"Well, tomorrow—"

A booming voice interrupted their conversation. "Adam, Michael."

"*Mon cher André,* you're back from the south."

"Several weeks ago. The ships had favorable winds. Come, join us for a banquet. It's a special celebration." André nudged Adam with one elbow and fell into step, walking between them. "The meal is almost ready. I have a new poem I've written—not as good as yours, but good enough. Tell me, how was your . . . exile? Did the monks treat you well?"

Adam nodded. "I will write of it sometime."

André paused, then looked away. "Come in, then. The food is ready."

"We'd be honored, André."

"Good. There are events to be discussed, and stories to be told. It's growing dark, and the servants are almost finished with preparations. Sit with me." He led the way into a courtyard.

"I have just brought two chairs covered with golden brocade from across the sea. You'll see they are quite exquisite."

Inside, some guests were seated at tapestry-covered tables. Servants brought fruit in silver bowls, while a boy carried a basin of lavender water into which each guest dipped his hands, then wiped them on a white cloth folded over the boy's arm. A server reached to fill the pots set between the guests. When he spilled wine on the priceless table coverings, the boisterous crowd paid no mind. André pointed to a raised circular table; Adam glanced up where two lavishly covered chairs were arranged on either side of a gilded chair shaped like a throne, its curved arms and high back draped in velvet decorated with golden tassels.

Guests near the head table sat on ermine cloaks carelessly draped behind them. Servants, dressed like squires in vests of damask and velvet, displayed the crest of each household, embroidered in threads of silver and gold woven by skillful seamstresses. Adam smiled inwardly. No royal display he had ever seen could outdo this, not even Paris. Thinking of his journey, he wondered if Catherine would think it unseemly if he stopped by. After all, Vitry was not that far out of the way.

He reached the table, and now, settled in his elaborate chair beside André, he wondered why he tormented himself with foolish thoughts.

A servant covered André's shoulders with a miniver stole. Horns blared from the musicians' gallery above the door, and the meal began.

Servants poured steaming soup from gilded urns. Platters of stuffed pigs and chickens with the heads carefully replaced, the eye sockets stuffed with grapes and berries, were rushed from the kitchen and placed on the tables as trumpets sounded again. Boiled vegetables followed platters of cheese molded into elaborate shapes.

Adam stared wordlessly at one of the cooks' creations: a complete battle scene with knights on horseback, their steeds wearing tiny saddles, carefully molded, with flower petals emerging from the cheeses that formed the lavish spectacle. He was used to André's lavish dinners, but even for him, this was notable. Adam wondered what André had found to celebrate this evening.

"My cooks are the best, eh, Adam?" André refilled his wine goblet. "Now the entertainment starts. I mean to make you forget your crude banishment, and convince you not all of Arras has lost its senses."

Two jokers ran between the tables, kneeling by the ladies, whispering and gesturing, laughter following them as they moved among the guests. Then a lady who claimed to be one of the *trobairitz* of the south sang a song of love, accompanied by a *vielle* and psaltery.

André pushed back his gilt chair and stood, clanging a knife against a silver bowl. "Friends! Friends!" he shouted, lifting his goblet high in the air. "Tonight, I want to make an announcement."

All eyes turned, eager to hear what new wonderment their host had planned. "I am beginning an important undertaking. I have decided to build a castle by the sea to the west. It will be made of imported stones, with jewels set into the walls, more valuable than the king's coffers. You will see a magnificent palace like no other in France, built by masons from Italy. I will hire artisans, who form the great colored windows in our cathedrals, to make even more impressive scenes than those in Paris. When it is finished, all of you, my friends," he said, gesturing from one end of the long hall to the other, "will be invited to share it with me.

"We will have a feast from the forests which teem with all manner of food. There are great animals there to hunt. Unicorns roam the land. That is what awaits us all, to repay us for our years of work and mutual support of the other merchants and bankers who have made all of this possible. A toast to the future!"

André unrolled vellum and read the poem he had written, detailing the days of pleasure, leisurely games and hunts that would take place on his castle grounds; guests would ride swift steeds, faster than the stallions in the king's stables. The verse told of unicorns which would be kept as pets, and exotic birds trained to fly beside falcons; courtyards would be filled with healing herbs and olive trees which would grow and thrive through cold winters.

His guests listened, rapt, evidently yearning to share in this spectacular dream.

When he ended, he rolled the parchment, returned to his chair, and handed the poem to Adam. "Will you find music that fits the words?"

"I will be honored, though it may take some time."

"I'll pay you well, Adam, as you know."

"Indeed, you've always been generous, you and the others." Adam refilled a goblet, then rubbed the ornately carved rim with his fingers and looked at the performers with a disinterested gaze, hardly noticing an acrobat contorting his body with impossible twists and turns through a large hoop.

When a juggler came out, Adam turned to André. "You may have to invent your own plays soon, dear friend. What happened before is just the beginning. Other minstrels will follow; they can no longer enjoy dramatic presentations, restricted as they are, and they'll go elsewhere, to a town where they can perform freely."

"They would leave, leave Arras?"

"They cannot feed themselves without the support of you

and your friends, and now most are fearful of unknown loyalties."

"Ah, Adam. As every member of the Puy knows, we had a bond that appears to be severed, thanks to outsiders and those who come here to Arras, at the king's direction. Or so they say." He settled back in the chair. "And who will insure the Legend of the Candle will be perpetuated? Until now it has been protected by you, the *trouvères*, who brought the nobility and us together. It's a heavy thought, Adam, and too much for my wine-soaked head."

"I beg your forgiveness. I have brought sad thoughts to your banquet here tonight, which should be a time of merriment. We'll talk of this more, of your worries and the concerns of other members of the Puy, when I return."

"Return, from where?"

"I'm thinking of going to Paris to study." He nodded towards Michael. "In the meantime, he will keep you entertained, and you will be busy with the plans you announced tonight. Your lofty visions inspire me, old friend." He put one arm on his host's shoulder.

"Not visions—plans, Adam. Now, if you'll forgive me, I must see to my other guests. Maybe next time you will tell me about Douai." He drained his wine goblet and rose from the ornate chair.

Adam himself was about to leave when he noticed a brown-haired girl rise from a nearby table, her back to him. His heart pounded. She turned, lifted a cup to her lips, and he saw the woman clearly. She was much older than Catherine.

Suddenly he wished he were somewhere else. He turned, relieved to see Michael waiting by the open door.

Outside, a heavy fog had moved in, its swirling mist visible only when they passed a lit torch. The path divided and Adam headed home. A nameless apprehension dogged his every step.

Was he wise to leave Arras? Childhood friends surrounded him here. Would he regret going to Paris to pursue a dream? What if it turned out Maroie was right?

The prior had suggested he was destined to lead a lifetime of searching, but for what? He pulled his cloak closer to his neck and continued down the lane leading to his own modest home. Maroie would be gone, as always. He opened the door to the only unlit home along the road. Inside, he lit a candle, then walked to the room where they slept. He undressed, pulled on a sleeping tunic, and slipped into bed, disturbed by conflicting thoughts, a mixture of failure at his ruined marriage and a determination to see all this through, to regain his reputation as an honored poet and composer, and to begin a new life, alone. But his final thought was of a slim girl with green eyes who sang in a tapestry shop.

After a dream-filled night, he woke the next morning and tried to shake the images of Catherine from his head. He needed to focus on the practical. He dressed and walked to the square, where he waited impatiently for his friends and watched the scene come to life. The chandler and his wife struggled with a horizontal shutter, finally latching it in place and steadying the two wooden legs beneath to support their display. A moment later, the shopkeeper hurriedly arranged candles on the lowered shutter.

Suddenly a goat, chased by a black dog, ran into the square and crossed in front of a loaded wagon. The bleating goat frightened the horse, causing it to pull its cargo to the left, and the youthful driver jerked back on the leather in his hands. Sensing the driver's incompetence, the horse broke into a run, pulling the wagon too fast on the rough cobbles. A rear wheel rolled off, pitching the driver and wagon into a table of fruits a merchant had carefully assembled for the day's display.

Adam heard Thomas's distinctive laughter and turned to see Michael and Thomas.

"It's the cobbler's half-witted son again," Thomas laughed, as they strolled from the scene to avoid the fruit merchant's shouted curses. "His father is kept busy working on his wagon. This is the second time I've seen him tumble. I would keep the lad on a shorter string."

They stopped at the *pâtissier* for a basket of cheese tarts. "So," Thomas said, as they resumed their walk, "you have already made plans to leave us here in Arras, while you seek fame and passion beyond these gates. We'll miss you."

"What I'll remember most," Michael said, "was how, when we studied with the friars, you always managed to keep them wondering. You found the quickest answers to their puzzles, and when you answered them in rhyme, I sometimes feared for your head."

Adam listened, remembering how his friends encouraged him to talk in verse, then howled in laughter at the nonsense, making him repeat a line over and over. "I haven't forgotten either, my friend, how you made me recite in the village, just to draw the young girls to our group."

Michael finished the tart and licked his fingers. "When you returned from Douai, did you think the town would have changed, that they would forgive those who speak their minds? It's the same as it was, Adam, and we understand why you want to leave. Things were not good, with you and others exiled. Now we weigh our words carefully and manage to stay out of trouble."

A legless beggar propelled his wooden cart in front of them, blocking the way, his palm outstretched. Adam reached into his purse, pulled out a coin, and put it in the man's palm.

"Anyway," Michael said, "a few minstrels can't persuade the corrupt ones who promote these new taxes. So many have fled rather than pay fines. One wonders who will levy the next one."

Thomas turned to Adam. "You can see we need your influence, now, more than ever."

Adam paused and laid his hand on Thomas's shoulder. "This is my home, as it always will be. You know that, dear friend, but shifting political powers still hover over Arras. I had hoped to finish the play I started, but I have done no writing of late. There is too much unrest."

"Ah, yes, the play. *Robin et Marion*, you called it. And you think you'll have time in Paris to finish it?" Michael asked.

"Perhaps. And I will return often to see you have not run all the magistrates from the city." They stopped as two children ran in front of them, chasing a frightened pig. "You know how many times I've spoken of leaving to study in Paris, and I can delay no longer. I'm in my thirty-second year, and opportunities are offered that will serve me well. It is true; I shall miss all of you, and these daily talks. But you, and others, will sustain the brotherhood, and poems will continue to come from your talented tongues. Write carefully of Arras, for I will hear of you from time to time."

They strolled in front of the fruit vendor who had once more carefully stacked the small amount of unbruised fruit into neat piles. Beside the table, in a ditch which now held broken pears and plums, lay a wagon wheel. Twenty paces beyond, near the entrance to the Crossbow Tavern, stood a horse, complacent, chewing contentedly on bruised fruit the driver had hurriedly salvaged from the merchant's losses.

The following day Adam embraced his friends and left the only home he had ever known, wondering what fate lay ahead.

CHAPTER THIRTEEN

In the second week of September, five months after Catherine's betrothal, icy winds, not expected until after All Hallows' Day, whistled around the corners of the tapestry shop, bringing her a new worry. Would the unseasonable weather prevent Gérard's messenger from contacting the *trouvère*? She'd sent the message out weeks before and now wondered if he'd ever received it.

As she and Francino sorted through a new shipment of tapestries, her father stepped inside the shop. "I just spoke with the man we sent to Arras. Seems the musician left town and no one knows his whereabouts, or if they do, they wouldn't tell the courier. We did contact the other entertainers, who all agreed to come. The *trouvère* was only one performer, at any rate, and I'm sure it will go as well without him."

She tried to hide her disappointment, lest her father guess how much she thought about the *trouvère* he so casually dismissed. Then, desperate to seize control of the situation, she recalled Adam's words the morning he left. "Oh, Papa. Gérard will think me a fool. I should have told him. The poet from Arras . . . he is often at some count's home, in Cambrai."

"There are many counts, Catherine. It would be like looking for—"

"*This* count is the king's nephew. I remember clearly."

"Oh?" He raised his brows. "It's hardly worth all this trouble, Catherine. Cambrai is two days' ride from here."

She laid down the tapestry. "Please, Papa. I will only marry this once."

"Very well. I'll tell him. I had no idea you were so taken with his singing."

"And why not? He is the best. He sings for kings. Besides, it will impress Guillaume's rich friends." She kissed her father's cheek, hoping he believed the half-truth, when in actuality the memory of Adam de la Halle had grown in her dreams. She wanted—no, needed—to see him again.

"Consider it done." Her father nodded to Francino and walked out the door.

As Adam approached Count Robert's castle in Cambrai, the walls blocked the sun, silhouetting columnar towers and the rectangular keep against a rose-colored halo of light. Gray stone merlons, jutting up from the highest part of the wall, reminded Adam of jagged teeth, impotent fangs bared to an uncaring sky. Between the notches were tiny moving figures, Robert's men-at-arms, walking to and fro on the wall walk.

Riding beside him, a *jongleur* he'd encountered north of Cambrai grinned at the imposing sight. "Just who is this count? Is he truly royalty?"

"He is the nephew of the king. Robert's father, the elder count, was killed in the last crusade, much to the sorrow of many artists he patronized. For a while, King Louis took over their patronage, until the younger Robert came of age and could manage the estate."

A squall blew up from the valley. Adam tightened his cape as loose branches fell onto the path and startled his horse. The *jongleur,* his gaze fixed on the mansion ahead, began to hum a popular tune, but as they approached the castle he abruptly ended the tune and spoke again.

"Aha, if Dame Fortune would smile on me so . . . a king for

a patron," the *jongleur* sighed. "Tell me more. How did you first meet the count?"

Adam laughed, remembering the brash young count who lived part of the year in a mansion outside Arras. "Everyone in Arras knows the count. In his younger years, he hosted tournaments in the square. Not only that, his companions were a rowdy bunch, given to pranks, although Robert seemed always to escape detection."

"What kind of pranks? Nothing serious, I suppose."

"It's a matter of record, so I suppose there's no harm in my saying. Once some of his friends went to a few of the outlying parishes and drove cattle into a churchyard. Others brought a falcon into mass at Notre Dame and loosed the bird there."

The *jongleur* threw back his head and let out a howl of laughter.

"Another time some young men broke into a church. That of course was serious enough to warrant excommunication." Adam turned in the saddle and smiled at the *jongleur,* amused at his interest in nobility, then continued. "The count is no longer that carefree boy, though, but a serious young man. As I said, after his father's death he took over the patronage of artists his father supported, most of whom joined the count's staff. The rest are free to move around as they see fit, but he still lends them his support."

"Aha, it's my good luck to have met you, Adam, for you move in noble circles. With your introduction, I may be fortunate enough to stay here through the winter."

"That is up to the count's staff minstrel. I'm invited here only as a friend. When Robert left his manor in Arras, he asked me to come here with their entourage. I had . . . appointments, which delayed me, but fortune blessed us both, my friend. We have traveled safely together, and I've enjoyed your companionship."

They crossed a creek that ran in front of the low wall surrounding the city, and the *jongleur* resumed his persistent humming. After a few moments he asked, "When were you here last?"

"Oh, two years, maybe three. But I saw Robert not long ago; early this spring, it was. He held a banquet at his manor in Arras, on the Feast of the Annunciation."

"This was before you left Arras?"

Adam nodded. His thoughts returned to the weeks that followed that banquet, when Robert had left Arras, and shortly after, a magistrate from Paris had seen fit to make an example of Adam in the public square. Still, had it not been for his exile, perhaps he'd not have met Catherine, the only bright light in what had turned into a week of catastrophic proportions. First, the encounter over his father's ring, when he'd been forced to hold a knife to a man's throat, and lastly, the final confrontation with Maroie.

He sensed the *jongleur* waited for more details about the count's banquet. "That evening helped me decide to go to university. The count had several guests from Paris. They told me all about the city."

"Were they scholars themselves?"

"No, no. Noblemen. Their time in Paris was spent hunting and with leisure pursuits, like airing their hawks." He chuckled. "But they told me much about the city, how it was crowded with students, how the streets were being paved, and businesses were thriving. I left the dinner determined to see for myself. But other . . . things . . . got in the way."

They rode in silence. A west wind blew the smell of the stables their way as they neared the moat that surrounded the lower wall of the castle. A squire ran to meet them, dodging the crowd of beggars congregated by the gate.

Adam showed Robert's seal, and the squire lifted a horn to

his lips and gave two short blows. As the portcullis was raised and the drawbridge lowered, a gong sounded at the bailey gate and another squire rushed to greet them. Already, the *jongleur* was chatting with one of the stablemen as they walked from the bailey.

The squire gave his name and waved Adam toward an entryway.

Inside, a servant greeted them in the dimly lit hall and bowed from the waist.

"Raoul. Is that you?" Adam embraced the manservant and they walked side by side down the dark hallway to a room that opened into the Great Hall, chatting amiably.

"The count is away but should return next week." Raoul clapped his hands, and a page rose from a nearby bench, carefully laying down the shield he had been polishing. "Show our visitor to the spare room." Raoul indicated an arched opening at the other end of the Great Hall.

He turned to Adam. "Supper will be early tonight; the cook's wife just had another daughter, and he asked early leave, no doubt to cry in the tavern."

Later, after sharing a simple meal of venison stew and vegetables from the fall harvest, Adam walked up the narrow staircase to his room. The only light in the passageway came from the family chapel. He paused, his eyes drawn to the statue of the Virgin surrounded by angels. The graceful serenity, the purity of the sculpted lines of the robe falling from her inclined head to rest gracefully at her feet, contrasted with the agonized stare of the chiseled wooden Victim hanging above the stone altar. Rays from the setting sun struck a circular pane of rose-and-sapphire glass above and behind the altar, reflecting jewel-toned crystals of light onto the pale walls.

Adam stood transfixed by the beauty, and remembered seeing it on an earlier visit.

"It's a gift from the artist," Robert had explained.

"One of the young apprentices you support?"

"He was," Robert had said, "but with all the new cathedrals being built to accommodate the growing number of faithful, his talent is now in demand."

Adam left the chapel, thinking that Robert was tireless in his pursuit of new talent. He had given many artists a start, including himself. He owed much to his patron.

He continued down the passageway to his room. After closing the door, he lit a candle on the table beside his bed, then pushed back the shutters at the window. He could hear Raoul below, scolding the dogs as he made his rounds, checking to make sure the drawbridge was raised and the sentries on duty.

Swifts flew past the window, a startling flap of wings. He watched them dip and soar, dip and soar, and was overcome with a sense of peace, an observer watching an endless duration of seasons, beginning to end, a lifetime away from the politics in Arras and the disillusion of his failed marriage.

The swifts left the courtyard and flew above a lower turret. Adam watched them dart toward the keep, its pointed top reaching for the crescent moon that hung above Cambrai. He reasoned this place would be standing after his death, when his body had been returned to the ground and his soul embraced by angels; would anyone then speak of who lived behind these walls in prior years? Would they remember a count or a wandering musician?

He turned from the window, closed the shutter against the cold and his own troublesome thoughts, and moved his *vielle* from the bed. He thought of Catherine with her lute in the tapestry shop, and heard her singing his songs. He saw her face, her hands holding the plectrum, guiding it expertly on the strings of the instrument.

She would be married soon, and he thought again of the

bridegroom. He hoped, for Catherine's sake, the man was nothing like his father. If so, he feared for Catherine, but what could he do? Fate had played a cruel trick, in bringing him to the tapestry shop and letting him become fond of someone who belonged to another. Strange, he thought. Both he and Guillaume had begun their lives in Arras, but they had taken different paths. Now Guillaume would marry Catherine, and happiness would be his. He hoped the man was worthy of someone like her.

He snuffed out the candle and lay back on his cot, exhausted from his thoughts and his journey. With a vague feeling of loss, he gave in to fatigue and slept.

He woke to a gray dawn and the sound of horses neighing in the stable not far from his room. Pushing back the coverlet, he rose to look out the opening and braced both arms on the sill. Gradually, the gray light changed to silver, then pink as the sun rose in the east, splashing pastel against the plaster facade of the castle wall. Beyond the courtyard the groom led animals from the far end of the stable to a small section on the hillside where the stubble had purposely been left high for grazing. Adam watched the sheep, amused by their roundness above the tall grass, creamy dollops of fleece gliding above the churning pasture.

Of all the houses the count owned, he liked this one best. Built on a ridge surrounded by forests of poplar and oak, it had once been a fortress; later, the count had windows cut into various rooms. In suitable weather, the shutters opened to the surrounding hills, allowing the air, filtered by the old forest below, to dry the damp stone walls. At midday, when the sun paused high above, the flowers and trees in the courtyard came to life; pigeons cooed in the rafters overhead. The scene reminded Adam of a great forest retreat. He inhaled deeply, smelled baking breads, and hurried to the kitchen.

The table where he had eaten the night before now held a wine pot and a bowl of stewed plums.

Raoul stood with his back to the table, cutting a long loaf with his knife.

Raoul turned and placed a trencher before Adam. "Here, *mon ami.*" He ladled cheese and fruit into a pastry. "These are the lightest pastries in all of France," he bragged. "My master has the best cooks in the region. But we will eat lighter this evening; I told the workers they could attend the fair in the village. Your young *jongleur* friend has made himself welcome, I am told, and is going with the minstrel and staff to the fair."

"My evening, then, should be quiet," Adam said, as a young boy entered and whispered to Raoul.

When Raoul nodded toward Adam, the boy reached inside a tube hanging from his neck and handed him a rolled parchment.

"And what is this?" Adam asked.

The boy shrugged. "I only know that a man in Vitry paid me to deliver it."

Puzzled at who would be writing him from Vitry, Adam broke the seal and smoothed the wrinkled parchment on the table. When he saw Catherine's name—coupled with Guillaume's—his heart pounded.

CHAPTER FOURTEEN

He read the message twice, trying to absorb it. The messenger sat on his heels, waiting. Raoul bustled about. Adam looked up and caught the expression of curiosity on the senechal's face.

"It is from an acquaintance," Adam explained. "The message invites me to meet with his daughter to plan the music and oversee the entertainment for her wedding."

The bride wanted his music, but the groom was not especially to his liking. Bittersweet, he reflected, like dark plums, sweet as honey, until the tongue reaches the sour pit.

"Will you go?"

Adam rose and walked to the window. A wild pear tree had been felled and the main trunk sawn into long planks, lain one above the other to promote drying, and now he watched as workers cut the planks and carried them away, no doubt for this winter's fires. He had a choice to make. To accept the appointment would mean seeing her again; unwise, given the situation. Why plant a barren tree?

He pictured her in the shop, perched on the stool with the lute in her hands, unaware she was more beautiful than the queens on her tapestries. Still, what harm could there be in doing her a favor? After all, he had done the same for others. He felt Raoul behind him, watching and waiting. Before he could change his mind, he turned from the window to face the messenger.

"Tell your man I will be there on Thursday," he said, "if it pleases the lady, to discuss the business of the music. I will arrive well before the nighthawk flies." He turned back to Raoul. "Her father must want a special fanfare written, or music for the jousts. Her husband-to-be is a wealthy landowner, and I suspect he plans a grand affair."

He hardly tasted the pastry Raoul had given him. Was she responsible for this? Probably not. Most likely her father heard him sing in the town square. Or it could have been Guillaume's idea.

"I sense an ambivalence. Is it something you want to do?"

Adam shrugged, trying to act unconcerned. "I will go, yes, but then I'll return here. I've a generous patron, and an unfettered life with no complicating distractions." *At least for now.*

Making his way to the stable by moonlight, Adam had an unfamiliar feeling of urgency, and of anticipation. He saw the stableman, candle in hand, checking on each of the count's prized horses. Agnès, a gift from the count, would be kicking the stall impatiently. Someday, Adam mused, he would own a stable of his own. Until then, the mare seemed content with her life, groomed and well-fed like the royal stallions themselves.

He cleared his throat, trying not to startle the groom. *"Bonjour,"* he called out. "Bring me the chestnut mare—the arrogant one on the end."

Once the groom was out of sight, Adam turned to the horse. "There you are," he whispered, "Eating as usual. I thought you would still be with your dreams, dark as it is."

The mare whickered and stomped one of her hooves. He backed away and held a hard yellow apple under her nose. "This is from the cook's larder. Now, let's be off to see about this business with the wedding music."

He allowed the horse free rein as she carried him from the stables to the lowered drawbridge, across the outer yard and away from the castle grounds. The path descended through the pasture, then joined the valley road to Vitry-en-Artois.

A haze of light seeped above the dark ridge, a glow that would become the day. Later, as the sun pierced the forest floor beside him, streaks of diaphanous gold and orange, a fox ran across the path ahead. The mare tensed, but kept up her steady trot, reminding him of the last time he'd ridden her. It had been at the fair before the Feast of Saint Denis, when he'd won the game of strength with the iron mallet. Village ladies had danced around him, tossing flowers, as he'd ridden Agnès into the victor's circle, her ears laid back, refusing to flinch in the pandemonium.

Adam leaned down to pat the mare's neck. "No, circles are not for you, Agnès, but long open roads like this one, where you can stretch your legs and have your freedom. At our destination, there's a quaint stable for you to rest."

Would Catherine have learned to ride? Perhaps, living near the Vitry stable. If not, would Guillaume buy her a horse and give her lessons? Suddenly, the pleasure of the morning dissipated in a wave of envy.

Two days later, Adam rode into Vitry-en-Artois. The previous night, not wanting to seem anxious to see her again, he'd stopped at a roadside inn, a remarkably clean establishment and free of fleas, which had offered good food and a place to wash. He had slept well, dreamed impossible dreams, and now, as the golden orb of the September sun warmed the village, a gentle breeze teased the hem of his surcoat and exposed his bright blue hose, an indulgence he'd bought when in Paris. He handed Agnès's lead to the stableman, then walked the short distance to the shop.

"*Bonjour, Monsieur,*" Francino called out. His face creased in a smile. "She's around back."

Adam nodded, wondering why Francino wore such a grin.
She stood beneath a tree, her hands cupped together.
This was not what he expected. For a moment he felt like an
intruder, but when her gaze softened, his heart raced. "Catherine, what's wrong?"

Her eyes locked with his and he felt suddenly lightheaded.
"I . . . a baby bird. It fell from a nest, or escaped from a
hawk."

Adam pulled a piece of linen from his waist. "Here, lay it in
this." He felt the touch of her warm hands against his. She laid
the bird on the linen, a welcome distraction which he hoped
would disguise his joy at seeing her again. When he spoke, he
wondered if his voice gave his feelings away. "I have a little
experience with birds; they are rather like a small falcon."

"Is it hurt?"

"Only stunned." He looked down at her. Why, she seemed to
be trembling! Was it from concern for the bird, or did she—
God help him—was she as overcome with the moment as he?

She lowered her gaze and he saw her cheeks flush. What were
they doing? What new torment had Fate devised?

"Oh, please . . . my manners." Her voice had taken on a
breathy quality, confirming his suspicions. "Come inside," she
said, walking ahead.

As they entered the shop, Francino offered a box for the bird,
then walked out the door.

Adam cleared his throat. "I got your message and came
straightaway." *Foolish,* he thought. She could see he was here.

She sat near the window, and he noticed how the sun glinted
from her hair. Cursing inwardly, he forced himself to concentrate
on her words.

"It was not my message, but my father's. Actually, the message came from Gérard, my father's business man. He's in
charge of the arrangements. I only suggested your name."

115

"No matter. I am honored by the request. We can decide together what music you want. Every bride dreams of a perfect wedding." He glanced back at the bird, totally discomposed and feeling absurd for chattering like a woman.

His voice caught her off guard; she had forgotten the low resonance, the intimate tone of his words that made her wonder what she would miss by marrying Guillaume. She breathed in the smell of him—the scent of outdoors, the earthy reminder of horses and warmed leather. It started a tingling in the pit of her stomach. She heard her own breathing, and noticed a half-amused smile play around his mouth.

Surely he didn't suspect her ruse. She felt her face redden and wondered if he had guessed her secret. Somehow, she had to convince him it was a practical matter.

"Your reputation. . . . I want only the best for. . . . You see, I just want you to be in charge of the music. I have little experience with this. But my betrothed. . . ." She bit her lip. "Just plan whatever you deem appropriate. Papa will pay what you ask." She turned away, hoping she sounded like any *clyent* securing an appointment.

She straightened a pile of small tapestries. Why didn't he answer? Oh, what a childish plan. She wanted to run behind the tapestries and upstairs to her room; he wouldn't dare follow.

Perspiration gathered on her upper lip and she silently cursed her own foolishness. Why had she been so unwise? He knew, and now she wanted him gone. At the same time she wanted to beg him to stay. What was wrong with her? How dare he act so composed?

"Tell me the songs you like best," he said, his voice soft.

She turned back. His brown eyes looked sincere; maybe he wasn't laughing after all.

"I'll see that they are sung. I will bring a *jongleur.* Perhaps

you would like the song we sang together when we were here . . .
after I stopped . . . the *Au Repairier en la Douce Contree.*"

"That, and any others. I leave it to you. 'Tis no matter."
That, she thought, was a foolish response. Bring him all the way
here, and it didn't matter?

He shifted uneasily, and she thought this was the most embarrassing moment of her life. Why hadn't she listened to her father
and left things as they were? She decided to change the subject,
anything but pursuing this madness about wedding music which
anyone with a pennyweight of sense would know had been a
contrivance to see him again.

"Have you always sung, I mean, for payment?"

He nodded. "As a child I loved songs and poetry. When I was
young, my father trained me to ride and hunt so I could manage his lands. He was a clerk and well-respected in Arras. I tried
to be like him, but my destiny was not to manage others' affairs."

Francino appeared with a platter of sweets, and Adam
reached for a pastry. He ate the tart, then crossed his feet,
uncrossed them, and leaned to smooth his breeches. "He gave
most of his land to the friars, as there were no other sons. I was
just thinking of him on my ride here and hoping he understood
why I must do the thing I love. Each must go after his own
heart's bidding."

"He didn't approve of his son being a troubadour?"

"Troubadour? How do you know the *langue d'oc?* Up here we
are called *trouvères.*"

"My father is from the south, and, from time to time, he
lapses into his childhood speech. I suppose I learned it from
him. Was it hard, going against your father's wishes?"

"Hard indeed, but I could not have lived with myself had I
taken another road. But you, you have no such difficulty, for
your life is opening up a new path, even now." He paused and

glanced outside. "I understand the groom is well landed, and your life will be full."

She started to object, then quickly dismissed the notion. He already knew too much about her.

A cart rolled by outside loaded with barrels. "That's the second cart I've seen," he said. "There must be a fair nearby."

Her flush deepened. The change of subject indicated he'd noticed her discomfiture. She nodded. "A small one. Nothing like the one Papa goes to every year—the Cold Fair in Troyes. He says it's the best, and worth the long trip."

"I, too, used to go every year." His face clouded.

She noticed his changed expression. Had she said something wrong? Did she ask too many questions?

"I went with the weavers, to buy supplies for the household. Most of the town went too. Of course, I've no need of that now."

"Why do you not—"

He stood abruptly. "I'll take my leave of you now. I may write something new, just for you, *Mademoiselle* Durant. And we'll sing those you mentioned. The music will make your heart glad, as befits such a charming lady." His demeanor had shifted; he'd become the professional *trouvère*, nothing more. "It will be a fine wedding."

He took her hand in his and bent to kiss her fingers. She quivered at the tenderness of his kiss, and before he lifted his head, his hair parted on both sides of his neck. She noticed the slight hump which must have given him the name that Francino said some of the villagers knew him by. She wanted to touch the spot, to tell him somehow that his deformity was endearing, as was he.

Her hand felt small and warm, the way her whole body would feel were he to dare to take her in his arms. He straightened, fighting the desire to hold her. To take advantage of her youth would be an egregious blunder, one he'd live to regret.

Hoping his demeanor belied his true feelings, he muttered the only words he could think of. "And now, I really must go." He studied her face, hoping for some reaction, but could see no expression in the green eyes—no denial, no affirmation.

As he left the shop, he felt her eyes on his back. He crossed the road and glanced back. She still watched him with an expression he couldn't read.

After paying the stableman, he mounted the mare. Once they were on the road to Cambrai, he leaned down to whisper in Agnès's ear. "I cannot guide you today, Agnès. You'll need to set the pace, for if it were up to me, we would lose our heads in the wind and ride like flying arrows."

As the mare followed the winding path, Adam tried to think of new words for the wedding songs, but his mind returned to Catherine—to her hands, her pale neck, her. . . . Suddenly, he realized the mare was standing still in the shade of a large oak tree, the reins dangling loosely at her sides.

"Agnès, my poor one. You deserve a rider with his wits intact." He urged the horse back to the Cambrai road and wondered if this parting from Catherine was an ending. Or a beginning.

Chapter Fifteen

Late the following day, Adam rode up the steep hill to Robert's castle. Leaves now covered the trail with a russet blanket that crunched under the mare's hooves. Beyond the trees to the east lay a clearing; wheat had been cut and bundled weeks ago, leaving a desolate field behind, waiting for October's cold.

He crossed the drawbridge to the outer bailey. "Feed her well, Simon," he called to the stableman as he dismounted. "She's been to Vitry and back, and deserves a rest and some fresh hay."

He walked under the arched entrance and into the courtyard. Robert sat on a low bench placed under an arbor. Overhead, a rose bush, which the gardener had coaxed onto trellises, offered its final blooms of the season. The young count wore a vermilion doublet trimmed in gold embroidery. A saffron-hued cloak decorated with the Lilies of France covered his shoulders. Beside him lay a gold sword, a reminder to Adam that his host was the nephew of a king.

"*Bonjour, mon ami.* I'm sorry I wasn't here when you arrived, Adam. I had business in Amiens. Did my men treat you well? Here, sit. There's room for us both." He moved his sword to the ground.

"As always, Robert; Raoul saw to my comfort. I was called away myself, and am just now returning." He leaned to embrace the count, then sat beside him.

"I heard—from informers—that you were sent into exile on

some false charge. Why did you not contact me?"

"There was little time. Besides, I expected only a fine. I saw no need of imposing on you."

"What happened?"

"A new magistrate was sent to Arras. Evidently some foreigner passing through thought that by reporting us, he would gain favor with the officials. He must have heard one of our plays and took our satire as a complaint against the crown."

"Ah, the ones your audience likes best, where you make fun of the officials, scoffing first at the monks, then the clergy." He shook his head. "Politics in Arras is confusing even to those who live there. But an outsider?" He laughed aloud. "I suppose, if one did not understand the rift between the clergy and the monastery, you would draw your own conclusions."

"Exactly. And the magistrate needed someone to use as an example. Unwittingly, he chose me. I believe he recognized me, after the sentencing, but, by then, it was too late. He had to carry it through. But that's behind us, Robert." He shifted uneasily, not wanting to dwell on the experience.

"Then let's speak of pleasant things, Adam. But first, I want a promise. If you need my help again, you will ask."

Adam nodded. Bells tinkled near the rose trellis. He leaned forward and saw the count's falcon, perched on top of a wooden cage, pacing across a slat on top. The bells attached to its claws jingled with each step.

Robert bent to retrieve the last small mouse from a box at his feet. "My newest peregrine." He fed the rodent to the eager falcon.

"He's a fine one, and my chief falconer has done well with him—trained him to catch a rabbit faster than a flying arrow. Notice the gold tip on his wing feathers. For the price I paid, he should be made of solid gold."

He laughed as he shoved the empty trap box beneath the

bench, then rose and extended his hand toward the cage to caress the bird even as it stabbed at the leather gauntlet with its deadly talon. The count covered the bird's head with a hood crafted of fine leather decorated with jewels and gold trim, hiding the eyes that had looked with hatred at everything except the small furry gift Robert had held to its beak.

Adam swallowed, then realized Robert was waiting for a reply. "He is truly beautiful," he said. "Will you take him hunting this morning?"

"No, the countess is preparing even now to leave Cambrai. We want to be far south of Paris before the winter turns too bitter." He signaled for a servant who stood not far away. "Take the bird inside, near the fire." He turned back to Adam. "Come inside. The cooks are preparing the meal. We will have time for a game of *tables* before we eat; and I want you to taste my newest acquisition—some Saint Pourcain wine. It is unmatched, I think." His eyes twinkled. "And you can tell me to what I owe this surprise visit." They walked past the buttery and entered the area adjacent to the Great Hall. Robert spoke to a servant who stood before the hearth, fanning the flame with leather bellows. "Fire's caught now. Go. Tell Raoul to send us some of the wine I brought back."

The count chose a chair beside the game board, facing the hearth. Placing the pieces carefully on the inlaid wood, he nodded toward the other seat. Adam pulled the chair nearer the board, commenting on the beauty of the gold and silver inlay.

"It is fine, isn't it, Adam? I traded a beautiful carved saddle for it when I was in Italy." Fingering the bone dice, he looked thoughtfully at his guest. "So, tell me. Have you finally decided to take up my offer to study in Paris?" He tossed the dice.

Raoul entered the room and set a pewter vessel and two cups on the table beside the game board.

Adam tasted the wine, stretched his legs to the crackling fire, then slid an ivory disk across the board. "I had planned to, Robert. As I said, I was called to Vitry-en-Artois. I agreed to entertain at a wedding there." He watched Robert move his opposing piece to another position. "A shopkeeper's daughter is marrying Guillaume Ridaut, a wealthy landowner. They want me to write the music and arrange for the *jongleurs* for her wedding. And I'm invited as an honored guest—to perform. It's to be held the first Tuesday in November." Adam aimed for a disinterested tone, not wishing to reveal the details of his broken marriage, nor his attraction to a comely young girl in a tapestry shop whose green eyes left him breathless at the thought of her.

"*Jongleurs?*" Robert smiled knowingly. "I thought they had fled the country, now that the king has banned them from performing." Robert's expression was one of guarded disinterest.

"Well, for now, they're out of favor, especially at court. They no longer get public funds, but citizens will always want entertainment. It's like prostitution—the ban is difficult to enforce."

Robert chuckled. "And the enforcers will readily accept a bribe. After all, the king's piety does not always extend to his representatives." He moved a game piece. "But back to this wedding music."

"I agreed to the commission," Adam said, "even though it will interfere with my leaving with you for Paris. As you know, I'm anxious to begin my studies, and will come later—if you agree."

"That's fine, Adam. When I get there, I'll make all the arrangements for your tuition and instructors. I'm anxious for you to meet fellow students, a few of whom I know, but there's time for that." He sipped his wine, then reached for a woven blanket and tossed it over his legs. "And some of the servants stay here to clean, so you'll not be alone. They'll close the house when you come to Paris. Later, when you're installed in the university, I'll travel south for holiday and leave you at the mercy of your teachers. They are the best. Some come from Greece and Italy—famous scholars. You'll be older than some of the students, but you are doubly talented, Adam, with both your poetry and music."

Robert leaned back in his chair, then waved his hand as a hovering servant approached with more wine. "You would write without my help, Adam; we both know that. At any rate, your teachers will find your talent uncommon; they'll be eager to push you further. Studying the ancients—such an education," he said dreamily. "Not for me, though, but you, with your talent . . . I expect someday your name will be inscribed with the gifted ones of Italy." He stared for a few moments into the fire.

A log fell, rolling dangerously near their feet. Robert rose, quickly lifted two pieces of kindling from a basket and pushed the glowing wood back into the fire. "My support of you is one of my greatest joys. You're like a brother to me, and no better use could come of the holdings my father left than to offer you subsistence and education, as he would have done. In the years my family has known you, you've made us proud."

Adam, embarrassed by his friend's flattery, lifted his wine cup and drained the contents.

"More wine?"

"No, Robert. I won't taste my dinner if I have more. It is a potent drink, this new wine."

"But it's the best," Robert said. "What do you plan now, for this wedding?"

"Well, it's a chance to use some of my newer *chansons* in a setting different than most. I've started on my new play, the one you wanted me to write. One player, the peasant, is Robin. And there is a charming shepherdess, of course. A knight will intrude on their peaceful rendezvous. It would make for an intriguing story, and a perfect chance for some of my new songs to be heard. I may include poems and songs from other *trouvères*, for variety." He turned back to watch the fire, rubbing his thumb on the curved lip of the empty wine cup. "It would be suitable for the wedding feast, if I can finish it by then. What do you think?"

"Ah, yes, it sounds like quite an undertaking—but an interesting proposal. Take your time with this wedding, and the new play; it may be your legacy, at least until your study in Paris is complete. Come now, and eat. The countess will want to talk with you again; be prepared for her endless questions about your poetry. She has tried a bit of writing herself, but sometimes gets furious when she cannot get a scribe who will listen, and she forgets her rhyme."

The talk at dinner centered on the countess's poetry, and when she insisted on hearing one of his, he spoke eloquently, of a fair maid whose knight returned from battle, a poem he had written in Arras. It brought tears to the countess's eyes, a reminder to him of what he did best. He could hardly wait for the final course to be served, sure the hex had broken.

Later, back in his room, he lifted a piece of parchment from a pile and smoothed the surface, dipped a quill in ink and wrote *neumes* across the scroll. He played the melody on his *vielle* and changed a few notes before playing it again.

To his dismay, thoughts of Catherine pierced his concentration. He could think of no words for the shepherdess, and the melody he thought would flow now seemed evasive. He laid the *vielle* aside and turned to study the written *neumes*.

He lifted the quill and scratched across the parchment, crossing out and rewriting, and at last he stopped, exhausted, wishing he had watered down the wine at dinner.

Knowing further efforts were futile, he tossed the quill aside and lay down on the bed. In a few minutes he fell into a deep sleep, dreaming of Catherine riding a steed through the streets of Paris, carrying a dove upon her wrist.

When he woke the next morning he remembered the dream, real and enticing. *Too much wine.*

He walked through the passageway to the kitchen. Someone had placed three bowls on a wooden shelf; one held brown eggs, the other two were heaped with ripening fruit. After fanning gnats from the bowl, he selected two pears and sat down at the long table. Robert entered, dressed for hawking: a warm tunic, leather leggings, and gauntlet of mail.

"I thought you were leaving for Paris today," Adam remarked.

"We decided to wait another day to leave. The preparations are too great, and the cook needs to lay in more stores for the journey. I wish you were coming with us, Adam. Don't wait too long; the roads will be impassable."

Robert picked his cup up from the trestle table, and Adam looked at the dark ring that remained on the oak plank. He saw a cracked jug, heard Maroie shouting, and remembered the promise he had made to himself. *I vow never again to place myself at the mercy of a beautiful woman.* Suddenly, he regretted his commitment to oversee the wedding entertainment. He had been bewitched, evidently, by Catherine's comeliness, and not fully recovered from the ordeal in Douai. He should never have answered her father's summons.

Robin et Marion, he decided, would have to wait until later. He must honor his promise to write new *chansons* for her marriage celebration. Once they were complete, he would simply teach them to a *jongleur* and pay the man to sing at the ceremony. It would be his wedding gift, and a polite way to avoid watching her marry another.

He hurried to his chamber, taking the steps two at a time, comfortable with his decision. After a few months at the university, Catherine would be only a dim memory.

On the Monday morning following the *trouvère*'s visit, as Catherine sorted through the latest delivery of tapestries, arranging them by color and quality, she heard someone at the door and turned around to face an out-of-breath man who smelled of sweat and the food he had evidently just finished.

Hoping the odor would not permeate the tapestries, she hurried to the entrance. "Can I help you?" She blotted her face on her sleeve. "Mind if I step outside?" She fanned her face with her hand. "Whew. Hot work."

He followed her outside, as she'd hoped he would. "I'm sent from Cambrai, with this." He reached inside the neck of his tunic, withdrew a purse, and handed her a folded piece of parchment that smelled much like the man himself.

Her heart raced. There was only one person she knew in Cambrai, and he was sending her a message, perhaps to arrange another meeting.

After handing the man a coin and watching him leave, she sat on a stool and unfolded the message, glad that no one was around. She wanted to enjoy it alone.

Mademoiselle Durant:

Regretfully, prior obligations will prevent me from attending your wedding in person, but, as promised, I have written chansons *to celebrate your special day. In my absence, I am sending, at my expense, two jongleurs whom I know personally. They are greatly respected for their talents, and I know they will entertain your guests to your satisfaction. Please forgive my absence, but it is unavoidable. Let your father know that there will be no fee, and that my songs are a gift from me to you. Best wishes.*

Adam de la Halle

She read it twice, fighting back tears, until a wave of anger washed over her. How dare he change his plans, just when she was hoping to see him again?

Francino walked in just as she crumpled the parchment in her fist. "Watch the store. I'm going upstairs for a moment."

She walked through the kitchen where the morning fire still smoldered, tossed the parchment into the ashes, then watched the edges curl and snap.

She'd been a fool. Had Isabel not told her it was a useless plan, reminding her he was patronized by royalty?

The whole idea was a childish one, not much different than her childish venture into the night. Francino was right. She needed to grow up and act like a woman. And it would begin now.

CHAPTER SIXTEEN

Catherine's wedding day dawned clear and cold. She shivered while waiting for the maid, hired by Guillaume, to pull the costly gown over her shoulders and arrange it like a spent lily on the rushes at her feet.

Later, walking from the chapel, arm in arm with Guillaume, she skimmed the crowd, hoping one moment for a last glimpse of Adam, hoping the next he had not come to witness the end of what had been their brief time together. She reminded herself of what Gérard had said, that all new brides were fearful of a new life, and that love would come. She dodged the grain being tossed by well-wishers, most of whom she did not know, then allowed her new husband to lift her into the two-wheeled coach, an extravagance that would have clothed the poor at Saint Mark's for an entire winter. The driver climbed up, and they were off. The last thing she saw was her father standing in the sunshine, waving his beret and smiling.

She clung to the image, all the way to Guillaume's estate. That night, as she lay beside her sleeping husband, she thought back over the past year. No miracle had come, and now it was too late; she lay with a man she was determined to love, come what may, and in truth, he had treated her kindly as the day of their wedding approached, evidently sensing the tension between them and determined that the marriage would endure. So be it; she would do her part, and perhaps, in time, a bridge could be built between them, for he seemed to have no such reservations about their life together. Truth be told, he may have grown to be the better part of Guillaume; perhaps, God be praised, the other Guillaume was no more.

The deed of coupling, explained in detail to her by Isabel, had not happened, though she'd been braced for the worst. At first, she'd lain still, trembling at what was to come, reminding herself the first night was the worst and that hundreds of women had gone through the same thing. Finally, she wanted nothing but to sleep, and hoped the deed would be finished soon. Into the wee hours, Guillaume had cursed and sweated until finally, exhausted and promising other nights would be different, he went to sleep, leaving her wondering if the ordeal would be repeated the following evening. Surely not, she thought. The image of the kitchen maid crossed before her eyes in spite of her determination to cleanse her mind of the past. Her thoughts drifted to Adam, and she lay awake, wresting with her conscience. What hope was there to love Guillaume when another had already captured her heart?

Fighting off tears, she tried to concentrate on what was good—her father's smile as he beamed approval when the priest gave his final blessing, Isabel's comforting hug as they left the church. Her mother, too, would have been pleased at her marriage, had she known. And in time, she herself would come to love Guillaume. She had to. She was bound to him for a lifetime.

Adam, hopeful that the isolation of Robert's castle would allow him to write again, had stayed three months in Cambrai after Robert's departure. With only a few poems to show for his isolation, he finally headed to Paris on a clear January day. It had been four months since he had sent the note to Catherine, but he could still see her perched on the stool, strumming the *vielle*, her great green eyes fixed on his soul.

His journey had been interrupted by bad weather and roads

covered with snow and slush, a distasteful way to travel which had made him spend days of idleness at wayside inns, where thoughts of Catherine played on his memory like a lute melody. She had married by now. His loss had been Guillaume's gain. But at least, to his everlasting relief, his thoughts turned less frequently to the tapestry shop and more often to his upcoming adventure at the university. Approaching the capital city, he urged the horse to a trot, hoping that all the rooms in Paris had not been let.

It was a cold February morning in the year 1266 that he passed through the city gates and stopped at the mule trader's. He handed the reins to the stable boy, paid the fee, then followed the paved street that ran from north to south through the town. He remembered coming here as a child; beggars had lined the road, grabbing at the pannier slung across the horse's back.

Now merchants displayed their wares in front of narrow storefronts, shops crowded together like compartments in a dovecote. New buildings and cathedrals altered the landscape, jutting into the sky. He saw the imposing Notre Dame that Robert had spoken of, its façade towering over the town, a silent reminder of the burgeoning strength of the Church.

He passed the king's chapel, a stone sanctuary that housed sacred objects, including the most venerated relic of the Passion, acquired from the emperor of Constantinople by King Louis. Even laying eyes on the Crown of Thorns would shorten the viewers' time in Purgatory and bring untold blessings to their families. Walking past bands of pilgrims waiting in the cold, Adam wondered if any of them would be blessed, allowed to marvel at this most precious relic, brought from its resting place in Saint-Chapelle to be held up to adoring crowds. Pausing near the church, he shifted his bundle to the other shoulder and fought the temptation to break into the crowd, shout at them to question how many coins were used to buy the relics, if indeed they were not stolen or taken as the spoils of an unjust war. He guessed that again today these peasants would go back to their cold hearths, another morning wasted, not having seen the revered relic.

Just beyond the saddle maker's was a goldsmith's shop, its lowered shutter displaying silver cups and knives carefully guarded by the olive-skinned wife of the master smith who stood inside loudly scolding an apprentice.

Adam paused to glance at the display. While admiring the craftsman's skill he noticed a belt crafted of narrow braided strands of silver, one end of which was shaped like the head of a bird. It reminded him of Catherine and the stunned bird.

Caught up in his memories of her, he crossed to the riverbank and stared at the waterbirds diving for food, listened to the waves slapping the shoreline, an endless irregular rhythm.

Shivering, he pulled the wool cape tighter around his shoulders, grateful for the fur-edged *pelisson* under his tunic. He pushed Catherine from his mind, trying to focus on his practical needs. His first task was to find a room for sleep and study. Later, he would find a way to explain to Robert his reluctance to live as a courtier; the lavish banquets and gaming rooms were not conducive to creativity. Sadly, earlier students had filled the halls near the university, and he regretted the delay in leaving Cambrai, for the few vacant rooms were costly; he intended to be miserly with the money Count Robert gave him so freely.

Standing at the river's edge he watched a barge drift by in the swift current. A puppy scampered along the muddy bank. Adam pursed his lips and whistled for the pup, intending to give him a bit of dried meat.

From his left a voice called out, "You are too close. Come, Jacques." The puppy ran from the water's edge, and he turned to see an old woman clutching a worn shawl around her shoulders. "He plays with the pigeons," she explained to Adam, her voice shocking him with its firmness, considering her age and general appearance. "He follows them to the water, not knowing yet that he can't fly."

As she stepped closer, Adam noticed her lean face and alert blue eyes. In one hand she held a basket; the other clasped a shawl. He wondered if she lived in the street with her dog.

She was walking away when he had an idea. "Madame," he called.

She turned back. *"Oui?"*

"Do you know of a place near here for rent, somewhere quiet?"

She narrowed her eyes. "Are you alone?"

"Yes. I'll be at the university."

"Studying to be a priest?"

"No. I'm a poet. My patron believes I should study the classics. I'll only be here a year or two."

"I thought you might be a musician."

"Oh, the *vielle*. I'm a *trouvère*. If you like"—he opened his bundle—"I've a note from a count who lives in Paris." The dog rubbed against his leg, then shook the water from its fur.

"Never mind. I see Jacques trusts you. That's enough for me." She shifted the basket from one hand to the other. "I live near here, but the owner is raising the rent, and I can't pay more. I suppose I could share the room a few days. It's more space than I need, now that I'm alone."

He tried not to sound too eager.

"If you have a place for me to sleep, I would pay you fairly. Here." He reached into the purse at his waist. "This is for two nights. If you will have me longer, I can pay that to you while I'm in Paris. Will that allow you to keep your room? I would hope it does, for I'm in need of a place to sleep."

She set the basket down and reached for the coins. He watched her sort them in her palm, evidently calculating their worth. When she finally looked up she spoke quietly. "I have prayed. You're the answer to my prayers. My name is Beatris. Come with us and I'll show you our room. There's even a cot for you, though at times you will have to share it with Jacques."

He fell in step beside her. "Let me carry this." He reached for the basket which he knew now held some kind of fish.

She looked at the bundle on his shoulder and shrugged. "You have enough. We're almost there, anyway."

They passed students sitting and standing beside the Seine, their hoods pulled up against winds that blew from the riverbank. He knew they were scholars; he overheard snatches of conversation—Albertus Magnus, Gratian's Decretum, *a priori* reasoning—and he admired their easy discourse over such lofty subjects. They spoke in mixed dialects, and he remembered Robert had said scholars from beyond the sea to the south came here in great numbers.

Suddenly, his good fortune in being here gave him a feeling akin to euphoria. Overwhelmed by gratitude and stimulated by the sights and sounds of Paris, he felt uncommonly blessed. Surely, in time, his new life would erase all thoughts of Catherine from his mind.

They approached a group of small houses fronting a narrow street. Vines formed a canopy between the roofs of adjacent buildings. They passed a baker's stall and the aroma from hot ovens wafted into the street, masking the fish smell from Beatris's basket and the stench of the carrion that lay in the ditch beside the road.

They walked beneath an arch that led into a narrow alley. The dog ran ahead, pausing by the door of a timber-framed structure that leaned precariously toward the street. A fire pit stood next to the building, and Adam wondered if this was where she cooked. He glanced up at the extended roofs of adjacent buildings which formed the thatched shelter overhead. Beatris fitted a key into the rotting wood. The latch, Adam noted, no longer offered any security, but only held the door closed.

Inside, the only light came from a narrow window that opened onto the alley. A small bed fit below the window. As his eyes adjusted to the dark he saw a hearth to his right. Across from the hearth was a table made of thick wooden planks supported on each end by trestles.

Beatris lit a candle and set it on the table. Tapestries, barely visible in the dim light, hung from a cord that stretched across the room behind the table and two benches. A sturdy chest evidently held her belongings. It was built of dark wood, and in the light from the window he could make out a crest carved into the top. A hunting scene was etched in the lid below the crest. The chest looked out of place in such a humble dwelling, and Adam guessed she had lived more comfortably in earlier times.

She pulled back one of the tapestries and pointed to a cot at the end of the room. "You can sleep there," she said. "We're seldom here, except at night, so you'll have it to yourself daytimes. I work at the fishmonger's stall when he brings new fish and needs help with cleaning."

"It's perfect," Adam answered. "I need only a place to read and sleep, and it is close enough to the university. Some clothes and a *vielle* are all I own."

"Good, then you stay. Now, will you build up the fire?" She walked outside with the dog, not waiting for an answer.

He put one of the logs in the ashes, and before he'd retrieved the flint at his waist, a small tongue of flame leaped from under the wood.

He glanced at the room that would be his home. Robert

would chastise him for renting a place, instead of finding accommodation with him, but he would handle that later.

The smell of cooking fish reminded him he hadn't eaten. He stood, intending to find a tavern, but just then Beatris walked in. "I have good fish stew and bread. You're welcome to eat with me."

She ladled the stew into a bowl, sliced some bread, then carried the bowl to the table.

While they ate, he looked closer at the tapestries dividing the room. They appeared to be of fine quality, and he vaguely wondered how they came to be here, in this unimposing room which reminded him of a garret in the tower of one of Robert's châteaus.

"You're admiring the tapestries. You've seen such work before?" She dipped her bread into the soup.

Her perception surprised him. "Yes. It is like those they make in Arras. I have sometimes seen them in manors where I entertain."

"Ah, I knew you were a *trouvère* from your *vielle,* and easy gait." She rose from the table.

He gazed absentmindedly at the tapestries and finished his wine alone, thinking of Arras and Catherine and what he'd left behind and what may lie ahead.

CHAPTER SEVENTEEN

As winter turned to spring, and servants cultivated the fields and sowers scattered seed, Guillaume worked alongside his foreman, supervising spring planting. His amorous efforts had waned. He took to sleeping in an adjacent room, citing an old back injury, but Catherine suspected more, a reason that had nothing to do with the greening wheat fields that surrounded his estate. Not a month after the wedding, he had returned from town late one evening smelling of horse and perfume, a strange mixture for a man buying leather goods, and when he mistakenly called her Jeanne, she knew his lust was satisfied at the *bordel* in Ypres, a tall wooden structure in a section of town her maid insisted they avoid on one of her infrequent trips to the shopping district. The knowledge had left her wondering what was different about her, different from the kitchen maid, or the harlot in town. Perhaps he simply wanted something forbidden, but whatever it was, it had made the whole idea of living with him easier.

The marriage, she now knew, was one of practicality. Not the worst kind of life, she thought, jabbing her needle into her sewing with such force she pricked her finger. Still, there were nights when she lay alone, thinking of Adam and how he made her feel, in spite of her determination to thrust his memory from her mind.

After wiping blood from her needlework, she laid the sewing aside. At least her life here was an easy one. When the nighttime visits to her room had come to an end, she found herself no longer afraid of him. Her feelings were more of pity for them both, although now she saw a new side of her husband—a man intent on wresting the last coin from the soil. And had he not insisted she spend a few weeks with her father before Advent? And did he not bring her expensive gifts on every feast day, saying how much he valued her help with the estate? He had even hired Louise, the young sister of one of the workers, as her personal maid, insisting every landowner's wife needed one. Catherine had objected, saying she could manage with the two maids already hired, but he ignored her objections. The girl had carved a cozy sleeping place in one corner of the pantry, and now she served both as personal maid to Catherine and part-time help for the cook.

Catherine rose and left the sewing corner, feeling a bit ungrateful. Other women would be pleased to have so many servants, and at least it gave her time to pursue other interests. She headed for the room set aside for records. The neatly bound ledgers stood on a shelf, filled with pages of her careful script. She prided herself on keeping accurate records, and even Guillaume commented on how the system was paying off. A quick glance told him what plantings bought the most money, what vendors offered better prices for certain quantities . . . all things she'd learned from both her father and Gérard. The ledgers had been a godsend, turning long lonely days into hours of pleasure as she notated each expense and receipt.

As the late afternoon sun slanted into the room from an open window on the west side of the house, she heard the pounding of hammers, the songs and curses of workmen, a reminder that Guillaume was still outside with the men. She walked to the kitchen where the cook sat nodding in one corner, and after pouring a spiced drink, she stepped outside.

Making her way across the courtyard, she thought how the

estate had changed over the last few months. The fields had been plowed and planted. The evenings had grown longer, the birds sang, and a faint sweet smell came from the stable. Now, the men were busy building a shed, one where the animals could seek shelter the following winter. Guillaume had vowed to complete it before the Feast of All Saints. The recent loss of two oxen had set him to drawing plans for the stable, detailed sketches of every post and stone. When Catherine first laid eyes on the drawings, she praised their accuracy and neatness, thinking it quite an accomplishment, given Guillaume could neither read nor write. Her glowing praise brought a smile to his lips. She could give her husband no love, but she could grant him respect, and any happiness it was in her power to give.

As she rounded the corner of the old dismantled stable, its roof gone and several boards taken for construction of the new one, she heard Guillaume's voice and paused, reluctant to interrupt the conversation, unseemly even for the landowner's own wife.

She stepped under the sagging door frame to wait, away from the gusty morning air.

A moment later she saw Guillaume heading her way, but before she could call out, a worker fell in step beside him, a broad-shouldered man who wore an air of meekness in spite of his powerful stature. The spokesman, she remembered, was respected by all the workers—too much so, according to Guillaume, who insisted the man's son was a troublemaker, having circulated stories of how serfs in neighboring towns received generous allotments of produce, and that some of the workers were given two days to work their own land.

The two men had reached the portico. Guillaume turned to the spokesman. "Go ahead," Guillaume said. "What's on your mind? This better be important. I have work to do."

The man lowered his head and rolled his tattered cap between his fingers, a gesture Catherine suspected was practiced to make him appear humble.

"Master, God has looked with favor on your lands, and bestowed upon us abundant crops last year." The spokesman wiped his face with a dirty piece of wool he pulled from the waist of his *braies,* then tucked it back and continued to roll the cap in his hands. He shuffled his feet, barely breathing, his eyes focused on the hem of Guillaume's surcoat. "Your faithful workers ask that you consider their part in bringing such a fine crop to you. They want only to be included in the fair division of these most abundant fields, and ask if their allotment can be increased as your wealth increases." He paused, still staring at the ground in front of his master as if afraid to lift his head. "They ask also, if it pleases you, to give them one extra day to work their own small plots so they may feed their families, to ensure you'll have strong and able serfs for this season's harvest."

Guillaume walked away, then stood a few moments with his back to the man. In spite of the worker's outward subservience, Catherine sensed the intense disdain this proud worker nurtured for Guillaume and his kind.

When Guillaume turned, he smiled at the messenger and scratched his beard, thoughtfully picking an offending particle from it which he examined before wiping it onto the opposite sleeve.

"You may tell them that, as always, I will give their request consideration. After the grain has been marketed, I will determine a fair adjustment, and will notify them of any change. My decision will be based on the swiftness and profit with which my crops are sold." He walked closer to the man who would repeat his words to them all. "And tell them they can have no more days to work their plots than what I already allow them, at the sacrifice of my own harvest. If they need more hoeing, they should see that their children work faster. Possibly if they rise earlier, they could work before they are due in the fields." He waved his hand, dismissing the man, then turned and walked past the abandoned stable.

Catherine held her breath. She felt sorry for the submissive worker and wished she had returned to the house and not overheard the exchange. She waited until Guillaume had almost reached the house before she stepped into the clearing, having decided not to mention the incident. He would think she had spied on him.

When she reached the courtyard, she saw a traveling tinker had arrived. He was displaying his tools, having boldly made his way as close to the kitchen area as possible. He loudly proclaimed the skill with which he promised to mend the cook's entire accumulation of worn pots in exchange for only his meals and a warm cloak for the next winter. She glanced from the tinker to the house. Guillaume stood by the door listening. Evidently the tinker's ramblings amused him, but he kept his eyes on a distant figure. Catherine turned to follow his gaze and saw the workers' spokesman still standing in the field, still rolling his tattered cap, looking back at the house.

The spokesman stood for a moment longer, then spit on the straw-covered ground and walked toward his shack.

Catherine mulled over the encounter she had seen. Perhaps Guillaume should have made some small gesture of negotiation. An uprising was the last thing he would want. She drank the cooled drink and refilled the cup from the fire, then carried it to the front room for Guillaume, wondering if she dared suggest a compromise, just to keep the peace.

I'd better let well enough alone, she thought. *As Guillaume has said many times, once you gave in, they will see you as weak.* She needed to remember that. No matter how lonely she often felt, she would never let Guillaume know. Perhaps that had been the kitchen maid's undoing.

By the end of August, the laborers' hard work had paid off; grain lay bundled and stacked, ready for market.

Catherine, sorting through a pile of linens, thought she had never witnessed such a cool August; the Flemish town never seemed to get warm, necessitating the need for bedcovers even now. While she was wondering if she should remind Guillaume to check on the winter's supply of wood, he came through the door and walked past her. "Bring us a cup of wine. We need to talk."

She laid the linens aside and brought two earthenware cups filled with wine to the main room. She handed him a cup and chose an adjacent seat, facing the empty hearth which would soon be blazing with fires, not to end until next spring.

"As you know," he said, "we'll take the grain to market tomorrow. We may have to stay a few days, give the animals a rest before returning. You're in charge while I'm gone."

She nodded, remembering how it was before, when he had gone for three days, leaving her alone as a young bride before she understood the workings of the estate. But she had managed, and quickly. Once the servants realized she intended to keep the place running as smoothly as it did when Guillaume was there, the men had set about their duties. By the time her husband had returned, the stables had been cleaned and all the linens aired.

"I can manage," she said. "You have the difficult part. The roads are filled with highwaymen this time of year, waiting to take advantage of a caravan of grain."

"True, but I'll have Emmanuel with me."

At the mention of the guard's name, she lowered her gaze and smoothed her linen tunic, glad Guillaume seemed not disposed to reading one's mind. Besides, how much of the story was true, after all? A cook could gossip as well as any hireling. Like a fast-moving play on a stage, she remembered the cook's words as he spoke to Louise about Guillaume.

"Some," the cook said, his gravely voice rising above the sound of clanging pots and pans, "think the master got his wealth from his father, but that's not all truth. A lot of people suspect he came by it another way, but since there's no proof, he was never convicted."

"Of what?" The girl's voice had a childlike whine, but the cook's words were what interested Catherine most.

"Of setting a fire that reaped him more land, that's what."

"And?"

"It happened one night, so the story goes. The master must have ridden his horse over that ridge." The cook pointed out the window, indicating a rise in the distance at the edge of a newly plowed field. "He evidently knew the Viauds were gone on their weekly trip to Madame Viaud's family estate nearby. Anyway, I was told he carried a lit taper into the drying room, bold as you please."

"Phew! I hate the smell of drying rooms. They all reek of old fodder."

Catherine started to intervene, thinking the conversation was going nowhere. Besides, it was most improper for servants to be speaking of their employer with such disregard. She gathered her courage, but stopped short when she heard the cook's next words.

"The fire, they say, was the master's doing. He probably thought Viaud would offer the land cheap, once he found out he'd have to rebuild. Anyway, evidently the hay was neatly stacked against the wall next to the house."

"So the hay stacks burst into flame."

"Exactly. He would have backed out the door and run to his

horse. No one knows exactly what happened after that, but they think he rode back, crossing that yonder ridge, and Emmanuel must have seen him riding from the fire. He was Guillaume's manservant then. According to what I heard, Emmanuel came from the bedchamber to get wood or something. Guillaume walked inside, right here, and knew his servant had seen the whole thing."

"And Guillaume did nothing to silence Emmanuel?"

"He probably wanted to kill him, but Guillaume's no murderer—cleverer than that. Instead, he elevated Emmanuel to foreman, then guard. Little enough to ensure any man's silence."

Remembering, Catherine could still hear the servants' laughter.

Now, across the table from her, Guillaume cleared his throat and leaned forward. "Are you listening to me?"

"Of course. You were speaking of Emmanuel."

He sat back, satisfied, and Catherine's mind spun back. Hopefully, what she'd heard was only gossip. She hated to think she lived with someone capable of burning down a man's house to get his land, but reason told her otherwise. She turned to her husband. "Emmanuel seems most loyal."

"Oh, he is, he is."

She waited for more, some denial of the rumor, but when none was forthcoming, she decided it was useless to pursue the subject. Judging from the way Emmanuel had been raised in rank, could he really be trusted? There were always rogues waiting for a caravan going to market. It was quite possible they would be ambushed on the road, and she would have her freedom.

Alarmed at the fleeting image, she excused herself and left the room, feigning sudden illness. Once in her bedchamber, she knelt at the altar and prayed forgiveness for the evil of her thoughts.

The next morning Catherine dutifully stood beside her husband in the shade of the granary, waiting to wish him Godspeed.

Guillaume called Emmanuel to his side. "Keep an eye on that new foreman. When he finishes, count the bales and look to see if the carts are full, then oversee the loading of the rear wagons. These cheating workers . . . if it weren't for them it wouldn't be necessary for me to spend my time riding into the village each week."

"You could hire more guards to take the foreman's place."

"Yes, but that would cut into our profits; each of them would want grain for their families." He coughed and leaned to spit.

Catherine cringed at Guillaume's insensitivity to the workers' plight.

He turned to her. "I hope to arrive before the merchants from the south; those monks move slowly when measuring grain, and by late morning there will be a long line of carts waiting at the scales."

A moment later Emmanuel mounted his horse and gave the signal to move out. Guillaume looked skyward, and seemingly satisfied with the cloudless weather, mounted his horse, and fell in line behind the last wagon as it rolled onto the path.

Catherine returned to the house and as she reached the paved area near the kitchen, a cloud passed over the sun. An owl hooted from the woods, a strange sound in daylight. She lifted the latch, opened the door, and crossed the threshold, trying to shake off the sudden premonition of impending doom.

CHAPTER EIGHTEEN

That evening, tired from the day's chores, Catherine climbed into bed, then glanced at the small altar in the corner where she had placed her mother's worn Book of Hours. Candlelight reflected from the illuminated cover, and she felt a trace of guilt, remembering the hours she had spent on bended knee, asking to be delivered from a loveless marriage. And what good had it done? Nothing had changed. She was married to Guillaume Ridaut, and her dreams of true love, made real by her brief time with Adam, had faded into yesterdays along with her girlhood.

She tugged at the coverlet and made a mental note to tell Louise not to tuck them so tightly beneath the mattress. And, beginning tomorrow, when Guillaume returned home, she would put all thoughts of love behind her. Marriage was a practical affair, meant to bring companionship to two people and provide a helpmate to both parties. At least that's what Guillaume had told her, when she had tried to talk to him about anything other than the crops, or the weather. He insisted marriage was never meant to be a fulfillment of childish dreams, but his recriminations had not stopped her wondering what life would have been with the *trouvère* from Arras.

During the first four days of her husband's absence, she found herself pleasantly engrossed in tasks she had postponed; supervising the salting of meat, ordering a supply of dried cod which, when cured, would last through months of bitter cold weather to provide a base for hot soup when nothing else was available. On the evening of the fifth day, she went to bed early. A torrential downpour pounded the roof and walls. She slid under the covers. According to plan, Guillaume would have returned today, but with weather like this, they would have stopped at an inn, even if close to home.

She heard the cook calling good night to Louise as he made his way out. He would be hurrying through the rainstorm to the room he shared with his wife. Sheets of water slammed against the shutters, and Catherine wiggled deeper under the covers, waiting for the worst of the squall to pass. She fell asleep and dreamed she was back in the tapestry shop. Voices sounded in her ears, low tones that transmuted into customers, and Adam stepped from the crowd, admiring a tapestry of vibrant colors. The sounds around them became louder, and she struggled to hear his words.

Suddenly she realized the sounds were not in the tapestry shop but here, in the house—yet she was alone. How could that be? Struggling from the haze of sleep, she propped her head on one elbow. The voices came from somewhere in the house.

"No! Please, no!"

That was Louise's voice.

Catherine scrambled out of bed and ran barefoot in her chemise, groping her way in the dark, moving ever closer to the sounds. Her heart pounded in her chest as she crept toward a faint glow of light. In the hall near the pantry she saw that the light came from the kitchen. Sounds of a struggle ensued and furniture scraped across the wood floor. She reached the cooking area. A lone candle burned. The scene became her worst dream, and she was back in her father's kitchen with Guillaume and the maid. She clamped her hand over her mouth. Was this some cruel trick of slumber?

Something hit the wall, and her breath caught in her throat. It was no dream, but very real. Had an intruder broken in? And what could she do, alone with no weapon? She reached the open doorway and caught sight of Louise's terrified face beside the shoulder of a black-cloaked man. Catherine stood immobile, frozen to the spot.

Suddenly the intruder turned, his face visible in the wavering candlelight.

Guillaume!

She uttered a silent cry. Not again, please God!

He turned away. The two figures struggled together like crazed shadows. Catherine's gaze fell on the cook's bread knife. She eased forward. Her hand closed around the hilt of the blade.

At that instant, Louise broke free, except for one arm caught in Guillaume's grip. He turned to face Catherine. "Go back to bed," he hissed.

She trembled under his glare, almost missing the girl's quick lunge for the knife, still held tight in Catherine's hand as she struggled to remain upright, dodging Guillaume's thrashing arm. He landed a blow to her head. She reeled in pain and he gripped her free arm.

Now the three were together. Catherine caught a glance of their shadows, a macabre dance of death against the white wall. She felt something warm run onto her wrist. A moment later Guillaume moaned and released his grip on her arm. He crumpled to the floor, pulling the girl down with him.

From somewhere behind Catherine a high-pitched cry rent the air. Too stunned to move, Catherine stared down at her husband.

Louise scrambled to her feet, mumbling incoherently. Only then did Catherine realize the housemaids were behind her in the doorway and had seen everything. Horrified, she tried to think what to do, then remembered the liquid on her hand.

Had she actually cut flesh with a knife?

She held her arm near the candle. Dark streaks covered her fingers and wrist.

Someone lit a lamp, and the room blazed to life. Louise stood before her, her face a white mask of terror except for the dark streak on her cheek. The girl's sleeping tunic was covered with blood.

The horror of what happened next would remain in Catherine's memory for a lifetime. One of the maids, who acted as midwife to the workers' wives, carried the lantern to where Guillaume lay motionless.

Catherine's teeth chattered, and she realized Louise was clinging tightly to her, sobbing and shaking as she stared at the limp form on the floor.

With the help of the other maid, the midwife rolled Guillaume over. She sought a pulse at his throat, then leaned near his mouth. He gave one violent jerk and lay still again. Only then did Catherine see the slow stream of blood trickling from his tunic onto his cloak, a great dark puddle that made her want to retch. Even before the midwife told her, she knew her husband was dead.

The realization struck her like a thunderbolt.

A shutter slammed. The room grew quiet, except for Louise's sobbing and the low talk between the maids.

The rain continued to pour, pelting great sheets of water onto the outer door. Later, Catherine would remember little except Louise's terrified eyes and the feel of blood on her own hand and the quick regret for a life cut short because of a man's own uncontrollable weakness.

Two months later, with the shock of Guillaume's death and the brief trial behind her, Catherine sat inside her father's shop, huddled beneath a woolen tapestry that her father had discarded as inferior, and listened to November winds whistling through the timbered house. All along the main street of Vitry, merchants had closed their shops, waiting for spring, but at times like these, wayfarers might stop for nothing more than to warm themselves at the fire. In so doing, a sale of tapestry might come unexpectedly.

She watched Francino idly carve a piece of wood and thought of that November a year ago when she had left Vitry to live with Guillaume in the Flemish town. How swiftly one's life could change, faster than the blink of an eye. She had missed living here, missed the ordinary townsfolk, but especially her father and Francino's sly humor. And now, with Guillaume's estate having reverted to the king's vast holdings, and the shop back in her father's hands as before, she found herself thinking nothing had changed, except her. Unrelenting guilt pursued her like one of Satan's angels, tormenting with memories of prayers to the Virgin, pleas that would finally deliver her from a marriage with Guillaume. That, together with her lingering doubt as to who had plunged the dagger, kept her awake nights. In spite of the maids' testimony, and the final verdict stating that Louise had acted in self-defense, a small part of Catherine remembered the struggle, the warm blood on her hand.

But that was not what worried her most. She knew that Guillaume's death had clearly been set in motion by a power stronger than anyone in that miserable kitchen, and now there was nothing to do but seek forgiveness for such a grievous sin. She must promise God something meaningful in return for redemption. A simple garland would not do.

Late that afternoon, while she and Francino lowered the poles that held up the front awning, a heavily laden wagon passed by carrying a woman and two children. A man rode between them, a red cross affixed to his tunic. Evidently, families were already heading south, making plans to join the next crusade, something the village priest had hinted about for weeks while cautioning no set plans had been put in place.

She stood stock still, knowing she had just seen a miracle. The family's passage was a sign of what she would promise God in exchange for redemption.

All that evening, she pondered what she had seen. This was not like one of those superstitious rituals promoted by gypsies, a trick with colored water or bean counting to divine one's future. Instead, it had appeared unbidden, no act of divination or sorcery, but a simple symbol of what God wanted.

The following afternoon, when she normally took advantage of the empty streets to rest, she made her way to Saint Mark's. Flickering candles lit the alcove that held the imposing statue of the Virgin. The smell of incense lingered from the previous mass, a sweet fragrance more noticeable in the small space. Bowing her head, she whispered a vow. "Holy Mother, I have seen His sign. My heart was troubled and heavy with guilt, but in His kindness, He allowed me to know the way to everlasting redemption. I will join the crusaders in their mission of faith. This prayer is for your guidance so that I can fulfill my destiny. Only then will I be free, cleansed of evil thoughts and prayers that have brought nothing but grief." She paused. Did she dare ask a favor, that somewhere on her journey she might see Adam again? Struck by the utter selfishness of her thoughts, she said a quick amen and hoped her unuttered plea had not been heard by the Virgin.

She rose, lit a candle, and left the chapel, walking purposefully across the cobbled walkway toward the rectory. Two quick taps with the iron knocker brought the priest to the door.

"Father Bretel, may I speak with you?"

"Why, Madame Ridaut, what brings you here? Of course,

come in, come in. I was sorry to hear of your loss. I pray for his soul."

"*Merci,* Father. But I have come about a different matter. A simple question, actually, to satisfy idle curiosity, I suppose."

"Yes, dear, go on. A question needs no defense." He waved his hand toward a cushioned bench.

"There is someone I know who has promised before God to make a pilgrimage." She paused, sliding one hand along a fold of her tunic, then lifted her head to meet his gaze. "If this person makes the journey with the crusaders in order to gain redemption, would the pilgrimage still be worthy?"

"Of course."

"And if—if this person is curious, and anxious to see sights along the way?"

"That has nothing to do with his intent, my dear. A crusade is a holy undertaking in its own right, regardless of other factors that may be involved. Your friend need not be concerned." His lips curled upward; he was obviously pleased to be the bearer of favorable news. "To support the crusade for any reason is admirable, and if there is a reward, so much the better. You are blessed to have such a devout believer as a friend. Tell him I wish him Godspeed."

Catherine hid her relief behind a grateful smile. "Thank you, Father." She handed him a coin, saved from those her father handed her at the end of every week. "Use this for the benefit of our poorest parishioners," she said, repeating what she'd heard wealthy matrons say when dropping purses into the priest's hands after mass.

She returned home, her mind awhirl. There was much to do in the months ahead. Thank goodness she had plenty of time. From what she knew, only tentative plans were in place for the crusade. The king might not leave for years, but she had to be ready. Her biggest worry was leaving her father, when he needed her most. And how could she travel alone?

She decided the best thing to do was to learn as much as she could, about the pilgrim roads, and how to stay safe. In the meantime, she would save every coin she could, and pray for guidance. By His grace, she had seen a vision of her salvation. The rest was up to her. She had only to bide her time, and pray for the guidance and wisdom she so desperately needed.

CHAPTER NINETEEN

Adam listened to the newly appointed Italian master of astronomy droning in a monotone as he read from the wood-bound codex propped on the lectern. Hard to believe, Adam mused, that several months of study were behind him. A short year before, he had ridden into Paris, as eager as any of the students who came to this great center of learning. The fact that he had written little of value during his stay he attributed to his preoccupation with learning. He had to believe that was true.

A youth in the front row nodded off, bringing muffled laughter to the students behind him. Adam took advantage of the interruption to rub his knees, stiff from sitting so long. He stifled a yawn. His bones ached from the cold bench, made colder by the March winds howling outside. The sound of the storm made him sleepy, made him want to pull his feet up and lay his head down. When the teacher closed the text, Adam stood up, relieved, and stomped to bring feeling to his stiffened joints.

Outside, a snowstorm had emptied the streets of Paris, and the few scholars who had braved the cold scattered in every direction, wading through drifts that had piled against the building during the class.

Adam held the hood of his cape tight to his chin, first with one hand and then the other, keeping one hand tucked under his arm. The skin on his fingers was raw; he had forgotten to buy gloves, lulled into complacency by unseasonably warm weather until now.

Storefronts were folded shut in deference to the wintry blast. Behind shuttered windows, vendors huddled near fires, waiting for spring.

As he walked up the path to the room he shared with Beatris, the only sound he heard was the crunch of his boots in fresh snow. The road rose and dipped, making it difficult to avoid roadside ditches. When he passed the baker's stall, planning to buy a loaf or sweet-tarts, he found it closed.

He turned from the main road and walked under the arch. The skimmer stood half-buried against the side of the fire pit. Using the hem of his cloak to grip the icy skimmer, he scooped away the snowdrift blocking the door to Beatris's room.

Inside, candles burned on the table; the window above her bed, sealed tight with oiled parchment, closed out the cold gray light. She sat by the hearth on a low stool, poking at embers that glowed beneath a pot, its three legs propped on stones nestled in the fire.

Adam removed his boots and wet hose. The leather was soaked through and he had no feeling in his feet.

"There's not much tonight," she said, ladling soup into two bowls. "Let's eat beside the fire, eh? Is it still snowing?"

"Yes, and the shops were all closed, else I would have brought something for our meal."

"We have enough—more than some have tonight. But this is the last of it; I'll have to go to the market tomorrow."

They ate in silence, savoring the hot soup and the end of a loaf of bread, while the dog trotted from one to the other, catching scraps as they fell. Later, Adam lay in bed, too tired to write or study. The usual street sounds were gone; no cats fighting, no far-off children's cries. Sometime in the night he felt the dog's warm body beside his feet, and he slept soundly, not dreaming.

When he woke in the morning, Beatris was poking at the fire.

"It's stopped snowing. The sun's out."

"Good. Then I'll get some more wood, and buy some food when the market opens." He wrapped his cloak around his shoulders. "After that, I'll pay a long overdue visit to my patron."

Patches of ice slid from thatched rooftops; frozen branches thawed in the sun, transforming the latest snow to a trickling slush. As he neared Robert's château, Adam saw beggars huddled beside the rampart and felt a twinge of pity.

He approached the iron gate. "I'm here to see the count."

"And I'm the King of France," the guard said, advancing with a dagger in his hand. "Now, get back with the others. We'll be giving no more food until dusk."

Adam realized that in his haste he'd grabbed a worn cloak, one used to haul wood and do odd jobs for Beatris. He reached to the purse at his waist, relieved he had not left the notice of safe passage lying on the table next to his bed. He held it out. The man lowered the weapon and reached for the document. After scrutinizing the seal, he handed it back.

"Forgive me, *Monsieur*. I thought no one but the beggars would be out in this weather." He unlocked the gate. "Please don't tell my master about this. You understand—"

"Indeed, my tongue is paralyzed. Just take me inside."

The gatekeeper swung wide the gate, and Adam crossed a courtyard, then followed a squire down a long hall.

Fires blazed from three hearths in the Great Room. As Adam entered, the count rose from his chair, hand outstretched, his pleasure evident by a wide grin. After the ritual kiss, he said, "Adam, my friend. I'm glad you're here."

Adam's gaze fell to an elaborate chess set, the pieces of which looked to be made of jasper. "Am I interrupting?"

"Not at all." The count looked a little embarrassed and set the game aside. "I was only trying to perfect the skill. I had no real opponent." He lowered his voice and glanced at the rooms above. "My wife is furious. The warm Advent lured us into complacency. I thought we had more time to leave before winter, and now she sulks with her maids, having been stuck here for months. My life is miserable. I'm trapped here in the city and fear spring will never come. I hope you can stay a few days. Besides, I'd like to hear how your classes are going."

"I could stay the night."

"Good. Simon, show our guest to a room, and have Christine prepare his bath." He turned to Adam. "We will eat well this evening, although I fear the cooks are not prepared. We have much to talk about, eh? In the meantime, I'll have wine sent to your room. Ah, it's good to see you. Go now, and make yourself comfortable."

Adam sat on the bed, sipping the wine and watching a servant girl toss petals into the tub. She stirred the water with her fingertips. He studied her face. In spite of her youthful stature he saw lines around her eyes and mouth. Had she spent her whole life here, or had she come to Paris to escape a demanding baron in some other province? She curtsied, then indicated the tub of water. After collecting his clothes, she laid them by the door. He smiled, thinking what he had missed by choosing Beatris's place over this. Truth to tell, he had probably gotten no more writing done than he would have at Robert's. He had done more studying, though. Robert was famous for his impromptu parties. A court was no place for a scholar.

He eased into the fragrant water, and she rubbed his back with heated oil that smelled faintly of lemon, then poured water onto his shoulders and back. The towel she handed him was so thick he suspected Robert had purchased it at some far-off trade fair.

Thinking he would rest before dinner, he sat on the side of

the bed and removed his slippers. Suddenly, the servant woman was back again, holding a sweet-smelling container in her hands and smiling down at him. She knelt and rubbed the concoction on his toes and feet. He could smell her hair, a faint almond scent. A few white hairs grew among the black ones near her brow. Her clothes carried a hint of hearth and burning wood. A musky fragrance rose from her body, and her breath came deep, her face very near his knees.

She rose, waiting for the damp towel he still wore. He could feel her eyes on his back as he removed it.

After quickly rolling onto the bed, he slid beneath the bed-cover. She walked to a chest under the window, retrieved a coverlet of linsey-woolsey and spread it over him, then walked quietly from the room. He fell asleep instantly, and when he woke it was dark. Someone stood close by. In the glow of a tall candle near the bed, he made out the form of the woman who had bathed him.

"I was . . . sleeping," he offered, feeling foolish, not yet awake.

"I know." She loosened the blanket she wore, let it fall to the floor, and stood naked before him. "My name is Christine." She leaned to pick up the blanket.

He inhaled her musky odor again. Her dark oval eyes matched her black hair, loosened around her face.

"I came to see if you needed . . . more help."

She put one knee beside him on the bed. Her breasts touched his face as she climbed across him. Then, she lifted the coverlet and crawled beneath.

Chapter Twenty

He closed his eyes, tried to quell the raging energy that drove his breathing. Suddenly she was astride him, and his body struggled to meet hers. A fleeting image came, unbidden, of Catherine at the shop door, then, a surge of pleasure. He opened his eyes, moist with unexpected tears, and silently cursed the persistent memory of the girl at the tapestry shop.

When he woke, the maid was gone. The candle on the wooden stand sputtered, threatening total darkness, and he rose to hastily replace it with another. Clean clothes hung from the perch overhead, and he dressed quickly. As he approached the Great Hall, he smelled cooked meats and the aroma of fresh bread.

Count Robert greeted him. "Ah, Adam, you're just in time. I was afraid you'd sleep through dinner. I'm glad to see you're rested. Did Christine give you a proper bath?" He winked.

"Yes . . . yes," he said, not looking at his friend. "I slept soundly."

"Good! Sit here now." Robert indicated a high-backed chair that faced the door. Servers ran to and fro, carrying platters and pots. "This is the same wine we had in Cambrai, remember?"

"I do remember, though it seems years ago."

Robert waited while serving men refilled the wine. "I felt bad about leaving last summer, so soon after you enrolled."

Adam shrugged. "Business before pleasure, especially when the king calls." They laughed together.

"And when I returned this past autumn," Robert said, "our

schedules never seemed to work. Tell me about life at the university. I always wondered what it was like, studying with other scholars—though I have no desire to do it myself."

Adam laughed, thinking of a younger Robert, the mischievous one who seemed always to outthink the officials in Arras. "There is nothing much to tell. Lately many students are not in class; some winter sickness has struck them down like babes. Even the young healthy ones have been staying home. I suppose it goes with the season, but the ones who are there—we rely on each other." He drained his cup. "I'm accepted as one of them, though I'm older by a few years."

A servant stoked the fire and he watched in silence until it caught. "Sometimes the studying gets so monotonous we have a quick game of dice behind the building. Most of the students are eager to learn, even though the subjects are difficult for some."

"I understand the scholars cause trouble in the city at night."

"Ah, yes. And because of that, any form of athletics is forbidden now. They have even banned chess." Adam shrugged. "The younger ones, I suppose, have energy to waste. The city officials have enforced new rules to protect the citizens, but gaming and drinking are still allowed. I think, though, drinking soon becomes old to even the most reluctant scholar."

He stared into the fire, watching the flames, and continued. "Pierre, a young man whom I've come to know, tells me fighting still erupts in the streets, and paid soldiers try to stop the rowdiest. Citizens protest, but during a brawl I've seen bystanders cheer loudly for winners and losers both—just to have something to do. Not long ago two Italians were accused of organizing crowds of protesters to defy the judging. They did this each time there was a fight, regardless of the outcome, just to amuse themselves. Finally, they were thrown in jail, or so I was told."

Robert chuckled. "Serves them right, the scoundrels." He winked at Adam. "So, do they ever study?"

"In truth, most students who room in the Latin Quarter study in their rooms at night, because morning comes early, and they can't be late for classes." He leaned his head back and rubbed his neck with both hands. "There are those who even sleep on the Street of Straw so they'll be on time for lectures."

"Speaking of that, Adam, you know if you change your mind and want to stay here, you're welcome—even when we are gone."

"I knew that. I just thought—I planned to get some writing done each evening, and keeping oneself locked in a room at night is hardly good manners."

A servant entered and announced that dinner was served.

Once seated, while servers poured more wine, Robert turned to face his protégé. "And did you manage any writing here? What about the play you started?"

Adam shook his head. "I wrote some poetry, but that's about all. My time is taken up with study. I suppose that is why the music is hard to concentrate upon—melodies are most evasive. I have struggled trying to think of it, but I have no inspiration. It will come, though. It will come."

"Ah, don't worry, Adam. You will finish it later. Did you complete that wedding music?"

"Yes, and sent a *jongleur* to the festivities to take my place. He sang some songs I'd written for her."

"Too bad about the groom, wasn't it? I knew Guillaume Ridaut's father. I suppose everyone in Arras knew the man, but I never knew the son. That poor girl, widowed so young. I suppose—"

"Widowed?" Adam held the wine cup in midair. "What are you saying? What happened to Ridaut?"

"No one told you? He died about six months ago in his own

home. I never heard the details. Seems he accosted a servant. There was a scuffle, and he died of a wound. The maid was vindicated. They said it was self-defense."

"No, I . . . no one told me." He stared at the tapestry covering the trestle table, stared at a red unicorn guarding the gates of a forest, refusing entry to a wood nymph. Robert's revelation turned his stomach. He hated to think of Catherine living with such a man. His worst fear had been validated; Guillaume was no better than his father. He regretted now not going to Vitry-en-Artois as promised. Perhaps, if he had insisted. . . . No, nothing he could have said or done then would have changed a thing. Besides, he had been falling in love. And now she was free. But what if this was all rumor?

"You are very sure of all this, Robert?" He felt his patron's eyes on him. *The man can practically read my mind.*

"Quite sure. Raoul told me about the man's death only because he remembered your mentioning the name. Adam, are you all right? Did you know him well?"

"No, no, Robert. I am just—surprised . . . a man married so short a time. It is sad."

"Not as sad as that scarce lamb's lettuce going to waste in front of you. I love the first greens after winter, and a peddler came through last week from the south. My cook bought all he had."

Adam forced himself to eat the lettuce, but his mind was on a poem sung by a *jongleur* about a knight who prayed for an adversary's death; the next day the enemy was found floating in the river. The knight's thoughts became so tortured from guilt he finally ended his life with his own sword. *I would not have had it this way.*

He could ride there and see her again. Would she think him insolent, so soon after Guillaume's death? Perhaps he should explain the real reason why he had not followed through with his promise to sing at her wedding.

He emptied his wine cup. What was he thinking? How could he leave Paris and go to her? What did he have to offer? A pallet on the floor of a hovel? Right now he was just another student. Even his talent had waned. No, he would stay here and finish at university. He owed Robert that much. Seeing her now was pointless. Whether she was married or not was no affair of his, nor was it of any importance now, and there was no place in his life for a woman. Had he not learned that already?

Trumpets sounded, and servants brought the final course to the head table. Later, as a servant passed by holding the alms bowl, Adam tossed his trencher in with the others and glanced down from the raised dais where he sat.

Across the room, men and women were laughing together, seated at a table near the kitchen. Then he saw Christine. She smiled, raised one brow, and tilted her head to the side.

The music began and dancers came to the floor. Christine whirled by in a group of three ladies, her tunic in disarray, sliding off one white shoulder. She laughed as she caught his eye and turned her head to watch him.

Her face became Catherine's, her hair, the color of Catherine's.

The dancers twirled to the other end of the room to be joined by three more. They joined hands and continued as the music played on and on, into the night. He drank more wine, wondering if Catherine had already promised her hand to another, or if she ever thought of him.

That night, when Christine again visited his quarters, filled with frustration and longing, he took her with a savagery that both gratified—and shamed—him.

CHAPTER TWENTY-ONE

That summer was one of the hottest Adam could remember. On the Kalends of September he sat by the Seine, lured by a breeze from the river and a group of students sharing a basket of sweets. He had had little time to cultivate friends, but Pierre—a lanky youth with a perpetual smile, from the southern border of Gascony—had taken a liking to him, and now urged him on the company of his own cohorts whenever Adam gave him the opportunity.

One of the youths leaned forward, raked his silky brown hair from his brow. His eyes, deep-set, lent an air of maturity to his otherwise youthful appearance. "They say you are a poet." He shifted his weight on the straw mat.

"He is," Pierre interrupted. "Adam de la Halle, meet my other friend. This poor lad, who fancies himself a student, is Wilbert."

A shy grin lit the pale face of another youth. "Are you really a celebrated *trouvère,* as we've been told?"

"Yes, I am a *trouvère,* or was. Right now I struggle with the books, as you do."

"Then you are truly a student"—Pierre poked Wilbert with his elbow—"unlike us. We occupy our time going to the tavern, and only come here to the Street of Straw to rest up for the evening. We stay in the tavern until the owner runs us out."

"Yes," Wilbert said, biting into a large apple he took from a cleverly concealed purse tucked beneath his arm, "but the lessons are becoming more difficult. Somehow the tavern is losing its appeal."

"For you, perhaps. You don't have such luck with the ladies as I do." Pierre turned back to Adam. "You should come along. Likely, you'd get a free ale for a poem. It's a new place, and the tavern keeper's wife knows us. She sometimes forgets to charge us for the cups we've had when the dancing starts, and her sottish husband whirls her around the floor." He cast a glance at Wilbert, whose face had turned dark rose. "There are winsome ladies there, too."

"No, Pierre." Adam looked across the grassy slope to the Seine. "The last time I went to the tavern, I was too tired to walk home. The next day, my head throbbed when I tried to listen to the teachers. If I go home after classes, I can sometimes study, or read from the text."

"You have real books? We walked to the bookstalls at Parvis Notre Dame, but they have only bound ones we couldn't afford. It costs nothing to look and feel them, though." He rubbed his hands together.

"These were given to me by a friend."

"A rich man, eh? Is he a student? We'll have to meet him."

"No, his name is Robert. He's my patron . . . and friend. He has a library, and it is easier to read the book than study notes from a tablet."

"Imagine, owning real books." Pierre rose from his worn mat and smashed an insect between his fingers that had crawled out from the flattened straw. "Now, about tonight—you're sure you won't come?"

"Perhaps, when our examinations are over, I will go and see this new tavern of yours. Enjoy yourselves, but remember, daylight comes early."

The next morning Adam walked partway with Beatris as she

headed north to the cathedral.

"We have a new window," she said. "Costly, but beautiful."

He nodded. "Some works of art in the royal chapel take one's breath."

Two bells rang from the church tower. "You've been there, where the king worships?

He nodded. "Once my patron's father invited me to mass. I sat in the upper chapel with the king's family. It was the Feast of Saint Lawrence. The king was gone from the city, and his brother was acting as his representative. He said he had never extended the privilege to another *trouvère,* so I was doubly honored."

"Did you see the great windows?"

"Ah, yes. They stunned me with their brilliance. And the icons," he shook his head, "they remind me of sentinels, and I suspect that is the intention, to give the idea of protecting the king in a safe cocoon." He said nothing more, having decided not to mention what it cost to build such a place.

A final bell rang and Beatris stepped inside the church. Adam left, making his way to the Street of Straw.

"Adam, we've been waiting. What kept you?" Pierre asked, tossing his mat onto the ground.

"The woman who gave me a place to live, I walked with her to the chapel."

"Funny, we were just discussing the new church being built north of here. It's supposed to rival all others."

"Hmph. As if the bishops need another church," Edward said.

Pierre spoke up. "Adam, you've not met Edward yet. He keeps us straight on all things religious."

Edward grinned at Adam. "Just saying what I believe. You'd think by now the peasants would rise up in arms."

Pierre nodded. "Perhaps they don't think, though Abelard

taught that reason, too, is a gift of God."

"Shh. Speak quietly, Pierre," Edward warned. "There is punishment for heretics."

"I agree with Edward," a third student said, putting a cushion on the ground to join the others. "Don't they know some of the coins they drop in the box go to enrich the very ones whose land they work, behind whose oxen they toil?"

"I can understand," Adam said, "how a serf, whose life is a daily struggle in the dusty earth behind a plow, would welcome the beauty of the cathedral. Those feast days, kneeling before that shimmering elevated chalice—that is the only time they see elegance and splendor."

"Yes, yes. Perhaps . . . the end justifies the means?" Pierre said, grinning.

They rose and walked up the hill. Adam smiled to himself, thinking how scholars took the other side of any argument, just for the sake of discourse. How different they seemed from the villagers in Arras who were mostly older, yet somehow more worldly, definitely more self-reliant than these favored youths.

"Adam." A voice called out from a narrow alley. "Slow down. I'll walk with you."

He dropped back and waited for Thomas, a disheveled student who had sat beside him during three weeks of lectures on Aristotle's Physics. Unlike Pierre and his friends, Thomas took pride in his studies and frequented no taverns.

As they made their way toward the university, Thomas confided he was almost finished with his study of rhetoric and would soon apply his knowledge in the courts of Paris.

"And what kind of official will you be, Thomas?" Adam asked. "Will you defend the farmer or the peasant when they are taxed ten sous for his hearth? Or have you learned to defend the velvet-robed lords who will pay you well? How have they taught you, and how do you decide?"

Thomas tucked his stringy hair behind one ear and looked curiously at Adam. "I thought you studied the arts alone. How is it you take an interest in politics?"

"One cannot be in the world and close his eyes to injustice. While we have a truly noble king to lead us—a pious one, too, as he is well known to be—greed is a human trait, not expunged with either punishment or prayers, my friend."

They stopped at a street vendor's cart where Adam bought a tart, then broke it in half and handed a piece to Thomas. "I have seen good men leave their homes to be magistrates, meaning to rule with fair and noble ideas." He leaned his head back to eat ripe cherries oozing from the pastry, then swiped his hand across his mouth. "And as they see corruption and greed around them, they are tempted beyond what man can refuse." He shrugged. "They become part of the problem."

He wiped his hands on the sides of his tunic and they resumed walking. "Perhaps it is not that way in Paris, as the king is here to rule, but in the provinces, the men he puts in charge, and whom he trusts to be as fair as he, are traitors to his ideals." Adam resisted the urge to tell Thomas more. No need to explain how the representatives in Arras manipulated edicts for their own benefit.

"And you, have you been the victim of these henchmen?" Thomas wiped his fingers across the front of his wrinkled tunic, leaving behind a streaky crimson stain.

"Not directly, not as much as others have." He had a fleeting memory of his attack in Douai, then glanced at Thomas. "Have you been promised a position in Paris? I can picture you, red-robed, pacing before the judges." He nudged Thomas with his elbow.

"Not yet, but I will be soon."

Adam patted Thomas's shoulder. "I know that to be true. And you'll be fair and just."

They reached the stone building where their classes met and Adam took the passage leading to the hall where he had spent so many hours. He sat on the hard bench to await the master, who would lecture all morning before assigning work for that day.

A hand slapped his shoulder and he turned to see Pierre, breathless from running to be on time to class. "Adam, you must say yes." Pierre bundled his tunic on the cold bench and sat down. "Edward and Wilbert are going to the Cold Fair at Troyes. They've asked me and want you to come with us, too. You will, won't you?"

He shook his head. "I've been there many times, Pierre. It seems a long way to go for nothing. It is three days to Troyes—a long trip to make."

"For nothing? It's one of the most important fairs in France. People come from all over with their goods. There are dancing girls and gypsies who tell the future."

"Do not believe everything you hear, Pierre. There are no dancing girls."

"Still, Adam, we would have a great holiday. No one will be in Paris. They probably close the shops."

"No, Pierre, not everyone goes. As I said, it's a long journey."

"What better way to spend the week? All Saints' Day falls on a Monday. We can leave Friday after classes, and since lessons are suspended that next week, we'll have plenty of time. Besides," Pierre continued, "Wilbert is taking his trick dog. Also, he will finish his studies here at semester end and leave for Avignon. Edward might not return, either."

The master entered and Pierre took out his wax tablet.

Later that afternoon, as Pierre and his friends walked with Adam to the Street of Straw, they coaxed him until he relented.

They cheered, lifted him above their heads, and carried him to a nearby tavern to celebrate their friendship and the well-deserved holiday they would take in Troyes.

While Adam and his friends celebrated their upcoming adventure at the neighborhood tavern, Catherine was sorting through a pile of new tapestries. When she had finished her task, she sat down to rest. The mixed smell of apples ripening in a nearby bowl, and the lingering odor of madder root and woad used to dye the tapestries, filled the shop with a strange scent she suspected clung to her clothes.

Her head ached and she had an odd feeling this had all happened before. It was the same, but not the same, and then she remembered. Apples ripened in the season before winter; that meant a year had passed since Guillaume's death.

So many *Pater Nosters* since then, but they did little good to free her from the nagging guilt. Confounded by the terrible strength of her prayers, she wanted desperately to believe she was not directly responsible for his death, but no amount of reasoning calmed her spirit. She had prayed to the Virgin for Guillaume's soul, and had tried to be sorrowful, but nothing could take the place of the promised pilgrimage. Somehow, someday, she must fulfill her oath.

From far away she heard the sound of a shepherd's pipe, a tuneful, rhythmic melody borne on the wind, carried into the shop, filtered among the tapestries. How did sound travel? Perhaps the scientists had an answer, or perhaps it was a miracle from heaven. *If I were a man I could go to a university, where I could learn what sound really is.* She thought, if she ever saw Adam again, he might know, but the chances of that happening were about the same as her meeting Queen Marguerite.

She shook her head, wishing she could discuss it all with

Francino, but he would only smile and tell her she was a bit daft.

That evening after dinner, as she cleared the pots from the table, her father spoke up, his voice serious. "Catherine, I believe it's time for you to learn the real workings of the business, beyond the shop. An enterprise is more than selling. I know you kept Guillaume's ledgers, but this is a bit different. And someday, when I'm gone, it will be yours."

She tried to hide her discomfort at the thought of his failing health, then reminded herself of the doctor's promptings, even before her marriage. Her father had paid no heed, had refused the prescribed soaks, and continued in his routine. True, she had noticed a marked difference in his agility when she returned to live at the shop again, but here he was, managing to still get around with the aid of a cane. It proved that doctors didn't know everything. Still, the reminder of his persistent infirmities chilled her heart. She kept her back turned, wiping the pots with more effort than was needed.

"I can show you the accounts, the shipping expenses and liveries. Gérard invented a clever system of receipts; it will be easy for you to keep records for me, though I wager you'll soon tire of it."

"Maybe not, Papa," she said, remembering how her record books had helped pass the days of her marriage to Guillaume. "And of course I'm willing to help."

"Fine. Now, there's something else I think you're old enough to handle. You know that Gérard and I always go to the Troyes Cold Fair. It's a wonderful experience. Traders come from all over. There's a lot of competition, so prices are good enough to warrant a trip there annually, though the fair is nothing like it was."

"Why, Papa?"

"The unrest has frightened some of the Flemish away, and the Italians have begun making their own cloth and have started going by sea to buy wool. Still, the fair has endured to serve the region. You'll find everything there we need."

He pulled a sheet from beneath the pile. "Ah, here it is. I've started a list of what we need, based on last year's purchases. Gérard can go along if you like, though I may need him here. I've arranged with Isabel's father for her to go with you. Francino, too. I have a friend in Arras—an almond importer. He takes his family every year, and you could go along with them. They travel with the cloth merchants, so you'd be safe."

Her brow furrowed. In spite of her initial excitement at the thought of seeing such an event, a small worry clouded her happiness. Had his chest pains returned? The doctor had assured her it had been a passing concern, nothing more, and the last year or so, it seemed her father's health had remained the same. Still, why would he be making all these plans to shift the management to her hands?

"I hope you don't mind, Catherine. It will relieve my mind. Besides, I no longer relish a journey during the winter season."

"Of course, Papa. I'll do as you say."

While Catherine wrung out a cloth and hung it to dry, her father sat down at his desk. As he sorted through a stack of parchment, she noticed a pronounced tremble in his hands.

A lump formed in her throat. He was getting old, and now it was time to show her how to run the shop. It had taken his lifetime to earn the trust of the weavers in Arras and of the buyers who placed orders for the tapestries from vendors as far away as Egypt and Italy. But did he honestly expect that people would deal with a woman?

And now he was turning over household purchases to her. *The Cold Fair*, he had said, of all places. She recalled a sunny afternoon, a rattling wagon passing by, and Adam telling her about the fair. Would he be there? Hadn't he said he had no home to buy for—before abruptly leaving the shop? Evidently she'd said something to offend. That had been over two years ago and she remembered his words like yesterday. Would she never get the man from her mind?

Chapter Twenty-Two

As the weeks passed, Catherine and Isabel spent hours going over their lists of household supplies: utensils, candles, cloth coverings, and items for personal use.

Autumn had stayed late, a blessing that would make the journey easier. Hopefully, by the time winter arrived, they would be near Troyes, a bit to the south.

The night before they were to leave, her father took to his bed, and Catherine summoned the town doctor.

"He complains of tiredness and difficulty breathing. What can be done? We were leaving on the morrow, but now I shan't."

"Nonsense," the physician said. "Your father has been working long hours again and needs a rest. He said you had taken over some of his accounts, and that was a help to him. When you return, I will have him fit again. Now, go on in. He's been asking for you."

When she stepped inside his room, he was sitting up in bed, pillows propped behind his back. "I am depending on you to lay in stores for the winter, Catherine, so no more talk about postponing the trip, which would worry me more. You need to watch our interests, and I trust you more than anyone, except Gérard. The cloth merchants will see you safely there, I've made sure of that.

"It will do you good to see the fair at Troyes; it is far superior to the small fairs you've seen before. Gérard has arranged for rooms at the inn there, and I know you will do well and make me proud. A good head you have on your pretty shoulders, as did your mother. Go now." He waved her away. "Let me rest, as that hovering physician insists. When you return, we will see how well you've spent my money."

During the first week of the journey, the excitement of watching tents raised at sunset, the entertainment from *jongleurs* who joined them from time to time as they moved through towns, helped to pass time as a slow-moving caravan of cloth merchants from Flanders led the way. Two horsemen rode on either side of the standard-bearer. Crossbowmen and pikemen, skilled protectors the merchants had hired, flanked the convoy on both sides. As the old Roman road narrowed through a stand of birch trees the archers closed ranks. Catherine stroked the mule's neck, a stubborn gray ride her father had selected from the stables across the street from the shop, and wondered how much further they had to go. She brushed strands of hair from her eyes, then sipped water from the bladder carried on the mule's back.

Five weeks after leaving Vitry, the convoy approached Troyes's sand-colored walls and entered through the Madeleine Gate, one of two through which travelers from the north passed into the city.

Passing over the wooden drawbridge, she gazed down into the dry moat where buzzards circled above an animal carcass. Beyond the drawbridge, the shouts of workmen and pounding of hammers assaulted her ears as townspeople hurried to finish new storefronts. When the caravan reached the *rue du Bois*, the cloth merchants took a side road to unload their goods at the *halle*.

Francino pointed east, and they headed toward the canal and into town. Wagons crowded the streets, moving in both directions, laden with goods. Local drivers cursed and dodged foreign vendors whose carts blocked the streets while they tried to select the most advantageous spots to unload their cargo.

"I imagined it would be like the open markets near our village, only larger," Catherine murmured, riding beside Isabel. They slowed the animals, watching the bustle of shopkeepers and householders clean and sweep elaborately decorated storefronts beneath newly hung flags, hoping for increased trade from travelers who would pass their way going to and from the heart of the fair district.

"Perhaps the king is coming to the fair, Isabel." She laughed.

Francino pointed to a modest steeple in the road ahead. "There's the Church of Saint-Rémi, and the graveyard. Gérard said the inn is just beyond."

They rode past the last row of graves to a thatch-roofed building on a rise where a blue-and-red banner, decorated with a chevron and three lilies, flapped from the rooftop.

They dismounted at the door of the hostel and handed the reins to a stable boy.

The innkeeper took Francino to his room, then returned to lead the women to a room above the main hall. "I'm giving you the Room of the New Bed," she said. "Mind you, no spilling wine on the bedcovers."

While waiting for their clothes chest, Catherine strolled to the window. "Look, Isabel. We can see passersby below, and watch all the activity from here."

"You'd best not lean so far out. You may fall. Besides, there's pigeons above."

"Oh, Isabel, don't fuss. We are on holiday." She turned away from the opening. "By tomorrow, the stalls should be finished. We'll be among the first to see the wares." She unfastened her cloak. "*Non!* Road dust has turned my blue cloak gray." She shook it out and hung it on a peg. "I'm going to bed. Who knows what tomorrow will bring?"

Shielding his eyes from the sun's sinking rays, Adam rode through the *Porte de Paris* into Troyes with his young friends from the university. They passed the grain market and the Viscount's Tower, and followed the *rue de l'Epicerie* to the Trévois Canal.

They came to a row of timber-framed buildings leaning together for support, uniformly braced against oncoming winds, and Adam suspected their proximity was all that kept the narrow structures from falling into the river.

"That's it!" shouted Edward, pointing at a blue two-story building on the end. "We're here."

They stabled their horses and walked inside.

"I'm going to the public baths tomorrow," Pierre announced. "And, from the smell of things, all of you should come with me."

"What is the charge?" Wilbert asked.

"It doesn't matter. I will charge you more if I have to sleep beside you again. We need to wash, and the canals are forbidden."

Adam walked to the window. "We can go to the baths at daybreak, then see the town."

"A noble plan," Edward said. "When the heralds come through announcing the fair opening, there'll be no sleeping anyway."

Catherine woke to the clamor of bells, a cacophonous tolling the likes of which she had never heard. She tossed back the covers. "Wake up, Isabel. The sun's been up for hours."

A short time later, dressed and having broken their fast, they met Francino, who led them through a narrow alley onto a wider street. The noise and smells of the city swirled around them, born on a crisp November wind from the Seine. Taking a footbridge across one of the numerous canals, they ended up in the main shopping district. The sun sent slivers of light between the shops, narrow gold rectangles spilling onto the road like priceless bullion.

Smoke curled skyward from numerous braziers where cooks basted fowl and pork on turning spits and shouted at stray dogs.

Not far away, the fishmonger opened his stall, and now the odor of sturgeon and pike blended with the smell of the roasts, creating an aroma that made Catherine's mouth water.

They strolled past tables covered with bolts of scarlet, green, and violet cloths intended to lure buyers inside. Another display showed raw wool hanging beside embroidered cloths, heavy with gold and silver threads woven through the vivid hues. Wedged between food vendors were dealers with gems and ornate stones.

Catherine heard the blast of a trumpet and followed the gaze of the townspeople as the heralds approached the city on horseback. The trumpeters came first, followed by standard-bearers; behind them rode counts and noblemen, their costly garments setting them apart. Last came the city officials. The scene took her breath away. Riders wore cloaks of red and gold that fell in folds onto horse blankets made of the same red and gold, moving tents of princely magnificence.

A blast of air blew from the north, and she drew her cloak close. When the trumpeters passed by, children covered their ears; nothing could be heard above the horns, not the cheering crowd, the flapping noise of flags and tapestries hung from every storefront, nor the bleat of animals in a makeshift corral nearby.

As the noblemen approached, the hooves of their mounts

clacked on the paved road. The heralds circled a platform set up for games, then proceeded to the outskirts of town, their trumpets announcing that the fair could now begin. Road workers and a boy pulling a small dung cart followed the horses. Throngs of people, oblivious of the street cleaners, spilled into the road, their attention now centered on the merchants putting finishing touches on displays. Cooks sliced dripping meats above the fire pits.

Catherine walked beside a table of knives and sickles and noticed the inlaid jewels on the knife handles, some of ivory, others trimmed with silver filigree. *I'll buy one of those for Father.* Pots of ground spices were displayed on tables, and bunches of aromatic plants hung from a cord tied between two posts.

Two tables later, they paused near a dark-haired woman with skin the color of candle wax who arranged stones and jewelry, placing them in circles and lines. She rubbed them with a linen cloth in a slow, seductive, circular motion. As Catherine approached the table, Francino walked up, munching on a tart.

The vendor stopped her polishing and pointed to the shiniest jewels, speaking loudly of their origin to no one in particular.

Catherine stepped closer and the woman hastily picked up a glittering necklace of ruby stones, exclaiming in a throaty voice how they set off Catherine's pale skin. Then Catherine noticed a spherical stone of amber, glints of dark captured in its lustrous translucence. The stone was attached to a silver rosary chain which held other less remarkable stones. The dark specks reminded Catherine of a bird's egg she had once found.

The vendor shook her head, and pointed to a larger stone set in a ring, then pushed it onto Catherine's finger.

She removed the ring, handed it to the woman, then picked up the rosary.

"The rosary is of common origin," the vendor insisted, still holding the ring between her fingers.

Catherine draped the silver chain of the rosary across her fingers and turned the honey-colored gem over in her palm.

"Look, Catherine." Francino nudged her arm. "Across the street. I'm sure it's the musician, the one who sang that night in the village, the one who's sweet on you."

She gripped the topaz and fought to control her swirling emotions. A deep breath did nothing to steady the pounding in her chest. Suddenly, she remembered the message he'd sent from Cambrai, the message that had erased girlish thoughts from her mind. It had been the message, as much as her father's honor and Gérard's persuasion, that had caused her to acquiesce to her father's wishes and marry Guillaume.

And now Adam was here, after all this time, unless Francino was merely teasing. Slowly, as if to brace herself for the cruel outcome, she turned around. There, at the boot maker's display, stood Adam, facing in her direction, conversing with a man whose back was turned to her. Her pulse quickened as he glanced her way. Their eyes locked, and a rush of joy crept from her toes to her cheeks. She wanted to cry out. Instead, she forced words from her mouth, words she hoped did not betray her excitement.

"I believe you are right, Francino. It is the *trouvère*."

And he's coming this way.

CHAPTER TWENTY-THREE

Adam left the boot maker's and crossed the road, followed by others near him. He walked toward her with deceptive calmness, trying to separate this vision from his own recurring memory. She had not changed. On the contrary, she was more beautiful than ever. And no man stood at her side, save Francino. Did he dare hope she was still free? He stood before her now, struggling to remember how he had lived without her.

From the searching look in her green eyes he suspected she was as stunned as he by what was passing between them. He reached her side and found his voice. "I'm surprised to see you here, so far from Vitry." He lowered his head. "I was sorry to hear of your loss. I knew him from my boyhood in Arras."

"Thank you," she said, her voice soft, and he knew she was trying to put the matter behind her. That suited him fine. They would never speak of it again.

A cold gust of air flapped the table coverings, and Adam grabbed his cap as wind whistled across the road, threatening to disturb the carefully arranged displays.

The jewel vendor cleared her throat, and Adam noticed the rosary stone in Catherine's hand. She returned it to the table and apologized.

The vendor prattled on, coaxing Adam to consider other jewelry.

Adam reached for the rosary Catherine had been admiring. "And would this be your choice, from all these lovely jewels?"

"I was only admiring it," Catherine said, ignoring the woman's comments. "We came to purchase household wares. I . . . we were . . . I have never been to a fair like this before. I am overwhelmed, I suppose, at the excitement."

Adam held the stone near her cheek. "It compliments you, though it dulls beside that crown of hair you wear." He laid the rosary back on the table. Color rose to Catherine's cheeks, and he berated himself for his forwardness. She would think him an affected courtier using fancy words.

Isabel and Francino waited at the next table, sorting through bolts of wool. Catherine stepped away from the jewelry display, and Adam fell in step beside her. "Did I embarrass you back there?"

"No, but you are indeed a poet, and you flatter with your comments."

Before he could reply, one of Adam's friends tapped him on the shoulder. "They're starting the games." Wilbert picked up his dog as they neared a pen of live geese.

"*Mademoiselle* Catherine, these are my friends from Paris. Pierre and Wilbert are studying law at the university. Edward is studying chess and taverns."

"*Bonjour, Messieurs.*" She rubbed the dog's silky fur, then turned to Adam. "You remember Francino. And this is Isabel, my closest friend."

A *jongleur* walked by singing loud, bawdy tunes and holding out a woven basket.

"Since this is your first time at the fair, you have a lot to see." Adam guided her through a group of men standing near a display of chamois-skin gloves. "It is a challenge to avoid the worst of the scoundrels." He gave her a broad smile. "We will see more of each other, I hope. I have attended many fairs; possibly I can help when you decide to purchase. Rogues, if they pay the fee, may exhibit here too."

"I thank you for that. I may need your help."

"I would pray so, Catherine. My travel to Troyes would have a reason then." He bent to kiss her hand, and when he straightened, he had an overwhelming urge to kiss her, here on the *Grand Rue*, in front of everyone. Instead, he released her hand and headed for the game tables.

He felt an odd sensation, as if he were above the crowd, looking down. Pigeons cooed from their resting places on the rooftops; banners flapped in the wind blowing through Troyes, mingling together all the odors of the merchants' wares. He shook his head, trying to clear his mind. If he were superstitious, he would think he'd walked beneath some magic potion or had been hexed by one of the magicians performing in the street.

Two hours later, having watched his friends squander a sizeable amount of money at the gaming tables, Adam coaxed them outside. A few minutes later, he spotted Catherine sitting in an area near a vendor who sold almond milk laced with cinnamon. He sat beside her on the bench.

"So, are you richer than before?"

"On the contrary. We all lost a bit."

"Some more than others," Wilbert said. "Pierre lost a week's allowance."

Pierre shrugged. "Adam suggested we all meet in the Tavern of the Crouching Lion at sunset."

Catherine glanced at Adam, saw he was watching her, waiting.

Isabel looked at Francino. "Let's do."

"Good," Adam said, his eyes locked with Catherine's. "At sunset, then."

That evening, the tavern filled with hungry and thirsty fairgoers. An entertainer with three bears kept the patrons amused.

Torches blazed against timber walls, and candles burned on every table, their orange flames wavering with each blast of cold as patrons came and went.

The owner's wife set pots of wine on the table, followed with bowls of hot soup and trenchers filled with steaming venison. While they ate, Adam's friends related tales of prowess at the game tables. Songs and dancing began, with villagers encouraging the crowd, thumping the tables in time to the music.

When six soldiers entered the tavern all eyes turned to the door, and the music stopped. Catherine gasped, surprised to see warriors in such a place. She glanced at Adam to gauge his reaction, but his face was indiscernible.

The men wore mail, prick spurs, and scabbards secured at their waist, but when they simply chose a table near the door and called loudly for a pot of ale, the music resumed, louder than ever.

Adam turned to Catherine. "There are rumblings of wars to the south."

"How close?"

He hesitated, and she knew he regretted mentioning the skirmishes.

He spread soft cheese onto a slice of dark bread. "They're far from here, mostly in outlying areas, away from towns. No need to worry. It's usually some petty disagreement among noblemen."

She sipped her wine. "We are in King Louis's care, and from the looks of things, prosperity is all around us."

He nodded, swallowing the last of the bread. "Commerce is fast coming to our cities, and traveling is safer now, else there would be no merchants here."

"You must see amazing things as you move through the countryside." She petted Wilbert's dog, which lay motionless on the bench, his head on the wool cloak covering her lap. "These wars . . . are they dangerous for the crusaders?"

"No more so than for other travelers. The crusaders travel in large groups. The skirmishes that are most dangerous are on outlying baronies. Greed or some unsettled fee is usually the cause."

The music stopped and the others returned to the table. A brawl started between two men in a far corner of the room, ending quickly as the largest of the two broke a pot over the other's head, then ran for the door, protesting the owner's demand that he pay for the broken vessel.

Catherine turned to Isabel. "It's time for us to be abed, I think."

Adam rose from the bench. "I, too, should leave, if I am to help you bargain with these sellers tomorrow." He helped Catherine adjust her cloak, fitting the hood over her hair below the coif.

Torches illuminated the streets which now were littered with scraps of discarded food. Loose animals rummaged for discarded morsels. Tired merchants slept under the tables, guarding their wares.

"Meet us at the game tables in the morning," Adam whispered when they reached the door of the inn. He brushed his lips against her cheek.

Isabel called from the doorway. "Hurry inside, Catherine. It's starting to rain."

Later, Catherine lay in bed, listening to muffled street sounds, glad Isabel was too tired to talk. She touched her cheek where his lips had pressed. She wanted him to kiss her on the mouth and hold her tight. Stifling a moan, she hugged the pillow and closed her eyes.

Adam lay on the cot in the room provided by his friend's uncle. He relived the day's events, trying to remember what she had

185

said, hoping for some hidden promise in a phrase, a nuance in the turn of her words. *I am smitten, and it is my own doing.* Words from one of his earlier *chansons* came to him:

> *My body begins to tremble*
> *And my tongue is tied*
> *As if a magic spell*
> *Surrounds me.*
> *And when I am myself again,*
> *The memory torments me.*

He turned on his side and lay staring into the dark. Rain blew against the shuttered window. He rolled onto his other side, folded one arm beneath his head, and remembered the promise he had made to himself: *Never again will I put myself at the mercy of a beautiful woman. It is better for a* trouvère *alone.*

His mind went back to the poem he had started for her wedding, and he fell into a deep, dream-filled sleep.

CHAPTER TWENTY-FOUR

Catherine awakened to street sounds coming through the window, closed against the night's cold.

"Isabel, wake up." Catherine pulled the coverlet to her side of the straw mattress, laughing as the cold air made Isabel shriek.

Isabel pulled the covers back up to her neck. Catherine rose, walked to the basin, and dipped icy water on her face.

"Today," Isabel said, "I am going to a fortune-teller. Yesterday, I saw one beside the moneychanger."

"Why visit a fortune-teller?"

"Don't you want to know your future? Or how the musician feels about you?"

She tossed a damp linen at Isabel. "You are very bold for someone so far from home."

They both laughed as Isabel reached for her shoes beside the bed. "Well, at any rate, we have work to do today; our two households are dependent on us, and we had best keep our wits about us."

Catherine spoke to the innkeeper and arranged to have the wagon and horses waiting at the east corner of the grain market to load their purchases.

They stepped outside. A sun the color of gold spilled over the rooftops. Wind from the north whistled between the buildings, and as they turned from the protection of the narrow alley Catherine pulled her cloak closer, grateful she remembered to bring a hooded one. A colder gust of air stung their faces as they walked into the square toward the area set aside for gaming tables.

The streets had been swept clean during the night and now were filled with people. Animals roamed between the stalls, ignoring officials who tried in vain to chase them away.

They approached an alchemist who rose from a stool behind his display. "Buy a piece of the true Philosopher's Stone; it will make you rich beyond the king's own treasury."

Curious, Catherine strolled to the display of shiny metal, molded into pots and urns of every conceivable shape. She lifted a small metallic bowl from the display. "Is this gold?" she asked.

"Indeed, yes. It was formed from my secret mixture, a pure product of fire, wind, and water. Solid gold, and priceless, but I offer it to you cheaply, as you appreciate its beauty."

She felt a hand on her shoulder and turned to face Adam. He reached for the pot and turned it over in his hand. With his thumb, he followed the rim on the bottom, the circle of hammered *orichalcum*. Looking straight into the alchemist's eyes he said, "You have fashioned this from common metal. Tell her the truth."

The man stared at Adam and ran his tongue over his curving upper lip, back and forth, his eyes shifting from one to the other. "It's true, it is not one of my best pieces. The Stone, though"—he reached to pick up a pebble from the display—"here is a piece of the true Philosopher's Stone." He held it up, closing one eye, squinting as he turned it between his thumb and forefinger. "See, a chip that matches perfectly. Surely, you recognize this as authentic." He handed it to Adam.

"It is a worthless piece of common stone. Come, Catherine."

They left the vendor who mumbled obscenities at their backs.

"How did you know the pot was fake?"

"The rim on the bottom, and the weight. It could not possibly have been gold. Besides, true alchemists work far from crowds such as this; they are disturbed by curious onlookers, and prefer the isolation of the forests for their work. Some noblemen dabble in alchemy, but lately, it has become a source of income for charlatans and wanderers who move from town to town, preying on unsuspecting purchasers."

"Then I'm grateful you were behind me; I might have bought his work. Papa would have been furious." They came to a spot where the street widened. "Ah, there's Isabel, just ahead." She pointed toward a tent that jutted into the road, obstructing the view of other vendors beyond.

As they neared the tent, a one-armed man stepped onto the path. He wore knee-length drawers tied at the bottom, and grayish-blue hose covered his long, skinny legs. His shoes, encasing amazingly long feet, were made of dark leather, bells sewn to the tops. His outer garment, tied at the waist with a narrow rope, was blue on one side, brown on the other, and hung from his shoulders to just above his cinched-in drawers, making him look like one of the fools who stopped at the village inn to furnish a night's entertainment in exchange for a meal from the kitchen.

As they approached, the man glanced at Adam, then at Catherine. "Come inside for a reading of your future, all of you. My wife can foresee riches, journeys, deaths. Find out what destiny awaits." He moved away, calling out to other shoppers.

"Please, let's do," Isabel said. "The last fortune-teller, the one who came to the marketplace that time in the village, told me fate would make a big change in my life. Then, my brother died." She pulled her cloak closer as a cold gust of wind flapped the cloths beneath the displays, forcing vendors to grab the corners of the table coverings that threatened to carry their wares into the crowded street.

"Isabel, those who see the future are evil. Father Bretel said not to believe them." She chewed her lip. "Well, perhaps . . . just this one time, though it will obligate me to say many *Pater Nosters* when I go to confession." She turned to Adam. "Will you wait?"

"I'll be with Pierre, just beyond that food vendor, at the saddle display."

Catherine and Isabel approached the tent, and the man hurried over, his hand extended. "Whatever you want to give. . . . She sets no price on her advice. It is a true gift from God."

Catherine gasped at his blasphemy, then reluctantly reached into the purse at her waist and placed three coins into the man's coarse palm. He grinned, showing two teeth, one below, one above, and gestured for them to follow. Catherine watched him walk and marveled that he did not trip over the pointed toes of such long shoes. He lifted back the flap which served as a doorway, and they stepped inside.

The room was in semi-darkness, illuminated only by three flickering candles placed beside two wooden boxes on a low table in the middle of the makeshift room. To Catherine, it all smelled of wax and burning weeds.

A voice called from the darkness. "Leave your cloaks on the bench and move toward the candles."

Isabel whispered, "This is unlike the village soothsayer."

"Do as I say, and don't be afraid." A woman eased from the shadows; her head bent beneath the weight of floor-length hair which framed a wrinkled face. She moved soundlessly across the dirt floor, then sat on a small stool close to the flickering light. "Sit," she said, indicating a bench on each end. "Pull them together. I must look directly into your faces. Ah, beautiful ladies, I see." Then, glancing from Catherine's hands to Isabel's, asked, "Who will have their fortune told?"

"Both of us," Catherine replied hastily, thinking of the three coins she had given the comical man outside.

"Very well. We will begin." The woman rose and brought a vial of liquid and an oval-shaped bowl to the table. She poured the contents of the vial into the bowl, then reached into the smaller of two boxes and sprinkled a fine powder over the liquid. She picked a slender reed from the table, touched it to one of the candles, and held it over the pot. A flame instantly leapt from the mixture.

Catherine gasped. *She is magic, or worse, a witch.* A cloud of dark smoke rose from the pot, and with it a strong odor Catherine could not identify, a mixture of smells, like the smell of burned meat and molten iron, like the smell near the street of tanners. The foul odor dissipated, and the woman withdrew little pieces of leather from one of the boxes.

Straining to get a glimpse of the tooled symbols, Catherine leaned forward; the fragments looked like figures and animals carved into hide, not clearly discernible in the flickering candlelight.

"You, first," the fortune-teller said, reaching for Isabel's hand. After turning it palm up, the woman reached into a flat dish and rubbed oil onto Isabel's skin.

"May the wheels of fate turn in obedience to this, the blessed ointment, and reveal the universal truth to me, your chosen truth-teller," she chanted, her melodramatic voice causing the sounds from the street to fade. "Look into the light of the candle, then close your eyes. I am beginning to see what lies ahead for you." She ceased rubbing Isabel's palm and began shuffling the leather pieces. "There is a journey in your future." Her voice slipped into a monotone. "You will marry." She moved the pieces again, placing one in Isabel's palm; holding it there, she intoned again in the singsongy voice that made Catherine think of Father Bretel at mass. "I see a child in your future." She stopped abruptly and looked up at Isabel. "You have lost someone very dear."

Her brother, Catherine thought.

"That is all. I am prevented from seeing more, and am warned not to try. I'm sorry." She blew into the pot of liquid, extinguishing the flame.

Isabel withdrew her hand, and Catherine chided herself, dismayed she had succumbed to Isabel's request to come in here. Indeed, this woman was part magic, part fake.

The woman pushed back from the low table and walked to the back corner. Catherine heard a rustling sound followed by sobbing coming from the shadows. She gripped Isabel's arm. "I want nothing of this. Let's go, quickly, while we can."

Just then the woman emerged again, carrying another vial. She again lit a fire.

Catherine sniffed. *Pure theater.*

The woman reached for Catherine's hand and rubbed the ointment into her right palm while intoning the same chant. Then she closed her eyes. "There is discord in your future, as well as a long journey. This journey will take you to unspeakable joy and despair."

She shuffled the leather pieces and placed one in Catherine's palm. "Yes, it is clear. This is the sign of the lovers. Love is in your future. Wait. I see swords—hundreds of them. This means a great conflict, though I hear no battle sounds. Now I hear the singing of angels transporting a soul to heaven. Wait . . . there is another soul, ascending. It is in a place far from here. You will suffer a great loss. No, there will be two. Two losses."

Catherine gasped aloud and shoved back the bench.

"That is enough," Isabel said. "You are trying to frighten us."

"Very well," the woman spoke again in the same monotone. "It matters not to me; I only speak the truth."

"The truth," Isabel sputtered. "No truth is in this sorry place."

The woman was still sitting at the low table as they snatched their cloaks from the bench and ducked under the tent flap into the daylight.

"I should never have encouraged you to go in there," Isabel said. "You're right, they are instruments of the devil, designed to steer people to the dark side with their concoctions."

"I suppose you're right, Isabel, but one wonders . . . she knew about your brother."

"She guessed—it was only a guess. The rest were lies. Come, we need to finish buying supplies."

Adam joined them at the next display. "Did she foretell your future?"

"No." Catherine shivered, adjusting her cloak. "She is a charlatan, bewitching with her oils and smelly fires. I vow never to listen to one again. She foretold of conflicts and journeys and death."

"Stories made up as she went along, for sure . . . the ravings of a mad woman," Isabel said.

They passed the boot maker and a long table displaying purses of every size, some with chains attached to girdles of the same material. Beside the purse maker, a small crowd stood by a display of combs, their attention focused on a vendor separating what appeared to be horsehair gathered tightly at one end by a thin rope, the loose ends blowing in the wind. The man pulled ivory teeth through the hairs, loudly proclaiming the strength and beauty of the comb.

Just past him was the black-haired jewel vendor, still caressing stones, still rearranging her display as if she had just set up her table. Catherine noticed the rosary she admired the day before was gone, no doubt bought by some dealer who would resell it at a higher price after putting the amber stone on a gold ring.

They walked past a large display of belts and leather goods. "I should leave," Isabel said. "They will be loading the wagons."

Catherine nodded. "I'll be there in a few minutes." She chose a sturdy leather coin purse for her father, then walked with Adam to the end of the street where the caravan was being loaded.

Adam reached to touch her shoulder, then withdrew his hand. "Never have I enjoyed a fair as much as this one."

His comment wrapped around her like a comforting shawl of fine wool.

"Nor I. Papa will be glad someone was here to help me with the bartering. You probably saved him many a sou."

Adam took her hand. "Then perhaps your father will allow me to visit when I finish at the university."

"He would be delighted." She heard the rumbling of wagons and horses' hooves on the cobbled street, and was dimly aware of Isabel complaining about the full load and how it would lengthen their journey, but nothing mattered except Adam's promise to see her again.

He helped her mount the mule. "God be with you." He stood out of earshot of the others. "Remember, after Paris."

She wanted to ask how long it would be. She wanted him to kiss her, and she wanted him to ask her to stay.

Their eyes locked for an instant before Francino maneuvered the wagon onto the path.

Her eyes clouded with tears. What if she never saw him again? She tore her gaze from Adam and bent her head into the cold north wind. *Would he really come? And if so, what then?*

Chapter Twenty-Five

Twelve days later, on a bitterly cold day in late December, a weary group approached the tapestry shop. Francino rode ahead to arrange for the wagon unloading. A short while later, Catherine saw him running back. As he drew near, she noticed his expression—a mix of confusion and abject misery. She gripped the reins and shaded her eyes. What had gone wrong? A chill of fear numbed her throat.

Francino's words came out in a rush. "Hurry, Catherine. Something's amiss. There are strangers in your house. One said she's a cousin of your father. They tell me nothing more. I told them who I was, but they—"

Prodding the mule, Catherine hurried to the shop and saw Marguerite, her father's cousin. She faintly remembered her from childhood.

Marguerite approached her with outstretched arms and a tearful expression. "I am sorry. I wanted to let you know, but there was no way. Two days ago . . . your father . . . I did not arrive in time."

Catherine jumped from the mule and shook the woman. "Tell me. Is Father ill? Where is he? God's breath! Has no one called the doctor?" She dashed past Marguerite and heard her cry out. "He's gone, Catherine. Gone."

Catherine lunged up the stairs and came face-to-face with the stableman from across the street. Then she saw Gérard, his reddened eyes confirming the worst.

It was true! Her father had died. Catherine felt the blood drain from her face.

Gérard walked forward, held her in a tight embrace. Tears sprang to her eyes. "When, Gérard?"

"Three days ago," he whispered, still holding her tight. "We could wait no longer."

She wailed with pain.

"I'm so sorry," he said, stroking her hair. "His last words were about you."

"Has he—is he—"

"He's buried in the parish cemetery, as he wanted. I'll take you there whenever you like."

"Now," she said, and clung to him.

The sun was setting behind the church as they reached the burial ground. A blast of cold air blew her hood from her face, but all she could think of was that she had not been here to say good-bye to her dear Papa.

She knelt at the fresh mound of earth and wept, while day turned into evening and her sobs mingled with the desolate cries of night birds. Hours later, she felt Isabel's arms around her, leading her to bed, and she could not remember returning home. She drank a warm potion, and just before she fell asleep, she remembered the fortune-teller's words. *There will be two.* Who would be next?

A heavy snowstorm came in January, and when bitter weather continued into February, Catherine locked the shop and stayed upstairs. Icy winds rattled the doors, and fires were no longer enough to heat the rooms. Staying warm, it seemed to her, occupied all her waking hours: pulling dry logs from beneath the snow-covered pile in the back, hanging wall coverings in drafty places, and thinking of new ways to make soup from the dried root vegetables.

When the sun began to warm the thatch, and ice no longer collected each morning between the cobblestones in the road, she dared to hope spring would return. Her knees were sore from hours at the altar in her room, praying for her father's soul, and for her transgressions.

As the Feast of the Purification of Mary was celebrated, slivers of hope cut through the grief that had consumed her during the long winter. She thought of the Troyes fair, and wondered if Adam would remember his promise to come to Vitry-en-Artois.

One morning in March, she awoke to the chirping of a songbird. She ran to the window, opened a shutter, and was rewarded by the sight of a warbler perched on a gnarled vine, thrusting out his chest, feathers atremble with each new song pattern.

Later that day, as Francino brushed dust from a tapestry, she sat on a stool, cupped her hands around a heated drink, and stared at the floor. "Soon, Francino, I must make a decision about the shop. Father's business is no longer profitable, no matter that Gérard has done his best. Truth is, the buyers all knew Papa, and now that he's gone, they've shifted loyalties."

She sipped the spiced wine. "I talked to the prioress at the Cloister of Benevolent Sisters. She told me I would be welcome there."

Francino's eyes grew round like plums. "You would go to a cloister?"

"Perhaps. But first I have a pilgrimage to make."

"Such an old promise." Francino shook his head. "God would not hold you to that. You were a young girl. Besides, I think a grief such as you have had is absolution in itself."

"It is not, Francino. I would never think of Papa's death as being anything but that God wanted him in heaven. I have every intention of fulfilling my earlier oath. Guillaume's death and Papa's have nothing to do with each other. I made a promise I mean to uphold, though I know not how, not as long as I own this house, which I thought of turning over to the monks at the abbey; Father would approve of that. What would happen to dear Gérard, though? He has been helpful to me in untold ways, helping me manage the accounts."

"Whoa," he said. "I meant no harm."

She forced a smile. Even now, there were times she would burst into tears, and now was no time to cry—not when she wanted to sort things out. "If I left, I suppose Gérard would go to a monastery, but Vitry is his home. I think the monk's lives are much the same as in a convent. It seems like such a peaceful existence, cloistered as they are, with no one to disturb their thoughts. I am not sure, though, that Gérard would be happy." She set the cup aside. "He could always stay here, of course. What do you think, Francino?"

He shrugged. "Ask him. How would I know? Besides, Catherine, he's a grown man. You cannot plan other people's lives. As for leaving, aren't you rushing into this? I hate to think of you going away." He rubbed the back of his hand and avoided her eyes. "I'd miss you, you know. And not just because of the work. Isabel's father has been wanting me to help at his shop, and I may, since . . . since our trade has slowed down. But Vitry wouldn't be the same without you."

She felt a new flood of tears, and rose from the stool, then set her empty cup on the wood table. She hated to leave too, in a way, but she could not put off forever her commitment to God. Perhaps, before too long, Adam would come, as he promised. Once she had seen him again, she could put her past behind her and depart Vitry with no regrets.

Adam's friends had delayed the return to Paris, stopping early each day to take advantage of what the roadside inns offered: good food, cheap ale, and country wenches. During these evenings, Adam watched the youths with amusement. He even allowed himself to be coaxed into entertaining in the evenings with a song or two as the roads became slick with ice, and the fire inside roared, and the wine flowed freely. Once, when a comely girl with black hair asked him to dance, he made an excuse, citing a sore knee in a fall from a horse. It was partly true, he reasoned, but the pain of the injury had left long ago. The pain of his ruined marriage, though, had come to his mind like a wound with the sight of the girl's slim ankles and long hair.

His thoughts slid back to Catherine. Instead of reaffirming his commitment to a solitary life, the time he had spent with her at the Cold Fair only undermined his resolve. He wished now he'd never allowed his young friends to talk him into going. Perhaps, he conceded, it was possible for others to love again and to trust. But, for him, in the light of day, he knew such lofty expectations belonged in a song, a tale of courtly love. He needed to finish this term, and concentrate on writing again. He'd been inspired in Troyes, had even scribbled a melody, about a girl with green eyes, and he dared to hope his creativity had returned.

Now, as they rode into Paris, a day late for classes, Adam determined to keep his mind on his studies and nothing else. He owed Robert that much.

In the weeks that followed, he never ventured far from the path that led from Beatris's modest dwelling to the rooms of the university. Beatris needed his help more than ever, and chopping wood and mending torn window coverings kept him occupied during the winter nights.

Finally, after weeks of bitter cold, an early spring came to Paris, warming the paved roads and seeping into the buildings in the capital city. As March turned to April, Adam knew he could no longer postpone telling his patron that he would not be returning to university for the next term.

He ascended the hill to the count's estate and found him in the courtyard.

Later, having broken the news to Robert, Adam waited for his patron's response, expecting scorn, but Robert simply reached for the wine ewer which sat on a stump between the two courtyard benches. "I agree, Adam, you're finished in Paris. Those who stay six years, I know, study law and ancient texts. You have no use for these. It's time to think of your future beyond the university."

"I thought you might disapprove of my decision to leave, but truly there is no point in paying more tuition, as I have no wish to be either a priest or a teacher." He sipped his wine, then looked directly at Robert. "You're not disappointed, then?"

Robert shook his head, apparently accepting Adam's decision, then bent forward to pet the hounds that paced between them.

It seemed Adam had worried for nothing. He said, "I've learned much of what others only dream of, thanks to your generosity. In addition, some of the teachers brought books with them, and I read a few."

"Better than those I loaned you?" Robert raised his brows in mock surprise.

Adam laughed. "I wonder they can afford them on the wages they are paid."

"They are paid more than you think, Adam. Perhaps not coins, but patrons. Many teach in royal homes during their time off. But back to your future. Why not complete this term, then come back to Cambrai? You always said writing came easily for you there."

"Yes. I'd like that." He leaned to pet one of the hounds. "I need to get back to what I do best."

Despite their agreement, it seemed to Adam that an uneasy

silence lay between them.

Robert cleared his throat. "It is not my affair, but I wondered, is there . . . someone, in Paris? I'm not prodding, but earlier, when you mentioned leaving Arras, you hinted that your marriage was ended. I never got to know your wife."

"It was a brief marriage—only a year, but still, a marriage. But our separation is for the best—I'm sure of that. A man focused on his writing makes a poor husband."

"You're being too hard on yourself, Adam. And don't forget, Raoul's talent for hearing gossip almost surpasses his abilities as a *baillif.* But you didn't answer my question. Is there someone here you've grown fond of? You could bring her here if—"

"You mean, a mistress? No, no." Adam pushed his hair behind his ear, ignoring the count's direct stare. "I've no such intentions, either. Affairs of the heart only complicate life."

"Very well. I only wondered . . . the wedding—you seemed somehow, when I told you of that groom's death, you seemed—"

"I knew his wife—before they married. She's not in Paris, but, yes—I did see her, after he died," Adam said, wanting to talk about her, yet not wanting to say her name. If he said her name she would become real again. As it was, she was a vision and would fade into obscurity. "She was at the Cold Fair in Troyes. She seemed genuinely glad to see me. As for me, I was taken with her from the moment we met, but she deserves someone with more to offer. Marrying another landowner would give her security and permanence—something I can't offer."

"Life at court? What could be better?" Suddenly an expression crossed Robert's face, as if he'd made a discovery. "Surely, you have terminated the marriage legally, Adam. You'd not be so foolish as to think you could—"

"No. We haven't divorced. As you know, we married young, and then my work took me away for long periods of time. I suppose . . . she was lonely. At any rate, she took a lover. And I have no appetite for seeing the townspeople ridicule her." His mind went back to a moment in his childhood, the first time he had seen a woman in a cart, caged like an animal. Liegart had been the one who explained the prisoner's crime. "Went to bed with another, and the husband caught them together." The image had never left his mind. He would never subject a woman to such torture.

"Besides," he continued, trying to put the incident in the back of his mind, "I've learned that women want a home. They don't want to be uprooted like a sapling in a windstorm. For myself, that's when I'm happiest—performing in some new town, before an audience of strangers. I suppose it's the challenge, but for whatever reason, it precludes my settling down. I was tempted, in Troyes, to court her, but thankfully she had to return home, and I had my classes to think of. She lives with her father now, and I daresay she'll be married before too many moons pass."

"Perhaps not, Adam. She may feel the same as you do about her. And not all women crave a home and hearth. What of Queen Eleanor, who practically launched a crusade by herself!"

They laughed together. A bell rang, and Robert turned toward the door. "Let's have some dinner. I'm thankful Lent is over; I was weary of cod and eels."

On the seventh of June, having finished the term at university, Adam prepared to leave the city, sure that with a change of landscape, he would write as before. He rolled some scrolls together and glanced around the room he had shared with Beatris, then stuffed the scrolls into his bundle. The wax tablet lay on the table, mocking his inactivity. He picked up the stylus and thought again of Catherine, of those two days in Troyes, and how he had told her when she left that he would come to Vitry when he finished in Paris. Most likely, after leaving the Cold

Fair, she had forgotten all about him.

Idly picking loose wax from the stylus, he remembered that night in the tavern, speaking to her as he never had to any woman; she was questioning and intelligent, something he admired as much as her comeliness.

Tightening the strap on his bundle, he wondered how soon the new scholar would arrive. Hopefully, it would be someone who would prove to be a little help to Beatris.

He sat on the bed and ran his hands through his hair. He would go back to Robert's castle in Cambrai and complete the unfinished work.

The next morning he kissed Beatris, then carried his belongings outside and headed to Cambrai, where he intended to bury his mind in his music. All would be as it was before he had met Catherine Durant.

CHAPTER TWENTY-SIX

Five days after leaving Paris and the university behind, Adam stood by the window gazing at a half-moon that lit the pointed keep at Robert's château in Cambrai. In spite of an earlier flush of creativity today, the words had once again become strangely evasive.

Robert had convinced him that he needed the time and solitude of Cambrai, but even here, the old tricks of looking at a note scratched hastily into the waxen tablet, or glancing at a few *neumes* on a piece of parchment did nothing to inspire him. He felt an odd thumping in his chest, and sweat broke out on his forehead. What if he could never write again? Had his time in Paris, instead of helping him, ended his writing?

He rose from the bed, wrapped the sheepskin over his shoulders, and felt for the candleholder. Ashes cast a dim glow from the hearth, and he went to the fire and held the candle near the crumbling embers until it ignited. He padded back and sorted through leaves of parchment until he found the one he was looking for. *Cançon, je t'envoieroie u ma dame est. . . .* He stared at the words, transfixed, then dipped the quill into the inkpot, willing the music to come. As he studied the *neumes* he had written earlier, he imagined the dark ovals were faces, the tiny specks where the ink had not covered the surface appeared to him as finite eyes, watching. He could imagine the judging *neumes* grinning, emboldened by his impotence. *I will go mad.*

Crumbling the parchment in his hand he rose and walked to

the hearth. The blackened ashes came to life as the parchment crackled to nothingness. *Good riddance. It was valueless, at any rate.* The fire smoked and smoldered. A flame reignited two slender branches. He stared while they writhed and crumbled. What wretched kind of life was he making for himself? He tried to remember the last time he had written anything of value. Only the poem written in Troyes, hastily scribbled on parchment while his youthful friends slept off their wine. It's as if, by seeing her, the joy had returned to his life. And what if, as Robert implied, Catherine felt the same? Was he being fair to her by staying away?

He poked at the ashes. How vain, he thought, to believe that a young girl would have more than a passing interest in an older man—and a musician, at that. What would a girl as young and beautiful as she see in a man of almost forty summers who was still married, owned no property, and wrote songs for a living? And when would he learn to leave her alone? Still, he felt a deep certainty that an unspoken promise lay between them. He'd felt it more than once. Why, when he had faced every facet of his life boldly, was he so reluctant to learn the truth about the two of them? Perhaps, by shutting her out of his life, he was avoiding a grim reality. Was he afraid of rejection? And who was he to say what was best for her? From what he knew of her, she was no fainting courtier, but a woman who faced her own lot head-on, and had a mind of her own.

He wandered aimlessly around the room, cursing his own irresolution until the gray light of dawn slipped through the open window, a reminder that another day had begun. He stretched out on the bed and fell into a deep sleep.

Hours later he woke with a start. Sometime during the long night he had made a decision. With a clarity the likes of which he had never experienced, he knew what he must do. He would go to Vitry and put an end to this agonizing. If by now she was betrothed to another, he could at least make sure the man was honorable. If not, he would move heaven and hell to persuade her father—

He stopped short. If she were betrothed, there was not a damned thing he could do about it.

As Adam rode toward Vitry, he felt a strange sense of calm. Clouds lay on the horizon, but here, the sky was clear. June had always been his favorite time of year, when the sun was at its longest and highest course, and the days lengthened, encroaching on the night. Along the roadside, amidst the ferns and irises, grew a few wake-robins, surprising this late in the year. Peasants believed the blooms were a sign of fertility, and gypsies used them for love potions. He chuckled. If only it were that easy.

He approached a bend in the road. Beyond that lay the town of Vitry. In spite of his earlier euphoria, now that he was here, anticipation made his heart race. He entered the village and saw the tapestry shop ahead on the right.

After tethering the mare, he walked inside. The room had been cleared, except for a few tapestries laid to one side. So, she had married, and her father was closing the shop.

When she stepped from behind a divider, his heart leapt. Her hair was in disarray, and her cheeks were flushed. She held a rush broom in one hand and a cloth in the other. As always, he wanted to kiss her. The thought brought warmth to his face, and he hoped she had not noticed.

"Adam!"

Her smile warmed him to his toes. "*Bonjour,* Catherine. I see I've come at a most inopportune time."

"Not at all." She laid the broom aside, then brushed the front of her tunic in a self-conscious gesture. "I . . . I thought you were in Paris, studying."

He stepped toward her and took her hand, then kissed both

cheeks. He fought the urge to hold her tight, fearing she'd pull away. She already would think him presumptuous, coming here unannounced.

She pulled two stools side-by-side.

"I finished my studies. And I told you in Troyes I would come." He made no mention of his earlier determination not to see her again. And standing here now, he could scarcely believe he had entertained such a notion.

"I did not expect you to."

They exchanged smiles. The color rose in her face, and she lowered her gaze.

He decided to change the subject. "Your inventory is dwindling. I suppose you'll have another shipment before long."

She shook her head, evidently relieved to speak of something else. "*Au contraire,* we have given no more orders to the weavers, and have cancelled orders from the south." She cast a quick glance around the shop.

"But why—"

"I forgot. You had no way of knowing. Papa died. I found out upon my return from the Cold Fair."

"Ah, Catherine. I'm so sorry." He noticed her eyes misting. He wanted to hold her close and blot her tears with kisses. Instead, he remained where he was.

After a moment, she looked away, but not before he caught a look of bewilderment in her eyes. Had she wanted comfort? He cursed himself for his inaction, but the moment had passed.

"A lot has happened since, but now I find myself alone. Gérard and I agreed. We had no heart to keep the store after Papa's death. Besides, Isabel and Francino will marry, and he's going to work in her father's shop. We've sold most of the stock, and now we're down to these."

His mind raced. Where would she go? How would she live? For one crazed moment, he wanted to speak up, to tell her how he would take care of her, and give her all the things she never had. He pictured her in court; she would outshine any woman there, with that crown of auburn hair and her lively green eyes. Besides, with her father gone, who would be her protector? Every woman needed a man to protect them, except for a cloistered nun. The worst part was, even if he declared his love, what could he offer? He wrested again with conscience. He was not free to offer her anything more, not now, not ever—not until he resolved the issue with Maroie.

He pushed the thought to the back of his mind. "And you . . . how will you manage, a woman alone?"

"Gérard has agreed to go with me on a journey, one I must make. After that, who knows?"

A cloud passed over the sun, and he was reminded this was the season of afternoon rainstorms. He needed a place for the night, and the horse would require a dry stable. He was about to take his leave when he decided he had nothing to lose. He would never see her again. "The inn where I stayed last time, they have excellent food. Would you consider eating with me tonight?"

Her face crinkled in a smile. "*Oui.* I've eaten there before. It was the mayor's birth date and they cook roasted pigs for the entire town. I would love to go back."

"Then I will return at sunset. *Au revoir.*"

She watched him lead the horse to the stable across the way. Then she pulled the door closed and hurried up the back stairs. Once in her room, she flung open the chest where she stored her best clothes. A green surcote, bought from a peddler, caught her eye. She shook out the folds, then walked to the light, hunting for insect holes, but evidently worms had no taste for the fabric. She laid it on the bed, then filled the basin with water from the jug. She decided to splurge and use the last of the soap bar to wash the dust from her hair. After her hair dried, she cleaned her boots and slipped on an undertunic.

By the time the sun set, she was waiting downstairs near the door, feeling foolish because her heart pounded erratically.

She took his arm, and they walked to the inn. Catherine studied Adam's face as he ordered food from the innkeeper's son. He looked more handsome than ever, although a few hairs had turned gray. How long had it been since she had seen him in Troyes?

Behind her she heard the shouts of the dancers as they joined hands in a line that stretched around two walls of the tavern.

"Come," he said. "They are dancing the *carole.* From the sound of it, they need someone in the circle who can sing the tune."

"It's your rondeau, the one you sang before."

"Let's join them," he whispered. "But sing only to me."

Moments later, Catherine found herself whirling in a large circle, one hand in Adam's, the other tightly clasped by an attractive woman she did not recognize. Musicians played louder, struggling to be heard above the boisterous guests. Suddenly the music changed and Catherine became separated from Adam as a long line of dancers broke through the circle. She caught a glimpse of him as he was pulled into another ring of dancers, and when the music stopped she was in the midst of strangers.

She searched the hall for him, finally finding him near the hallway surrounded by three of the ladies. In the second before she looked away, she saw a white hand, adorned with a gauzy veil flowing downward from a ringed finger, reach to touch his cheek, then slide quickly down to disappear beneath his cape.

Clutching the edge of her surcote she hurried to the table, one eye on the door. When the music began, she would make her way out, unnoticed. Why had she agreed to come here with him? And what did she expect? He was used to fawning courtiers and was recognized in a crowd. She blinked, fighting back tears.

"There you are! I'm sorry—met some old friends."

She nodded. "Not old, young and beautiful." She hated her words, knew they sounded petulant and incriminating, but what did it matter? She had no business trying to complete with women like that.

"Beautiful on the outside, Catherine, but I know their husbands. Life at court sometimes turns young women into shrews. Everything is about politics and appointments." He poured their wine. "Tonight, though, let's not talk of them. Let's talk about you. You didn't tell me about your plans, the journey you will make once you close the shop."

"I have . . . no plans, not yet, not exactly." How could she explain all that to him, about Guillaume, about her unrelenting guilt for his death? How could anyone understand how it feels to be responsible for ending someone's life?

She clamped her lips. The less said, the better.

Hours later Adam lay awake on the pallet next to a snoring *jongleur.* He recalled the conversation he had with Catherine, and thought of the vow he had made to himself, remembered his determination to pursue the solitary life of a *trouvère.* Unwittingly, he was making a mockery of his own commitment, for he wanted nothing more than to be with her, and yet, she was elusive, about her plans for the future, about some journey she seemed set upon making. It was obvious she didn't want to share her plans with him.

He dozed, then woke and turned sideways on the pallet. He had dreamed she danced the *carole* beside him, singing the words he had written. The circle of dancers had metamorphosed into a whirling spinning abyss twirling drowning him, nullifying all reason.

CHAPTER TWENTY-SEVEN

Catherine opened the shutters to a sunny, cool Saturday and wondered if Adam would come again today, or leave Vitry straightaway. They had parted last evening in silence, a quiet that followed her mention of a journey. Perhaps she had seen him for the last time.

She closed one shutter and walked to the perch that hung from the rafters. *I may as well wear yesterday's tunic. He probably spent the night with one of those fawning women, and even now is on his way back to Cambrai.*

Once downstairs, she swung open the wood door leading outside and saw Adam was securing his horse to the apple tree out by the road. He turned at the sound of the squeaky door.

"Bonjour!" she called.

For an instant their eyes met, his look so intense she almost stumbled. He tossed the leather strap over a low branch and walked her way.

"Bonjour, Catherine. It's a fine morning for riding. Would you like to? I'll rent a mule if you prefer, but a horse is better. Can you manage a gelding?"

She nodded. "I can, but not well. I usually rode behind Papa the few times he rented a horse."

"I'll make sure the stableman gives you a gentle one."

"Why spend the money? I'll ride double with you." She lowered her voice. "That is, if you don't mind. Father got thrown once. He said the stableman's horses weren't to be trusted."

"You'll not have to worry about Agnès. She's gentle as a babe." His eyes grazed her form. "You may want to dress warmer. It's turning cool."

"*Oui.* I'll only be a minute." She ran upstairs and grabbed her cloak, then remembered she hadn't broken her fast. She crossed to the room that held food and dishes, then reached for a basket which she stuffed with an assortment of cheese, bread, and some ripe berries.

He was waiting for her beside the horse. Self-consciously, she twisted the tie on her coif. He cleared his throat and adjusted his beret.

This trouvère, whose words echo in châteaus throughout France, is without words, like me. "I brought a bite to eat later," she said, breaking the silence.

Adam reached for the basket and secured it to his horse, helped her mount, then swung into the saddle.

"You'll have to tell me the paths. I only know the main road."

"Go straight ahead. I'll show you the farms, beyond the city gate. They're beautiful this time of year, with the grazing sheep and all the wildflowers."

"All of France is beautiful," he said. "Each region offers the wayfarer something different as you pass from town to town."

"Ah, you are blessed, Adam, to be able to travel at will and enjoy the countryside." She waved to the sheep herder as they passed. "Sometimes, I think the shepherd is a most fortunate man; he has his animals and the peace of the meadow. Shepherds seem always happy, and with little."

"I have thought the same many times. Nights I spent with them make for some of my best poems." They came to a branch road. "Which way?"

"Follow the creek. I'll show you a place I know of, a place I came to as a child. Later Isabel and I went there, when she had free days and when Francino would mind the shop." They passed a hedge of roses, and she inhaled the fragrance.

She waited while he took the horse around a wide trough in the road. "The place was used as a chapel, I believe, before they built the monastery."

They entered a copse of trees, and when they came to a clearing he reined in the mare. "It's beautiful here."

"I know." She could smell the soap he'd used to wash, and suddenly felt as though her life was changing, and she would never be the same again. She had never known the honest pleasure of a man's company before, aside from her father's, and Francino's, of course, who was one of her best friends. But with Adam, she loved the world and everything in it. Blooms were more fragrant; the skies more fair.

He shifted in the saddle and met her eyes. Would he kiss her?

Suddenly she remembered her promise, the one she made to the Virgin. She had no right to claim another's life, and she wanted no harm to come to this man for whom she was beginning to care.

She cleared her throat and looked away. "Go to the right— the path along the wood."

He turned away, and she wondered if he had felt, in that moment, the same thing as she. Carefully maneuvering Agnès around large boulders, they came to a stone grotto nestled in a tangle of vines. A stream ran beside the crumbling stones, and water cascaded from rocks, forming a pool that overflowed to boulders below.

The only sounds were the splash of water and the warning cry of birds perched in trees overhead. They rode to the stream and dismounted.

An animal path led up to the grotto. Lizards darted in and out of the rocks, throats undulating pink and gray.

She glanced back at Adam, and, for the second time that morning, he seemed to be without words.

"Is it not a lovely place?" she asked.

"Indeed, a secret bower; and why would it be abandoned?" He tossed the reins across Agnès's back.

"I suppose the monks have no time for reflection now, this far from the monastery." She stopped to remove a pebble from her shoe, felt his eyes on her, and looked up. His glance registered pleasure and intimacy, taking her off guard.

She unpacked the basket. When they had almost finished eating, the mare came to Adam's side and nuzzled his wool cape.

"Agnès is fond of you," she said.

"She knows me well. Though she stays at the count's stables, I consider her mine. We have ridden together many times."

He boosted Catherine back up, and his hand covered hers. Their eyes locked briefly. He looked away and mounted the horse.

They followed the stream past a thicket and onto the path that led to the main road. Turning south, he told her about some of the sights he had seen along the old Roman road.

"You lead a charmed life, going to court and mixing with royalty."

"I am not so footloose as I once was, as a young poet. Count Robert commissioned me to provide entertainment at his courts. My future is committed. Whereas you . . . why, you have the freedom to pursue your dreams."

Mesmerized by the slow, steady gate of the mare, and Adam's voice, she imagined herself with Adam, at court. She would take his arm, and proceed toward the king.

She blinked, startled by her own childish fantasy. He had come as a friend, not a suitor. Still, something had passed between them, or was that, too, a product of her imagination?

They were approaching the tapestry shop. The horse's hooves

echoed on the cobbles, and she wondered what he was thinking. He turned his head, and she thought his jaw had tightened.
Did he regret coming here? She had been a fool to believe a
man who sang for kings could have feelings for the daughter of
a shopkeeper. When would she learn?

During the week following Adam's visit, Catherine decided she
could no longer postpone her promise to God. Besides, she
needed to keep busy. It was the only way to rid her mind of
Adam.

The first thing she needed to do was to convince Gérard to
leave Vitry with her and journey south. Drawing on what she
knew would appeal to him most, she had reminded him of his
relatives in southern France.

When he suggested that if they wanted to see him, they knew
where he was, she appealed to his softer side. "Just stay with me
until we spot a caravan moving to join the crusade—an easy
task once you know what to look for. I've seen them pass the
shop. The larger caravans have guards who carry a plain banner
with a cross. You could return then, to Vitry, or take your time
to visit the oldest monasteries, the ones you said dated from
earliest times."

She had watched for his reaction, praying that his love of
architecture would be the one temptation he couldn't resist.

"I would only be a burden, and I hate riding mules."

"Nonsense," she had insisted. "Besides, Gérard, you have no
family here, and you say yourself you could not stay with the
monks; you told me you never understood their cloistered life
of sacrifice. So where will you go?"

"I'll stay here in my room in Vitry. There is always work for
an old clerk."

She sat down now on a three-legged stool, crossing her arms
in front of her, and turned her head to stare at the wall. "Well,

then, I guess I shan't get to see France after all, as I cannot go alone and without a guardian." She pinched her lower lip tightly to the upper one, the corners of her mouth turned down for emphasis.

He slammed down the wax tablet, pushed back the bench, and stared at the rafters. After several moments he turned to her. "Very well. You are a self-indulgent woman, spoiled by your father, but it's true you need someone to look after you."

She brought both hands to her cheeks and opened her mouth in feigned surprise.

He looked away and began tapping his fingers on the wood table, scowling, then turned sideways in the chair to look at her. "But I will buy a horse. With the right trappings, I will look like a knight." He shoved the wax tablet to the back of the desk. "It's true. The endless days afford too much solitude. I miss your father, and the routine. Besides, the numbers are becoming difficult for me to read. At any rate, I promised your father I would stay with you until you remarried. I thought you'd be wed before this, but instead you have some wild notion to leave. Very well. I'll go along. A girl like you needs a guardian more than most. You're daring and headstrong, two qualities that bring danger to a woman."

He leaned back, locked both hands behind his head and stared at the empty shelves. She knew from his look he was proud of his accomplishments. He had negotiated the sale of most of the tapestries, and she had a sizeable sum on which to live, if she were frugal. As for Gérard, the income from his father's lands was more than enough to see him through his final years.

She watched him secure the last of the records with twine, brush the shock of white hair from his forehead, and place the stacks beside books to be turned over to the monastery. He lowered his ample frame into a chair.

On impulse, she rose and hugged his neck.

As she left the room, he got in the last word. "I wonder how far we will get before you want to turn back."

CHAPTER TWENTY-EIGHT

Within a month, they had started on their journey. At the edge of town, they passed the land her father had owned. She watched until it was out of sight. When she returned, she might sell the land, but for now, she was content to let sheep from a neighboring farm graze the plot. She glanced to her left. Dense patches of forest blocked her view. Then, where the forest met the lowland, the landscape opened to a silvery river that wound through the grassland. Herds of game milled near the water, escaping the heat of early July which settled on northern France like a woolen cape.

The trade route from the village proved wide and flat, with only occasional holes and bumps. The hooves of numerous horses and wheels from passing carts kept the dirt packed on either side of the path.

As the path narrowed, the hair on the back of Catherine's neck rose.

Before she could catch her breath, the rustle of tree limbs warned her of an ambush.

"Go, Catherine. Run for your life!"

The highwaymen rushed toward her. She struggled to turn the horse around.

Gérard shouted again, heading her way, but already one of her attackers reached for the purse at her waist. With a quick swipe of his knife, the bag of coins fell into his hands.

The thief waved the purse in the air, displaying it to his

companions, and Gérard closed in. A flailing hoof knocked the thief to the ground. Before Gérard could dismount, one of the others grabbed the coin purse and disappeared into the woods.

Gérard slid from his horse and within moments the assailants set upon him with their fists, pummeling and kicking him.

As the largest of the men raised his fist to strike, Gérard covered his face with his hands. She watched in horror. The bastards were crushing his arm. He writhed in agony. At a call from the woods, they fled the scene, while Catherine shouted oaths at their backs. She looked down at Gérard. Would they both die, here on this godforsaken road just outside the city gates?

"They've gone." She said, wiping blood from her cheek.

"Catherine! What happened to you? You should have run." He winced in a failed attempt to hide his pain. "Where are the paid protectors when you need them? So much for the king's promise of safe passage for travelers!"

"Never mind me. It's only a cut. Your arm—what's wrong?" She stooped to examine his twisted limb. "*Mon Dieu!* You need a doctor."

"It's a long way to the next town," he said. "Shorter to turn back." He glanced at his arm and looked quickly away.

She wanted to retch. It looked nothing like his arm at all; she wondered why the bone hadn't come through the skin.

She struggled to help him to his feet. "If we can get you up, can you manage the horse, clear back to the village?"

"*Oui.*" He grimaced.

She hoped he wouldn't pass out from the pain. It was a long way to the ground.

"A bad break," the doctor said. "Give him some of this." He handed her a potion. "It'll ease the pain."

An hour later, Gérard slept soundly, and Catherine rubbed

some salve on her face wound.

What now? She needed to unpack their necessities and return food to the larder. Perhaps this was a sign. Once again, she had endangered someone's life by pursuing her own interests. From now on, she would act by herself. Hadn't she harmed enough lives? First Guillaume, then Gérard. Where would it all end? Everything she touched turned to trouble.

Gérard stirred, and she went to his side. "I'll fix you some broth. After that, go back to sleep. The physician said the pain would leave in a day or two. Until then, he wants you to rest."

He took another sip of the potion, laid back on the pillow, and fell fast asleep.

Four days later, after settling Gérard into his favorite chair and giving him the ledger he demanded, she set out to speak with Isabel. Taking the short path to her friend's house, Catherine wondered if Isabel could be any help at all. She clicked her tongue. The disastrous event with the robbers had only made things worse, and she could tell that Gérard had little interest in another trip—an escapade, he'd said, as if she intentionally looked for misadventures.

Isabel's house was even warmer than the tapestry shop, and Catherine chose a seat by the open window and fanned her face with her hand. She locked both hands around her drawn-up knees. "Help me think of something, Isabel. Gérard's arm is mending, and while I'm determined to leave, I'll not endanger his life again. Besides, he refuses to travel with just the two of us."

"No wonder. He's aging, and while he's in good health, he still knows he's not as agile when confronted like the two of you were. And what did it get you? Almost everything your father saved is gone, taken by a bunch of ruffians—not even proper soldiers. He knows he can't protect you, not now when there's highwaymen and such, waiting for travelers just like you."

Catherine nodded. "I suspect he wants to live out his days here in the village. Since we returned, he's made friends with some of the widowers who play board games all day. I think that's what he aspires to."

"And why not? He deserves it. You said yourself he helped your father for years, when things were lean. And he has enough to make his days easy. Why should he endanger life and limb traipsing around France?"

Catherine picked at her nail. Isabel was right, of course. But how could she leave him here, alone? And how could she now afford to travel so far on her own? She needed money to stay at inns, and even monasteries expected a decent donation. She bit her lip, thinking that at least her father would never know that badlings had benefited from his savings. But she had made a holy vow, one she dared not turn from. There was no way out. Surely terrible punishment awaited one who lied to God.

She left Isabel's no less confused than before, and made her way straight to Father Bretel's.

He listened with interest, and seemed to be considering her dilemma. A short while later, he sent her away. "Wait a few days, Catherine. I need time to pray on this. God will give me an answer, all in good time."

Two weeks passed. She had almost begun to think the priest had forgotten all about her, when he took her aside one morning after mass. His solution had shaken her to her bones. "Go to a convent, Catherine. You cannot make your journey alone, and it's clear the clerk wants no part of travel. Dedicate your good works to God. That will please Him as much, or more so, than joining the crusaders. Besides, it's folly to think you can make it to the port city, with no family or guardian."

And so, after a few sleepless nights, she had made a decision. She would take the priest's advice. Now, with everything packed, she waited for the promised caravan of merchants, which Gérard said would see her safely to the convent.

The long-awaited day arrived, and after she tossed her bundle in the wagon and climbed aboard, she waved good-bye to Isabel and Gérard. The tapestry shop blurred from sight as her eyes filled with tears.

CHAPTER TWENTY-NINE

They headed west, toward the seacoast, stopping along the way to sleep in tents. On the sixth day, they approached a marshy area, then crossed a bridge. A fine mist swirled around them, making it difficult to see the landscape. One of the merchants, who seemed to be in charge, shouted from his seat atop the wagon. "Can you walk from here? We need to reach the seaport by nightfall."

She lifted her bundle and pasted a smile on her face, trying to look brave. Through the fog, she could barely make out the convent. Massive stone walls guarded the inner sanctuary that would become her home. It reminded her of a fort.

Behind her, the wagon rumbled away, crossing the bridge, leaving her alone in the vast empty space that led to the looming structure. She remembered Father Bretel telling her it used to be a monastery; now it was a convent school. He had also said you could smell the sea when the wind was right. All she smelled was some poor animal lying along the banks of the canal. Vultures balanced precariously on seaplants, pecking at what was left of the wretched carcass.

She hastened her steps, anxious to be inside, away from the damp wind. Perhaps warm drinks would be served, and she could make friends. She walked through an entry and found herself in a courtyard. All was quiet and gray, as different from the tapestry shop as she could have imagined.

Once inside, she was taken to a small office. After what

seemed like hours, a stern-faced nun entered wearing a gray robe with something stiff beneath that crackled when she walked.

She introduced herself as the abbess and handed Catherine a list of rules. "I presume you read."

"Yes," she said, squaring her shoulders, while inwardly trembling under the woman's scrutiny.

"Very well. Then I'll expect by tomorrow you'll know how to address an abbess correctly. You may go now. A novice will show you to your room. Don't be late for services."

As she left the abbess's office, a freckle-faced girl who looked to be about eighteen rose from a bench and fell in step beside her. At the end of the hall, the novice grabbed Catherine's hand, made a quick turn and continued down another corridor. She looked over her shoulder. "We're not allowed to talk," she whispered, "so keep your voice down. My name's Gabrielle."

"I'm Catherine," she mouthed. She certainly didn't want to break the rules her first night here.

The room where she would sleep proved to be nothing more than a small space large enough to hold a bed and desk. A large wooden cross hung on one of the whitewashed walls, and over her bed was an unpainted statue of the Virgin.

Gabrielle squeezed her hand. "I hope we can be friends. There aren't many our age." She left the room, and Catherine sank onto the bed. At last she would fulfill her vow. Father Bretel had told her that nuns came to God pure, their past sins forgiven. She would pay the price for her transgressions. With his grace, she would find peace, and forgiveness.

During dinner, she kept her silence, thinking the task of silence would be the most difficult of all. After the meal, she followed the others to the chapel. As the reader droned on, she stifled a yawn. The long journey, the flickering candles and warm room made her want to curl up and sleep.

She felt a strong hand on her shoulder, and realized she had nodded off. Turning, her heart sank. It was the abbess herself.

That incident, she thought later, had been the beginning of what was to follow.

Two days after her arrival, she'd been assigned to the vineyards. Several days later, she had been working under a sweltering summer sun. Overcome by thirst, she tossed some grapes into her mouth and continued down the row. Her punishment for that had been a week of isolation.

Then one afternoon, she had been bitten by a spider. Without thinking she flung it away, and it landed on a nun's prayerbook, causing muffled giggles from a group of novices nearby.

Her worst offense, though, had taken place one afternoon in the courtyard. Gabrielle had pulled her aside. "Everyone's busy, inside with important visitors. Keep scrubbing the fountain and we can talk."

She had learned, by then, of Gabrielle's past. Married at fourteen and widowed two years later, she had gone to work in a tavern. "It wasn't bad, really. There was singing at night, and all the food I wanted. Plus the men were free with their coins."

"But you decided it wasn't for you."

"*Au contraire.* I liked the work, but one day the officials came. They said the owner was watering the wine. He couldn't pay the fine so they shut the place down. I was out of work, and couldn't find another job. I was pregnant, too, from a liar who'd said he'd marry me." She shook her head. "How dumb can a person be?"

Catherine was about to reply when a nun came their way. "I've been watching the two of you. You both know the rules. The abbess will hear of this. Finish your task, then go to your rooms."

That incident had brought the worst punishment. She would remain in the chapel eight hours a day, except for the midday meal. As if that were not enough, she was forced to wear a hair shirt. The prickly itching made her skin raw and sore to the touch.

Now, as she contemplated her future, she wondered if she had made a terrible mistake in coming here. Father Bretel had warned her it was a grievous sin to enter into a mystical union with Christ with no sense of vocation. To take the veil and not have experienced a true calling would risk your being unfaithful to God.

Fearful of committing another sin, she decided to ask the Virgin for guidance.

She knelt at the foot of her cot and was distracted by what looked like a movement coming from the wooden icon above her head. Had she been sent a signal? Surely it was a trick of light and shadow, but she could have sworn that the icon winked. *Blessed Mother!*

She rose and rubbed her knees, sure she had received a message. Somehow, she had to leave this place. It had been a mistake to come here. Besides, she was sure the Virgin knew that her heart was not in the undertaking. That alone made it a useless endeavor.

After spending another hour on her knees, asking for direction in what she was about to undertake, she rose, stuffed her few belongings in a bundle, and went to her classes. She passed a note to Gabrielle, risking the abbess's wrath. Later, in the latrine, Gabrielle caught her by the wrist. "You'll never get away with it, you know."

"I have to try."

"Where will you go? Back home?"

"To Amiens. After that, to Paris."

Gabrielle covered her laugh with her hand. "Paris! Well, wish you luck." A bell clanged. They exchanged kisses. "Good luck,

Catherine. You're very brave." She scampered out.

Following mass that evening, Catherine returned to her room and waited for the others to fall asleep. When nothing could be heard but owls and night birds, she tiptoed down the hall until she came to the open window at the end of the corridor. It led outside, into the cook's herb garden. She swung one leg over the sill, pulled her bundle out, and crept across the stone courtyard, hoping the dogs that Sister Lucia kept fed with scraps would not bark and waken the entire dormitory.

Once past the gate and onto the road, she paused to get her bearings. Abbyville was the closest town. From there, she would head for Amiens, then Paris, but that was weeks away. She shifted her bundle and sighed. There was nothing to do but walk. A half-moon lit the way as she trudged southward, hoping her dark clothes would make her invisible to anyone traveling this way at night.

She kept to the main road. Tomorrow, if luck was hers, she could snare a ride, hopefully with a family who would take her along in exchange for watching their children or feeding the animals. She could cook, too, and even knew how to mend a wagon, having watched Papa fix his.

In an attempt to lighten her mood she hummed a tune; the very shadows seemed to taunt her with whispers, and the cries of wild beasts reminded her she carried no weapon. Perhaps she should have tried to smuggle a message to Gérard before attempting this, but if she had been caught trying to break the rule that allowed no correspondence the first six months after her arrival . . . she shuddered, imagining what would have befallen her then.

She thought of Adam, of how he had told her to follow her heart, to do what she thought best. But even he would see this as foolhardy. Still, she couldn't stay and risk damning her soul when she felt no calling. She would just have to rely on God and the Virgin to protect her against highwaymen and wild beasts.

At last she saw a rosy glow to the east. Her legs ached, and her stomach rumbled, but now was no time to quit. Later, when she had put more distance between her and the convent, she could stop and rest. When the sun rose above the trees, and she thought she could not take another step, she heard the rattle of a wagon behind her. It was driven by a swarthy man who sang loud and boisterously, his songs a mixture of war cries and obscenities. In his cups, she thought, and hurried to the side of the road and into the treeline.

After he passed, she wondered if she could make it any further.

Before long, another wagon pulled alongside, catching her off guard, and she feared the worst. Her hunger and thirst would be her downfall, for not only had she not heard them coming, but had almost tripped in front of the cart.

A friendly voice called out. "*Mademoiselle.* What're you doing out here alone?"

Catherine's knees gave way and she fell to the ground. She lifted her head and saw a woman peering over the man's shoulder.

"Why, it's a girl. Where're you headin'?"

"South."

"Well, if you don't mind riding with my younguns and some melons, get on in."

She stumbled to her feet, used the last of her strength to climb up, and collapsed beside a girl she judged was a few years younger than her. Juice dripped from the girl's lips, and Catherine couldn't pull her eyes away.

"Want some? Pa says no more after this. The others are for sale. You can buy one if you like."

"Hush, Mara. Can't you see she's tired? Been walkin' all

night, have you?"

Catherine nodded.

The melon was the best she had ever tasted. A moment later she wavered between wakefulness and sleep.

Someone shook her shoulder. "Wake up. Ma'am. We leave the main road here, unless you want to go west with us."

Feeling somewhat refreshed, but still rubbing sleep from her eyes, Catherine scrambled up. "No, I need to stay on this road, and thanks for the ride."

"Never you mind. Glad to do it."

She jumped down, and the girl waved to her until the wagon turned at a bend in the road and rolled out of sight.

All that day she kept to the edge of the woods, ready to hide in case of an encounter like the drunken man from last night. As dusk settled over the land, she approached a village which lay below a ridge. The town appeared to be about the size of Vitry-en-Artois.

After passing beside a row of timber-framed shacks, she came to the main street and walked past a bakery which still held the fragrance of breads baked that morning. A little further along, the smell of roasting meat came from a tavern.

She paused, inhaling, and her stomach rumbled, reminding her she had only eaten melon and a piece of bread since night before last. She shifted her bundle to the other shoulder. The place looked like any ordinary tavern, where workers came to have an ale at day's end. And this one had good food, too. She squared her shoulders. If Gabrielle worked in a tavern, so could she. Besides, what did she have to lose? Another night of hunger and sleeping with wild beasts? She smoothed her hair, straightened her dark tunic, and walked inside. A bell on the door rang, but no one looked up. A group of men sat at a long table, and a boy cranked a skewer over the fire pit.

A heavyset woman appeared, wiping her hands on a dirty

apron. "You alone?"

Catherine nodded, and felt six pairs of eyes turn her way. She licked her parched lips. "Are you the owner's wife, and, if so, could I speak with you?"

"Well, well, Miss High-an'-Mighty is here, though she don't look so mighty no longer."

She ignored the man's remark and followed the woman to another room where dishes were lined in a row.

"I suppose you're lookin' for work, like all the ones who come by like you."

Catherine nodded. "I know how to cook and clean."

The woman eyed her up and down, then finally nodded. "You look like you're accustomed to work, and there's honesty in your eyes. I can't pay you nuthin', but if you'll help out, I can see you get food an' a place to sleep. You get to keep any coins they leave behind."

"That's all I need," Catherine said, calculating that at least she could stay a few nights, eat some hearty food, and return to the road feeling better than she did right now.

In fact, if things worked out here, she might stay until she saved enough for the whole journey.

CHAPTER THIRTY

During the two months since Adam had last seen Catherine, he had kept busy, entertaining first at Robert's castle in Cambrai, and later, in Paris, where an Officer of the Crown had summoned him to recite poems for the enjoyment of the guests who had come from distant provinces to celebrate the birthday of the king's son, Pierre. He left Paris in August and headed to Cambrai, where Raoul greeted him with the news that Robert had gone to his château in Arras. "I'm sure he'd welcome you, Adam. He will be entertaining some emissaries from the south."

Adam wrestled with his conscience. He had no desire to go to Arras, not now. But the tapestry shop was tantalizingly close.

He bid good-bye to Raoul and headed toward Arras with no clear destination in mind. The last time he'd seen Catherine she had been evasive about her future. He remembered thinking there may be another suitor in her life, one younger, more settled than he.

He had been riding for three hours when the sky turned gray and thunder rumbled in the distance, adding to his black mood. He stopped at a wayside inn, ate slabs of meat from a roasted pig, and drank too much wine.

Early the next morning he saddled the horse, tucked his coin purse, heavy with gold from the grateful king, inside the waist of his breeches, and headed for Vitry. The girl could sing, and had lovely green eyes, but he now suspected her evasiveness was contrived to send him away. Where did that leave him? With a pang of regret, he realized he may have waited too long, fearful of scaring her away. No more of that. This time he would take her dancing and buy an expensive jug of wine. Over dinner, he would ask her to stay with him for a lifetime.

The thought brought him back to reality. She would think he was joking. Still, what did he have to lose? He would declare his intentions and his past. If she refused, so be it. Besides, he told himself, there was that play, waiting to be finished.

In Vitry, he tied the mare to the apple tree before he realized the sign for the tapestry shop was gone and the door boarded. His heart lurched. Taking the path beside the low wall dividing the shop from the house next door, he hurried around back and rapped on the door. "Catherine? Catherine, are you there?"

A shutter upstairs slammed back, and a white-haired man wearing a knitted cap stuck his head out the window. "Who are you? Why do you come banging a door like a tax collector?" He scratched his chin. "*Are* you a tax collector?"

Adam stepped back and looked up. "*Bonjour, Monsieur.* You must be Gérard."

The head disappeared and the shutter closed. Adam was about to walk away when the back door flew open.

The man tied a leather strip around his waist and adjusted the sleeves of his tunic. "You know me, but I don't know you, which puts me at a disadvantage."

Adam smiled. No wonder Catherine liked the man. His eyes were expressive and kind, set in a weathered face that bespoke of many summers. And he had a sense of humor.

"I know of you from Catherine. I've been here before. She and I are . . . friends."

"I think you'd better come in."

Adam walked into a tidy kitchen area. He smelled her fragrance, sweet and persistent. Or was his mind playing tricks? If he closed his eyes, he might hear her laughter.

He swiped a hand across his brow, then, remembering his manners, apologized to Gérard for the interruption, and sat down at the table.

"I've not broken my fast. Will you join me?"

"*Merci.*" Adam took a bite of apple tart. "Is she still sleeping? If so, I can come back."

The look on Gérard's face left him feeling more alarmed than before.

"Catherine isn't here." Gérard licked his fingers and refilled his cup. "She joined a nunnery."

Thoughts reeling, Adam let the bite of tart slide down, afraid he would choke.

"Several weeks ago, she insisted she wanted to join the crusaders going south. Somehow, she talked me into going along, but we were ambushed. I ended up with a broken arm and no desire to ride a horse through the countryside. We returned, and when she was ready to leave I begged off." Gérard shrugged. "She has it in her mind she has to make amends for the death of her husband. She had nothing to do with it, but somehow she believes it was her fault. Once she saw I was adamant about staying, she decided the next best thing was a nunnery. It's redemption she's looking for, for something she didn't do. No amount of lecturing convinced her otherwise."

Adam's mind churned. Catherine, in a nunnery. It made no sense. Her restive spirit encased in cold walls of silence, contemplating a sin that never happened? The image burned his mind. He should have come sooner. He would have kept her from making so grave a mistake.

"Does she—is she intent on taking vows?"

"I've no idea. Once she told me her plans, I felt lost as to what to do. I know nothing of women's cloisters. We had a bit of an argument. I could see she was determined, so I arranged for her to travel with a caravan of merchants, where at least she'd be safe. I've heard nothing since."

Adam's throat knotted, thinking of Thomas à Becket's suffering a century ago. Hearing the story as a child he'd been horrified at the man's mortification. Surely, Catherine would not fall prey to such extremes. But would she have the choice? Most nuns, of course, had taken the veil to serve God, but still—how to keep every barrel of wine pure?

A shutter banged closed, bringing his thoughts to the present. Gérard rose to latch it open. "Just what interest do you have in Durant's daughter?"

Gérard's back was turned, which gave Adam time to contemplate an answer. What interest indeed? How much should he tell this man, a perfect stranger, albeit a man dear to Catherine's heart? He decided he could trust him.

"I came back intending to make her mine."

"Ah, then you are free to marry? Well, if she so chooses—"

"I am not free, not now."

Gérard scowled. "Then you should not complicate her life, not if, as you say, you care about her. She has had enough of sorrow these last few years."

"Hear me out, Gérard. I am not free to marry, although I have no wife."

"Explain."

"My wife found happiness with another. We separated. I have no heart for revenge. You know what is done to adulterous wives."

Gérard nodded. "I've heard they could be burned at the stake, though more often they are punished in some other way. I know of one whose nose was slit."

Adam shook his head. "I bear part of the blame, and could not live with myself were I to cause Maroie pain. There has been pain enough."

"Then there is no future for you and Catherine. Not unless

you want to leave northern France, or at least leave here. This is too close to Arras. People gossip."

Adam wiped his brow. "Right now, I only want to know that she is safe. Her happiness means more to me than my own." He circled the rim of the cup with his fingers. "I must find her somehow. If she tells me she wants to live as a nun, and truly wants to see me no more, I will accept that, though it will break my heart."

During the long silence that followed, Gérard wiped the dishes clean. When he finally turned to face Adam, he wore a smile. "I have become disillusioned with my life of leisure, one I thought I wanted. If you are going to the convent, I want to come along. There's nothing for me here. Besides, I want to be there to hear you convince her to change her mind." He chuckled.

Adam's heart soared. Not only would Gérard's company be a welcome change from his lonely existence, but perhaps this man could help convince Catherine that the cloistered life was not for her. It might be the most important task of his life.

On her first day of work in the tavern, Catherine pulled the apron over her head and was dismayed to find it fell almost to the floor. It needed a new hem when she had a moment to spare.

She tucked her bundle beneath the bed she would share with the owner's three-year-old daughter and walked downstairs to seek out the tavern owner's wife.

"Madame Borée, how can I help?"

The owner's wife glared. "Can't you see what to do? Look around you. They all want ale. Here, take these." She shoved two heavy flagons at Catherine and turned her back.

Catherine made her way to the table, struggling with the heavy iron pitchers and praying she wouldn't trip.

"Ho! A comely wench here, friends. Where'd you come from, my sweet?" The man pulled her close with his muscular arm, so close she could see the fine red hair that covered his chin. He looked at her from beneath sun-reddened lids.

She held her breath, repelled by his nearness, and tried to turn away.

His grasp tightened. "There now. Not so fast. Do you know who we are?"

She shook her head and tried to smile.

"We're the town's officials, girl, just come from a meeting. Best you learn who's who around here." He tapped the table. "Pour my ale."

She bent across to do as he bid, and felt him fumble her side. Before she could jump away, he squeezed her breast. "Mm, nice goods here."

His words brought a shout of laughter from his companions. She tried to push him away, but he rose and shoved her into a corner.

She screamed, raising her voice above the general melee that filled the little tavern. She struggled and kicked, and from the corner of her eye she saw Madame Borée coming her way with a pot in her hand.

"Unhand her, you lout, or I'll throw you all out. She's a simple serving wench."

The man wiped his mouth and straightened his tunic. "Then you'd do well to keep the whore in the kitchen. Them globes don't belong to any common maid I've ever seen."

Catherine's face burned. Evidently the men thought she was there not only to serve food, but to satisfy their lust. She followed Madame Borée to the side room.

"Help Leon in the kitchen 'til they leave," the woman hissed. "And try not to get Leon going like you did them out there."

Catherine started to object, but her words were cut off.

"Mind you, Leon's as bad as the councilmen for goin' after wenches. That's the hardest part of my job, keeping them all straight. And my husband upstairs in bed sick, leavin' me with all the work. Men!" She slammed the pot onto a shelf.

Catherine scurried away, glad to be assigned another task, away from the men's stares and the woman's snide accusations.

CHAPTER THIRTY-ONE

Leon, Catherine quickly learned, was given to fits of bad temper, tossing pots and food when angered or upset over Madame Borée's orders.

It took Catherine only a few hours to see why she had been given the position. No one with other options would put up with these working conditions, but she had little choice. She'd hoped that she'd be able to save enough to see her way clear to leave, but, so far, there seemed little likelihood of that. She had only managed to anger some rich patrons and had been sent to work in the kitchen, well away from any hope of an extra *sou* coming her way.

Leon wiped his face with his apron and backed away from the heat. "You know anything about cooking?"

"Yes, some. In my own house. But I can learn to cook larger portions. Just show me what to do."

"Hmph. Your own house? Uppity aren't you? What brings you so low? Your husband find you in bed with a scoundrel?"

"No." She shook her head. "Nothing like that."

"Then what?"

"I . . . I fell on hard times." *Let him think what he may. It's none of his affair.*

"Just like I thought. Whorin' around'll catch up with you every time. Take it from me. Go to church. Learn to lead a clean life, else you'll burn in hell." He stirred one of the pots. "Or so they say. For myself, when I hear them priests rant on, I wonder how much they know about what life is really like, I mean, workin' for a meager pittance, day in and day out. Working this stove. That's all I know. This stove and poverty."

He took a pot from the fire. "Here. This goes outside to that table in the corner."

"But she told me—"

"I don't care what she told you. It's my kitchen, and I'm telling you get it outta here."

She lifted the pot with both hands, and her skirt caught on the rough edge of the wood table. Boiling liquid sloshed onto her arm. She cried out, but kept on walking to the table.

After setting the pot down, she hurried back to the kitchen. "Do you have any leeks? I burned my arm." She showed him a reddened oblong area between wrist and elbow.

"None I can spare," he said. "But there's wild beets out back." He wiped his hands. "Hold on. I'll get some. Best painkiller for a burn, and I should know."

She sat on a stool, wondering how she could endure the pain and finish the day's work, but there was nothing to be done. She needed food and a bed. Beyond that, she would just have to make the best of things.

Leon walked back in and set about mashing the roots of the plant. "Here, smear some of this on your arm. Pain will be gone by tomorrow."

She grimaced. The pain in her arm might be gone, but the pain in her heart hurt more than ever.

Adam and Gérard listened as the prioress spoke in halting sentences, "She just up and left. There was nothing . . . no reason for her to leave. Why, the nuns under my care are all happy. You can see that for yourself. Of course, a novice—there are certain rules we have—nothing too strict, mind you."

She worried the edge of a parchment, and Adam had the

sinking feeling the prioress knew exactly why Catherine had left. Still, there was nothing more he could do, not here.

A sudden sense of urgency caused him to rise abruptly. "Very well. Thank you for your time."

Once outside, he felt his anger rise—at the prioress, but more, to himself, for having allowed all this to happen. And now, he had no idea where Catherine would turn. If she had returned home, she would have arrived long before now. A quick and disturbing thought stabbed at his heart. What if she were lying alone on a road, hurt and unable to go for help? Anything could have happened to her, out there, alone.

They untied the horses and were leading the animals to a well near the gate when a young novice stepped from beneath the shade of an oak tree. Her upturned nose was covered with freckles, as if she had stayed too long in the sun. Adam felt a twinge of pity. The girl looked to be younger even than Catherine.

"Sirs, I overheard . . . inside. You're looking for Catherine, from Vitry?"

"Yes. Can you help?"

"That depends. Why do you want her? Is she in trouble?"

Adam stepped forward. "No. I only wanted—"

He felt a hand on his shoulder, and Gérard interrupted. "I'm her father's bookkeeper. I'd like to see her, but if she's gone, she'll be needing what's in here." He tapped the purse at his waist. "She shouldn't be alone on the roads with no money."

The girl seemed to be considering, shifting her eyes from one to the other. "Well, I'm not sure it's the truth, but she talked to me about jobs, for women like us, and I told her I once worked in a tavern. She asked me all about it. She may be looking for work. I doubt she'll go to another convent." She paused, as if gauging their honesty. After a quick glance over her shoulder she spoke again. "I'm not sure I believed her, but she had some

240

notion about going to Paris."

Adam saw two black-robed nuns, buckets in hand, heading their way. Before either of them could thank the girl she spun on her heel and was gone.

Ignoring the blaze of the August sun, they rode south. At noon, they stopped to rest the horses, and themselves.

An hour later, Adam slipped the last of the cheese into the pannier hanging from the horse's back, then mounted and rode up the incline with Gérard. They headed out again. "Do you have any ideas, Gérard? If that young novice can be believed, we'd have—"

"I've no doubt the girl spoke the truth, Adam. It sounds not unlike Catherine to try to make her way. As for working in a tavern, well, perhaps it's the only place for employment. She had mathematical skills, but who'd hire a woman to keep ledgers? She'd have no choice but maid's work, since she seemed bent on making her way alone."

"But Catherine, a common serving girl. I hate to think of what could be happening to her." Adam swallowed the fear in his throat.

"So do I, but I fear it's our next best hope of ever seeing her again, unless she would decide to return." He shrugged. "Who knows? She may have headed back. We might have missed her somehow."

"I'll not give up, not unless poor Agnès does. But if you want to return, Gérard, I'll well understand. As for myself, I cannot write or sing until I know she is safe and well. After that, I will find a way to make her mine."

Over the next two days, they rode in virtual silence, each consumed by fearful thoughts for Catherine. By the third day, they had ridden through two more villages, and had asked at the neighborhood taverns after a young woman who might have requested employment. No, no new hires. No visitors either, except merchants and the occasional bondsman or family making their way to join the crusaders to the south. No auburn-haired girl of comely face and green eyes. "I'd have remembered her," was the common answer.

That evening they stayed at an inn five leagues north of Amiens. As usual, questioning the owner's wife was futile. She'd seen no one like Catherine.

Later that evening, Adam, unable to drown his creeping fear in the bitter wine, and too restless to sleep, agreed to a game of *tables* with the owner, a slight man of medium build whose hands shook as he moved the game pieces. Adam soon learned that the doctor had given the man a year to live.

"And that was ten years ago," the man laughed, showing his four teeth. "I'd hire some help if I could afford it. My wife works night and day." He lifted a cup with shaking hands and drained it dry. "Just the other day, a looker came through, wanting work." He shrugged. "Much as I hated to, I sent her on her way. She inquired as to the shortest way to Amiens. It's a thriving town, but around here, the drought ruined the crops. If it weren't for travelers coming through, we'd starve. The locals come here, drink, and leave."

Adam could hardly contain his excitement. "A looker? A young woman, wanting to work?"

"Sure. Like I said, she was something."

Adam leaned forward. "What did she look like?"

He man laughed again. "Don't get excited. She's long gone. On the skinny side, but pretty. A head of red hair. You know what they say about red-haired women? They're the devil's spawn."

Adam clenched his fists beneath the table. His heart raced. "You say she was going to Amiens?"

"I didn't say that. I said the next town is Amiens, and she asked how far. Maybe she was lost." He looked up as a man entered, asking for a room.

The owner called to his wife, and Adam bid him good night. He took the stairs two at a time, anxious to tell Gérard the news.

"Don't get your hopes up, Adam. That description could be anyone. And she could be anywhere by now," Gérard said. "From here on, there are roads running east and west. I'm sad to say it, but our one hope is that she might have returned home."

Adam nodded, crushed by Gérard's logical assessment. They were on a fool's errand, prompted by his unrelenting need to find her. The horses were tired, and the heat was getting to Gérard. "What say we go to Amiens tomorrow? Then we'll head to Vitry. If she's not there, I'll return to Amiens and take the only road from there to Paris. I'll not rest until I find her."

The next afternoon, they rode into Amiens. Plodding along the marshland near the Somme, they came to the magnificent cathedral, its spires shimmering in the sun. Adam wondered if Catherine had passed this way. Had she stopped there to pray?

Gérard interrupted his thoughts. "I'll go east. You check to the west. We can meet at the city gates before sunset."

Adam nodded. He fastened his cloak against the dry wind, then took the unpaved branch road west. Coming alongside a wayfarer, he slowed the mare and inquired as to a tavern.

"There's only Borée's inn, and the tavern on the main road out near the gates, but they may have closed down. Had a kitchen fire in there."

Merci, Monsieur. Adam touched his beret and spurred Agnès back to the main road, trying not to hope. If Borée's inn was like all the others, that left only one place to look before returning to Vitry. His options were dwindling fast.

He spotted the inn's rusty sign on the left before he saw the building. After looping the reins over a post, he went inside and was greeted by loud music and the smell of roasting meat.

No sooner had he sat down than a heavyset woman came to his side. His heart sank.

"You alone?"

He nodded and ordered an ale, one he would finish quickly. He had wasted time here, and they still had a ways to go.

The patrons appeared to be locals, except for three men who wore the distinctive cloaks common to squires in the king's service. He stared into the fire where a pig roasted on a spit, and wondered if he should have been asking the village officials along the way. He swiped his hands through his hair, feeling a sense of despair settling in. The woman brought his ale, and he drank it fast. If Catherine was not in Vitry, perhaps he could enlist Count Robert's help. At any other time, that would be an unreasonable request, to locate a girl who might be anywhere along the long Roman road, but now, nothing mattered but finding her. He would use every bit of influence he had.

"Adam?"

He looked up, startled, and his heart pounded. It was a dream. He was sleeping, and had only dreamed he had found her. Involuntarily, he reached out to touch her. Her flesh was warm. Real. She wore a too-long apron dirtied with wine, and her hair was pulled back in a coif, but those eyes—he would know them anywhere. "Catherine? Oh, praise God. Catherine. It's really you."

She rubbed her hands on the front of the apron, and the smile she sent him washed away the days and nights of worry. "Yes. Yes, it is me."

He took her hands in his, and his mind went back to the tapestry shop, to the ride on his horse on the path along the wood. He pulled her close and was about to kiss her.

"Ho, a little service over here!"

She scooted away, then returned with a full pitcher of ale

which she set on the table where three men sat staring at the newcomer.

"What brings you here, Adam?"

"You. It's a long story. When are you free?"

"Not until the last man leaves. It is usually very late."

"I will wait. In the meantime, I'll get a room at the inn back in town. Gérard is with me."

"Gérard? How did you manage—"

Someone called her from the kitchen. "I must go."

"I will come back at closing. We need to talk. You must come with me, Catherine. This is no place for you."

Late that evening, making his way from the inn and back to the tavern along the empty street, Adam looked cautiously to both sides, keeping a keen eye on the shadows. As he neared the tavern, he saw a group of three men stumble across the threshold and into the night.

Once they disappeared into the darkness, he tied Agnès to a post and walked inside. The room was empty, except for the tavern keeper's wife, and Catherine, who swept the floor with a rush broom.

Madame Borée glanced up. "We're closed. Come back tomorrow." She picked up a pot and walked to the kitchen.

Catherine pushed back a loose strand of hair and smiled, a disarming smile that melted his heart.

"Where do you stay, Catherine?"

"Here. They gave me a bed with their child."

"Pack your belongings tonight. We leave in the morning."

"But Adam, I can't. I've only saved—"

"I'll not see you here another night, nor will Gérard. I'm taking you away."

She caught her breath. What did he mean? For a day? For a lifetime? Visions of the capital city sprang to her mind.

"We're heading for Vitry tomorrow."

"Vitry? What of Paris?" Her earlier elation dissipated, leaving a heaviness centered in her chest. So, he intended to deliver her safely home, like a willful child, much like the constable had on that night so many years ago. Where would that leave her? She needed to get to Paris. Enough time had already been wasted.

A wolf howled from somewhere in the woods behind the tavern.

She swallowed her disappointment. "I—I cannot leave, Adam, not just yet. I am constrained more than a footloose *trouvère*."

"Is it money? What money you need I can give you." His eyes locked with hers, and he smiled that beguiling smile.

Determined to see it through, she chose her words carefully. "I cannot take money from you, nor from Gérard, not after I went against his wishes. This is my doing. Don't you see? There's nothing for me but to stay here a few more months. Perhaps then—"

"No, Catherine. Be ready at Prime. I'll not let you go again."

She spoke now with a quiet firmness. "I left Vitry once. I'll not go back. I cannot, not until—"

"Until what, Catherine? Why do you resist me?"

"I made plans to go to Paris. I thought—I don't know what I thought, when you came. Perhaps that we could go together."

He rewarded her with a broad smile. "Then we shall go to Paris."

That night, she lay on the mat, trying to sort her thoughts. It seemed a miracle that he was here, and that he wanted her to leave with him. Her excitement built, even as she wrestled with her conscience. How could she travel so far with a man? In Paris, they would think her a common courtesan. Still, if Gérard came along, it would all be respectable, a woman with her guardian and a friend.

Blessed Mother, he had come for her, and just in time. Lately Madame Borée had become insistent, hinting that a tryst with one of the noblemen who frequented the tavern would bring them all a nice piece of change. She shivered, thinking again of what the woman had suggested.

How had Adam found her here? Tears of happiness welled in her eyes. She would be with him all the way to Paris. After that, somehow, she would find her way to the port city. Perhaps he would help. Or could she convince him to take the cross? If not, they would have to part.

Thunder rumbled in the distance, and she rose, crossed to the window, and pulled the shutters snug. She stuffed her cloak in the crack beneath in case it rained, and padded back to bed, her mind churning and her heart racing. There were too many unanswered questions, but one thing was clear. She was going with Adam.

CHAPTER THIRTY-TWO

Catherine woke clearheaded and determined. She washed as best she could in the little time remaining, packed her bundle, and left by the side door. When Adam rode up, with Gérard a short way behind, she ran to kiss her father's longtime friend. He had helped to fill the void in her life from her father's death.

Gérard glanced ahead. Adam was engrossed in examining the mare's hoof. Evidently satisfied that Adam was out of earshot, he leaned forward. "There's something you should know, Catherine. The man has fallen for you—he claims to love you. I sense you have a growing affection for him, making it necessary for me to tell you something that may change your mind about him. He is married, to a woman in Arras."

She stepped away. Her hand flew to her mouth to stifle a cry, and she felt the blood drain from her cheeks.

"Their marriage is finished, but I doubt there will ever be a divorce. She was unfaithful, but he is reluctant to make their separation legal. She would be the brunt of town jokes, and worse. I'm sure you've seen women in stocks for the same thing."

She had ceased her trembling. Her head swirled with doubts. If, as Gérard said, the marriage was finished, then what did their being together matter? What mattered was if she were falling in love with a man who might return to his wife.

Adam was walking their way, and Gérard quickly changed the subject. "So, why did you leave the convent?"

She lowered her gaze and felt Adam beside her. In that moment, she remembered why she was here, standing in front of a tavern, about to ride off with the only man she'd ever cared about. She had an obligation, and would see it through. He could help her. That was all she needed to know.

She remembered Gérard was waiting, and she forced a smile. "I simply had no calling for the veil. Even the Virgin agreed." Later, she might tell them both of what had transpired between her and the statue, but could a man ever understand?

"Well, I'd like to hear more, but for now, let's head out for Paris," Adam said.

She handed her bundle to Gérard for safekeeping, then walked to where Agnès waited. She mounted the horse behind Adam. He loosened the reins, and Agnès set off at a trot. Catherine clung to Adam with one arm and clutched her cloak against the autumn wind with the other, determined to make the best of the time they might have together. She needed to get to Paris.

The first night away from the inn, they set up tents beside a retinue of squires riding north to Saint Omer. Adam and Gérard slept near the fire on blankets spread on open ground, and two musicians who had joined them set up a tent not far from the one in which she slept.

Fires blazed, and torches burned from poles placed strategically throughout the camp to discourage animals and thieves.

She lay listening to muted voices of the men camped nearby and the sound of an entertainer singing familiar *chansons*. Later, while the camp slept, she heard wolves howling and owls hooting in the darkness deep in the forest.

She wondered if Adam already slept, or if he heard the animal sounds too. Would he give her a thought, or did he only lie in the blackness, thinking ahead to his destiny at Robert's court? Would he agree to join the crusaders with her? She turned on her side, wriggled into the straw pallet, and fell asleep.

The next morning, after breaking their fast, they rode down the hillside, waving to the men who had shared their tent site. Back on the main road, they traveled single file as the path narrowed; the trade route wound southwest, hugging the terrain. Barren fields lay on both sides of the road.

The previous evening, Gérard had said that he wished to see Reims. "I will go alone and can meet you in Paris later."

"Indeed, no," Adam said. "It's an empty and dangerous road from here." He looked sideways at Catherine. "Perhaps, if Catherine doesn't object—"

"I'd love to see the city, but what's there?"

"They are building a new cathedral," Gérard said, "to replace the one that burned." He ate the last of a dried apple. "They're building it on the same spot where the other stood, and before that, where the Romans built a large public bath."

Catherine winked at Adam. "For a man who worked with numbers all his life, I think he should have been an architect."

Adam chuckled. "Then it's settled. Besides, we're in no hurry to go anywhere."

Catherine and Gérard exchanged a quick glance. Thanks goodness Gérard had agreed not to mention the crusade. He'd even seemed a bit interested himself, asking questions she couldn't answer. She pulled her drifting thoughts together. Truthfully, she had time to spare; the next crusade was at least a year away, from what she'd learned at the convent. Everything depended on the king, and his readiness, and favorable weather.

"So Reims it is," Gérard said, unrolling his sleeping mat.

Later, as Gérard snored by the fire, Catherine turned to Adam. "The road to Reims—is it very dangerous?"

"Not if we go together. They're more likely to attack a man alone. That's why we *trouvères* travel together. Pilgrims sometimes use the route, and the king's soldiers, too."

The following day they left for Reims, joined by two men on

horseback, thanks to Gérard and his propensity to make friends of strangers. That evening, a thunderstorm drove them inside a tavern overnight. The next day they set out again, and after riding for hours along an empty road, they saw a cart approaching, heading north. Inside were a man and woman, three dogs, and a squealing pig. As they rode past, Catherine heard the woman laugh and was reminded of her parents and her youth and the past she left behind. She kept her eyes on the road ahead, determined to look ahead, not back.

Four days later, as they rode a narrow path guarded by trees on both sides, she heard a noise in the woods. Startled by the unexpected sound, she instinctively tightened her hold on Adam's waist.

"Don't be alarmed," he said, feeling suddenly protective. He had an urge to ride into the forest where shaded trees would hide them from the others. In the forest, he would kiss her cheek again, as he had first dared to do in Troyes.

He mopped his forehead with his sleeve and heard her mention something about animal noises, bringing his mind back to the present.

"I'm not afraid," she continued. "It's just that I can't see them, yet I know they are in there."

"So many animals live in those woods that we are bound to see some. Most are harmless." He hoped he sounded convincing.

Behind them, a steady howl rose from the forest, taken up by another and another, followed by what sounded like yelping pups. "Only young wolves, I think." He reached for the flask of water tied below the saddle. He wanted now, more than ever, to get them all safely to Reims.

The trees on the west of the path cast long shadows on the dirt road, making it more difficult to avoid the ruts made by earlier carts. As they neared a clearing, Adam stopped to wait for Gérard. "We would have to travel after sunset to reach the abbey I had in mind. I had hoped to spend the night there." Thunder rumbled in the distance. "It is safer to stop now and sleep outside than ride spread out along the path after dark."

After they set up tents and built a fire, they shared food saved from the morning meal.

Catherine sat at the base of a broad tree trunk, keeping her eyes on the fire, watching the flames leap, orange, blue, blood-red into the black night as one of the two men traveling with them added fresh branches to the pile.

Adam lay nearby, his head propped on one arm, the other hand holding his wine cup. She imagined lying on the blanket beside him; he would reach for her as he had before, only this time she would not stop him.

She pulled her cape close and leaned her head against the rough bark. Clouds drifted idly across the moon-man's benevolent face.

She heard the men talking, discussing the weather and possible delay.

Later, she lay in the tent on her mat, waiting for sleep to come, and heard footsteps outside. Her body tensed under the coverlet as she recognized human footfalls, distinctive from those of a four-legged beast. Then, to her relief, she heard Adam whisper her name. She rose, wrapped a coverlet around her shoulders, and walked out into the night where he waited, silhouetted in the firelight.

He reached for her hand, and she walked beside him, not knowing, not caring where he led her. Just beyond the small clearing where the men lay snoring by the dwindling fire, he stopped, and they reached for each other, quickly, naturally. He lifted her hair and kissed her neck, her lips. He lowered her to the ground. His whispered words were coaxing, comforting, insistent.

Waves of desire rose from her loins to her chest. She had no fear of what was happening, only a deep sense of wonder at the sensations. She clung to him, trembling, and wrapped her arms around his back, pulling him closer, yearning for some evasive fulfillment. She felt his heart beating against her own, then a sudden quick pain, and uncontrollable joy.

Hours later, as he carried her back to the tent, she asked him if the wolves had heard her cries, her moans of pleasure.

"Of course," he whispered. "They are very wise, the wolves, and tonight they are happy."

CHAPTER THIRTY-THREE

Delayed by early winter storms, they finally arrived at Reims in early November and, coaxed by a friendly innkeeper, decided to stay through Advent. Gérard, delighted at the prospect of a chance to visit neighboring hamlets, set out alone on the first warm day in December.

During their weeks alone, they shared bits of their past, sometimes talking into the night until the fire dwindled to ashes. One evening, after a lively game of *tables*, she asked him to play her a tune. He retrieved his *vielle* from a corner of the room. After two songs, he laid the instrument aside. For too long, he had kept from her his greatest fear, but that was no longer possible. She had every right to know, if in truth, his talent had abandoned him. If they had a life together, it may not be what she thought. After all, he had told her he sang for kings. If the vessel of creativity were truly drying up, he would be nothing more than a *jongleur*, hired to sing someone else's songs.

She had listened intently, her brow furrowed, as he poured out his torment. When he finished, she moved to a stool at his feet. "If that is so, then you can write only for me."

She pulled him close and he held her tight, long into the night, as if to let her go was to let go all he held dear: his music and his dreams for the future.

The following day, he set to work on a pile of half-completed poems. That evening, bursting with pride, he had shown her his day's work. She said it was one of God's miracles. He only smiled, thinking the real blessing was her presence.

Two weeks later, Gérard returned to the inn, sick and miserable, having gotten lost in a blizzard. On the Feast of the Nativity, they gathered in a large room at the inn. A Yule log burned, helping to warm the cold stone walls, now covered with tapestries and woven fabrics against the chill of winter. Gérard, almost recovered from his ordeal, drank wine and danced with the innkeeper's wife. Adam and Catherine sat to one side, enjoying the festivities and each other's company.

Later, after returning to their room, Adam reached into the leather purse at his waist. He pulled out a rosary and placed it in her hand.

She stared at the amber on her open palm. "How did you get this? It's the one from the Cold Fair in Troyes."

He nodded. "The vendor was glad to part with it when I returned to her table later that day. I thought it a perfect gift for the season."

Catherine smiled. She opened the small purse at her waist and put the rosary inside. "I will treasure it. Perhaps I will someday give you something you will love as well."

She kissed him soundly, and he swooped her up and carried her to bed. A single candle wavered, putting the room in shadow. He loosened her chemise and they celebrated the season together in the best way they knew how.

That January brought more snow, light dustings that left the roads impassable, but by February the mountain roads cleared enough for them to set out for Paris.

They arrived in the capital city in early March. Beside the road, apple trees stood in clumps, bare limbs now erupting verdigris and olive.

They followed the paved road into town, heading toward the left bank. New storefronts lined the road. Moneychangers were on every corner. The streets were cleaner now, bustling with city life even this far from the river.

It was late afternoon when they reached the street where Beatris lived. They tied the animals together and tethered them to a vine that grew between two buildings across the alley.

Adam rapped on the door and heard the dog bark. "Beatris. It's Adam. Are you in there?"

She flung open the door, grinned at Adam, then hugged him. "You said you'd come back, and you did." She saw the others and backed away, wiping her hands on her skirt.

"Beatris, these are friends of mine, from Vitry-en-Artois."

She waved them inside. "You're just in time for dinner. I'll add more to the pot, and we can eat in a few minutes."

Adam leaned down to pet Jacques, tried to calm him as he ran in circles at their feet. "We can eat in the tavern, the one beside the old inn. I see the owner put up a new sign. Business must be good."

"Indeed. The university gets more students each year. Two scholars just moved from here last week; they slept in your old bed. But I won't hear of you eating in the tavern, not when my good stew would go to waste. There is plenty, now. Jacques and I eat like royalty." She stirred the pot with a wooden spoon. "I found work at two markets, and one sells cheese, good goat cheese. Remember, Adam, when we had fish stew every night? But good talk, too, eh, *mon trouvère?*" She poked him with her elbow. "I have blankets aplenty, and you're all welcome. Besides, the inn is probably full." She turned to Gérard. "I hope you like fish stew."

Beatris bustled about, setting trenchers on the table. A crow called loudly and Adam felt a chill. He looked out the small opening above Beatris's bed and watched the crow walking along the edge of a thatched roof. *That is only a woman's silly superstition.*

He rose, hugged Beatris, and turned to stir the pot. "Do you truly have room for us to stay? I don't want to impose—"

"Yes, yes. You can all stay." She turned to Catherine. "Can you cook?"

"I am a better cook," Gérard interrupted. "Let Catherine and Adam buy the food, and I will be the cook."

"Very well. It's decided."

"I can pay you, Beatris," Catherine said. "I have a little saved."

"Only buy the bread and wine. I have no need of your money." She clucked her tongue. "Young people need to save for their futures."

Catherine averted her eyes, and Adam felt the blood rise to his cheeks.

Suddenly an expression of awareness lit Beatris's face. She glanced at Adam, then back to Catherine. "You've all ridden too long. You need a good night's sleep."

After the meal, Beatris placed the empty pot on the floor for the dog to lick. "And now, my head hurts. I'm going to bed," she said, leaving them to find a spot to sleep.

Adam spent his days writing and showing Catherine the sites of Paris. Gérard, enamored of the new buildings springing up in the capital city, opted to browse the cathedrals, something that made Catherine suspect he was getting restless.

On a cool April morning, Beatris shook Catherine awake. "Almost time to leave. You said you wanted to see Saint-Julien-le-Pauvre."

After Catherine dressed, they walked the short distance to Beatris's parish church. When Catherine stepped inside the chapel she understood Beatris's fondness for the church; smaller than most cathedrals, its interior was cool and dark and quiet, the noise of the city shut out by thick walls. The only sound came from the murmuring devout, kneeling before statues that lined the walls. Flickering candles and minute shafts of daylight from modest wall openings below the eaves illuminated the interior.

Catherine lit two candles and prayed for her parents' departed souls, then walked to the fading statue of the Virgin, convinced only Mary, of all the saints, would intercede for her, would understand her sin of happiness and save her from endless Purgatory.

What she needed now was strength to resist Adam's touch, to avoid his glance, in spite of his presence that made her heart soar.

She tried to keep her mind on her prayers but kept thinking of their nights together in the abandoned chapel he had discovered, not far from Beatris's home. Stone walls, covered with vines, obscured the ruins. The roof, collapsed inward, provided a clear view of the night sky. When he told her of it, insisting it would be the perfect meeting place, she had resisted, but after sleepless nights, had succumbed to her desires and met him at the chapel.

After making love, he held her close. "Don't ever leave, Catherine. It is because of you that I write again. Poems and songs come unbidden, as before. So, you see, for the king's own pleasure, you must remain at my side." He smiled and kissed her soundly.

She laughed, scoffing at such an idea. "You simply needed time. I had nothing to do with it." She tickled his nose with a leaf, then confessed her own inner turmoil and her desperate attempt to lead a pious life, stopping short of confiding her intention to join the crusaders or her plan to ask him to join the expedition.

Other evenings she had cried in his arms. "This must be the last time, Adam. Help me resist what I know is wrong. God watches us both."

"The God that I know wants us to be happy, Catherine. He's

not a cruel father who'd deny pleasure to his children. I believe he gave us thirsts and feelings to enjoy our time on earth."

She nodded, wanting to believe him. When he spoke like that, all the warnings she remembered from her childhood, echoed by Father Bretel's own lips, drifted away like thistle blooms.

And now, kneeling with Beatris in the quiet church, she begged forgiveness of the Virgin for her frequent falls from grace.

Later that afternoon, while helping Beatris bring the tapestries inside from the line where they aired that morning, Catherine told her about the tapestry shop.

"Ah, I wondered why you knew so much about the weave. These, my husband created."

"He was a weaver?"

"No, but just as important. His job was to make small drawings bigger; he had to design a model weavers could follow." She rubbed her hand across one of the tapestries. "He learned from another designer who came through here from the north on his way to a fair. The man decided to stay in Paris instead of returning to his home." Beatris removed her shawl and made her way to a chair. "This designer told us the new laws made it hard for guild members; when they raised the price so the taxes could be paid, no one could buy. They were under great pressure, so he said, to pay even higher fees. When he saw *mon mari* was a talented artist, he decided to remain here. My husband was his apprentice.

"It's from the northerner that my husband learned to enlarge the designs. He became quite skilled at it and made a good livelihood for us. We used to own a house not far from here." She nodded toward the tapestries. "These are some he was allowed to keep, ones with small defects in them. People have bought tapestries worked from his patterns to take far away. They warm the laps of bishops and kings."

Catherine hung the last tapestry. "Your *mari* . . . ?"

"In his fifty-fourth year, the plague came to the town where he'd gone to purchase inks. Overnight he took sick, and only months later did I find out what had befallen him. They told me he got the fever and died three days later. His last words were about me." She rubbed the back of one hand, sighing, then looked up. "So I kept his tapestries here, with me. I have others, too, packed away in those chests. Someday, I will give them to my church, to do with as they wish."

"They would bring a handsome price, Beatris, if you took them to the street market."

"Ah, yes, I know," she said. "But they mean more to me than a few coins."

Three days later, Beatris took to her bed, lying with the dog at her feet and a cloth on her forehead, insisting the pain at her temples would leave soon. Catherine treated her with valerian and put cloths soaked in herbs gathered under the new moon on her forehead, but in spite of all her effort, the headaches became more frequent.

The following week, on a blustery cold day, Catherine woke with a start. Trying not to disturb Gérard or Adam, she ran to the bed and looked at Beatris's face, drawn with pain, then fled the room to find a priest.

The young cleric hurried through the streets, following Catherine, with his surplice and stole in disarray, the Blessed Sacrament in one hand, a lantern and bell hung from the other.

Inside, he rushed to Beatris's bedside. "I'm afraid it's too late," he said and murmured a blessing.

Catherine kneeled, her tears falling on the tapestry that covered Beatris. The dog whimpered at the foot of the bed.

Chapter Thirty-Four

Rain dampened the cobbled street as they bore the plain wooden box from the main street down a narrow alley leading to Saint-Julien-le-Pauvre.

Adam and Gérard walked behind Catherine. Fishmongers and their families followed the procession, having closed their stores to mourn this plain woman who had been their loyal employee.

At the church a priest in black vestments ushered them in as the funereal sound of pealing bells echoed from the belfry. Coffin bearers lowered the box beside the stone altar and covered it with a black pall while priests intoned the Office of the Dead, and Adam mourned the loss of a dear friend.

When he returned home, he took his *vielle* outside to the fire pit where he had spent hours with Beatris. Time, he reflected, was fleeting. Something had brought him here, allowed him to see an old friend again, and he marveled at the turn of fate. His own demise, he reckoned, might come within the decade and he had only begun the life he had always dreamed. But was Catherine happy? She seemed content, but there were times he caught a glimpse of some inner struggle, something she had not yet shared with him. He rose and walked inside. She would tell him in her own good time, if he was meant to know.

Early in May, Adam received a summons from his patron. He donned a surcoat, and walked to Robert's mansion, where he was greeted by the count himself. "Thank you for coming, Adam." A servant took Adam's cloak as Robert led the way to the solar. "I am sorry for your loss. I know you were fond of the woman."

Adam took a proffered cup and sat near the fire.

"And now for the reason I brought you here. Are you free to leave Paris?"

"Of course. I only wanted my friends to see the city. As luck would have it, I obtained some small commissions. Word travels fast in Paris."

"Perhaps I did mention your name, once or twice." Robert chuckled, then grew serious. He leaned forward, locking eyes with Adam. "I have a favor to ask."

"Anything."

"As you know," Robert said, "I'm committed to this crusade. The king's young brother, Charles, has persuaded Uncle Louis to go to Tunis first. He convinced him that the Caliph of Tunis might join the Christian cause. To complicate matters, there's a pocket of unrest in southern Italy. The Saracens insist on provoking constant skirmishes."

"Does King Louis anticipate a full-fledged war?"

"No, not at all. But the infidels there supported the Hohenstaufen forces, and after Charles executed Conradin, some have refused to accept Charles as their liege lord. They are few in number, but Louis thought if I went there, perhaps made a show of French solidarity, they would settle down once and for all. I'll be going to Orléans first, where an army of knights and squires will assemble, then we'll go south. Once the crusade is behind me, I'll be at Charles's estate in Naples."

"How can I help?"

"I'd like you to come to Orléans. I was thinking . . . if you've finished that play. . . ."

"*Robin et Marion?* No, but I shall." He had no interest in the ritual celebration Robert intended to host, but he owed his patron more than he could ever repay. It was little enough to do.

"Fine. You could go on from there to Naples, as I know you're not inclined to go on Louis's crusade." The silence in the room reminded Adam of their differences, no matter their deep affection for one another.

Robert broke the quiet. "If you would, write a tribute to King Charles, and when he and I return, it could be performed. It would validate his victory over the German forces and help to secure his reign." He drained his cup and continued. "I dread the long journey south, but one does not disobey the king's orders, even when the king is your uncle." He chuckled. "Besides, my wife wants no part of Paris this next winter. So think about what I've said, and do whatever you need to do for your work."

Catherine packed her few belongings, then stood at the open shutter and took a deep breath. Below, she could hear Gérard and Adam as they walked to and fro, loading the packhorse for the trip, discussing the temperament of her rented horse and the dangers of the road ahead. How much longer could she postpone telling Adam of her intentions to join the crusade? Even Gérard had quizzed her, after learning that Adam's final destination was Naples, as to how far she planned to ride with Adam. She had had to admit she had no set plan, but assured Gérard things would work out.

When Adam had told her of Robert's request and of his obligation to his patron, she had tried to hide her excitement, but the whole thing seemed preordained. If Adam was being encouraged by Robert to leave Paris, it was just another sign that she should join the crusade. Everything seemed to be moving her way. She had studied the map, curious as to where

Naples was, and had made a mental picture of their route. They would be far to the south before the road divided, time enough to persuade him to stay with her, at least through the crusade. Hadn't he said that Robert would give him ample time to get to Naples?

As they left Paris, a cathedral bell rang. Adam felt a sudden chill, though the sun was warm and the day clear. Two days outside Paris, the road narrowed.

"We need to stay together along here," he warned, easing an arrow from his quiver.

When the sun dropped behind the trees, they came to a stand of birch where they stopped to let the horses drink from a shallow stream. "This path is little used now, and I cannot judge the direction without the sun. We're too far from the river to continue unguided."

Gérard rode his horse alongside Adam's. "Just before the last bend, there was a cave we might use . . . or should we go on?"

"Ah, no, it would be good to stop." Adam glanced overhead. "Looks like a heavy rain later. We'd better seek it out."

Gérard pointed to an opening at the foot of a hill.

"I'll see if it's safe," Adam said. "Wait here."

He entered the cave and the rank odor of an animal den assailed him. Once convinced the lair was abandoned, he headed out to tell the others.

"We'll be safe here for the night, though you may want to leave most of the supplies out here with the horses. An animal has lived here, not too long ago—probably a bear or wolf, but it's better than sleeping in the rain."

He lit candles from the flint at his waist and handed one to Catherine.

After they shared cheese and bread, Adam unhooked a bundle from the packhorse and brought blankets inside the cave.

Gérard carried two straw pallets inside.

Adam snuffed the candle flames and reached for her hand across the woolen blankets. When he heard her breathing gentle as she slipped into sleep, he smiled to himself. She reminded him of an innocent, though from what he'd heard of Guillaume, she had lived through a hell on earth. Still, had he himself not made her cry? He cursed at the thought. Was he no better than Guillaume? Someday, when the time was right, he would tell her of Maroie, and why he could never marry again. Until that time, he would love and honor her, and be everything a husband could be, except in name. God help his selfish soul, he could not let her go.

He had almost fallen asleep when the dog licked his face. "Jacques, no." The dog continued, alternately growling and digging at the blanket. One of the horses whinnied.

He reached for his bow and remembered he left it outside.

The dog ran to the opening with Adam close behind.

Footsteps crackled the dry leaves, and the dog tore out into the black night.

CHAPTER THIRTY-FIVE

Shadowy figures darted into the woods, the dog at their heels. Adam cursed. With no moon to light his way, pursuit was futile. He called to Jacques, then walked to check on the horses. The packhorse was gone, its burden lying safely on the ground next to Agnès and Gérard's horse, but Catherine's rented gelding was gone, as was his crossbow and a flask of wine. In the faint light rising from the east, Adam saw a severed leather tie hanging from the branch where he had secured the horse. Cursing again, but without any recourse open to him, he returned to his bed.

The following morning, he told the others what had happened. Strapping blankets onto the horses, he noticed Catherine's worried look. "At least they left us with the other horses, so we can travel mostly as before, only now we are without protection, so must move during daylight. We'll have to ride double."

On the main path, the road narrowed. Trees closed in on both sides, forming an arc of branches overhead. Vines and thorny bushes covered the path, making progress slow and laborious. Rustlings and cries from animals in the woods. He felt Catherine's hands tense as she tightened her hold on his sides. The smell of the forest floor, thick with rotted leaves, gave off an odor not unlike plowed earth. Later, after they had stopped to eat, Catherine suggested switching places. "Let me see if Agnès will tolerate my guidance."

266

He laughed and helped her up, then mounted the horse behind her. "Loosen the reins. Give her her head."

His arms were around her waist, and he felt the familiar warmth moving from the center of his body to his groin. The path leveled out, and the horse trotted steadily, rhythmically. Catherine relaxed against him. He pulled her hair aside and kissed her ear. "We are safe. The wolf family protects us. They have already devoured the bandits. Listen to the wind—it tells their story."

"Which way now, Adam?" Gérard called from ahead where he had paused at a divide in the road.

"Stay to the left, down the hill to the valley."

Agnès whickered and shook her head. They crested the ridge and entered a clearing that sloped steeply down to the water's edge.

Twelve days later, they crossed through Orléans and neared the southern gates of the city. Visible on a high cliff beyond the town, ragged peaks of stone reached to the sky. After a long ascent, they reached the path that climbed even higher to Robert's château. A guard, his horse caparisoned in brocade embroidered with a crest of lions and fleur-de-lis, rode to meet them. They crossed the drawbridge and entered the bailey, where workers scurried past, unmindful of visitors.

The smell of roasting meat mingled with the smell of baking bread. Stonemasons chiseled at a boulder while squires hung banners from parapets high above the keep.

As they dismounted, Count Robert approached. "*Bonjour, Mademoiselle.* You are Catherine Durant?" He kissed her hand. "I'm glad to see you both." He glanced at their traveling clothes. "You must be exhausted."

Adam introduced Gérard and handed the reins to the stableman. "We rode through heavy rain. Would you be willing to lend another horse for the journey to Naples? Thieves stole one of our mounts. Today we took turns riding these two, sometimes doubled on them, so they will need extra rations." He patted Agnès's broad back.

"You are in luck. I have bought new blood for my stable, and there are fine riding horses among them. You can have your pick, except the black pair from Spain; they are for breeding." He nodded to a servant. "Maurice will show you to your rooms. Tonight we'll eat at sundown. Now I'll leave you to rest, as I have to see to the preparations."

With Robert out of earshot, Gérard stepped to Adam's side. "You said you'd be entertaining. From what I see, it's a coronation."

"Hardly, but it's important to all of Christendom. Robert is honoring the knights who'll be stopping here on their way to the crusade. That's why I needed to finish *Robin et Marion*. He wants it performed for their entertainment. I'm glad we arrived early. I need to speak with the actors and musicians and arrange the stage."

"Looks like you'll have a large audience for your play."

Adam nodded. "Noble families want to be represented on this crusade, especially with the king's nephew, even though they may support it only halfheartedly."

Gérard gave Adam a sidewise glance and wondered how his friend could hide his conflicting ideas from his patron, the nephew of the most pious king France had ever known. The man flirted with danger.

All that week, Catherine witnessed new arrivals, knights from every part of France, coming to stay at the castle. The bailey was scarcely emptied of horses than others arrived. On a pleasant evening in late June, Catherine dressed carefully, thinking she was as excited at the culmination of the week's activities as were the knights in whose honor the banquet would be held. She took the walkway that led to the Great Hall. A squire offered his arm and showed her to a seat beside Adam on a raised dais near the count, not far from where Gérard had been seated with a group of minor dignitaries. Introduced as Catherine's guardian, Gérard bowed formally, and Catherine could hardly repress a smile.

Mingled smells of imported perfumes and strongly flavored meats permeated the air. Servers scurried about, setting bowls and pots of wine on the tables. A fanfare of trumpets brought waiting guests to tables bedecked with layered tapestries that hung to the floor. Servers refilled platters of steaming vegetables and brought new loaves from the baker's oven while a minstrel played tunes on a lute.

Adam spooned plums into the trencher between them. "These are stewed in wine, probably very sweet."

"I have eaten more than you already. Your meat is untouched, and it was tender and well-seasoned."

"You sound like my father. He thought I would die of some sickness without meat, but I never wanted it. He and his friends hunted animals north of Arras. Once I saw them disemboweling a young deer, and the blood and the accusing stare of the dead animal made me sick. I never forgot. After that they stopped asking me to go with them." He shook his head. "Father and I grew apart, but once I reached manhood, I realized all he had done for me, and we became close again."

"Tell me, what was he like? You've said he was a clerk, one of the few in town who could write. But what do you remember about him?"

Adam spoke of the old timber-frame house where he had spent his childhood. "The last time I saw Father—I remember it like yesterday. He was huddled beside the hearth, wool wrapped around his shoulders while the howling, raging wind spread a white blanket over the frozen town. The chickens had been brought in because of frigid weather. They clucked and pecked through reeds on the floor before settling into the straw. Father cursed them, but I knew better. He had named them all.

"His eyes, a piercing blue when I was a child, had softened to gray, and were now almost hidden by brows turned white. In spite of being a respected clerk, admired for his careful attention to detail, a trait that earned him the gratitude of the town's officials, old age had spared him none of its vagaries; his knees creaked when he walked, and his fingers were swollen and twisted. At fifty-six, he could no longer hold a quill.

"I remember his exact words. 'So you have decided to go with the count.' He looked not at me, but at the fire, as if he could will the heat to his body.

"I told him I'd made no decision. The roads were impassable in any case. Then I asked him to go with me. He was alone—had been for years. Mother had died young. He refused my entreaties, saying he was too old to wander the countryside atop a horse of questionable temperament. He wanted to stay in Arras, where Mother had been buried. Then he insisted I go with my patron, that there was no reason for me to stay. I left that spring and never saw him alive again."

He blinked, and Catherine touched his sleeve. "You did all you could. We all have regrets. It was his choice to remain there."

Even as she tried to console him, she felt a pang of fear. His work had taken him away. If the same thing happened to them, what would be his choice? She trembled at the thought. What if he would not take the cross? They might part and never see each other again. She felt a chill of foreboding race down her spine, and reached for her wine cup, hoping to dispel the disturbing image.

A hush came over the room. Catherine, grateful for the distraction, turned to see Robert had risen and was about to make an announcement.

The count raised his cup. "To Adam de la Halle, the celebrated *trouvère* from Arras, and to the knights who will ride in the king's crusade and proudly carry our banner." He pointed to an emblem on the wall, emblazoned with the Lily of France and the cross of red.

Catherine turned back to Adam, thinking the timing perfect. "I have been told women will go on this next crusade as they did before." She watched for a reaction, but beneath his thick brows she saw only the intelligent brown eyes, intent, sincere.

He drank from their bowl of wine. "Many are disenchanted with the constant crusades, Catherine. Women may be going, but there are mercenaries going, too. It is a desperate undertaking." He lowered his voice. "Frenchmen have perished, and the cost has been too high."

She took a dark plum from the dish between them. Her gaze shifted to the count, surrounded by his knights. How could she tell Adam her intentions? If he knew about her promise of a pilgrimage to the Virgin, he might remind her, as Isabel and Francino both had, that a youthful oath would be forgiven. He would try to convince her to abandon her plans. She could not take that risk. That she should find herself here, surrounded by crusaders, was a validation of her mission. She would try every way she knew to convince him to go with her, but if he refused, she would meet him later, when she had this behind her. But what if, in the meantime, he met another? What if, by honoring her vow, she lost Adam?

Chapter Thirty-Six

After dinner, the tables were cleared and benches rearranged. A bell rang, and Robert stood to make another announcement. "In a few days, I will take up the cross. I know not whether I will return, and therefore, if there are those here to whom I've done wrong, come forward, and I will right it, and I will redress all grievances against me or my servants."

The room stilled; no one spoke, and he continued. "Very well. On to more pleasant business. I have arranged special entertainment for you tonight, a way of thanking those who will wear the cross during this dangerous undertaking. A new *pastourelle, Robin et Marion,* will be performed for the first time. It was written by my guest, the *trouvère* from Arras, whom many of you know. The actors come to us from Paris, but the shepherdess will be played by Nicholas Cosset from Orléans."

A raised platform had been constructed at one end of the hall, opposite the dais. Catherine watched as an actor, dressed as a shepherdess and carrying a crook in one hand, came from behind a curtain stretched across the back of the platform. The shepherdess walked to a partially enclosed structure that resembled a bowery, and sat down on a bench. Nearby was a sheep, and scattered over the stage were other sheep.

"Her sheep are clever, Adam. They look almost real."

He nodded and whispered in her ear. "They're wooden, but covered with real sheepskin." He looked back at the stage as the shepherdess sang the opening line:

Robin loves me, Robin has me;

All conversation in the room stopped and servers stood silent as the castrato voice continued.

Robin asked for me, and he will have me.
Robin bought me a dress
Of fine, good, and beautiful cloth,
A long gown and a little belt,
A leur i va!
Robin loves me, Robin has me,
Robin has asked for me and will have me.

A knight came from behind the curtain, entered the bowery, and walked to Marion's side.

I was returning from the tournament,
I found the beautiful Marion all alone.

Catherine leaned toward Adam and whispered, "He will carry her away."

"No, I changed that part, to make my play different from other *pastourelles*. Watch what happens after the shepherdess rebuffs him."

You are wasting your time, Sir Aubert.
I will never love anyone but my Robin.

The knight retreated behind the curtain, and when Robin entered the stage, Catherine leaned forward, listening.

A man on horseback came here
Who was wearing gloves,
And carrying something like a rapacious kite

On his wrist. And he started to beg me fervently to
  love him,
But he did not gain anything from me by this,
For I will never do you wrong.

Marion, you would have killed me.
If I had come in time,
With my stubborn Gautier
And Baudon, my first cousin,
Even if little devils were tangled in it,
He would not have left without a fight.

Catherine watched, laughing, as Marion pulled cheese from
her bodice and shared lunch with Robin, who then left the
bowery, promising to bring back his cousins and Peronnelle,
Marion's shepherdess companion.

Robin walked to the side of the stage opposite the bowery
and called to his cousins offstage.

Gentlemen, listen to me for a moment.
I came here to get both of you,
For I don't know what ruffian on horseback
Forced his attentions a while ago
On Marion; and I fear he may
Come back there again.

The knight reentered and walked to center stage, then asked
Marion about his lost falcon. Robin came from behind the
curtain.

Catherine gasped, then leaned toward Adam and whispered,
"Now there will be trouble."

When the knight accosted Robin, accusing him of mishan-
dling the falcon, Marion turned to face the knight.

In the name of God, sir, you are wrong
Thus to have torn his clothes to rags.

And how has he dealt with
My falcon? Look at him, shepherdess!

He doesn't know how to manage it:
For the love of God, sir, pardon him!

Willingly, if you will come with me.

I shall do no such thing!

You certainly will . . . I don't want to have any other
Girlfriend than you, and I want my horse
To carry you away with me.

You plan to do violence to me.
Robin, why don't you help me?

Robin walked forward, addressing the seated guests:

Oh, how unfortunate I am. I have lost everything!
My cousins will come too late!
I am losing Marion, I have been smacked about,
My tunic and my surcoat have been torn!

Suddenly Robin's cousins came on stage, and Robin turned to them.

Let's see what has become of them.
Please, all three of us, let's hide behind these bushes;
For I want to go to Marion's aid,
If you will help me rescue her.
My courage has returned to me a little.

The knight walked to where Marion stood, entreating her to

come with him. When she refused, he spoke one last time.

I am indeed foolish
To have stopped for this silly girl!
Good-bye, shepherdess!

When the knight retreated behind the curtain, the audience cheered.

At the end of the first act, Catherine said, "You added parts I had not heard: the knight looking for his falcon, and Robin's cousins—a rough lot, they are. I remember, that is the scene you labored over in Paris, worried if the actors could convey the humor, but they did. And poor Robin. He is not so brave, after all."

"Oh, but in the second act he redeems himself by saving one of Marion's sheep from a wolf. That is the best part of the second act. The rest is just games and dancing."

Catherine covered her ears. "Now you are spoiling it for me, Adam. Tell me no more."

Near the end of the play, with the audience clapping in time with the music, the actors danced the *farandole,* then left the stage. Only Robin and Marion remained, seated together in the bowery.

Adam reached for Catherine's hand. "This song came to me months ago, when I dared to hope you would come with me. It is even more meaningful for us now."

From somewhere a horn sounded, a seductive, haunting sound, to accompany Robin's final words to Marion:

Follow me, come down the path,
The path, the path along the wood.

Tears came to Catherine's eyes. She turned her head and

wiped her damp cheek with her free hand, hoping Adam had not seen her tears. She heard him whisper, "Catherine, why do you cry?"

She turned to him. "Your play, of course. The ending is beautiful." After a moment she looked away and realized everyone in the hall was standing, clapping, looking his way. Shouts of "Bravo! Bravo!" echoed in the room. Some guests shouted Adam's name as they stood at their tables and cheered.

"Look," she said. "They loved it. They will never forget it. After tonight, you will be famous."

The following morning, as Catherine broke her fast, Gérard came down from his room wearing riding clothes. "Is Adam still sleeping?"

He looked at her appraisingly, and she was suddenly conscious of her tunic. She'd gained a little weight, with so much rich food, and no longer lifting heavy tapestries. Leave it to Gérard to notice. In all things, he was moderate, a reflection of his carefully calculating mind.

"They have gone hawking," she said. "According to Adam, the count is an expert falconer." She smeared jam on a bite of bread. "Perhaps you can catch up with them. They've not been gone long."

"I've no taste for hawking." He glanced over his shoulder, and once assured they were alone, he continued.

"A group of the knights and men-at-arms are leaving this morning. They invited me along." He broke off a piece of bread, then washed it down with watered wine. "There will be no women. These are men whose wives stayed behind, else I'd have asked you to come."

"No! You were turning back. You said—"

"I've changed my mind. I've been considering this, even in Paris. When Beatris died, who was younger than me, it gave me pause. I asked myself, do I want to spend the rest of my life playing board games with old men, or reading about foreign lands I'll never visit? Besides, some of these men are older than I. And don't you think this pretense of guardianship has worn a bit thin?" He winked, then finished his wine. "So if you've no objection. . . ."

From the gleam in his eye, she knew his mind was made up.

"I've no objection, but—when are you leaving?"

"Right away. We'll be taking a different route from the others, to pick up supplies at an armorer's shop. They will issue emblems and crosses to those who have none—like me. I understand they give us boots and heavy clothing, even arrows, along with instructions to guide us as to the proper equipment and sailing date. Once we get to the port city, we'll bivouac and complete our training there." He lifted her chin with his finger, evidently intent on setting her mind at ease. "Don't worry, now. I'll be fine."

"But you're not needing arrows, are you? You'll not go in the midst of fighting, Gérard."

He shrugged. "I've not come this far to stay with the women. Besides, I need stories to take back." He laughed at his joke, but Catherine cringed. He was putting his life in danger. The words of the fortune-teller came back to her. *There will be two.*

"I beg you, don't be foolish, Gérard." She clamped her lips together, waiting for his assurance.

"I make no promises, Catherine. And don't spoil my fun. By the way, shouldn't you tell Adam your plans soon?"

"I will, when the time is right." She looked away, and he kissed her cheek.

As Gérard joined the line of riders, she watched from the portico. He mounted the stallion, and she caught sight of his moneybag, heavy with coins. It held his life savings. No one could handle money like Gérard.

278

On impulse, she called out. "Wait, Gérard."

He dropped from the line and turned back. She ran to his side and reached into the pouch at her waist. "I've far more than I need, and it's safer with you." She crinkled her eyes and handed him most of her money. "I still dream of those highwaymen taking my purse."

"Very well." He put the coins in a separate purse, then stuffed it all into the heavy leather pouch. "I will see you at Aigues-Mortes, if I can find you in the mob. Our ship may sail before you arrive. If so, I'll see you when we return, God willing."

He eased his horse into the moving line. She felt a tear roll down her cheek, remembering how he'd insisted on a white horse. And he was right. He did look like a knight, but would a bookkeeper, no longer young, be safe on such a journey?

CHAPTER THIRTY-SEVEN

Four days later, Robert stood in the bailey with Adam, watching the stableman ready Agnès and another mount for Catherine. "I wish we could leave together, but my wife and her ladies simply refuse to rush." The count gave a sigh and swiped one hand through his hair.

Adam smiled. "*Au revoir,* my friend. I'll see you when you get to Naples."

A groom adjusted a lady's saddle on Catherine's horse. "Please, I'll ride astride," she said and waited for him to bring another saddle.

He helped her mount the roan palfrey, a broad-chested gelding that had, the count insisted, the temperament of a lamb. After Adam had settled Jacques into his cleverly contrived sling, he adjusted one of Catherine's stirrups, then swung onto Agnès's back. He followed Catherine across the moat, keeping a careful eye on the roan, then looked away as she expertly guided the horse across the planks. When the road widened, he brought his mare alongside Catherine's mount. She was about to say how much she enjoyed meeting Robert, but the serious expression he wore made her realize he wanted to talk.

"There is something I should have told you before, Catherine, or perhaps you already know. It's no secret, but somehow, I suppose I feared it would come between us."

"About your religious convictions?"

He smiled. "I love that about you, Catherine. You never waste words. But, no, it's about my past."

"You mean, in Arras? If it's about your marriage, Gérard told me long ago. I was hurt, of course, and wondered why you didn't tell me. Later, I came to accept it. Do you think of her often?" She wanted to get it all out, to have it talked about, instead of buried inside them both.

"Never when I'm with you. There's only a sense of wasted years, for both of us. My biggest regret is that I'm not free to marry."

"Gérard explained why," she said, trying to let him know she had long ago resigned herself to that. She knew men had mistresses, that wives could be discarded on a man's whim. She also knew Adam well enough to know it would be no mere whim that would lead him to break a vow, even one to a woman. "I'd not want to build our future on someone else's pain," she said, hoping the admission would put the subject to rest. For now, being with him was enough. Besides, she had learned that a wedding was no guarantee of love. And right now, her own commitment to God was uppermost in her mind.

"Would you ever go back to Arras?"

"Not without you."

They rode in silence, and after several minutes had passed, he spoke again. "Arras is not like Paris, but you would love the town. There's a beautiful church, and a labyrinth of tunnels beneath the city where vintners keep their barrels cool. And in town, there is a monument, celebrating the brotherhood of *trouvères*. It holds the Jewel of Arras."

Catherine gave the palfrey free rein as it trotted beside Agnès. "A jewel the city owns?"

"Not exactly. Many years ago, so the story goes, two minstrels who were enemies fought bitterly. The arguments were so intense that civil leaders approached the two, begging they reconcile their differences. Lambert, one of the minstrels, went to pray about this new demand. During his prayers, the Virgin came to him and gave him a wax candle."

Adam grew silent as Agnès waded across a rocky stream. They reached the other bank, and he continued. "Plague ran rampant in the region, and the Virgin told the minstrel to put drops from the candle into the holy water, and people who drank it would be cured."

"And were they?"

"There is disagreement. One man, according to the legend, said he preferred wine, and went up in flames. Whether faith or weather made the plague finally leave, everyone was afraid to doubt, as they knew full well what had happened to the one who scorned the cure of holy water."

"So, the candle is the Jewel of Arras?"

"Yes, and was given to the *trouvères* to keep. A fraternity was started to perpetuate the memory of the candle's appearance in Arras. Only the most highly respected noblemen and bourgeoisie are eligible to belong, but they are members secondary in standing to the *trouvères*, who actually were given the candle by Our Lady. That is why the Jewel of Arras is held in such esteem by *trouvères*."

"You sound as though you miss Arras greatly."

"I do, but I tell you this now, so you can know how I feel. I left Arras for many reasons, and one of them was the constant harassment of citizens for funds to support the crusade. I have little understanding of their dedication, and I know the crusaders are not always aware how the funds are obtained, but I feel only disdain for the tolls and fees extracted from citizens of France for the interests of the papacy. The escalating taxes in Arras are the cause of arguments among my friends, and I see no way a crusade furthers the cause of France."

Her hands tightened on the reins as she guided the horse over a patch of brambles. His opposition to the crusades was like a blow to her stomach. He would never agree to come.

"I have no quarrel with those who choose to go," he continued, evidently unaware her world was in shambles. "As you know, the count is going again, even though he lost his father on the last crusade. I fear for Robert's safety—for all of them. Even the king's own recorder, John of Joinville, is staying home this time. He perhaps is wiser than the others."

For a long while, she made no reply, intent on guiding the gelding up the bank. Once they reached the plateau, she took a deep breath, determined to have her say, knowing the attempt to change his mind was futile. Still, he'd been honest with her. He deserved the same. "I know some scoff at the crusaders, Adam, but I believe most of those who take the cross do it with noble intentions. They only want to serve God and ensure their spot in heaven. I always wondered if I should go." She glanced sidewise, trying to gauge his reaction. The color had washed from his face. She plunged ahead. "Then, while in Orléans, I was encouraged to join the women. Some are with their men, but there are others, all ages, who will be going to Aigues-Mortes to make a holy pilgrimage. They gave me directions to—"

"Aigues-Mortes? That is the port city King Louis built amidst ponds and marshes. Why go there?"

"There is an abbey where the women will stay until the men leave. Some of the women will return to their homes, but others will wait there until the men come back." He made no reply and she continued. "There will be a smaller ship for women to go partway, but I'll make that decision when I have to."

Adam brought the horse to a halt. "What are you telling me, Catherine? Are you leaving me?"

She rode the palfrey alongside his mount, bracing herself for what was to come.

He spoke in a low, tormented voice. "I would be especially

fearful for you, Catherine. A port city on the Mediterranean . . . *Mon Dieu,* you must know by now how much I am smitten by you. I want us to have a future together." He loosened the reins and studied her face as they rode through the woods.

She stared at the horse's head, determined to finish what she'd started, but the despair on Adam's face was weakening her resolve. "I'm not leaving . . . only taking another path, for a short while. I was hoping you would come with me. I wish I'd known earlier, about your . . . your disdain for the crusades."

He looked ahead and for a long while he didn't speak. "I could be burned for what I'm about to tell you, Catherine, but perhaps it's the only way you can understand. Not that I try to persuade you to my beliefs, but I owe it to you to tell you how I feel. If you reject me, so be it, but we need no secrets between us."

He looked so serious she almost dreaded what he would say. What new complication was coming? She felt a chill in spite of the mid-summer heat.

A muscle in his jaw twitched, and after a long moment, he spoke. "As you know, I travel through France, and like most travelers, I see and hear things others might miss. A few years ago, before Count Robert brought me to court, I visited Languedoc. How much do you know about the inquisitors, and their opposition to the Cathars?"

"I know the inquisitors were sent to weed out heretics, but what has this to do with anything?"

"Not only heretics, Catherine, unless you would call a pious and devout Cathar a heretic. The crusades are only a continuation of the same type of persecution. There were men who were persecuted for their beliefs, men who found it easier to leave their homes than face the authorities. They built their houses on hillsides, far into the cliffs near the sea, where they thought they could worship freely and live as men and women of peace."

His voice carried a conviction she had never heard before, and she listened guardedly. "The pope sent representatives to route them from their homes. Then they were burned alive."

"I don't believe that. It's a sin, and an act clearly against the teachings of the Church."

"Indeed, you are right, Catherine. Trouble is, once the minor sentences of these prisoners were carried out, whether fines, or some other punishment the Church allows, they were then turned over to civil authorities, who were not bound by the strict rules of the Church. I saw one of the abandoned homes. A large pen still stands on the grounds, a reminder of what can happen under the guise of faith. The secular authorities forced the men into the pen and burned them alive. What is worse is that the inquisitors who routed these pious men from their peaceful dwellings had the sanction of the king."

She caught her breath. What he said was indeed traitorous. "But you serve him loyally."

"That I do. In many respects he is a benevolent and fair ruler. He is kind to the poor, and has ruled France wisely and well. Because of him, we live in an era of unmatched peace. He's also a generous patron of the arts, but I don't always agree with his laws." He turned sideways in the saddle. "Did you notice the wagon that just passed by?"

Trying to catch another glimpse, Catherine guided her horse around a boulder that blocked the path, wondering what she'd missed. "An ordinary wagon."

"Did you not see the yellow badges?"

"I took no notice."

"Most people don't. It is another of King Louis's laws. Jews in France now must wear a yellow badge. In some places the women wear blue stripes on their headcoverings. If a Jew is caught without the badge a fine of ten silver *livres* can be imposed, though the law is not always enforced."

"I didn't know. There are few Jews in Vitry-en-Artois. It would seem a senseless law." She frowned. "The only Jews I know are the ones who lend money to the tapestry importers. They are clever and educated, for the most part. I've never thought them different than anyone else."

"But the king does. He believes they are a threat to Christendom, much like the Cathars were, holding fast to their beliefs, living in their hideouts to escape the inquisitors."

"What beliefs are those, Adam?"

"Tolerance of other religions. And it wasn't only the Cathars who were tolerant, but the lords who protected them and welcomed them to the region. They were powerful men, and bold. Loyal to France, but tolerant in their beliefs, like the men they protected. And like them, I've no mind to judge another's piety, especially the king's. I am a loyal subject, but not blind."

"Do you believe as the Cathars do?"

"No, Catherine, I don't. My faith is the same as yours, but the massacres carried out in the name of Christianity make me wonder where it will all end. To me, the crusades are tainted by what I saw firsthand. Faith can be kind and just, or cruel."

"You think this crusade cruel?"

"Not in and of itself. Unjust, perhaps. There will be needless deaths. But men are free to choose. I only wanted you to understand why I cannot go with you."

"I do understand. I will go alone."

She blinked back tears. He was right, of course. But wasn't there good and bad in everything? Her convent stay had proven that. She had to remember that her mission was the only way her soul would be redeemed. Adam had no such worries. Perhaps, if she told him the whole truth, he would understand. She shook her head. She could no more change his mind than he could hers. They were at an impasse, and, much as it hurt, she would have to say good-bye.

Light rain began to fall, and she nudged the gelding up an incline. A cold panic constricted her throat. The only sound was the horses' breathing, their steady rhythm on the path, and the undergrowth crushed beneath hooves. They followed the river, and finally he broke the silence. "Please understand, Catherine. I am obligated to the king, and equally to my patron. I give them my quiet support, despite my views. What puzzles me most is why you would give up what we have."

"You aren't the only one with convictions, Adam. I, too, am obligated."

"Obligated? To whom?"

"To the Virgin at Saint Mark's."

He looked away, but not before she caught the expression on his face—a mixture of disdain and restraint, evident in the set of his jaw. "Why did you not tell me earlier?"

"I . . . I thought you might leave, if you knew the truth. Oh, Adam, I wanted to tell you, but the more we were together, the less I wanted to lose you. Besides, I had no clear plan, not until I spoke with the women at Orléans."

He said nothing, only followed the narrow lane as it became steeper, taking them between the hills where chestnut trees blocked their view of the valley below. They ascended another peak, and heavy mists enveloped the mountaintop, wrapping them in a vaporous cocoon.

The road leveled through a forest, and they passed an abandoned grotto. It reminded her of the first time they had ridden together. As she followed him through a narrow pass, she studied his back, remembering the feel of his shoulders beneath her hands in moments of intimacy. Tears sprung to her eyes. How could she bear a future without him?

Chapter Thirty-Eight

One morning, following a week of uncomfortable silence during which they had slept side by side without touching, Adam woke to find her watching him. He turned his head, and she buried her face against his neck. He clasped her body tight to his and whispered in her ear. She returned his kisses, eagerly, and they came together in a new intimacy, leaving her to wonder why they had wasted the week.

Later, as they left the inn, skylarks and greenfinches sang a cacophony that echoed from the valley below, almost drowning out the *clack, clack* of the animals' hooves on the cobbled lane. The path ran alongside a swift creek. A row of prominent cottages lined the water's edge, facing three sunken huts that sprouted from the creek bank on the meadow side.

Neat rows of turnips and beans and parsnips lined the road. The last furrow was short, ending at the water, lined with fragile carrot tops that tossed in the breeze like so many green feathers. The greenery curved down to a stand of willow trees at the water's edge where a wooden mill wheel turned, the groan of the axle the only sound except the splash of the paddles. Adam remembered coming this way before, years earlier. They were not far from the divide where the road to Naples branched off. Earlier, they had passed a caravan of men and women. The men wore crosses on their garments, but she had not uttered a word.

He dreaded the road ahead, remembering the steep path that waited; it would tire the animals more than a full day's ride on level ground.

He glanced at Catherine. When her eyes met his, she lifted her hand, a slight gesture, and smiled. She blinked before looking away, then fanned at a flying insect. The coronet which bound her head earlier was in disarray. Her hair flowed loose, making her face appear small. She needed a protector, but had made it clear she intended to fulfill her vow, with or without him. How could he convince her to come to Naples instead? Time was running out.

They rode into a clearing, and he slowed his horse. "We'll stop just ahead. An old hermit has made a shelter by a stream—if he still lives. I remember him because he knew all my songs, and those of others, too, yet he lived away from men. I stayed a night with him when I came this way before. We can replenish the water and have a bite to eat. The road beyond, on the way to Naples, is easier. The path is wider, more traveled." He watched her for a sign, anything to give him hope, but her next words sent chills of apprehension down his spine.

"Adam, the women at Orléans . . . they will meet me at a monastery, a famed place of pilgrimage, where they will pray for the crusaders' safety before going on to Aigues-Mortes."

He reined in the mare. His expression conveyed desperation. "Where? What monastery?"

"In Arles. I tried to tell you before."

He made no response, just urged his horse forward again. Finally, he decided to make one last effort to persuade her from this dangerous mission. "Come with me to Naples, Catherine. We could be happy there. It's a land of fruit and honey," he added, trying to lighten the moment.

Minutes, then hours passed. She remained quiet so long, he began to think she would never speak again, that they would ride in silence to the end of their days, hearing only the steady thump of the animals' hooves, only screeches from squirrels and songs and wing-flapping of birds. The silence became an entity, a being apart from the woods, a stillness that moved with them, cloaking them in an embryonic cloud of wordlessness. *Perhaps I am going quite mad.*

Finally, softly, she replied. "I cannot."

He wanted to press her further, but his emotions—anger at her stubbornness, fear for her safety, sadness at her impending departure—warred in his breast. "When do you leave me, then?"

"Not until the road divides in Arles. I'll join the women. We will take the Pilgrim road a bit, then turn south to Aigues-Mortes."

"I see you've studied a map." He smiled at her now, trying to disguise his smothering pain.

She returned his smile, evidently unaware of his anguish. The silence lengthened between them as he searched his mind for words that might convince her, although he knew it was futile. His verses had made audiences laugh and cry, had influenced kings and convinced barons of the futility of petty skirmishes, but he could think of no phrases now.

He masked his inner turmoil and said simply, "I never want us to be apart, Catherine, but I cannot go, for the reasons I told you about, and because of my work."

"I will join you, then, in Naples, when this is behind me." As she spoke, the sky around them darkened, and a fresh breeze stirred the trees. "Please don't worry. We will have many other crusaders around us. You said travelers together are safe." She nudged the gelding to a trot.

He watched her handle the horse, and thought how quickly she had learned. Any man would be proud to have such a woman. A branch caught at her coif, and she pulled back, almost losing her balance. He winced. Trouble was, he wanted to protect her from everything—from discomfort, from misplaced guilt, from political discord—and he wondered if, with his refusal to go on the crusade, he had endangered her life. She had mentioned a separate ship for the women. He had to hope she would do her penance, or whatever it was she sought to do, on dry land. For the first time in years, he thought of making his way to a chapel, but how could he pray, and for what? The irony of his predicament made him want to laugh—or cry.

An hour later found them on the well-traveled road that hugged the Loire Valley. The scenery changed abruptly; forests and rugged mountains met them at every turn along the path. They camped that night in a clearing, beset by nighthawks and the occasional prowling wolf. Late the next morning, they arrived in a village on the banks of the Rhone River, from where they would make their way to Arles, and after that was the day she dreaded most, the day they would part.

They followed the Rhone for more than three days. On the fourth day, the sky turned dark. Little eddies of leaves swirled around the horses' hooves as they made their way along the path.

Catherine glanced upward, taking note of the swift-moving clouds. "Looks like a bad storm."

"We should hurry on then. Weather this time of year is unpredictable in these parts."

The road wound close to the river. As they approached the riverbank, Catherine noticed the rushing current, swifter than any she'd ever seen.

"It's as though it is in a hurry to reach the sea," she said, brushing a strand of hair from her eyes. She glanced at Adam, noticed the furrowed brow. "You look tired, Adam."

"No, not tired."

Something in his tone, his quick answer, gave her pause. The wind had picked up, whipping her hair from the coif and blowing debris into the road. The horses whickered, as if sensing

291

some unseen enemy.

"Hurry," Adam shouted. "We need to take cover."

They had just left the riverbank when she heard wind whistle through the trees, ancient cedars permanently bent, like old men carrying the weight of life on their shoulders as they headed to the sea. Shepherds guided their flocks from the fields, hurrying to safety, and she recalled a story her father told her of a great wind in southern France. He called it the Master Wind and claimed it was like no other. People were tossed about like insects, he said, and entire roofs flew through the air as if carried by demons. She hoped this was not one of those winds, for they could be blown away.

With the village behind them, and the wind growing ever stronger, she slowed her mount and removed her cloak from a leather pouch. While struggling to hook the clasp, the fabric caught in the wind, blew over her head like giant wings, and was carried into the sky.

"Can't we stop?" she shouted.

"No!" Adam reached in a pouch and pulled out a blanket. Hard-pressed to keep it from blowing away, too, he handed it to her. "Put this around your shoulders. It may get worse. We have to find shelter for the night. We should have stayed in the village, but there will be another town before long."

The animals, she noticed, needed no prodding. On the contrary, they rushed along as if whipped, and Catherine suspected they, too, feared this unseen element that now blew with a fury.

As the dry wind turned more ferocious, she rode with bowed head, intent only on remaining upright and keeping the palfrey under control. From somewhere behind them, she heard what sounded like thunder. She turned to look just as Adam jerked at the reins. "Get to the side!"

She struggled to bring the gelding to the left. A horseless

wagon rolled past, careening toward a canal. With a great crashing sound that could be heard even above the roaring storm, the wagon plunged into the water.

Frozen in fear, she spurred her horse back to the road. A moment later she heard Adam shout and looked up. He pointed to a weathered building set back from the road. She followed him to the sheltering side and caught her breath, grateful for a moment's respite from the tumult.

Adam jumped from the horse and tossed her the reins. "Hold them tight."

Jacques whined, and she lifted him from the pouch with her free hand, then slid down from the gelding. She heard Adam banging on the door at the front. A nearby tree heaved a shuddering sigh. Her heart stopped as the roots came free of the earth. The tree twisted to the ground. She flung herself down as the wind tore at her hair. A piece of debris flew by. Panicked, the horses reared. The reins slipped from her hands, cutting her flesh. She rolled to the side in time to see the horses disappear from sight.

"Damn!" she shouted into the relentless wind. "Damn you both!"

She covered her head and eyes. Jacques whimpered in her arms. Something brushed her shoulder and she looked up to see Adam, kneeling at her side.

"Where are the horses?"

"They pulled loose!" She wiped dirt from her face. "Can we get inside?"

"No. Door was bolted tight—solid oak. We have to keep moving. It's not safe here; the building could go at any minute."

They locked arms and struggled back to the main road. A loose board flew by, narrowly missing their heads as they hurried forward, propelled by driving winds. She thought the whirling tempest more punishing than a winter blizzard. When she stumbled, she felt Adam's arms close around her. She glanced at his face, saw his brow was creased with worry. Only then did she realize the full extent of the danger they faced.

CHAPTER THIRTY-NINE

Adam clamped his jaw, fighting a sense of growing remorse. He had made a dangerous error in judgment in not stopping sooner, risking Catherine's life for a few extra miles. Had he not been warned about this river valley, a wind tunnel that lifted buildings and laid them in adjacent fields? They needed a cover of some sort, and soon. The dog trembled beneath his cloak. A cooking pot flew by, and Adam began to fear in earnest for their lives.

They plodded on, Adam hanging onto Catherine with one hand, the other half-covering his eyes. Limbs and debris sailed overhead. He tried to follow the road, obscured now with leaves and broken branches. His mind raced. He had risked her life needlessly and was no more able to change the course of the wind than to change the course on which she had embarked.

They rounded a bend in the road, and Catherine cried out. "The horses!"

The animals cowered in a thicket of trees, their ears laid back, evidently terrorized by the unrelenting windstorm. Overhead limbs whipped like leather straps.

"Better to lead them now," Adam said, coaxing Agnès from the trees. "This can't last much longer." But he knew better; a mistral could last for days.

They set out again, and when he had almost lost hope of finding shelter, they came to a wooden house sitting in a bosk. They tethered the horses to a sturdy tree on the windless side of the house, then hurried to the door. Adam pounded with his fist. When no one answered, he used his shoulder, determined to get inside. As he took aim again, the door slammed open, caught by the wind. Catherine rushed past. Adam struggled to pull the door shut, only dimly aware of a man at his side.

A gray-haired woman led Catherine to a bench.

An older man pulled a stool near a fire, and turned to Adam. "Sit here. You'll dry out faster." The man had only one useful eye; the other was a dark mass half-covered by a drooping lid.

Adam glanced around. It was a peasant's shack. The walls were made of wattles and interwoven thatch, blackened like the floor and stools; even the candles were covered with soot. The few openings in the room had been stuffed with straw, and a pallet lay on the floor in one corner. Outside the wind continued to roar, but the structure seemed unaffected except for a persistent flap on the roof. Adam suspected the loose thatch would soon join the other debris swirling outside.

One of the men offered them a meal. Exhausted, stomachs full, they fell asleep near what was left of the fire, while the wind howled with a fury.

The next morning, Adam struggled from the abyss of dreamless sleep, sure some unskilled trumpeter played a cruel joke. Then, he heard giggling. The trumpet was a duck, squawking loudly as two boys chased it around the room. He lay still, gazing up at the hole in the thatched roof, watching as smoke drifted out of it, listening to the sizzle as drops of moisture from the opening landed in the fire below. From somewhere close by a calf bawled. He glanced around the room and saw Catherine sleeping peacefully with the children. The scene caught at his throat. Was it too much to hope that someday . . . ?

He tore the thought from his mind. The likelihood of a future together was dwindling with each day that passed.

The smell of food reached his nostrils; whatever it was, he

wanted some. He marveled that these peasants, living in such poverty, would have wood to burn and food to cook. They had been more prepared than he, and evidently took these terrible winds as an ordinary event.

The woman left her cooking and sat down beside Adam. "Your wife's very pretty." She smiled and nibbled on a crust of bread. "What's your name?"

"I am Adam, from Arras."

"I'm Borgine," the woman said. She pointed to the older man who sat on a stool near the fire, scraping a piece of leather. "That's my husband, Miles."

"Those two are Gautier and Jean, our sons that lived, and their young ones," she said, indicating two pale-looking boys and a girl about the same age. "And that's my daughter." She pointed to a girl still asleep on the mat. Her black hair lay twisted around her shoulders, and Adam had a fleeting image of Maroie, then looked away. That seemed like a lifetime ago.

Miles called to the two boys who were once again chasing the duck. "Go. Feed the animals," he said.

Outside, a calf lowed. A goat bleated.

"Maman," one of the boys said, pulling on the sleeve of Borgine's daughter. She rose from the bed, yawning. "We've used the last hay."

"Shh! Feed the hens, then."

The boys tossed seeds onto the floor. The chickens scrambled for the food, clucking and scratching in the hard earth. A rooster chased the older boy, pecking at his bare legs.

The boy shrieked, *"Maman! Maman!"*

Miles left the fire, clapping his hands, coming between the rooster and the boy.

His daughter, a girl of about eighteen years, entered the room. Her unbrushed hair hung to her shoulders and covered half her face. She stood silhouetted in front of the fire that lit the near-dark room, and Adam could clearly see her rounded hips and muscled thighs beneath the garment she wore. Their eyes met and for a brief second she smiled, then straightened, arching her back. He saw the folds of the tunic, not touching her stomach, the thin fabric of her chemise held away from her body by high rounded breasts. The image changed to one of Catherine, an image that flooded his mind and made his loins ache. He looked away.

Suddenly the room seemed overly warm. He wiped his brow with the tattered end of a coverlet and saw Miles looking at Catherine, his one good eye roaming her form.

Appalled, Adam's first reaction was to challenge the man, in spite of his hospitality, but no sooner did the thought cross his mind than he realized he had done the same to the black-haired girl. Besides, a confrontation would only embarrass Catherine. And what right did he have to interfere? What was he, after all, to Catherine? Clearly, she felt something for him—he could sense it in her gaze, in her laughter. And their lovemaking had brought them close as any two people could be, but she had her own mission, one he could not share. And if this peasant dared to ogle her, what of the lords and knights she would meet, once she joined the crusaders at Aigues-Mortes? On what ground could he object?

Miles had turned away, and Adam hoped the man's lust was only temporary. Still, the sooner he and Catherine left, the better.

Miles sidled over and sat down beside Catherine. A rush of anger singed Adam. "Catherine, we really must leave. I've a long trip to Naples."

She shot him a curious glance. "Can't we wait a while? This can't last forever."

"It's died down a bit. We'll have no trouble now."

Borgine looked up from her mending. "Why not stay a while?

It's little company we get, and there's food aplenty."

"We're both grateful to you," Adam said. "But we have to be—I have an appointment, not far from here."

Catherine blinked. "An appointment? I thought—"

"Yes. We have to leave."

"But where are we now, Adam?"

"A few leagues north of Arles, I think."

"You're an hour's walk from the monastery at Arles," Miles said, "just off a road that leads to the good road. I know because the master's house is on the paved road. Heading south, you'll pass his sheepfold and storage shed."

Adam fixed his eyes on Catherine. "We've enjoyed their hospitality long enough and must be gone."

"Please stay a bit longer. The horses deserve a rest. They were frightened to death."

He acquiesced, knowing she was right. Still, he would keep one eye on Miles, and if Catherine insisted on staying the night, he would sleep beside her, even if it meant sleeping on the dirt floor.

Just before sunset, the wind died down. After leaving Miles a generous payment for his hospitality, they left his home. Before dark, they reached the town. The Benedictine Abbey of Montmajour, the arranged meeting place the women had promised, rose to greet them, perched in plain sight on a rocky hill like a sentinel guarding the town.

"In spite of the storm, we are still early, Adam—a chance to rest my bones." She rubbed the palfrey's neck. "I daresay the animals can use a few days' rest too." She studied his face, trying to ascertain his mood. He'd been quiet since leaving Miles's shack, and she suspected he dreaded, like her, their parting. To make matters worse, the monastery would have separate quarters for women, far from the men. The thought of sleeping alone, with him so close, and yet, so far, brought her to the edge of tears. She struggled to capture her composure. There would be many nights alone. She had made her choice, and so had he.

After stabling the horses, they walked inside. A welcoming monk led Adam away, and she was shown the dormitory set aside for women. Later, she made her way to the visitor's chapel, where she prayed for Adam's safety on the journey to Naples. Comforted that he would travel partway with a caravan of traders, she turned her petitions to the crusaders and to her own future redemption which was sure to come. She was only days away from joining the main band of crusaders, the swarming movement of humanity inching toward Aigues-Mortes. From there, King Louis's army would sail to victory.

As she left the chapel, she saw Adam waiting in the cloister.

"I suspected I'd find you here. Walk with me. We can find a tavern somewhere and eat together."

She nodded, grateful he had thought ahead. She had no wish to sit tonight at a table of women. That would come soon enough.

They walked out the gate, then took a path that led past the Chapel of the Holy Cross. Tombs, hewn into rock, marked the resting place of monks and bishops alike. They paused at a grotto.

"Does this remind you of something, Catherine?"

She nodded. "I thought you would have forgotten—it was so long ago. So much has changed."

"But not my love, Catherine. It has not changed, except to grow stronger."

He pulled her close and kissed her, and neither heard the squawk of ducks at the grotto pond, or a passing cart or a woman's laughter, but only felt the pain of parting, looming like a dark cloud over their passion.

Chapter Forty

On the Ides of August, they approached the divided road. To the east lay Aigues-Mortes, and far to the southwest the town of Naples. Adam slowed his horse, his mind racing, searching for words he knew to be futile.

"We part here, Adam." Her trembling voice belied her resolute pose as she sat straight-backed on the gelding.

She guided her horse from the path to a shaded cove beside a stream, where other horses stood saddled and ready.

He dismounted and walked to her side. "You will come to Naples afterward?"

"Yes. It won't be long."

He rubbed the horse's flank. No use protesting. They had been through all that. "When you reach the city, come to the Sicilian king's château, just inside the northern gate. They will know where you can find me." His voice sounded thick and unsteady, even to his own ears. He fought the doubts that clouded his mind, and clung to the hope they would meet again. He would barter his soul for that to be true.

He tightened the girth on her gelding, then opened his coin purse. "Here. Take this. There may be things you need."

She shook her head. "I've plenty, Adam. Gérard saw to that."

He suspected her reticence was because he opposed the journey. It would be like her, to refuse subsidy for that reason alone. "Very well, if you're sure." He refused to quarrel, with so little time left. He shook his head. There was nothing left but to say good-bye. "I wish you Godspeed to Aigues-Mortes, Catherine. Naples will be a barren city until you come to share it with me."

Catherine smiled and slipped down from the horse. "You've made me happy, Adam, and I'm grateful you brought me along with you these months. If I should not live to see the morrow, I would die happy having spent these months with you."

Her words sent a chill of apprehension down his spine, one he refused to acknowledge. He kissed her soundly while travelers formed a line and sang hymns as they made ready to follow the knights who moved out, making their way along the old Pilgrim road to Saint-Gilles, where they would turn south for the trip to Aigues-Mortes.

Adam could not recall a hotter August; the punishing sun glared down on his back as he rode the dusty path from Arles. Soon the road would join the great trade route that hugged the sea on the way to Italy, but until then this narrow trail would take him monotonously through foothills and plateaus, forests and meadows.

Golden eagles and peregrine falcons soared overhead, hunting for food. Foxes stalked below, sometimes stopping to sniff as the wind carried the scent of man to the wary beasts.

A sharp whistling call pierced the silence, alarming Agnès. A low growl came from the leather pouch where Jacques rode. A marmot stood erect beside the path, its reddish-brown fur reflecting sunlight, its call warning the colony of approaching danger before it disappeared into a hole.

Adam drank wine from the pig bladder, not seeing the beauty of the unfamiliar land through which he rode; melancholia followed him, a hovering cloud of despondency that had been his companion since leaving Arles. He tried to concentrate on the landscape; at times he sang out, listening to the echo of his voice coming back from the hills, but in spite of his efforts to distract himself, he thought again of Catherine and relived the days with her in Paris. His mind returned to the danger she might face.

He had heard tales of looters who preyed on crusaders, stories repeated as *jongleurs* moved from court to court; they told of whole groups of men and women who had been set upon by highwaymen or who perished by the road from strange diseases as they moved through unfamiliar lands. What worried him most, though, was the thought of another man touching her, having his way with her. If, God forbid, something happened, how would he live with himself? He'd known from the outset she was obstinate and strong-willed, but so was he. Had he not clung stubbornly to his convictions, as she did to hers? But convictions be damned—he loved her.

I will think of nothing but my work, until she comes to Naples, else the worry will drive me mad.

He met a merchant caravan heading north from Montpellier, and he knew he neared the trade route; he thought he could smell the water. Soon, the humid air of the valleys changed to a drier, cooler breeze. He reached the well-traveled road that followed the sea. Crossing into the fertile land, he caught a glimpse of harriers over the wetlands; he knew them by their long legs and longer tails, saw the ordinary brown of their feathers as they swooped and cruised over the marshes, not far from their nests, searching for prey in the lagoons.

He shifted in the saddle, and wondered how far the women had traveled, and if they had enjoyed fair weather. She'd been wearing a green tunic that matched her eyes. He wished he had told her to wear a surcoat, but even with that, she'd not be safe. She had no idea the effect she had on men. The thought made him curse the things he'd left unsaid.

Another group of merchants passed by, their wagons loaded

with oranges and lemons. Parisians, he mused, will pay dearly for those. He passed the silvery groves of olive trees growing on both sides of the road, and wished Catherine were there to see them.

It was October, 1269, when he finally rode into Naples. By the following autumn he had finished *Le Roi de Sicile,* written some new chansons, and pined for Catherine.

Catherine fell in line behind a group of ladies, two of whom had children at their side.

"Have you gone with previous crusades?" Catherine asked, noting their sturdy traveling clothes and the calm demeanor of their children.

"*Oui.* The king's last one, but they made us turn back. This time, though, we are determined, even though we have to walk, not like some I know who have a grand horse to ride." The woman looked sidewise at the gelding.

"The horse is not mine. He is loaned to me," Catherine said, trying to change the subject and determined to make friends among the women. "Were there this many women before?"

"More," the woman said.

Catherine looked around at the crowd. They had gathered some along the way. There must be hundreds—no, thousands—of people.

"More?" Catherine said, her voice small.

"Looks like a lot, but there'll be less later," the woman's companion replied. "Some will drop out, once they find it's no royal parade." She nudged her friend, and they laughed together.

Catherine felt someone tap her ankle and looked down. A girl with hair the color of hazelnuts walked alongside the palfrey. Her cheeks were rouged and her head uncovered, reminding Catherine of the courtesans at Robert's, except this girl was no courtesan. Her brown frock had worn thin and did little to hide her ample bosom. "Pay them no mind," she said. "They're a pain in the arse, an' everyone knows it. Where did you come from?"

"North of Paris."

"Hmm. That's a long way I guess. I've only traveled two days. Came along when I saw them comin' through town. Mind if I ride a bit?"

Catherine reined in the horse and patted the gelding's rump.

"My name's Maryse," the girl said, climbing up.

"I'm Catherine. Is your husband with you?"

"Ha! I've no husband, not a real one. Mind you, if I did, I'd not be here now."

Catherine nudged the horse ahead, trying to sift through the girl's meaning, but what she said made no sense. "You wouldn't want him along?"

Maryse laughed. "Well, I wouldn't want him here, if that's what you mean. He'd put an end to my fun, sure would, like all husbands. No, I plan to snare me one of these rich squires the king takes along to do the fightin.' That is, if I can get one before they go taking theirselves on a ship, which prob'ly won't make it across the sea."

"You came to—"

"I'm not the only one here. You think all these women are so pious?" She laughed, a deep throaty laugh that made Catherine smile. "By the way—why are you here?"

Catherine weighed her words. How could she explain that she wanted to rid herself of guilt for a man's death? How could she tell someone she dared not go back on her word to God? "My priest said it was a holy undertaking."

Maryse fell silent. Catherine wondered if Maryse was considering what *she* had said, trying to make sense of it. They lived in different worlds.

Sundown streaked the sky orange and gold when the caravan

wound through a valley and up to a wide ridge.

"Guess this is where we'll sleep," Maryse said, and slid from the horse's rump.

Catherine dismounted, then removed the saddle and checked the palfrey's back. Satisfied there were no chaffed spots, she checked the hooves for stones, grateful that Adam had shown her the proper care of a horse. There were no grooms here, not for a woman. She tossed a blanket on the horse's back, then walked him slowly across the clearing. Later, she would let him graze, but for now, he needed to cool down. Besides, she wanted to see the sights.

The campsite bustled with pilgrims. Ordinary villagers worked alongside squires, helping to set up the tents. Smoke rose from campfires. Dogs ran free, prompting curses from the cooks. Children pitched a wooden ball, and when it rolled near the feet of a young girl, her mother picked it up and threatened to keep it forever unless they moved away.

"Look," Maryse said. "Bowmen. Notice their brawny legs. You can always tell a good bowman, for sure." She winked at Catherine and gave her a smile. "If I had a coin to bet, I'd pick the one on the left." An arrow flew through the air, hitting the makeshift target and bringing a round of applause from the onlookers. "See? I told you so. I know a good man when I see one."

Catherine suppressed a smile, amused at the girl's good-humored banter. The clang of mallets drew her attention to a ridge. Shading her eyes, Catherine studied the scene. A large tent had been raised, surrounded by several smaller, more color-ful ones. "Who sleeps there, do you think?"

Maryse followed her gaze. "The red and blue ones, you mean?" She shrugged. "Knights, or noblemen. The big one might belong to a Count or a Duke. Their tents may be prettier, but ours go up quicker."

The horse nudged Catherine's shoulder. She led him to a meadow and tied him with the others.

Later that evening, after a meal that tasted surprisingly good, she crept inside one of the four tents designated for the women. Pausing momentarily, she was reminded of the convent dormitory she had left so many months before—a lifetime ago.

She blinked her eyes, then scanned the interior, wondering where she was to sleep.

Maryse called out. "Over here. I saved a place."

Later, lying on her back wide awake, Catherine listened to shouts and singing from nearby campfires. Finally all was dark, and she knew the men had extinguished the fires and were sleeping.

Somewhere in the distance, wolves howled a series of distant, lonesome wails, and Catherine remembered the first night she had lain with Adam. A tear rolled down the side of her temple. He'd given her his heart as he had shown her the world. Still, she must go on to Aigues-Mortes. There was no turning back. Her promise to the Virgin must be fulfilled.

She closed her eyes and lay still, trying not to waken Maryse or the other women, and prayed for Adam's safety on the road to Naples.

The next morning after mass, colorful banners were hoisted in the breeze. Catherine mounted the gelding with Maryse and fell in line behind the others.

As they moved out and ascended a rise, Catherine felt a twinge of pain. She eased the water holder from the pannier and sipped, but a moment later the pain returned. Perspiration beaded her brow, and she slowed the horse.

"What's wrong?" Maryse asked. "Is the horse lame?"

Catherine started to reply but instead found she was unable to sit upright. She gripped the horse's mane with both hands and leaned forward to keep from falling. "I'm going to be sick."

She felt Maryse's arms around her.

"I thought as much. I can always tell, though I've never had a babe myself."

The words hit her full force. Was that possible? She was too stunned to speak. Another wave of pain and nausea made her gasp for breath, and the realization that she carried a child within her womb, Adam's child, made her want to shout to the world in spite of the pain. She tried to steady her thoughts, but her mind was numb with happiness. Could it be? She tried to remember her last flow. Weeks ago, but she had thought it because of the riding and eating at odd hours. But her breasts, more tender now . . . she had all the signs.

"I'm fine now. Let's go." She gripped the reins to steady the horse, but a cramp so violent she thought she would retch grabbed at her stomach. Sweat drenched her face. She clung to Maryse to keep from falling.

"Help me," Maryse shouted. "God's Wounds, someone help."

CHAPTER FORTY-ONE

When Catherine woke, she found herself in an unfamiliar setting where a warm breeze carried the smell of cut grain. For a moment, she was in her own room at Guillaume's estate, but then an unfamiliar voice shouted nearby.

"*Maman,* she's awake!"

Catherine blinked and saw a woman with gray hair and kind brown eyes studying her face. "They said your name is Catherine. I'm called Mathilde."

"Where am I? What happened?"

"You are lucky. A girl brought you here. Seems she caught you before you fell from the horse, else you'd be worse off than you are." On Catherine's forehead, the woman laid a linen that smelled of mint and cloves. "Your husband one of the crusaders?"

"I have no husband."

Mathilde's expression changed to one of pity. "You running away then, eh? Did he beat you?" She pulled a coverlet from the foot of the bed. "Then it's just as well you left, before the little one's born."

Catherine swallowed. Full awareness returned with a jolt. She was with child, a child conceived one of those glorious nights with Adam. She touched her abdomen, in wonder of the miracle. But what if Mathilde was wrong? What if there was no child at all? Only then did she realize how much she wanted it to be true. She pressed the woman further. "How can you be certain . . . that I carry a child?"

"My dear girl, I've had eight of my own, and helped the local midwife birth several more. I knew what to look for. I could feel it inside. That's not to say you'll have a healthy one."

Panic gripped Catherine. Her joy spiraled to despair. Suddenly, the child within her had become more important than anything—an unbreakable tie to Adam. She desperately wanted it to survive, to come squealing, protesting into the world. Slowly, Mathilde's words took on a deeper meaning. Had the woman implied that all was not quite right? She gripped the edge of the coverlet and covered her pounding chest. She had to know the worst. "Is something wrong? I mean, what did you feel?"

The woman shrugged. "They all feel the same, it's not that. Just that when you bleed like you've done, it's a sign things aren't quite right."

Catherine felt a cold chill move the length of her body, from her feet to her throat. "How much . . . how much did I bleed?"

"Enough so's they knew you needed help. At least they had that much sense, though even that surprises me. Why those women come all this way, when there's little chance their men will come back. . . ." She shook her head. "For the likes of me, I can't see what good it does. Now for the men, that's a different story. They can make their own way."

The room became suddenly warm. Mathilde's words had brought a new worry to quell Catherine's fragile happiness. What if, during his stay in Naples, Adam found another? She flinched at the thought, but it was something she had to face. How could she support another life? She hadn't planned on this.

Braced with a new resolve, she thought of her future; come what may, she would do whatever was needed. A woman willing to work, especially one who could read, could find employment anywhere. She was no longer the frightened waif in a tavern, but a mother with hopes and dreams for her unborn child. She would learn to spin—even to weave. There was always a shortage of weavers. If she started now. . . .

Catherine turned her head. "How long—could you tell how long before the birth?"

"If you're lucky, um, I'd say another four full moons at the most. Less than that, he'll be a weaklin' and may not live."

"I see." She laid her head back and tried to calm her racing mind. The other women would be far away by now. She would have to make her way alone to Aigues-Mortes and find the convent. There, one of the nuns could teach her a skill, while the child grew inside her, and she did her penance. She pushed back the coverlet.

"The horse—what did they do with my horse?"

"He's in the pasture, safe for now, but you may as well forget riding anytime soon. Like I said, you're lucky, *Mademoiselle,* that I knew what to do."

"I can't pay you much," she said, remembering she had asked Gérard to keep the little money she had.

"I want no pay. You don't look like you eat much. Later, when the babe's born, maybe you can do some light chores, cooking and such." Catherine nodded, and the woman crossed to the window and shook a coverlet, then turned back and placed it at the foot of the bed. "My husband works the post, so he's gone a lot. I have the full care of the young ones, and the little plot of land out back."

"I will be gone soon, but I'll see that you are repaid for what you've done."

"You'll not go anywhere, not if you want to give that little one a chance. Bleeding's a sign you have to rest. Stay off your feet, for the most part, 'til it's born. Then you may have a live birth."

Catherine listened to Mathilde with a sense of helplessness. After all this, coming so far, it looked as though she was fast losing the chance to redeem her soul. The notion stabbed at her heart. Already, she had postponed her mission too many times— first with the convent, then risking His wrath by seeking happiness with Adam. Even a kind and understanding God would lose patience with such capriciousness. She caught her breath. Was this all a sign that she had fallen from grace? What if He saw fit to take the babe in retribution? The image gave rise to an image she refused to believe. A tear rolled from her eyes, down her temple, and onto the mattress.

"No use crying, Catherine. Melancholia will bring on early labor for sure. Better to say your prayers and rest. Later I'll bring you a bit of supper."

She padded from the room. Catherine thought she had never felt so alone in all her life.

"Push! Push!"

Catherine leaned forward, unable to see through the haze of burning pain. The room turned and spun, and she held tight to the hands that kept her from plunging forward into nothingness.

She heard someone whisper above her. "Too long . . . she's lost too much blood."

Too long. . . .

Then she was going to die, in a stranger's house on the way to joining a crusade. Perhaps He would know she had wanted to fulfill her vow. Maybe He would at least spare her child. . . . The pain ended and she fell into the waiting abyss.

Gérard approached Naples, traveling on horseback in the company of two knights he'd befriended in the monastic hospital. The serenity of the town contrasted with the loneliness and desolation in Aigues-Mortes where families waited for the crusaders to return. He inhaled the smell of the sea, carried by a salty breeze, so different from the smells of burning wood and death.

He breathed deeply, trying to clear his mind of the memories, but his thoughts drifted back to the accursed crusader ship, one of two that had never made it to Africa. Halfway there, she had harbored in a cove, having been separated from other ships in a squall. As the men slept, pirates had sneaked aboard. The crew had fought bravely to protect her, and after a heated battle, the surviving pirates had fled, leaving the deck strewn with bodies, pirates alongside crusaders. The distraught captain had ordered the crew to set sail. Once in deep water, the uninjured men had lowered their shipmates and the marauders overboard, then sailed for their lives, back across the choppy sea to Aigues-Mortes and safety.

He could still smell the stench of rope and vomit and salt air as the ship plunged northward, an endless monotony of churning waves until they entered calmer waters near the port city. He had arrived in June, unharmed except for a leg broken by tumbling cargo and cracked ribs that ached when he moved. In spite of the pain, he had managed to get to the monastery, an ancient stone fortress that now served as a hospital for wounded crusaders.

The monks had set the bone and treated his wounds. He tried to erase the memories, wanted to tell them of the wasted men, but they treated his flesh, letting his mind rot. He promised himself that once he found Catherine, they would join Adam in Naples. A better life awaited them there.

As he began to heal, he was taken to an inn in a neighboring village, where he met the woman who nursed him back to health. It was there he learned that King Louis died that August, two months after Gérard's ship had returned.

Sara had taught him that later years were for joy, not loneliness. With her he no longer felt the guilt of desertion that had followed him as he sailed for his life back across the sea in the limping vessel. His leg had finally healed enough to ride, with only occasional pain to remind him of his injury. He wondered that love should come to him so late; he would be fifty-two this year, he thought, shaking his head.

His first venture from Sara's inn had been to the convent in Aigues-Mortes, where he expected to find Catherine, but instead, heard words that sent him reeling. "No record of a Catherine Durant or a Catherine Ridaut."

"You must be mistaken. She came here with the women, the wives who waited for the men. Our ship sailed before she arrived, but I know she would not have left without me." He leaned forward. "She was on her own pilgrimage, in a way."

The prioress shook her head. "I'm sorry. She must have been with the others—the women who sailed to Tunis. There was a special ship for the wives. I was told it sank before reaching Tunis."

"No! It can't be." He swiped his hand across his face. Nine short months ago he had waved good-bye to her at Orléans. In all the confusion at Aigues-Mortes, the teeming mobs of humanity waiting for fair weather to sail, and the arrival of the king, he had never been able to find her. He regretted that now. Perhaps he could have convinced her to turn back—to give up her misdirected endeavor.

The prioress straightened the pile of parchment and gave him a look so full of pity he began to feel a cold creeping sensation in his chest. Surely not. . . .

He had returned to Sara with a heavy heart. She soothed his angst, reminding him that Catherine could have changed her mind and gone with Adam. But Gérard knew better. Catherine was too dedicated to her mission. Two days later he saddled his horse and left the inn on the saddest journey of his life.

After a month of riding, Gérard rode into Naples, still trying to think of words he should use. How did you tell someone his dreams were ended? How to say he would never see his love again, and that he would spend the rest of his life without Catherine? There were no words, or if there were, he didn't know them.

Approaching the city gates, he waved good-bye to his two companions as they reined in their mounts at the Inn of Olive Groves. Gérard glanced at the sketch Adam had drawn. The next drawbridge would lead to the château of the Sicilian king.

A guard at the gate told him Adam had left for the square after chapel.

He rode back across the drawbridge and into town. A volcanic mountain loomed ahead. Snow lay draped in the shade of its jagged peak like a priestly chasuble.

The road led past a university, situated on a narrow street that sloped to the bay. Women carried baskets to and fro. Fishermen cursed as they unloaded their catch, and the smithy's hammer clanged. Ahead was the town hall. Two musicians sang near the baker's stall, one playing a lute, the other pacing nearby, his hat extended to passersby. On one side of the square was a park, built on a gentle knoll. Stone benches, cleverly placed, afforded the user a view of the cathedral across the way.

He turned his horse from the cobblestone road and crossed to the benches. From here he could see worshippers as they left the church. Adam might be among them. He tried to recall how long it had been since seeing Adam. A year and three months, to be exact. It seemed longer than that.

He dismounted and tied his horse to a sturdy bough, then doubled his riding cape beneath him on the cold stone and sat down.

Behind him, a dog barked, and he turned to see one running his way. He whistled, then bent to pet the animal as it sat at his feet. The dog tilted its head, bringing his short ears forward, then jumped on the bench.

"*Bonjour, Monsieur.* Get down, Jacques. No one wants your fleas."

Adam's voice. Gérard spun around. A man, his back to him, stood gazing at the harbor.

"Adam?"

Adam turned, shading his face with his hand. When he recognized Gérard, he smiled, a wide joyous smile, and for a moment Gérard wished he were back on the ship, back with the stench of violence and death, anywhere but here.

CHAPTER FORTY-TWO

Glancing past Gérard's shoulder at the single horse, Adam stiffened, his countenance registering both happiness and confusion. After they embraced, Gérard stepped back, dreading the next few moments.

"Gérard—why are you here? Why have you come . . . without her?"

Gérard swallowed and lowered his head, trying to remember the words he had rehearsed.

Adam grasped his shoulders. "Tell me, my friend."

The carefully rehearsed speech refused to come. Gérard looked up at Adam, fighting back tears. Adam whitened, even before he heard the words. "She . . . she is gone. She may have taken a ship, part of a convoy. It sank at sea."

Adam turned away, and for a long moment Gérard wondered if he understood. Adam moaned, an animal sound that turned to great wracking sobs, his cry containing more pain than Gérard had ever heard before. It echoed across the knoll, rolling to the sea, rolling back on the waves to the knoll again, filling the square and echoing from the cathedral. Adam sank to his knees beside the bench, his hands and head against the stone. Tortured wails wracked his body as Gérard stood helplessly by, paralyzed by what he witnessed.

Across the square, church bells pealed and worshippers streamed out the cathedral doors, children clutching their parents' hands, women chatting with their neighbors before scattering in all directions.

At dusk they rode to Robert's castle in silence; the only sounds the horses' hooves on the old road and Jacques's soft whimpering.

For three days, Adam stayed in his room. Servants came and went, carrying trays of food, and returned each time with the food untouched.

On the fourth day Gérard could stand it no more. He entered, cursing his inadequacy. Still, someone had to pierce Adam's solitude. Somehow he had to make the man see that he had to go on. Starvation was a cruel death.

The room was dark except for slits of light around the windows. Gérard opened the shutters and turned toward Adam. A jug of wine rested on the table. He picked it up and drank, hoping it would give him courage to speak.

He glanced at the rumpled clothes, the unkempt hair, and after looking at Adam's swollen eyes it came to him that his friend had not slept at all. The room smelled to Gérard of despondency. "My God, Adam." He sat down across the table, drank more wine, and said, "May I speak of something else you should know?"

"Yes, my friend, go ahead. A mortal wound cannot be worsened."

Gérard paused, remembering that last day in Orléans when he'd noticed Catherine's waist had thickened. He'd suspected then, but kept quiet. If was none of his affair. Should he keep quiet now? He argued with himself. Would it pain Adam more to know? Still, what right had he to know, and not share it with the child's own father? He gathered his courage and spoke. "When I last saw her, I suspect she was with child. I've known her for many years. Women change in a certain way, even before the babe grows in their belly. On a sea voyage, if it was anything like mine, she may have—"

"She was . . . with child?" Adam rose unsteadily, walked to the window, then turned back. "Why did she not tell me?" He looked away, beyond the stone walls, across the field, and Gérard wondered if he were crying, if the wound had opened wider, until he heard him speak again. "If I had been with her . . . or if she had stayed with me. . . ."

"I cannot be certain, of course. But you should be comforted by knowing she loved you, Adam."

"Comforted?" He sat, took a drink from the jug and rubbed the back of his hand across his mouth. His eyes blazed. "I'm to be comforted because of some misguided vow to the Church? The cross lays a heavy obligation on one, does it not, Gérard?"

Gérard recoiled from the bitter words, and Adam continued. "So many have lost so much, in the name of the Church." He shook his head. "I've had a lot of time to think, here in Naples, alone, and in spite of my beliefs, I've come to admire her resolution. All of us need ideals, and her commitment and passion for a cause she thought just, is one of the reasons I love her." He shrugged. "I suppose I've learned that her dedication is little different from mine, to my work, which she always supported. I wish it weren't too late to tell her that—that I understand."

After a long moment he reached across the table, grasped Gérard's wrist. "I thank you for coming, my friend. I know it was not easy to bring such news. Now," he said, "I suppose I should wash."

"Perhaps." Gérard said, knowing the forced smile on Adam's face covered a world of misery.

The silver-green leaves of ancient olive trees shimmered in the September sun as Adam crossed the patch of grass to where Gérard dozed in the shaded garden. "I thought I might find you here," Adam said. He took a seat.

Gérard sat up, startled. He ran one hand through his hair and put on his cap.

Adam laced his hands, half wishing he'd stayed in the room. He had forced himself to eat a bit of bread, and wondered why. Why should a man live in a world that no longer mattered?

"I was told the king returns home tonight," Gérard said. "You may want to know, his staff made arrangements—before they knew of your loss, of course—they made plans for the performance of your poem, the one you wrote in the Sicilian king's honor. They have built a makeshift stage in the Great Hall where we assemble after dinner. They beg you to come." He rose from the bench. "And now it's me who must wash. I'll leave you alone."

"Truly, I had forgotten about the poem." Adam rubbed the stubble on his cheeks. "I have no stomach for the merrymaking at dinner, though. Perhaps you could have the cook send up some soup."

"Of course, Adam. After dinner, then."

That evening, Adam listened to an artist from Crete reading *Le Roi de Sicily*. At the end of the first part Adam rose to accept the applause the king directed his way. The accolades failed to move him. All he could think about was Catherine, picturing her struggling in the depths of the ocean, breathing her last. It was hard to imagine her gone, that he'd never see her again.

The narrator continued, and now a *mimi* performed bodily movements, adapting himself to characters in the poem. Adam, ignoring the actor, leaned across Jacques toward Gérard. "You say the prioress knew nothing of her? Don't they keep records?"

From behind them an elderly matron hissed, "Did you come to hear the poem or to talk?"

Adam looked at the stage again. The reader finished the last page, but Adam was not listening to the words he had created.

After the performance, Gérard told him that King Charles

would remain at the castle until the following evening. "They've arranged a performance of *Robin et Marion* for tomorrow night. They will use the same stage they used tonight. I look forward to seeing your play again."

"That's right. You saw it with Catherine, in Orléans." He struggled to continue. "She liked it that night. She told me I would be famous." They followed behind a group of noblemen, and from a side door he noticed the figure of a woman. Her head was turned to the side, and he almost cried out. The woman reminded him of Catherine. He rubbed his temples. Was he to be forever tormented with her face? This was the torture saved for Purgatory.

When he looked again, the woman was still there. She stepped from the shadows. She even had Catherine's eyes.

He gripped Gérard's arm, feared his mind was going, or his weakened state was making him dream while awake. Sweat beaded his forehead. "Gérard. Do you see—"

"Adam?"

It was her voice. Catherine's voice. He froze. If it was a dream, let him stay dreaming. If a mirage, let his mind live in the world she had left. His memories were better than reality.

Gérard gasped, then urged him forward.

"Catherine!"

She smiled and held out her arms. Adam rushed to embrace her, wrapping her slight figure tight, feeling the tremor in her limbs. He kissed her cheeks, her forehead, and found her lips. They were warm. Real. She had come to him. Tears rolled down his cheeks. Still gripping her, he stepped back, afraid to believe. He raised a finger to touch her face, ran his trembling hand across her chin.

Behind them, Gérard cleared his throat. "Catherine." They turned toward him. Tears had filled his eyes. "But the prioress said—"

"Come," Adam interrupted. "I know a quiet place where we can talk."

In the king's garden—where only hours ago Adam had come to Gérard, bereft of the will to live—Catherine and he sat together, across from Gérard. Overhead, silver leaves on the olive trees blocked the setting sun. Catherine glanced at Adam. Shadows danced on his face. The dark specks in his eyes were the same, and he smiled the same lopsided smile. Through a haze of emotions, she struggled with where to begin. She had strived these past four months to put her grief behind her, and as time passed, the pain had diminished. For him, it would be fresh and new. Still, he was waiting, as was Gérard. She owed them both the truth.

She took a deep breath and told them of her discovery of her condition, wincing as she remembered, and then of her delivery. As she talked, she watched Adam's face, his expression reflecting the pain in her voice. She reached for his hand.

"Don't talk if it pains you. You're here, and that's all I want or need."

"No, I need to tell you."

Adam drew her near. She turned in his embrace, the comforting embrace she had denied herself since their parting. "Our daughter lived, Adam, for almost a half year. But each day, she grew weaker. I prayed, but my prayers were not answered. At first, I thought it punishment as I'd been unable to fulfill my vow, but later I realized God, and not me—not my prayers—controls our destiny."

She burrowed against his chest and cried, for her lost babe, for the pain she had brought them both with her strongminded will, and when her tears were dried he kissed her again.

"We will have other children, Catherine. I'm only grateful no harm came to you. If only I had known—"

322

"There was nothing anyone could do, Adam. And besides, my loss convinced me more than anyone, or anything, could have."

Gérard leaned forward. "How did you come here? Surely not alone."

Her eyes crinkled into a smile. "I relied on some royal friends. I sent a message to Count Robert. It took a few months, but he was finally located, and he sent six of his men to bring me here."

Adam chuckled. "Ah, I see you've learned your way around court circles. That will serve you well in the future."

"The future. . . ." Catherine smiled up at him.

Gérard rose from the bench. "Have you put it all behind you, then? Are you freed from the obligation you've felt?"

"Freed? Yes, I suppose so, and I'm wiser. I found that there is redemption in love—in real love, like what I had for the babe." She turned and looked into Adam's eyes. "And in the love I have for you."

Gérard walked to the chapel to offer a special prayer. There was much to be thankful for. Catherine was safe. And she was fortunate. Redemption is what everyone struggles to attain, but few recognize it when it arrives. Catherine had, and in time to make a life with Adam. No matter that Adam had little use for the trappings of faith, preferring instead his own private commune with God, which seemed to be enough for men like him. But in Gérard's experience, a little prayer never hurt.

Adam slipped his arm around Catherine's waist. "Let's walk across the meadow. The air in Naples, since you've arrived, suddenly smells very sweet."

"Ah, still the poet." She pulled a veil over her hair. "I must tell you more, but the rest can wait."

"Come then. We have an hour before sunset. We can take the path along the wood."

AUTHOR'S NOTES

This fictional biography is based on what little is known about Adam de la Halle, also known as "Adam d'Arras" and "Adam le Bossu" ("Adam the Hunchback"). One of Adam's works, *Le Jeu de la Feuillée*, is believed to be autobiographical, and from that we may conjecture something about his family and studies.

Although Adam's name is not listed in the *Nécrologe de la Confrérie des Jongleurs et des Bourgeois d'Arras*, a necrology of a literary confraternity, it is generally understood that he must have been active in the group and took part in literary competitions known as the "Puy d'Arras."

Adam may have married young, to a Maroie, and probably studied in Paris. There are references to an exile in Douai. It is almost certain that he was patronized by Count Robert II of Artois and that he went to Naples, where he wrote *Le Roi de Sicile* in honor of the count's uncle, Charles d'Anjou.

Adam was probably born sometime between 1220 and 1250 to Henri de la Halle, a municipal employee in Arras. Adam's death may have been in Naples around 1289, but some believe he lived as late as 1306. This is supported by a document referencing payment to minstrels who were hired to perform at the dubbing of Prince Edward in Westminster.

Drawing on this, I join with others in speculating that Adam's *Robin et Marion* may have been the first penned version of what we know today as the legend of Robin Hood. The language of the trouvères, *langue d'oil,* was also spoken in the Norman court (now England). It is also likely that trouvères frequented the court, and a popular play like Adam's *Robin et Marion* surely would have been performed there.

The English version of Robin Hood has many elements of Adam's play, *Robin et Marion:* game-playing, Robin's pure heart (a trait not usually associated with outlaws), and Robin's cousins, who may very well have become the "merry men." If nothing else, the similarity in the protagonists' names suggests a tie to the popular legend.

The Tapestry Shop is not a scholarly work, but I wanted to use dates, people, and places that form the basis of what we know of Adam's life in order to be true to his legacy. In the interest of story, I created a fictional Catherine, who shares his journey, and Gérard, a clerk, as well as other secondary characters.

A woodcut of Adam, which appears in one of my college textbooks, was my inspiration for the novel, sending me on a search that ends with the writing of this novel.

Adam's works have been copied, translated, and recorded on CDs, a lasting tribute to a little-known poet and musician whose songs and poems have endured through the ages and whose plays led to the birth of the comic opera form.

ABOUT THE AUTHOR

Since leaving the teaching field to pursue writing full-time, **Joyce Elson Moore** has reached a widening audience with her books, beginning with historical nonfiction and later, with a historical romance, *Jeanne of Clairmonde,* which garnered an RPLA award. Now she writes historical novels with settings that range from ancient Rome to Early Modern Venice. Conservatory-trained, Joyce's background in music is evident in *The Tapestry Shop,* a historical novel based on the life of a medieval poet/musician who wrote what many consider to be the earliest documented representation of the Robin Hood legend.

Joyce lives on the west coast of Florida with her rescued boxer dog, rabbits, tree squirrels, a resident coyote, and several gopher tortoises that call her wooded three acres their home.